RUSSIAN MOJITO

A Detective Emilia Cruz Novel

Carmen Amato

Published 2023 by Laurel & Croton (second edition)
Trade Paperback Edition

Identifiers: ISBN: 979-8-9885363-7-6 (print)
ISBN: 978-0-9997122-3-8 (ebook)

Praise for Detective Emilia Cruz

CLIFF DIVER

"From the moment I started the first one, I couldn't put it down. . . Her work touches on important issues affecting Mexico in a real, human way and is exciting, fast paced and utterly gripping." – *Mexico Retold*

HAT DANCE

[Emilia] is a force to be reckoned with." – *Mystery Sequels*

DIABLO NIGHTS

"Amato brings her characters to life with her vivid writing style and sets them on the streets of a Mexico steeped in Catholicism and corruption." – *OnlineBookClub.org*

KING PESO

"Danger and betrayal never more than a few pages away." – *Kirkus Reviews*

PACIFIC REAPER

"Carmen Amato . . . out does many of the best crime authors out there." – *Artisan Book Reviews*

43 MISSING

"A fast-paced procedural . . . a real page-turner . . . a very original plot." – *The BookLife Prize*

Also by Carmen Amato

DETECTIVE EMILIA CRUZ SERIES
CLIFF DIVER: Detective Emilia Cruz Book 1
HAT DANCE: Detective Emilia Cruz Book 2
DIABLO NIGHTS: Detective Emilia Cruz Book 3
KING PESO: Detective Emilia Cruz Book 4
PACIFIC REAPER: Detective Emilia Cruz Book 5
43 MISSING: Detective Emilia Cruz Book 6
RUSSIAN MOJITO: Detective Emilia Cruz Book 7
NARCO NOIR: Detective Emilia Cruz Book 8
MADE IN ACAPULCO: The Emilia Cruz Stories
THE ARTIST/EL ARTISTA: A Bilingual Short Story
FELIZ NAVIDAD FROM ACAPULCO: A Detective Emilia
Cruz Novella
THE LISTMAKER OF ACAPULCO: A Detective Emilia Cruz
Novella

GALLIANO CLUB SERIES
ROAD TO THE GALLIANO CLUB: Prequel
MURDER AT THE GALLIANO CLUB: Book 1
BLACKMAIL AT THE GALLIANO CLUB: Book 2
REVENGE AT THE GALLIANO CLUB: Book 3

THRILLERS
AWAKENING MACBETH
THE HIDDEN LIGHT OF MEXICO CITY

Regarding names and monetary conversion

Regarding Mexican names: It is the custom in Mexico to use two surnames. The first is from the father's family and is always used. The second surname is the name of the mother's father. The second is sometimes dropped in conversation and/or to shorten the name in keeping with American and European naming conventions.

Conversion rate: For the purposes of this novel, $US1.00 = 10 Mexican pesos.

Spanish words: A glossary of Spanish words and terms commonly used in the Detective Emilia Cruz series is included.

Trouble never comes alone.

Russian proverb

CHAPTER 1

"All rise," the sergeant-at-arms bellowed.

Emilia Cruz Encinos and the others in the courtroom got to their feet. The court-appointed lawyer, Hector Martinez Mora, smoothed the lapels of his tailored suit as he stood next to Emilia.

A door opened in the wood paneled wall behind the judge's bench. Emilia watched as a trio of judges—two men and one woman—climbed two steps and entered a bulletproof glass enclosure. The massive structure was mounted on a dais decorated with the seal of Mexico. The snake writhed endlessly in the eagle's talon.

The last judge bolted the door, effectively locking himself and his colleagues into a protective square bubble.

The sergeant-at-arms locked a door near a workstation staffed by officers of the court. Half a dozen other uniformed officers closed and locked double doors at the rear of the courtroom before taking up guard positions around the perimeter. Security cameras hung from the ceiling switched on with an electronic whine and swiveled into position, watching for danger.

Emilia's heart thundered in her ears, louder than the indistinct murmurs of the judges and the swish of their robes. Of its own accord, her right thumb slid over the comforting ridge formed by the key in her skirt pocket.

The thick glass threw a greenish tinge across the

unsmiling faces of the judges. No nameplates or announcement identified them. In Mexico, for judges as well as cops, the secret of longevity was anonymity.

"Please be seated," the female judge said. Her voice was faintly distorted by a microphone.

Once again, chairs scraped against the tile floor. Martinez Mora, who'd let Emilia know from the start she should address him by the honorific Avocat, as befitting a practicing criminal attorney, glanced at her as he pinched the creases in his trousers and sat. They were in the front row of seats, behind a long table. The courtroom was less than half full, with representatives from the office of the Attorney General, a Mexican military contingent, officials from the Secretaría de Relaciones Exteriores, and a small delegation from the embassy of the United States.

Emilia gave the lawyer a taut nod in return as she settled into her chair and tucked her hands in her lap. Avocat Martinez was not there as her defense attorney, but as a legal guardian to ensure that documentation was properly compiled, affidavits pertaining to her character were filed, and Emilia answered questions as needed by the tribunal process.

The center judge rapped a gavel. Emilia gave an involuntary start at the loud noise, terrified he was going to stand, point to her, and shout "LIAR!"

"This tribunal is now in session to share preliminary findings," the judge announced to the courtroom. "Regarding the escape of convicted criminal Diego Barrielos

Luna while being transported by Special Operations personnel and law enforcement officers to Brownsville, Texas in the Estados Unidos under an extradition agreement between Mexico and Washington."

Someone behind Emilia shifted restlessly, shoe leather scraping the floor. Otherwise, the room was silent with anticipation.

"Over the past six weeks," the judge continued. "This tribunal has reviewed all available evidence. Detective Emilia Cruz Encinos of Acapulco, the lone survivor of the team transporting Señor Barrielos Luna, has made herself available for over 100 hours of testimony."

That was the understatement of the century. The judge more accurately could have said that the combined gears of military fury, Mexican law, and the secret that could end her police career had ground Detective Emilia Cruz Encinos of Acapulco into emotional sawdust.

After all, in Mexico, surviving a cartel ambush meant only one thing.

Collusion.

The assumption of guilt was immediate. Emilia had practically been a prisoner at a military base near Mexico City during the tribunal's investigation, answering the same questions day after day.

"The primary phase of the tribunal has reached its conclusion." The judge looked up as if to reassure himself that he had everyone's full attention. "Detective Miguel Anaya Vargas of Reynosa, working alone, accepted significant funds from the Barrielos Luna organization in return for carrying a concealed tracking device while participating in the extradition convoy. This allowed Barrielos Luna's sicarios to pinpoint the convoy and mount an attack with armored vehicles and a helicopter armed with missiles. Detective Anaya activated the tracking device shortly after the extradition convoy bearing Barrielos Luna departed the Multifoco prison in the state of Michoacán. The failure of Special Operations personnel to discover the device's signal is under review."

Emilia felt eyes boring into her. If she turned around, the resentment sparking off the Special Operations officers in the back of the courtroom would probably set her on fire.

The judge turned a page and kept reading. "Beyond Detective Cruz's testimony, evidence supporting this finding includes recovery of the tracking device, the absence of other fingerprints on it besides those of Detective Anaya, the transfer of 30 million pesos on the day of the convoy into a bank account used to pay his wife's medical bills, and a record of unauthorized visits by Detective Anaya to the Multifoco facility prior to the prisoner's departure. Detective Anaya made little effort to hide his treason, no doubt aware that he would not survive the ambush. This tribunal believes that Detective Anaya's law enforcement colleagues were unaware of his actions."

As he droned on, the locked room felt like a coffin.

Special Operations was Mexico's paramilitary black-ops unit. Emilia and Anaya, along with Lieutenant Leonel

Cardenas, were invited by the unit commander to participate in the extradition convoy as a reward for solving the disappearance of 43 students, a crime orchestrated by Barrielos Luna and his extended family. The invitation had been extended as an honor and Emilia had accepted it as such.

She was the first and only woman ever included in the unit, albeit for the single operation.

What happened during the extradition wasn't Emilia's fault, but she knew the men staring fixedly at the back of her neck didn't see it that way. A woman had been brought into the tightly knit Special Operations brotherhood and brought nothing but bad luck.

A tap sounded at the side door of the courtroom. Emilia's pulse jumped again.

All three judges looked at the sergeant-at-arms. He surveyed the bank of computer screens at the big workstation. Nods were exchanged. The sergeant opened the door, accepted an envelope from whomever was on the other side, and passed it through a slot in the bulletproof shield to the judge on the end.

The three judges held a hushed conference, chairs and heads pushed together. On the other side of the glass, whispered conspiracy theories circled the courtroom.

Emilia watched the dais, dry-mouthed as her heart pounded. Had someone discovered her secret? Her sin of omission?

The judges separated and straightened in their chairs. The

judge in the middle banged his gavel.

"To resume," he said. "Due to Detective Anaya's treason against his team and country, the Barrielos Luna organization was able to pinpoint the extradition convoy, blockade the highway, and mount a successful attack. Evidence at the scene corroborated Detective Cruz's testimony, which may be considered incomplete as she was in the prisoner vehicle for most of the event, with restricted visibility."

Avocat Martinez nodded knowingly. He'd pointed that out several times during her questioning.

Her heart was beating so fast, Emilia felt light-headed. She forced herself to focus on her breathing. Two breaths in, two breaths out. Two breaths in, two breaths out.

"The prisoner vehicle was attacked after the other vehicles in the convoy were disabled," the judge said. "The doors were opened with explosive devices, which left a chemical signature consistent with the Barrielos Luna organization's history. Lieutenant Leonel Cardenas and Detective Cruz attempted to defend themselves and remain in custody of the prisoner. Lieutenant Cardenas was killed in the exchange of gunfire. Detective Cruz was not seriously injured, because she was shielded by Lieutenant Cardenas during the firefight."

Emilia pressed a hand to her mouth, momentarily overwhelmed by the clinical description of Cardenas's last moments. Irreverent, handsome, and extroverted, Cardenas had been her closest colleague during the politically-charged investigation into the missing students.

"Barrielos Luna and his rescuers," the judge said. "Fled the scene via helicopter, sparing the life of Detective Cruz out of deference for her as a woman."

Emilia dropped her hand. Her knuckles were white.

"This completes the preliminary findings." The judge put aside his paper. "The second phase will examine Special Operations protocols to determine why the convoy did not turn back when an irregular traffic pattern was noticed and why the airspace above the convoy's route was not adequately monitored, allowing for the intrusion of an unlicensed helicopter."

The female judge rapped her gavel to silence a murmur from the back row. "This tribunal has the authority to examine all aspects of the event in question," she said. "You are all reminded that Detective Cruz's participation in the failed extradition operation is classified and will not be released to the public. The penalties for revealing classified information will be severe. In this case, exceptionally severe."

The warning was plain.

The female judge looked directly at Emilia through the thick glass. "The tribunal salutes Detective Cruz's bravery," she said. "We wish you a swift recovery from the trauma of this tragic episode. Detective Cruz, you will not be needed for further questioning and are free to go at the end of this session."

"Thank you, Your Honor," Avocat Martinez said loudly.

The third judge held up the envelope from the sergeant-at-arms. "The tribunal has two more announcements. First, a reward for the capture of Diego Barrielos Luna has been set at 20 million pesos."

He permitted a brief hum of approval from the courtroom. "Second, in recognition of his gallantry saving the life of his colleague and sacrificing his own, the nation will posthumously award Lieutenant Leonel Cardenas the Condecoración al Valor Heroico. To receive this military honor, the lieutenant will be posthumously inducted into the Special Operations forces."

A gavel banged. The sergeant-at-arms barked an order. All stood.

The judges filed out of their bulletproof enclosure and left the courtroom. As soon as the door closed behind them, the room erupted with agitated conversation. Emilia could almost taste the outrage that a law enforcement officer would receive a medal when nine dead Special Operations men on the same mission went unrecognized.

The double doors at the rear opened and fresh air surged in. Emilia inhaled greedily, feeling sweaty and shaky.

Avocat Martinez extended his hand. "I'm sure you are pleased by the finding, Detective Cruz," he said.

Emilia gave a thin smile and took the proffered hand. "I'm glad it's over."

"Home to Acapulco, now?" Avocat Martinez asked.

"I'm not sure," Emilia said.

"Whatever you decide, I wish you all the best." Avocat

Martinez picked up his briefcase. "You acquitted yourself well, Detective. You are a resilient young woman."

A bitter laugh escaped before Emilia could swallow it back. "Thank you," she managed. "For all your help during the tribunal process."

"An honor to be of service." He gave her a slight bow and walked away.

Emilia watched him go, sure that Avocat Martinez had no idea how helpful he'd been.

Before the extradition convoy, Emilia had visited Barrielos Luna in prison to find out what the kingpin knew about a man who called himself El Acólito. A murderer, rapist, and human trafficker, El Acólito had possibly procured girls for Barrielos Luna. Undercover during an investigation, Emilia had broken El Acólito's trafficking operation and sent him on the run, but at the cost of a sexual assault she could not remember.

Meeting Barrielos Luna in prison had been a costly mistake. As flames from the ambush engulfed the extradition convoy vehicles, helicopter rotors churned impatiently, and Cardenas lay dying, Barrielos Luna let Emilia know why he was going to let her live.

El Acólito.

I know where he is and I'll find him before you do. You'll trade for him. Yes, mi corazón, you're going to be very useful to me . . . Whatever he is to you, you want him that much.

Barrielos Luna had spared her, not because she was a

woman, but because he believed he could use her. In his eyes, Emilia was an up and coming detective in one of Mexico's largest police departments, a rising star with federal connections, and soon to be famous in law enforcement circles for being the lone survivor. Every cartel had cops on its payroll, to look the other way, make charges disappear, arrest rivals, and otherwise ensure the smooth flow of drugs to the insatiable appetites across the border. The more influential and notable the cop, the more useful they were.

If the tribunal ever found out Barrielos Luna's intention, Emilia knew her life would be twisted apart. She'd be dangled as bait to catch Mexico's most wanted fugitive. Sacrificed for some politician's ten minutes of fame.

But Avocat Martinez had unwittingly come to her rescue.

Sitting beside her during the first round of questioning, Avocat Martinez made the assumption that she survived because not even a man with Barrielos Luna's notorious reputation for cruelty could kill a woman in cold blood. The military interrogators swallowed the narrative and by the second day, Avocat Martinez's assumption solidified into fact, providing Emilia with a veil of protection and sympathy.

Weeks later, her secret was still safe.

But Emilia wasn't.

She didn't know how or when the fugitive drug lord would show his hand, only that he would. And what would she do?

Emilia walked out of the courtroom, ignoring the stabbing glances of the Special Operations officers. She slid her hand into her skirt pocket and touched the key again. If she found El Acólito before Barrielos Luna did, perhaps she could beat the fugitive drug lord at his own game.

Once a rising television actor known as Rafa Gamboa, El Acólito's real name was Rafael Gamboa Escobar. After getting fired from a movie set, he recast himself as a priest dedicated to Santa Muerte, Mexico's forbidden saint of death. Gamboa began roaming western Mexico using his evangelical rallies as a cover for a sophisticated human trafficking operation.

After Emilia exposed his activities, he disappeared into thin air. She knew Mexican law enforcement wasn't hustling to find the legendary El Acólito, who could trade on his fearsome influence with Santa Muerte to access sanctuary and protection. No doubt both cops and cartels were in his thrall; if they weren't, there was always bribery and blackmail.

Barrielos Luna was also on the run, but his worldwide notoriety made it harder to hide. The huge price on his head and the global news coverage of his daring escape meant that he had to stay on the move. Emilia hoped that the norteamericanos were hunting him; they had responded harshly in the press to Mexico's failure to deliver the extradited prisoner.

The cartel kingpin had virtually unlimited resources with which to buy safe houses and loyal sicarios. A Santa Muerte disciple, Barrielos Luna also had a network of fellow worshippers. It wasn't hard to imagine a scenario in which Barrielos Luna found El Acólito before Emilia could even start her search.

The key in her pocket came from Rafa Gamboa's long-abandoned apartment in Mexico City. It was a barely a clue as to the fugitive's whereabouts, but it was the only one she had.

Mexico City's afternoon sky was white and hazy as she left the building. Despite relief that the tribunal process was over and she was exonerated, a familiar apprehension dogged her.

What if Barrielos Luna discovered the improbable truth even El Acólito didn't know?

El Acólito, the former actor Rafa Gamboa, had been born Ernesto Cruz Encinos, Junior.

El Acólito was Emilia's brother.

CHAPTER 2

Two days later, Emilia sat in the restaurant of the Palacio Réal hotel, inarguably Acapulco's most luxurious accommodation, and watched general manager Kurt Rucker fill two champagne flutes. The gentle ocean breeze ruffled his short blonde hair.

"To second chances," he said and handed her a glass.

"Second chances," Emilia echoed.

Her heart constricted as their fingers touched. It was the day they met all over again, when she was mesmerized by the combination of sharp intellect, mental toughness, and compelling self confidence, all poured into an athlete's body.

They touched glasses in a toast to the future. Emilia took a sip of champagne and followed his gaze beyond their table to the setting sun as it spread ribbons of color over Puerto Marques, the bay-within-a-bay on Acapulco's southeastern side.

The curving shoreline was dominated by the Palacio Réal complex, including the flagship restaurant. Cantilevered over the ocean, the fine dining establishment was built to resemble a masted sailing ship. A cunning confection of canvas sails created a roof over the long teak hull as tables skirted in white linen and laid with antique sterling flatware evoked the dining room of a Spanish galleon.

"How does it feel to be home?" Kurt asked. His posture was relaxed and comfortable but his ocean-colored eyes betrayed his concern for her.

"Awkward," Emilia admitted. Her smile failed and she drank some champagne to hide her shakiness.

Emilia ran away from Kurt and their life together in the Palacio Réal penthouse after the assault by Rafa Gamboa and the DNA proof that he was her brother. But even as police work took her to a task force in Mexico City and the abortive assignment with Special Operations, she'd been unable to break away from Kurt. Every long-distance conversation was both reassuring and agonizing; neither could say a final goodbye.

A waiter materialized with swirls of caramelized shrimp on gold-rimmed plates. The sweet scent of apple from the Calvados liquor tickled Emilia's nose.

"Compliments of Chef Jacques, señora," the waiter murmured. He set down the appetizer and lit the candle on the table before melting away.

"It doesn't have to be awkward," Kurt said. "This is just the two of us."

"And all the ghosts of my past." Emilia heard the tremor in her voice and tried to pull herself together before she sabotaged Kurt's romantic homecoming dinner.

"We can leave the past where it is and move on." Kurt flipped his napkin into his lap. "Eat your shrimp before Jacques comes out of the kitchen and quits."

Emilia picked up her fork. In another life, the hotel's head chef had created his signature appetizer for her.

"I can't forget what happened," she blurted.

"No one expects you to forget, Em. But you still have a life."

"Rafa Gamboa is still out there," Emilia whispered, ignoring the beautiful food in front of her. "So is Barrielos Luna. He's like a snake. He's going to wrap himself around me and squeeze until none of us can breathe."

The man across the table from her was the only person who knew the truth about why Barrielos Luna let her live. Kurt had taken the news without flinching.

Now he put down his fork. "Em, you don't know how this thing with him is going to play out. Nobody does."

"He's out there," Emilia insisted. She was ruining the evening but she couldn't stop herself. "Him and his army of faceless *sicarios*. Waiting for me on some street corner. On the beach. *Madre de Dios*, at the next table eating Jacques's food."

"Or maybe he's dead in a ditch," Kurt said quietly.

"You once said," Emilia reminded him with a lift of one shoulder to indicate the hotel soaring up the cliff behind them like the architectural marvel it was. "If I'm in danger so is everyone in this hotel. I want to be with you and call this place my home again, but I can't put you in that position."

Kurt pushed aside his plate. "Tomorrow, Ronaldo Olivas and I are going to review the hotel's security program and make some upgrades," he said, naming the hotel's chief of security. "A beautiful woman who means a great deal to me once said she wouldn't live scared and I'm going to make sure when she's home, she's safe. And if she's safe, so is everybody else."

Emilia swallowed hard against a sudden lump in her throat. "That sounds like a lot of trouble for one crazy cop."

"She's worth it," Kurt said and stretched a hand across the table. "You're home, Em. We'll work it out, one day at a time."

Emilia wrapped her fingers around his. His hand was a lifeline pulsing with vitality and courage, pulling her out of a well of self-recrimination and fear.

"Okay," she breathed. "One day at a time."

"In a couple of years we'll step back, see how it's going."

The flippant remark made Emilia laugh, but Kurt's gaze was steady and unblinking.

He had a strength like steel, tempered long before he came to Mexico by years in his country's military. Kurt might manage a hotel now, but he'd been to war, confronted the enemy, seen pain and death.

That was why he understood her so well. They were both fighters.

Before she could say anything, a blur of white buttons and checked pants swept across the restaurant to their table. "Emilia!"

Jacques Anatole, a swarthy, lanky Frenchman in a chef's jacket, kissed her passionately on either cheek, half lifting Emilia out of her seat. "Your presence elevates us all. And this ogre is again tamed." He lifted his chin at Kurt. "You are a terrible boss."

"I can't be good at everything," Kurt said.

"He used to be modest," Jacques said to Emilia. "Now he is perfect."

Emilia laughed. The chef was the first member of the hotel staff who became a friend when she previously moved into the penthouse with Kurt.

"Now, to welcome back our prodigal daughter, I have for you a meal you will remember in song and verse and describe to your grandchildren with tears in your eyes." Jacques gestured dramatically to the plates in front of them. "First, you have my famous *camarones en Calvados*. Next a risotto with the essence of white truffle. Then, a morsel of fish that will melt in your mouth. A piece of skate like the wing of an angel, perfumed with herbs and posed with a mélange of vegetables. And for dessert, my fair lady's favorite cannoli with sweet *crema*."

"That sounds wonderful, Jacques," Emilia said. His fabled risotto was second cousin to *arroz rojo* but infinitely more exotic.

"I'll have the same," Kurt said.

Jacques glared at Kurt. "We're in training for the Ixtapa Half Ironman," he said. "I have beat you to the swimming dock four out of the last five mornings. No, my friend, you'll get a couple of chicken breasts, brown rice, and a spinach and beet salad. No dessert."

He pressed Emilia's knuckles to his lips and disappeared

through the kitchen door.

"You didn't tell me you were in training for a race," Emilia said.

"It's not for six weeks," Kurt replied, gazing at the gently swinging kitchen door. "I should fire him."

"He's your best friend."

"Depends on what's for dinner," Kurt said.

Emilia laughed again. Familiarity was gently closing her wounds.

She felt . . . safe.

Almost.

She'd feel better once she attacked the long to-do list in her shoulder bag. Go back to work and wear a gun every day. Check the police database for any recent sightings of Rafa Gamboa and Barrielos Luna. Visit her mother and stepfather, and the rest of her extended family. Enlist the help of Padre Ricardo, the priest who'd been her mentor since grade school, to trace the original owners of the key.

Emilia's mushroom risotto was delicious and the fish was a work of art. She shared with Kurt, who was duly served with the high protein meal Jacques had promised. As they ate, Emilia thought of her suitcase, upstairs in the penthouse, waiting to be unpacked.

In the bedroom that used to be theirs . . .

She hadn't been with a man since the assault. She wondered if that part of her life with Kurt could be what it had been, or if Rafa Gamboa had stolen that from her, too.

"Where's your car?" Kurt asked.

"At the police station," Emilia replied. She put a piece of asparagus on his plate, punctuating his beet salad with a stripe of green. "Silvio has the keys."

Kurt smiled his thanks and pronged the extra vegetable. "That's Lieutenant Silvio now, isn't it?"

"It'll be strange having Franco as my boss," Emilia admitted. "With him as the lieutenant, I'll be assigned a new partner. I hope it won't be a rookie like—."

She'd lost Kurt's attention. He was staring beyond her right shoulder.

"What's going on?" Before she knew it, Emilia was on high alert. Was Barrielos Luna behind her? Or a dozen armed *sicarios* as she sat in front of a half-eaten plate of fish and asparagus?

"Don't turn around," Kurt said.

"Tell me what's happening, Kurt." Was Rafa Gamboa and his sinister tattoo of Santa Muerte invading the Palacio Réal?

Emilia darted glances at the tables in her field of vision. Whatever was happening, the diners were unaware and focused only on themselves and their meals.

"Em, it's okay," Kurt said gently. "I just saw something odd."

Emilia couldn't shake her fear. "How odd?"

"Do you remember Sergei Porchenko?" Kurt asked. "Russian. Owns the Pacific Lotus hotel downtown. On the Acapulco Hotel Association board with me. He came to our World Cup party."

"His wife is named Magda," Emilia recalled, her heart still thumping. "I spilled red wine on her."

"He's sitting in the corner in an Armani suit," Kurt said. "Opposite the bar. He gave his dinner companion a big wad of US dollars and thinks nobody saw."

"Oh." The tension that surged through her body ebbed. Emilia relaxed, but Kurt was right to be concerned. In Mexico, private cash transactions always meant trouble. Money laundering, bribes, cartel deals.

To make matters worse, Sergei Porchenko was Russian. Across Mexico, but especially in resort areas, the Russian mafia was making its presence felt, buying up condominiums, running prostitutes, and opening huge casinos. Money flowed through each operation, and in Mexico, money and drugs always swam in the same river.

Kurt raised a finger and the waiter materialized by his side.

"The two gentlemen at Table 16," Kurt said quietly. "What was the name on the reservation?"

"One moment, *jefe*," the waiter whispered.

Emilia barely had time to take another mouthful of food before the waiter was back. He handed Kurt a folded slip of paper.

"Will you be needing anything else, *jefe*?"

Kurt skimmed the note and shook his head. "No, thank you."

The waiter left and Kurt slid the note across the table to Emilia.

Bogdan Andropov. Room 316. Checked in 4 days ago. Russian passport.

"Well," Kurt said, when Emilia handed him back the little slip of paper. "Would you like to have coffee with a couple of Russians?"

Emilia managed a small smile. "Of course. Who wouldn't?"

Kurt came around to pull out her chair, moving with the athletic grace and assertive confidence that nearly made Emilia's knees buckle. "Come on," he said. "I promise to make it quick."

Porchenko rose to intercept them, a meaty paw extended to Kurt. "Rucker, we've been enjoying your overpriced hospitality this evening. Gotta pay your five star chef, eh?"

"It's good to see you somewhere besides a board meeting, Sergei," Kurt said, as the two men shook hands. "May we join you?"

"Of course," Porchenko said after an awkward beat. "Your place. Sit where you like."

Introductions were made all around. The conversation was in English and Emilia struggled through the sudden language switch and Porchenko's heavy accent. Coffee for four appeared on a silver tray, and the waiter left a small trolley of desserts. Emilia sat across from Bogdan Andropov as Kurt and Porchenko faced each other at opposite ends of the table.

"I told you that Rucker keeps a classy hotel," Porchenko said to Andropov.

"Yes, you have a beautiful hotel, Mister Rucker," Andropov said.

Unlike Porchenko, Andropov's English sounded like a certain British television program Kurt liked. Otherwise, Andropov did not stand out. He was Emilia's age, with a slim build, deep-set brown eyes, and wavy hair cut stylishly short on the sides and long on top. His gray suit was anonymous and inexpensive, worn with a black shirt open at the collar.

Kurt stirred sugar into his coffee. "Please, call me Kurt," he said. "Are you here for business or pleasure?"

"Some of both," Andropov replied. "I'm a travel writer."

"Are your readers interested in Acapulco's beautiful beaches?" Emilia's English felt rusty but serviceable. "Or our exploding crime rate?"

Before Andropov could answer, Porchenko clattered a spoon against his coffee cup. "Russians want to know about places that are warm," he declared.

"Yes." Andropov gave Emilia a smile of apology for his dinner companion's rudeness. "Anything to make winters in Moscow a little shorter."

"Have you seen the cliff divers at La Quebrada yet?" Kurt asked Andropov.

"No, but I plan to soon." Andropov casually slid a hand over a cell phone lying screen side up. His fingers were long and thin.

Porchenko cleared his throat noisily and shoved up his jacket cuff to glance at his watch, a gold Rolex ringed with diamonds.

"Perhaps the water park downtown," Emilia offered. "There's a dolphin show."

"Do they perform tricks?" Andropov's face lit with interest.

"Yes," Emilia said. "They're amazing."

Andropov sipped some coffee. "I'd love to see it."

She hadn't seen him flip it, but Emilia was sure that the cell phone was now lying face down.

"Our concierge would be happy to arrange a tour for you," Kurt added.

"Your entire staff has been outstanding, Mister Rucker. You run a fine establishment."

"Thank you." Kurt acknowledged the compliment with a nod. "How long do you plan on staying in Acapulco?"

"As long as I can convince my editor," Andropov said. His smile was surprisingly boyish. "The warmth of your sun is quite addictive."

The phone under his hand vibrated, creating a barely perceptible muffled buzz against the tablecloth.

"That's why we all come to Mexico," Porchenko boomed out. "Sun and heat. The rest of the world's too fucking cold." He thrust an arm toward the dessert trolley. "Lemme taste that pudding thing."

Emilia passed him an exquisite dish of flan custard, the top glistening with swirls of spun sugar.

"You got a Mexican dessert chef, Rucker?" Porchenko punched his spoon through the delicate caramelized crust.

"They know sweets."

"This cheesecake is quite delicious," Andropov said, scraping the last bite off the plate with his fork.

"In Mexico it's called *pastel de tres leches*," Emilia said. She realized that his phone was no longer on the table.

The man might be a travel writer, but he was also a magician.

"If I may beg your pardon," Andropov said. He patted his lips with his napkin. "I have a conference call scheduled with my editor. The different time zones must be accommodated."

The Russian shook hands with Kurt and bowed over Emilia's fingertips as if she was the queen of Mexico. "It was a pleasure to meet you, señora."

"*Egualmente*," Emilia murmured. Andropov had lovely manners. Maybe all Russians weren't mobsters after all.

Andropov turned to Porchenko. "Thank you for all your assistance."

Porchenko heaved himself to his feet. "Enjoy Acapulco," he said, without offering his hand.

Andropov executed another courtly bow and walked rapidly out of the restaurant.

Pulling a monogrammed handkerchief out of his back pocket, Porchenko wiped his nose. "Gotta head back to the Pacific Lotus myself," he said. "You gotta come by and see what Magda's done. Japanese gardens all over."

"Emilia and I will walk you to the lobby," Kurt said. He signaled the waiter with a gesture that Emilia knew meant *put this on my bill.*

Porchenko barreled ahead as the three strolled along the wide path from the restaurant towards the main body of the hotel. As they skirted the beach, the path widened into broad steps leading into the soaring hotel lobby and the famous open-air Pasodoble Bar.

Emilia had forgotten the opulent drama of the Palacio Réal lobby at night. Thousands of tiny lights wrapped around the trunks of royal palms, which soared to the vaulted ceiling from blue and white *talavera* pots as tall as her shoulder. A white grand piano, the polished lid propped open, dominated the center of the cathedral-like space. A jazz quartet accompanied the pianist, turning the magnificent three-story lobby into an intimate club.

Several couples swayed to the music; other guests took advantage of clusters of sofas and chairs to enjoy quiet conversations and post-dinner cocktails in the romantic atmosphere.

Porchenko flicked a finger at two men sitting in the shadows beyond the palms. Both stood, revealing themselves to be massive *gringos* in jeans and suit jackets. As one of them headed for the exit, presumably to get Porchenko's car, Emilia caught a glimpse of an earpiece connected to a coiled wire snaking into the man's collar. The second bodyguard waited for his boss, ready for trouble but staying out of earshot.

"Your friend Andropov must be doing well," Kurt said to Porchenko. "Not many journalists can afford the Palacio

Réal."

Porchenko shrugged. "How much they pay hacks in Moscow is none of my business. I don't know him all that well."

"Ah, of course not." Kurt punctuated his softly spoken words with a tight smile. "By the way, did you know we have a zero tolerance policy at the Palacio Réal for solicitation?"

It took a moment for Porchenko to register what Kurt was saying. Obviously, what the Russian thought was a discreet transfer had indeed been seen. Porchenko covered his pause with a forced laugh, his belly jiggling under the expensive suit jacket.

The handkerchief came out again. Porchenko plied it across his face. Emilia watched the two men. Kurt was lithe and taut, with an unspoken authority that made strangers stop to look at him. Porchenko looked both unhappy and unhealthy, despite obvious wealth. His jowly face was a mix of pasty skin and broken red veins.

"These Russians," Porchenko said, wadding the handkerchief into a pocket. "They come to Mexico and are surprised they have to pay in pesos. So now and then, I change a few rubles for them. They get pesos to spend here, Magda gets rubles to spend when we go back to Moscow."

"What about dollars?" Kurt asked.

The bodyguard gave Porchenko a discreet signal that the car was at the entrance, earning a brief glare from the Russian.

"Sometimes they want dollars," Porchenko said with a

heavy shrug. "So I exchange those, too. No one trusts the banks. They're all thieves in Russia. Same here."

"You need to be careful about informal money exchanges," Kurt said. He tipped his head toward the bodyguard. "People could get the wrong idea."

"Kurt, I must ask a favor," Porchenko said. He massaged Kurt's shoulder but dropped his hand when there was no response. "There's no need to mention any of this to Magda. She still believes rubles magically appear in her purse."

Kurt gave a nod. "Good night, Sergei."

Porchenko planted a wet kiss on Emilia's hand and clapped Kurt on the back with false heartiness.

"Hell of a performance," Kurt muttered as the Russian and his bodyguard finally left the hotel.

Emilia lifted her eyebrows. "Indeed."

"Come dance with me, Em," Kurt said.

It felt natural to press against him. As they turned slowly in the glow of the fairy lights, Emilia saw familiar faces. Luis, the night concierge, smiled behind the desk as he spoke to an elderly gentleman. Benny, the head doorman, waited respectfully to usher guests to the valet service. The pianist, whose name she couldn't recall, gave her a smile as Kurt pulled her closer.

"Sorry," Kurt said, his lips against the top of Emilia's head. "That was the unplanned portion of the evening."

She inhaled his subtle cologne of bay rum and citrus. "Did you believe what Porchenko said about changing money for Russian visitors?"

"Not on your life," Kurt said. He tightened his hold on Emilia as they moved to the music. "But I made my point. He knows my hotel is off limits for his business deals. Beyond that, whatever he's up to doesn't concern me."

"Porchenko really didn't want Magda to know," Emilia mused. "You could blackmail him."

Kurt laughed.

If she stretched up, she could run her lips over his jaw. Taste his skin. Make his blue-green eyes widen with desire.

"Let's go upstairs," Emilia said abruptly.

Kurt stopped moving.

Emilia met his stare.

They made love in the dark penthouse bedroom. The only light to guide their hands came from the moon's reflection on the ocean far below.

As much as Emilia wanted to be with Kurt again, nothing was the same. When she took off her clothes, the rush of desire fizzled and she nearly flinched when he touched her bare skin. The end result was two strangers who regretted having a one night stand halfway through but were too embarrassed to stop.

When it was over, the fiasco elicited a little half-hearted laughter. Kurt closed his eyes. Emilia went into the bathroom and cried.

CHAPTER 3

The Palacio Réal driver dropped her off early at the police station in central Acapulco that housed the detectives unit. Dressed for work in skinny jeans, black tee, denim jacket and detective badge hanging from its lanyard around her neck, Emilia got a half-hearted salute from the uniformed guard at the gate as he let her into the secure compound.

Her official vehicle, a big white Suburban, was parked where Silvio said it would be. In its youth, the lumbering SUV had been modified to conceal a load of cocaine by a couple of clever *norteamericano* drug mules. The undercarriage had never really recovered. Emilia noted a distinct droop to the rear fender. A few months sitting idle while she was in Mexico City had not helped.

Emilia shoved open the rear door and nodded to the uniformed officer behind the desk by the holding cells. He mumbled something that might have been *Buenos dias*.

Emilia strode down the hallway to the detectives squadroom and promptly collided with detectives Macias and Sandor as they charged out.

"*Rayos*, Cruz," Sandor exclaimed, grabbing her arm to keep from knocking her over. "How long has it been?"

"Long enough," Emilia said with a laugh as she caught her balance.

She was glad to run into the two men, figuratively if not literally. José Macias Trevino and Vidal Sandor Moreno were both decent investigators who had given her less trouble than most when she became the first female detective. Clean cops, as far as she knew. They were always a little removed from the rest of the squadroom, which Emilia chalked up to being college men as opposed to former beat cops like her and Silvio. Still, she wouldn't mind partnering with either of them.

"You starting back today?" Macias asked.

"As soon as I talk to Silvio," Emilia replied.

"You want to talk to him now?" Macias exchanged a look with Sandor.

"Isn't he in?"

"He'd better be," Sandor said.

Both men were uncharacteristically nervous. Macias kept rubbing the fingers of his right hand together, while Sandor's eyes scanned the hallway behind her. "What's going on?" she asked warily.

Macias glanced at his watch. "Sorry, Cruz," he said. "Gotta go. Welcome back and all that shit."

"Yeah, sure." Emilia stepped out of the way.

Neither man took more than two steps before checked by the approach of Victor Obregon Sosa.

Emilia's mouth went dry. Of all the people she wanted to deal with on her first day back, the head of the police union for the state of Guerrero was last on the list.

"Gentlemen," Obregon said in the mocking drawl she

remembered. As usual, he was dressed like the devil's own fashionista: black suit, black dress shirt, black satin tie. "I take it you won't be joining us?"

"Excuse us," Sandor said shortly. He and Macias pushed by Obregon. The two detectives trotted down the hall toward the holding cells and the rear door to the parking lot.

"Well, well." The corner of Obregon's mouth quirked up as he saw Emilia. "If it isn't Detective Cruz. Back from her triumph in Mexico City."

"Hello," Emilia said.

Obregon had run the union for years, using the position to amass political power and hidden wealth. Several run-ins had taught Emilia that he was not a man to be trusted.

"I expect congratulations are in order," Obregon said. "You're quite the celebrity these days."

"Hardly." Emilia wondered what he was doing there. In her experience, his presence meant trouble.

Obregon smiled like a hawk assessing its prey. "Call my office and arrange a meeting. I'd like to hear how the task force solved the disappearance of those 43 students after all the previous investigations failed."

Like almost everyone else, Obregon only knew about her original assignment to the task force in Mexico City and nothing about the Special Operations extradition team.

"The Attorney General's office would be glad to brief you," Emilia parried.

"Modesty doesn't suit you, Detective." Obregon dragged his eyes away from Emilia as a short man in a tan trench coat came striding down the hallway as if he owned the place. "Ah, Enrique."

"Obregon," the man said, coming to a halt next to the union chief. "I hope we can make it fast. This place is a dump."

"Detective Emilia Cruz, may I introduce Enrique Santibañez, the mayor's new chief of staff." Obregon ignored the slur amid introductions. "Enrique, this is Detective Emilia Cruz, someone you need to know."

"A pleasure to meet you, señor," Emilia said.

Santibañez didn't offer to shake her hand. "Is she going to be in the meeting?" he asked Obregon.

"Yes." The rumble of Silvio's voice reverberated off the wall.

Emilia stifled a grin. The newly minted chief of detectives for the city of Acapulco filled the doorway with meter-wide shoulders and an expression like thunder. His white button-down shirt was an obvious concession to the new rank and responsibilities but at variance with the rest of his look: jeans, wiry crew cut, shoulder holster under the left arm, unconscious air of menace.

Santibañez took a step back. The two men had obviously never met. Silvio, a former champion heavyweight boxer, had the same effect on the mayor's man as he did in hundreds of lively interrogations.

Obregon made the introductions and Silvio ushered them into the squadroom.

Emilia looked around. The desks sprouted more computer

monitors, but otherwise the space was the same. Battered metal file cabinets. Walls segmented into murder boards, with photos and notes plastered on every vertical surface.

On the other side of the room, near the newish copier, a dark wood hutch held the coffee maker, a tray of clean mugs, and a built-in mini refrigerator. Silvio had kept the conference table across the room which his predecessor had installed, and Emilia knew it would be used for the daily 9:00 am meeting in an hour.

But the squadroom was eerily empty. Nobody typing up reports, pinning up crime scene photos, or looking through the latest missives from Dispatch.

Again, Emilia had a strong suspicion that she'd picked the wrong day.

She yanked Silvio over to the copier as Obregon and Santibañez settled themselves at the table. "What's going on?" she hissed.

"Just agree with whatever the fuck I say," Silvio growled.

"How do I know if you're right?"

"For fuck's sake, Cruz." Silvio glared at her. "Just do what I fucking say for fucking once in your life."

"I'm not fetching them coffee," Emilia warned.

Silvio snorted and led the way back to the table.

As soon as they were all seated, Santibañez announced that his time was limited.

"I'm sure that Lieutenant Silvio has a number of demands on his time as well," Obregon said silkily.

The air crackled with tension. Silvio responded by

opening a laptop.

Obregon and Silvio had been sworn enemies for decades. The animosity began when Silvio married Obregon's sister and his new brother-in-law launched a campaign of career-killing innuendo. The murder of Silvio's wife Isabel changed the dynamic, especially when Emilia and Silvio linked her death to Obregon's involvement in a money laundering scheme.

A few months later, Silvio was promoted to lieutenant.

"In response to the mayor's concerns of a growing theft problem at the airport," Silvio said so formally that Emilia nearly did a double take. "We've been able to make a preliminary identification of those responsible."

A wall-mounted television blinked on, showing the laptop's display. He moved the cursor around the screen and clicked a link.

"Preliminary?" Santibañez scoffed. "You've been working this problem for weeks, Lieutenant."

Silvio raised his eyes from the keyboard and focused on Obregon. Emilia could almost hear tension humming like an overstressed generator.

"Let's get on with it," Obregon urged.

The grainy feed from a security camera bloomed across the television, with a date-time stamp in the lower right corner. The view appeared to be of a packaging warehouse. As figures walked in and out of range, the focus sharpened and Emilia realized that the packages were suitcases circulating on a conveyor belt. Workers in security vests took some suitcases off the conveyor and left others to ride out of sight.

"This is the baggage handling zone in the airport," Silvio said. "In back of the ticket counters."

The silent camera feed blinked and the view zoomed toward the conveyor belt. Three men moved across the screen. One pulled a suitcase off the belt. A second man opened it. Both rifled through the contents, taking out small items. When they were done, the third man closed the case and replaced it on the conveyor. They were fast and efficient; the suitcase was delayed less than a minute. They plundered a dozen cases in less than eight minutes.

"What are they looking for?" Emilia asked, eyes glued to the video. "Drugs?"

"Jewelry," Obregon answered. "Watches, small electronics."

Emilia darted a look at the union chief. He looked bored and she guessed that he'd watched this footage before.

The camera view shifted again, although the conveyor was still in sight. A new date and time appeared in the corner. Suitcases were lined up in rows on the floor near the conveyor. Again, figures in security vests opened random suitcases and combed through the contents, taking out small items. The men were selective, Emilia realized. They only took large, hard sided suitcases off the conveyor. This time after the hard-sided suitcases were picked over, they were stacked on baggage carts.

"They're opening cases at various points in the luggage

handling system," Silvio said. "It depends on their shift assignment."

"What about identification?" Santibañez asked. He obviously hadn't seen the video before and was glued to the screen. "Do we know who the thieves are?"

"Coming up," Silvio muttered.

Another date and time change appeared on the screen, and yet another theft was carried out in grainy black and white.

The camera zoomed in close enough to see faces and the identification badges clipped to the workers' vests.

Silvio stopped the video. "We've got more, but it's more of the same."

"Why haven't these men been arrested?" Santibañez demanded.

"The video was obtained illegally," Obregon answered him.

"Is that true?" Santibañez shrilled.

"The baggage handlers union claims that police cameras in the airport are a violation of worker privacy," Obregon said. "In which case, it cannot be used as the basis for an arrest."

"That's ridiculous," Emilia said. The video evidence was more than solid.

"Thank you, Detective Cruz," Obregon said, his voice loaded with sarcasm. "Nonetheless, as things now stand, this video is inadmissible evidence. However, the police union has agreed to a joint investigation with the baggage handlers union to determine if worker rights have been violated."

"We all know that if you decide they have been," Silvio said. "It's precedent to argue against body cameras for cops. Workers rights, etcetera."

"The mayor is an advocate of police body cameras," Santibañez interjected.

The issue of body cameras for Acapulco cops was a hot button issue, Emilia knew. Cops across Mexico had a terrible reputation as thugs and thieves. Without body cameras, the charges were hard to refute. Advocacy groups argued the cameras would curb abusive police behavior. But many cops opposed the cameras, fearing they were a hindrance against the tough tactics needed against rising cartel violence.

"Of course the mayor is in favor of cameras," Obregon assured the chief of staff. "But that's a separate discussion. The two issues should not be conflated."

Silvio slammed down the laptop lid. The television screen went dark.

"Is that all?" Santibañez asked. "Do you have anything else to show us?"

"Just names, shift logs, addresses, and cell phone records," Silvio said.

"All obtained by illegal and inadmissible video," Obregon pointed out.

"So what do I tell the mayor?" Santibañez demanded. "Culprits identified but no arrests? When the press is eating us alive?" He dropped a folded copy of *La Jornada de Acapulco* on the table.

Emilia pulled the newspaper toward her. The bold

headline "Acapulco's Tourism Lifeline Under Threat" jumped off the front page. Starting with a shrill statement from the office of Carlota Montoya Perez, the city's popular mayor, the article chronicled dozens of complaints from travelers transiting the Acapulco airport.

"I'm sure the mayor will understand the need for the union investigation to go forward," Obregon said. "Half her electorate is union affiliated. They'll be watching to see if she supports them or not."

Silvio folded his arms. Emilia marveled at his composure.

Santibañez wasn't so sanguine. "You're suggesting we let the thefts continue until the union investigation wraps up?"

"Those complaints," Obregon said pointedly. "Were not made by Acapulco voters."

The meeting ended in a draw. Santibañez left the newspaper and grabbed his trench. Cell phone in hand, he scurried out ahead of Obregon.

At the door to the squadroom, Obregon confronted Silvio. "You understand, Franco," he said. "The cameras have to be removed."

A muscle jumped in Silvio's jaw. "The union's request is noted."

The hawkish expression slid over Obregon's face and faded, to be replaced by a look of bland interest. "Congratulations on the counterfeit seizure. I hear it was quite an impressive haul."

"Three million dollars," Silvio replied. "Washington is sending the Secret Service to come and collect it."

Disappointment hovered in the air as Obregon turned back to Emilia. The hawk was still hunting but circling higher, looking for easier prey.

"Welcome back, Detective," he said. "I'm sure we'll be seeing more of each other."

When the union chief headed down the corridor, Silvio turned on his heel, stalked through the empty squadroom, and disappeared into his office.

"*Madre de Dios*." Emilia took a deep breath as oxygen rushed back into the room. Her first day back and she'd fallen into the deep end of the always dangerous rivalry between the union chief and her former partner.

She made a pot of coffee and carried two steaming mugs past the placard proclaiming *Lieutenant Franco Silvio*.

"Obregon never liked cameras," she said, shoving the door open with her foot in lieu of knocking. "Means accountability. Possible unpopular union disciplinary action. But what is the deal with counterfeit—."

She stopped. The lieutenant's office was awash in case files. Silvio's ancient metal desk was nearly hidden beneath towers of manila folders gushing out random papers and photographs. More files teetered on the two visitor chairs and others formed an undulating barricade against the walls.

Despite the mess, the smell of lemon furniture polish thickened the air.

"Yeah, move those and sit down," Silvio said from behind the desk.

Emilia and looked around for a handy place to set the

mugs, kicking the door closed in the process. "Where . . . uhh . . . where . . ."

She handed him the mugs, scooped an armful of files from a chair, and balanced them on an already precarious stack on the filing cabinet. The pile obscured the bottom half of a poster advertising a championship boxing match. Emilia knew that fight had been Silvio's last bout on the heavyweight circuit.

There was no other decoration in the office. No photo of his late wife, Isabel. No evidence of a current romance.

"So what is all this?" Emilia asked. She sat in the empty chair and took back one of the mugs. "The Records department explode or something?"

"New database," Silvio said. "Fucked up everything."

"So we're back to paper files?" Emilia felt her jaw drop.

"It'll get fixed, Cruz," Silvio said tiredly. "Are you at the hotel again?"

"Yes." Emilia sipped the coffee, which wasn't bad. "Kurt drove me back from Mexico City."

"Good, I don't have to change your address in 15 different personnel databases." Silvio slurped from his mug. "How's Hollywood doing?"

"Worried about Russian funny business in his hotel."

Silvio snorted. "Yeah, that's a tragedy."

"It is to him," Emilia shot back.

"I assume the tribunal didn't find you guilty of treason." Silvio tipped his chair back and raised his mug in a sardonic toast.

"No." Emilia resisted the urge to throw her mug at his head. "Like I told you before, Anaya sold us out."

Only two cops in Acapulco knew about Emilia's role in the Special Operations extradition convoy: Silvio and Chief of Police Rodrigo Salazar. The tribunal had called both of them as character witnesses. Chief Salazar phoned in his testimony but Silvio went to Mexico City.

"*Rayos*," Silvio swore. He'd known Anaya, who'd also been a boxer before becoming a cop.

"Yeah." Emilia didn't want to talk about the ambush, too afraid she'd let something slip. They'd been partners long enough for her to know that Silvio's menacing exterior masked a shrewd observer. "Look, I'm ready to get back to work," she said. "Just need my gun and a new partner."

Silvio grunted, set his mug on a paper avalanche, and tapped at his keyboard. A printer hidden behind the stacks whirred. He plucked a sheet out of the hopper and shoved it at her.

Emilia expected to see the brief personnel description of a new detective. Her new partner.

It was the name and address of a doctor.

"What's this?" she asked blankly. "We're hiring doctors as detectives?"

"He's the police psychiatrist," Silvio said. "An expert on post traumatic stress. You have to schedule an appointment. Today. In person."

Emilia sucked in her breath and was rewarded with a gust of lemon polish. "Why the—."

"You're on medical leave for the next six weeks." Silvio toasted the paper with his mug. "After that, the doctor will evaluate your fitness for duty."

"Fitness for duty?" The conversation was suddenly rushing past her. "Who the hell says I'm not fit for duty? You?"

"You're on medical leave," Silvio said. He threw a set of car keys across the mountain of paper. "Go make your appointment."

Emilia scooped up the keys to the Suburban. "Don't be an idiot, Franco," she said, trying to get the situation under control. She needed that gun and she needed access to the police system. "With Obregon and that twerp from Carlota's office breathing down your neck, you need all the help you can get. I'm ready to work. Give me back my gun."

"No gun until the psychiatrist clears you for duty," Silvio said.

"Is this a joke?" Emilia looked around dramatically. "Is somebody going to jump out of this mess and yell 'Surprise?'"

"See you in six weeks, Cruz."

"Wait a minute." Emilia couldn't believe he'd stoop so low. "Is this your way of finally getting a woman out of the squadroom? Not cleared for duty? That's fucking convenient."

"Think what you want," Silvio shot back. "I don't owe you anything."

Madre de Dios, but the man was a pigheaded *pendejo*.

"You owe me a fucking explanation!" Emilia jabbed a finger at him. "You came to Mexico City. Testified to the tribunal. You never said a thing about fitness for duty or medical leave."

Silvio inhaled some coffee but didn't break eye contact. "I hadn't decided then."

He'd decided after seeing her in Mexico City? Because she was such a wreck? To her utter horror, Emilia made a choking sound as she was hit by an unstoppable gush of hot tears.

Silvio set his mug down with a thump. Coffee slopped out. A dark stain spread across the file folders.

They sat in silence. Silvio stared woodenly at his screensaver. Emilia scrabbled through her shoulder bag for a tissue, furious with herself.

Silvio finally cleared his throat. "Emilia, look," he began, his voice uncharacteristically gentle. "You—."

"Fuck your pity," Emilia interrupted harshly. "I'll be fine."

She launched herself out of the chair and scooped up the psychiatrist's information.

Silvio rose. "My regards to Hollywood."

Emilia yanked open the office door, causing papers to flutter off the filing cabinet and stir the over-scented air.

Lemon, for sure, but there was a spicy note, too.

Maybe not furniture polish.

She glanced back at Silvio, for the first time seeing the starched crispness of his white shirt, the new braided belt, the crease in his jeans. She was used to seeing him in a sweat-stained tee, smelling vaguely of carbolic soap, old leather, and salt.

"Are you wearing cologne?" Emilia asked, hearing the incredulity in her voice.

A familiar scowl tightened Silvio's features. "Get out, Cruz."

The Suburban sounded like an asthmatic bulldozer as Emilia waited for the guard to lift the barrier and allow her to drive out of the police station lot. As she headed toward the main artery that wrapped around the lip of the bay, Emilia kept a watchful eye on her mirrors. If Barrielos Luna's *sicarios* were out there, the big white Suburban would be relatively easy to follow.

After 20 minutes of aimless driving, it was clear no one was tailing her.

This time.

As the Suburban wheezed and rattled, Emilia pulled into a PEMEX station for gas. The national oil and gas company's green, white, and red colors blared across the plaza. To Emilia's surprise, the station was closed. Decorated with a logo featuring a stylized eagle's head superimposed on a solid drop of oil, each bright green pump was locked with plastic sheeting around the handle, along with signs reading *CERRADO! NO HAY GASOLINA!*

Closed! There is no gas!

The next PEMEX station she tried was open but jammed. Under the wide silver roof, at least two cars waited for each of the dozen pumps. PEMEX stations were not self-serve, making for slow progress. Attendants in their ubiquitous gray PEMEX uniforms and ball caps trotted from car to car, making change from rolls of peso bills, enticing motorists to get their oil checked or buy the fuel additives stacked in colorful displays at either end of the plaza.

When she finally got to a pump, Emilia cut the engine and winced as the Suburban gave an exhausted groan. An attendant in a mostly clean uniform appeared at her window. "*Hola*, señora. A full tank today?"

"Yes, thank you."

The attendant rushed to the pump, peered at the meter, and reset the counters for gallons and pesos with exaggerated motions. He tapped the display, making sure Emilia saw that everything was set to zero.

Once Emilia nodded her acknowledgment, he lifted the handle with a flourish. Gas glugged into the Suburban.

Every PEMEX attendant did the same thing in a ritual to demonstrate that the driver wasn't being cheated. In return for this pantomime of honesty, the tip should be an appropriate reflection of the driver's gratitude.

Emilia gave the attendant an extra 10 pesos.

She wasn't that grateful today.

Okay, so she'd had the last word in an exchange with Franco Silvio. That was emotional money in the bank. But without access to the national police database, she just lost six precious weeks in the hunt for Rafa Gamboa.

And without her gun, Emilia was never going to feel safe again.

CHAPTER 4

Emilia reeled out of the police psychiatrist's office, clutching a schedule of appointments and a small notebook. She was exhausted by a combination of unwelcome scrutiny and utter frustration.

She also had homework.

Every evening she was to write down three things for which she was grateful. The psychiatrist called the notebook a gratitude journal, as if she was a child preparing for First Holy Communion.

They'd review her entries at the twice-weekly appointments.

The *pendejo* of a doctor had actually clicked his tongue at her when she asked about being cleared for duty sooner than six weeks. Six weeks was the minimum, he informed her, with the maximum as much as a year. He was honest, but totally unaware that his new patient felt his words like a punch to the gut.

Resisting the urge to scream at the man, Emilia went back to the Palacio Réal and threw the journal in a drawer. Kurt came up to the penthouse from his office on the ground floor of the hotel. They ate dinner on the balcony overlooking the Pasodoble Bar, neither mentioning last night's disappointment. Afterwards, Emilia organized her closet.

Kurt read a book before turning out his light.

The next morning, he was out of the penthouse by 5:00 am to work out. Emilia flipped her hair into a ponytail and treated herself to the gauzy plum-colored sundress she'd bought in Mexico City. Flat sandals, a swipe of mascara, and a slash of bright lipstick. A skinny leather belt made her waist look tiny.

The woman in the mirror was fit and attractive.

Not some crazy *bruja* who was afraid of sex or needed to spill her innermost fears to some psychiatrist.

"Hello, Mama," Emilia said, practicing the line to her reflection. "How are you?"

Despite the brave outfit and practice in front of the mirror, Emilia knew she wasn't in the best mood for the challenge ahead as she coaxed the Suburban up the steep cobbled hill that ran between the hotel complex and the highway. While in Mexico City, she'd called a few times, gritting her teeth as her mother Sophia Encinos prattled on about her husband Ernesto's knife grinding business, cousin Alvaro's children, or fresh *jitomates* at the market. For Emilia, the confrontation with her mother over Rafa Gamboa was still unresolved.

But the topic no longer existed for Sophia. The argument over the son she'd given away so long ago blew away like tears in the wind, never to be mentioned again.

Once in the central Acapulco *barrio* where Emilia grew up and Sophia and her husband still lived, Emilia made for a small shopping center. "Reinforcements," she murmured to herself.

The Suburban emitted a series of sighing clicks before the engine shut off. The white beast, confiscated from drug mules and assigned to Emilia as her official police vehicle, was long overdue for a check-up. Or possibly a replacement.

The sign for Mercedes Sandoval's dance studio glinted in the mid-morning sunshine. The brown metal slab of a door was protected by a heavy iron security grille. Light shone through the curtained windows, also fortified by decorative ironwork. Emilia rang the intercom bell and was rewarded by a metallic voice asking for identification.

"Emilia Cruz to see Mercedes Sandoval," Emilia shouted into the retrofitted speaker jammed into the stucco. Two beats later, the deadbolt clunked.

"Oh, Emilia!" Mercedes squealed. She pulled Emilia through both doors and into a rollicking hug in the middle of the empty studio. "I've missed you!"

Mercedes was deceptively strong and Emilia was nearly breathless by the time they broke apart. The former ballroom dance champion was several years older but her camisole and capri leggings revealed the musculature and lithe movements of a teenager.

"I missed you, too." Emilia was buoyed by the fierce show of friendship. "It's been a crazy couple of months."

"I want to hear all about Mexico City," Mercedes said. She held Emilia at arm's length and studied her dress and bare arms with approval. "You look amazing. Tell me you did something besides go to the gym. Did you get to the

Ballet Folklórico? A concert at the Palacio de Bellas Artes? You at least had drinks at the Gran Hotel under the stained glass roof?"

I worked. Later, I got shot at.

But Mercedes, like the rest of the public, didn't—and couldn't— know about the assignment with Special Operations.

"I had lunch once at El Péndulo," Emilia said with a rueful smile. "But mostly Mexico City looked like the inside of an office building."

"What about Kurt? Was he glad to see you again? Of course he was." Mercedes hooked an arm through Emilia's and steered her toward the single room off the dance floor that functioned as living room, bedroom, kitchen, and office. "Come into my boudoir. I'll make us a cup of tea and we can talk all morning. I don't have any students until this afternoon."

Emilia tugged Mercedes to a stop. "I need a big favor," she said. "A huge favor."

Mercedes searched Emilia's face. "What's wrong?"

"Can you come to my mother's with me?"

"Oh, Emilia." Mercedes covered her mouth in dismay. "You haven't seen her yet?"

Emilia shook her head. There was no need to explain.

Mercedes knew the whole story.

She knew the awful way Emilia discovered that she had a brother. She knew that Sophia admitted to giving him away after her first husband Ernesto died in a car accident.

Mercedes even knew the rest of the story, which Emilia got from the woman who raised Rafa Gamboa.

Emilia's father had been the chauffeur for Karina Escobar de la Vega's husband, a doctor who also died in the accident. After both husbands were buried, Sophia demanded that Karina, who was childless, take one of the two Cruz toddlers. If not, they'd be abandoned in the street.

As Sophia shoved the children forward, Ernesto Junior became hysterical. He was 3 years old and knew something was wrong. Emilia was younger and quiet, clinging to a doll for comfort.

Doubtful that Sophia could manage the screaming boy, Karina chose him. The brother got a new name and every advantage in life. Sophia took Emilia and raised her in poverty.

Karina never saw or heard anything about the Cruz family again.

Until almost 30 years later, when a cop named Emilia Cruz Encinos came to Karina's mansion in Las Brisas, asking questions about a man named Rafael Gamboa Escobar, aka Rafa Gamboa, aka El Acólito.

Simple iron gates bisected the wall surrounding the little yellow stucco house. Through the bars, Emilia saw Ernesto Cruz in his usual spot in the courtyard, hunched on the small stool by the grinding wheel.

He worked the foot pedal and the sun glinted on the wheel as it spun faster. His leather apron was stained with oil and absorbed the sparks flying from the blade of a scissors as he pressed it to the coarse surface of the wheel, the steel keening a protest. Spread on a cloth on the paving stones, several more blades awaited their turn.

As the Suburban wheezed like a racehorse, Emilia tooted the horn. Ernesto stopped the wheel and trotted to the gate latch.

A bronzed and wiry man in his late 40s, he looked much healthier than when he entered their lives as a vagrant Sophia found wandering in the market. His name was the same as Emilia's father, prompting Sophia to merge the two men in her mind. Even now that her mother and Ernesto were properly married, Emilia wasn't totally sure her mother understood that this Ernesto Cruz was not the same Ernesto Cruz who'd died in that fateful car accident so many years ago.

Ernesto charged a few pesos apiece to sharpen blades for the *barrio* and the grinding wheel quickly became a neighborhood fixture. Housewives brought knives, dulled by hacking up chicken bones and rope and plastic bottles. Gardeners brought their machetes and clippers. A small sewing workshop down the street provided a steady stream of commercial shears.

Emilia and Mercedes watched as Ernesto lifted the iron rod that kept the left side of the gate pinned in place and walked the gate open. The metal shavings clinging to his apron winked in the sunlight as he trotted to the other side. Only when both halves of the gate stood ajar, pinned in place by the attached drop rods, did Emilia drive in. Everyone knew the damage a free-swinging iron gate could do to a car.

"*Hola*, Ernesto," Emilia called as she climbed out. "How's business?"

"A good day," Ernesto said as he closed and secured the gates behind the Suburban.

"Is Mama at home?"

"She's in the kitchen with your Tía Lourdes."

With that, the conversation was over. Ernesto was a man of few words. He seated himself on the stool by the wheel and picked up the scissors. His foot worked the pedal, the wheel spun, and the two women hastened inside as the sharpening process screeched into the glorious blue sky.

Emilia called out a greeting and two voices replied from the back of the house. She ushered Mercedes into the small kitchen to see Sophia and Tía Lourdes with the makings for tamales.

"Mercedes Sandoval!" Sophia froze by the table, startled in the act of wiping her hands on the flowered apron she wore over a checkered dress, her hair in a loose braid and brown plastic flip flops on her feet. Her high cheekbones and almond eyes were untouched by age; strangers invariably assumed Sophia and Emilia were sisters.

"Mercedes Sandoval!" Tía Lourdes chorused with her sister-in-law.

The presence of the former ballroom champion, whom

her mother and aunt regarded as the biggest celebrity Acapulco boasted, had the intended effect. As Sophia whisked away the corn husks and Lourdes flew around with cups and saucers, there was no time for animosity between mother and daughter.

"Please, don't go to any trouble." Mercedes waved her hands in graceful protest and winked at Emilia. In a strapless sundress that kissed the floor, with her thick brown hair swept into a stylishly messy twist, the dancer was ready to play her role to perfection.

Sophia and Lourdes gazed at Mercedes in adoration as they served tea.

"You should have called first," Sophia said. "I have a cell phone."

"Of course, Mama." Emilia had bought the phone for her mother but Sophia didn't remember things like that.

"Did you like Mexico City, Emilia?" Lourdes asked.

"It was big," Emilia said. "Very big."

Lourdes peered at the doorway between the kitchen and living room as if expecting to see a suitcase. "Where are your things?"

Small and slender, her thin face creased with squint lines, Lourdes was the wife of Raul Cruz, the brother of Emilia's late father. After the fateful car accident, Lourdes and Raul took in the widowed sister-in-law and toddler daughter. Emilia grew up in the small apartment over Raul's car repair business, where Lourdes was perpetually in motion, cooking, cleaning, mending clothes, and stretching Tío

Raul's paltry income to feed her husband and two sons as well as the newcomers.

"I'm living at the Palacio Réal again," Emilia said.

"Is Carlos there?" Sophia asked, as if Emilia could afford to live alone in a hotel that cost 8000 pesos a night.

"Yes, Carlos is fine, Mama," Emilia said. Sophia always called Kurt by the closest Mexican approximation of his name. "I'll tell him you said hello."

"Have you spoken to Padre Ricardo?" Lourdes asked pointedly.

"I wanted to see Mama first," Emilia replied, hoping to avoid an argument.

Lourdes greeted Emilia with outstretched hands and an exchange of kisses, but she was deeply Catholic. To her, Emilia and Kurt were living in sin, compounded by the fact that he was a *gringo*. Emilia knew he was not welcome in her home.

"I saw you on *Bailando por un Sueño,*" Sophia said to Mercedes, unwittingly diffusing the moment. "Did you win?"

"I wish I had." Mercedes laughed. "But I've never been on the show."

"You wore a blue dress in the finale," Sophia said, as if Mercedes had forgotten.

As the other three women chatted awkwardly about the popular dance competition show, Emilia sipped tea and looked around, realizing that she hadn't been back to her mother's house since the day Sophia had angrily admitted that she'd given her eldest child to Karina Escobar de la Vega. It was the only time Sophia had ever acted like an adult instead of the childlike woman who'd never recovered from a nervous breakdown.

Emilia's glance lingered on the wall behind the table, as if expecting to see the remains of the mug Sophia had hurled at her.

But all she saw was painted stucco. Tile countertops, a pot simmering on the stove, a bottle of iodine by the sink for soaking raw fruit and vegetables. A breeze puffed the cotton curtains framing the open window, carrying the sounds of Ernesto's work from the other side of the house. The constant whirr of the spinning wheel, the intermittent rasp of dull steel against coarse stone.

"Mama, Tía Lourdes," Emilia interjected when there was a lull in the conversation. "I need to talk to you all about something."

"You're getting married," Lourdes said immediately.

Mercedes lifted her eyebrows and kicked Emilia under the table.

"No, that's not it," Emilia said and returned the favor. "It's about my work."

Lourdes pursed her lips. Mercedes frowned. Sophia blithely went to the counter and began refilling the tea kettle from the big *garrafon* of bottled water.

"Mama!" Emilia jumped up and took the kettle out of Sophia's hands. "This is important. I need you to listen."

Sophia blinked. "If you got a bad grade at school,

Emilia," she said with a vague smile. "It's all right. I know you try your best."

"It's not about school," Emilia said, hearing the annoyance in her voice.

She led Sophia back to the table amid her mother's fluttery protests about making more tea. "I met some people in Mexico City when I was there," Emilia began again. "They might come looking for me."

"New friends," Sophia said with approval.

"No, they aren't nice people and I don't want to see them again. So if strangers ask about me, say I'm still in Mexico City and call me right away."

Sophia cocked her head. "Are you in Mexico City?"

"No, Mama." Emilia swallowed her impatience with her mother, the way she'd done thousands of times before. "But it's better if the bad people think I am."

"Well, all right," Sophia said uncertainly. "Should Ernesto say that, too?"

"Yes, Mama. You should all say the same thing. Even Tía Lourdes and Tío Raul." Emilia took a deep breath. "These bad people? They might be looking for Rafael Escobar Gamboa, too."

Lourdes gasped. Mercedes was motionless.

Sophia shrugged, her expression still one of happy confusion. "I don't know him."

"You know who he is, Mama," Emilia said, struggling to keep her voice even. "We talked about him. Rafa Gamboa is your son. My brother. The boy Karina raised."

To Emilia's surprise, her mother patted Emilia's cheek. "You're being so silly, Emilia. Saying that strangers are going to come around and ask questions. There aren't any strangers in our *barrio*."

"That's good, Mama," Emilia said, oddly deflated by the way her mother had sidestepped discussion of Rafa Gamboa. "So you'll know if they're strangers. We never tell strangers personal things, right?"

"My Emilia, she worries about everything," Sophia said to Mercedes as a car engine revved outside. "Even when she was a little girl."

"Is there a problem, Emilia?" Lourdes asked quietly. "Shall I say something to Alvaro?"

A few years older than Emilia, her cousin Alvaro was also a cop. Sergeant Alvaro Cruz ran the central police evidence locker, a position which afforded him the ability to both grant and receive favors. He and his wife Daysi had a house with a washer and dryer and the latest electronic gadgets. They owned two cars and sent their children to an exclusive pre-school.

"Don't worry," Emilia said. "I'll talk to—."

The air filled with the screech of metal on metal and a tremendous bang shook the house as if two trains had collided in the courtyard. The overhead light flickered, the floor heaved up, and Emilia lost her balance. She crashed into the table hard enough to flip it over and Sophia screamed as cups and saucers crumbled into a thousand shards of pottery scattered across the tile floor.

"It's an earthquake!" Lourdes shrilled. Sophia screamed again, eyes wide in fright.

Mercedes helped Emilia right the table and quickly shepherd the older women into a huddle underneath it. Emilia held her breath, hands flat on the floor as if she could push a quake into submission.

But instead of another tremor, they heard doors slam and Ernesto shout. A big engine rumbled and the grinding wheel's clackety-clackety rhythm slowed. Emilia smelled car exhaust as thick dust played in the sunlight streaming through the kitchen curtains and settled on the dark fabric of her dress. She wondered if the front of the house had crumbled.

"Stay under the table," she said to the women cowering against the wall. She cautiously raised herself into a crouch, only to be checked when Mercedes grabbed her hem.

"Where are you going?" Mercedes demanded. "There could be another tremor."

"I don't think so," Emilia said. "I think something hit the house."

"Be careful," Mercedes warned.

Emilia squeezed out from under the table. Pebbly grit crunched under the soles of her sandals as she hurried into the living room, following the unmistakable sounds of a scuffle.

The big window which faced the courtyard was a blank hole. Instead of a sheet of glass, the radiator of her Suburban filled the opening. A carpet of glass and cement debris spread over Sophia's pristine furniture. The air was so thick with dust that Emilia began to choke.

She stumbled back into the kitchen and dropped to her knees next to Mercedes. "Call the police, tell them I'm here and that it's a home invasion."

Her friend already had her phone in hand as Emilia turned to Sophia. "Mama, you stay here. Don't make a sound."

"Ernesto?" Sophia quavered.

"I'll go find him," Emilia said. She snatched up the big knife Sophia used for cutting bones and grabbed the lid off a pot on the stove.

Thus armed, Emilia slipped out the back door to the patio, a blank piece of cement littered with battered trash cans and clay troughs for Sophia's spindly cilantro and parsley plants. It narrowed into a path that wound around the house to the front courtyard where Ernesto kept his wheel.

Staying in the shadow of the house, Emilia crept along the path, knife in one hand, pot lid in the other, the throb of a car engine and the grunts and thrusts of a fistfight louder with every step. Her own shallow breathing sounded like waves crashing on rocks as she alternated between straining to hear a siren and silently cursing Silvio for hanging onto her gun.

At the corner of the house, Emilia eased herself into the shade of a young jacaranda tree that softened the side of the house. Gathering her courage, and thankful that the color of her dress blended into the foliage, she poked her head out far enough to see into the courtyard.

It was a crime scene in process. The gates were open but each half was bent and buckled, creaking dangerously from a single hinge. An enormous black SUV with tinted windows and a crossbar welded to its front bumper idled behind the Suburban. Wearing black military balaclavas covering their entire heads except for their eyes, two men struggled to lever Ernesto into the rear of the big vehicle. Another masked man stood at the ready, a long black rifle swinging in an arc over his field of vision.

With his head covered by a plastic bag and his hands tied behind his back, Ernesto jackknifed his body like a gymnast but to no avail. The two men wrestled him into the back seat, jumped in after him, and slammed the doors.

The engine roared. The SUV vibrated. A second later, the Suburban did the same.

The two vehicles were locked together. The black SUV had obviously rammed through the gates with its cross bar and hit the Suburban hard enough to propel it into the living room window. Now the cross bar was caught on the Suburban's rear end.

With a ringing clang, the SUV lurched backwards. The Suburban's bumper flew into the bright afternoon sky. Emilia flinched as tires screaming, the black SUV backed out of the courtyard. It cleared the broken gates and roared into the street. In an instant, the black monster vanished, taking her mother's husband with it.

The Suburban's bumper clanged onto the paving stones like a dead meteor falling to the earth.

CHAPTER 5

Emilia cut the twine and peeled a handkerchief-sized piece of muslin away from the chunk of cement block. She smoothed the fabric on the kitchen table and they all stared silently at the message inked in crude block letters.

NO COPS
SOPHIA
WAIT FOR
THE CALL

"Whatever's going on," Lieutenant Franco Silvio said. "They're making it public and personal."

Emilia found her mother's cell phone plugged into the charger and brought it to the table.

"So now what?" Mercedes asked.

"We wait," Emilia and Silvio said at the same time.

The immediate aftermath of Ernesto's kidnapping was chaos. Neighbors streamed into the courtyard to gasp and gawk. Two patrol cars of uniforms shouted conflicting orders. Sophia screamed and screamed.

Along with her cousin Alvaro, Silvio arrived less than ten minutes after Emilia dialed his cellphone. Her former partner, now chief of detectives, took control of the onlookers, the over-excited uniforms, and the crime scene techs who could do little more than photograph the damage.

Alvaro brought his father—Emilia's Tío Raul. Eventually they were able to push the Suburban out of the way and board up the gaping hole left by the shattered living room window.

Sophia subsided into shell shock. When the crime scene techs departed, Mercedes and Lourdes swept the living room and found the fabric-wrapped cement missile.

"I don't understand," Sophia said. "How do they know me?"

Because of me.

Emilia's chest was so tight she couldn't speak. None of the scenarios that dominated her thoughts for weeks included kidnapping her mother's husband to get her attention. Barrielos Luna was craftier beyond her wildest dreams.

Alvaro took out his own cell phone. "We need a plan for handling the call."

The sound of a saw ripped through the air. "I'll check on your father," Lourdes said. Mercedes followed her out, leaving Emilia and her mother seated at the kitchen table with Silvio and Alvaro.

"Señora," Silvio said gently to Sophia. "Is there something only you and Ernesto would know? Not exactly a secret but something you know about him that no one else could know?"

Sophia blinked and turned to Emilia in confusion.

"For when they call, Mama," Emilia explained. The first priority was always to get proof the victim of a kidnapping was alive. "If we can't talk to him, we need to at least prove they really have Ernesto and aren't trying to trick you."

"I made *albondigas* for him yesterday," Sophia offered. Her eyes filled with tears.

"That's good, *tía,*" Alvaro said encouragingly. "Did you tell anyone besides Ernesto what you cooked?"

"No." Sophia gestured to the refrigerator. "There's extra, if you want some."

Silvio caught Emilia's eye and cocked his head towards the back door. She followed him outside to the patio, fully expecting him to say he knew that Barrielos Luna was behind this. Silvio had to know. He always knew.

"What's the deal with your mother's husband?" Silvio threw out as soon as the back door closed. "Is he some sort of low level courier or *halcone*?"

"You think Ernesto's working for a gang?" Emilia didn't know whether to laugh or cry. "No, he's a knife grinder."

"You've known him two years. What the fuck was he doing before that?"

"He was a knife grinder in Mexico City."

"Maybe trouble followed him."

"This has everything to do with Barrielos Luna," Emilia said.

"That's out of the fucking blue," Silvio said.

"We've both been a cop too long to believe in coincidences," Emilia insisted. "I watch the *cabrón* escape custody, then something real bad happens to my family right after I get home? This has Barrielos Luna written all over it."

Silvio scowled. "The Barrel Bomber's got better things to

do than snatch some Acapulco knife grinder."

"He's got a long arm," Emilia countered.

"Look, Cruz," Silvio said, with an air of patience she didn't like. "You might have seen Barrielos Luna kill a bunch of people but that doesn't mean he's got any interest in your mother's husband. Let's work on the most probable theories, first. Ernesto is probably up to his neck in local gang shit."

"*Madre de Dios*, Franco." Emilia had to tell him after all, but Silvio wasn't listening, the *pendejo*. "I know Barrielos Luna is behind this."

"Does Ernesto have any tattoos?" Silvio pushed his own agenda. "Where does he hang out in the evenings? A bar? Pool hall? What do you know about his friends?"

"Ernesto is not some criminal!"

"Okay," Silvio said with a glare. "We'll leave Ernesto's habits for now. How about we focus on the immediate future? Whenever the call comes, your mother's in no shape to work the conversation."

His sharp left turn gave Emilia a moment to catch her breath before she spilled out her secret. She crossed her arms. "I know."

"You'll have to pretend to be her," Silvio ordered. "Verify they've got Ernesto and find out what they want."

"Okay."

The back door banged open. "It's ringing!" Alvaro shouted, startling them both.

Emilia skidded into a chair next to her mother and took a

deep breath. Her mother's phone vibrated on the table, the display lit with Ernesto's number.

It was a hopeful sign. Express kidnappers invariably used the victim's own phone to contact family. A ransom of a few thousand pesos, usually the limit that could be withdrawn in one day from a local ATM, was all that was needed to release the victim, shaken but unharmed.

"Mama," Emilia said hurriedly. "I'm going to pretend to be you. Don't say anything. Let me talk."

Silvio tapped the screen, activating the speaker.

"*Bueno*?" Emilia answered the call. "Ernesto? Is that you?"

"Sophia Encinos, we have your husband." The words were spoken by a robotic and distorted male voice.

Sophia gasped.

"Let me talk to him," Emilia said. "Prove that—."

"The debts of Ricardo and Rubén are due." The voice cut her off. "Los Colectores has set the ransom for Ernesto Cruz at two million dollars in cash money."

Ricardo and Rubén. The names meant nothing to Emilia. "Let me talk to Ernesto," she insisted.

"Two million dollars," the voice intoned. "In five days you will receive a text message from a different number. Follow the instructions. Do not waste time. Do not let Ernesto suffer."

"I want to hear Ernesto—." The words were barely out of Emilia's mouth before a soft electronic pop ended the call.

Emilia stared numbly at the black screen.

"It was a pre-recorded message with a voice masking app," Silvio said. "This Los Colectores group planned this in advance."

Los Colectores.

The Collectors.

"Five days to raise two million dollars?" Alvaro gulped. "They have to know we can't pay that."

Sophia grabbed Emilia's arm. "Was Ernesto kidnapped?"

"Yes, Mama." Emilia heard her voice crack with tension.

"Maybe they took the wrong Ernesto Cruz," Alvaro speculated.

"Mama, who are Ricardo and Rubén?" Emilia asked.

"I don't know," Sophia said wonderingly.

Lourdes and Raul took Sophia home with them. Mercedes returned to the studio to teach her afternoon dance classes, shaken but wholly the professional.

Silvio and her cousin Alvaro decamped to the back yard to look through the shed where Ernesto kept tools. Emilia didn't follow but wearily went upstairs.

At least Kurt was on the way.

She had to admit that Silvio's question about Ernesto's life before coming to Acapulco hit a sore spot. Ernesto had arrived on their doorstep with little besides the clothes on his back and the grinding wheel in a sack. Later, he revealed that he left a wife in Mexico City. Eventually, Emilia helped him reestablish contact so he could get a divorce.

Ricardo and Rubén.

Ernesto's ex-wife Beatriz was the only person Emilia could think of who might have information about the men named by the kidnapper. Emilia could ask everybody who knew Ernesto in Acapulco, but she already knew what they would say. Sophia's husband did virtually nothing without her. Their lives were predictable. Church on Sunday, occasional meals with Lourdes and Raul or visits to her cousin Alvaro's house to see the children.

Mostly Ernesto worked. No clubs, sports, or meals in restaurants.

Emilia went into the larger of the two bedrooms. It was as feminine as before Ernesto came into their lives. Sophia's floral dresses hung from wall hooks. Frilly curtains decorated the windows. The well-worn bedspread was pink.

When Emilia and her mother lived in the house, they had no secrets from each other apart from a stash of condoms Emilia hid in a pair of socks. But now Emilia felt like an intruder, come to secretly rifle through a married couple's privacy.

As an uncomfortable mixture of curiosity and guilt churned in the back of her mind, Emilia methodically looked through the tiny closet and her mother's dresser. In the bottom drawer she found a battered accordion folder. She sat on the bed and opened it.

A thick piece of paper was on top, embossed with the elaborate seal of the bishop of Mexico City. The sacrament of marriage between Ernesto Cruz Centeno and Beatriz Parrales de Cruz was hereby sundered as neither had entered into the sacrament with the understanding required. The folded civil divorce decree was less elaborate, the wording more clinical.

Emilia expanded the accordion and fished out two wrinkled handwritten letters.

On lined paper torn from a student notebook, the first letter from Beatriz to Ernesto was a plea for him to return. The second apparently was a response to Ernesto's reply that he wanted a divorce to remarry. Now Beatriz was a woman spurned, angrily agreeing to the divorce.

The same cell phone number was scrawled on the bottom of both letters. Neither mentioned Ricardo or Rubén.

Ten minutes later, after a thorough search of the rest of the bedroom, as well as the smaller room that used to be hers, Emilia brought Beatriz's letters downstairs and showed them to Silvio and Alvaro.

"So call her," Silvio said as they sat in the kitchen. "See if she knows who Ricardo and Rubén are."

"Here goes," Emilia said. She punched in the number and hit the speaker button.

After the third ring, a woman's voice answered with a cautious "*Bueno*?"

"This is Detective Emilia Cruz from the Acapulco police," Emilia introduced herself. "May I speak with Beatriz Parrales de Cruz?"

"Speaking," the woman said warily.

"Beatriz, my mother Sophia is married to Ernesto, your ex-husband."

"Good for him." Beatriz obviously had little affection left for her ex-husband.

"Ernesto's run into a little trouble here in Acapulco."

"You're police?"

"I'm Sophia's daughter," Emilia said.

"Huh."

At least the woman hadn't hung up. "We've been informed," Emilia said. "That Ernesto . . . uh . . . owes a significant sum of money."

"That's not my problem," Beatriz said swiftly. "I don't have any money."

"Apparently he owes money," Emilia said. "Because of someone else. Two men named Ricardo and Rubén. We don't know their full names and thought you might."

Emilia paused, hearing nothing from the other end.

"Do you have any information about these men?" Emilia plowed on. "Perhaps Ricardo and Rubén were associates of Ernesto's in Mexico City? Are the names even remotely familiar?"

Sobbing filled the phone.

"Beatriz?"

"He left me, you know." Beatriz's voice acquired a distant quality as if she'd put the phone down and was speaking past it. "When we heard the boys were dead, he walked away and never came back."

A sudden chill raced down Emilia's spine and lodged in

the pit of her stomach. How could she have forgotten that Ernesto had two sons who died trying to cross the desert into *El Norte*? She never knew their names, only that Ernesto left Mexico City after learning of their deaths.

"Ricardo and Rubén were your sons?" Emilia tried to make the blunt question as gentle as possible. "Did they owe anyone money, Beatriz?"

"El Cripo." Beatriz coughed, a soupy hack that sounded as if her lungs were underwater. "A man named El Cripo. He made a contract with Ernesto to guide the boys. When they got to *El Norte* they'd pay him back. Send us money, too."

Silvio rubbed fingers against his thumb. *How much*?

Emilia nodded. "How much was the contract for, Beatriz?"

"I don't know." Beatriz sounded even more distant. She coughed again.

"Tell me about this El Cripo?" Emilia regrouped. "Was he from Mexico City? Does he have a real name?"

"I don't remember."

Silvio mouthed *Los Colectores*.

Emilia nodded, grateful for the prompt. "Beatriz, you're being so helpful. Did this El Cripo work for a group called Los Colectores?"

"What?"

"Los Colectores," Emilia said.

"No, no. We never saw him. Only Luca."

It was a thread and Emilia grabbed it. "Who is Luca?"

"Ricardo and Rubén went with Luca," Beatriz said. "That

was the last time we ever saw them. Rubén was 14 years old."

"I'm so sorry for your loss, Beatriz," Emilia said, her heart breaking at the other woman's distress. "I hate to think this call is causing you pain, but Ernesto is in trouble and you've been so helpful." She gathered herself for one last effort. "What was Luca's full name?"

"Luca . . . maybe Diaz. Luca Diaz."

"No second name?"

"I'm not sure . . ." Beatriz coughed again. "Maybe Alonso. Luca Diaz Alonso."

"Luca Diaz Alonso," Emilia repeated as Silvio wrote it down. "Was he from your *barrio* in Mexico City?"

"Ernesto said the boys would be fine," Beatriz said angrily. "They'd have a better life in *El Norte*. Instead, they're dead, he's married to someone else, and I'm sick with the cancer. In my lungs. Ernesto's your problem now."

The connection cut off.

"See, not Barrielos Luna," Silvio said pointedly to Emilia.

Alvaro looked confused. "What's the Barrel Bomber got to do with anything?"

"Nothing, *primo*," Emilia snapped. "A fucking lieutenant and he still doesn't know what he's saying."

"Is there a problem—," Alvaro started.

"They died," Emilia cut him off. Her emotions sparked like lightning in a bottle. "Didn't you hear her? The boys died. So why blame Ernesto?"

"Doesn't matter if they're dead," Silvio observed. "*Coyotes* still want their money. With interest."

"*Madre de Dios*," Emilia burst out. "We're living in hell."

The kitchen was small and cramped and closing in on her. Emilia rushed through the living room, the floor twinkling with grains of glass too small for her aunt's broom. The front door gave way to the courtyard.

The Suburban still rested against the house like a beached whale caught in a cement net.

Above the vehicle, the window was covered with plywood. Orange traffic cones marched across the gap in the wall where the gates had once protected the house. The two panels of wrought iron were propped against the inside wall, like the broken shields of a vanquished giant. The bumper was on the ground next to Sophia's geraniums.

Emilia leaned against the driver's side of the Suburban. Supposedly a police tow truck was coming to haul it off to car heaven. She closed her eyes and lifted her face to catch the waning rays of the setting sun. Silvio would have to find her a new official vehicle.

She heard two sets of footsteps come out of the front door and circle around the Suburban. Emilia cracked an eye. A hand held out a sweaty beer bottle.

"Apparently, Ernesto drinks Negra Modelo," Alvaro said. "I would have put him down for a Pacifico man."

"Thanks," Emilia said gratefully and took the bottle. Her stomach growled and she realized she hadn't eaten all day. As Silvio joined them, another bottle in hand, the beer hit her stomach like a cool, yeasty bomb.

The three cops watched the sun bid another spectacular farewell to the day. At street level, Acapulco was gray and broken and riddled with crime, but above the mess, the city was painted with a shimmering palette of rose and gold.

"We have to call Hostage Negotiations, *prima*," Alvaro said quietly.

"No," Emilia said. "The more police are involved the worse it will be for Ernesto."

"Hostage Negotiations has the horsepower to connect with Mexico City," Alvaro pointed out. "Dig up Ernesto's contacts. Work the ransom negotiations."

Emilia closed her eyes. She was still stuck on the hamster wheel named Barrielos Luna. If he was behind Ernesto's kidnapping and Hostage Negotiations somehow connected with the drug kingpin . . .

"Lemme tell you something, Cruz." Silvio's voice ripped through her thoughts like a buzz saw. "You're on medical leave. No gun until the counselor signs off. Your stepfather getting kidnapped doesn't change anything. So don't think for one minute that you're gonna mount some fucking one-woman show."

Emilia cut her eyes to him, standing there like king of the mountain in his clean white shirt, pressed jeans and shoulder holster. "I know," she said. "I'm simply not convinced that the Hostage Negotiations unit and their crap reputation is the way to go."

"Wait a minute," Alvaro jumped in, handsome face full

of alarm. "You just got back from that assignment in Mexico City and you're already on medical leave?"

Silvio's face tightened and Emilia took grim satisfaction that the *pendejo* knew he'd made a mistake.

And wasn't going to fix it.

"Headaches," she said to Alvaro. It was all she could come up with on the spur of the moment but it was better than *pain in my ass*. "Migraines."

"In five days you need to have either a two million dollar ransom," Silvio said to refocus Alvaro's attention. "Or a plan to negotiate it down."

"I know!" Emilia exploded. Beer bottle in hand, she launched herself off the side of the car and confronted the other two. "I know we only have five days and this Los Colectores outfit is asking for the fucking moon. We're never going to be able to pay two million pesos, let alone dollars. But the crew from Hostage Negotiations is as likely to team up with the kidnappers to get a piece of the ransom as they are to rescue Ernesto."

Alvaro held up a hand to stop her rant. "There's a new lieutenant in the unit, *prima*," he said. "Chief Salazar cleaned house and brought in a guy named Javier Plano Mendoza."

"A new lieutenant," Emilia scoffed. "Come to grab what he can, like all the rest."

Silvio scowled at her. "Remember Hugo Chen Garcia? From my old unit. He's in Hostage Negotiations now."

"So?"

"Says Plano is clean. Runs a clean shop."

Clean. As in no overt links to cartels, dirty money, murder-for-hire, or any other crimes associated with cops climbing the ladder of success.

"There has to be another option," Emilia insisted. "What about a private company? Pinkerton manages kidnappings. I could call Alan Denton."

"Cruz, you're dreaming," Silvio said, voice larded with derision. "Denton is not going to take on a case for the family of an Acapulco cop."

They all knew Pinkerton was an elite security agency with branches all over the world. The agency cossetted and protected diplomats, movie stars, and business tycoons. Emilia had traded information with Denton before, but he was paranoid about any connection to local law enforcement that might sully Pinkerton's reputation.

"Even if they did, who's going to pay for it?" Alvaro wiped his forehead with the back of a hand. His tailored blue uniform was damp with sweat. "Their fees could be as much as the ransom."

"What about your mother?" Silvio asked. "What does she want to do?"

Emilia nearly choked on a mouthful of beer.

"Tía Sophia isn't well," Alvaro admitted. "This should be Emilia's choice."

"Listen, Cruz," Silvio said. "Alvaro's right. This is what Hostage Negotiations does. If Plano goes sideways, my buddy will let us know."

For once, Emilia wished she could be like her mother.

Dissolve into tears. Be led away by the hand. Let someone else do hard things.

Find options that didn't exist.

Five days.

"Fine," she said finally. "We'll ask Hostage Negotiations."

"I'll make the call," Alvaro said and walked across the darkening courtyard.

"It's the right decision, Cruz," Silvio said. He kicked the Suburban's fender and dislodged a piece the size of a dinner plate. It clanked onto the pavement, leaving a long shred of white painted metal dangling over the tire. "*Rayos*, your ride looks like a thousand hours of paperwork."

Emilia tasted beer in the back of her throat as her temper flared. She didn't like the way he'd mentioned Barrielos Luna and her medical leave, didn't like the way he'd automatically aligned with Alvaro, didn't like the way his friend Chen Garcia was now going to play babysitter.

She punched her beer into Silvio's chest. Caught him by surprise but he didn't budge as froth surged out of the neck of the bottle, spilled over her hand, and stained his white shirt.

"If they fuck us over, Franco," Emilia warned. "It's on you."

CHAPTER 6

"This is my cousin," Alvaro said. "Detective Emilia Cruz Encinos."

"I'm Lieutenant Javier Plano Mendoza," the other man said and held out his hand.

Emilia gave his hand a perfunctory shake.

Plano didn't try to squeeze her hand or tickle her as so many other male cops did but he raked his eyes over Emilia's ponytail, white tee, skinny jeans, and focused on the detective badge hanging from its lanyard around her neck. "I've heard about you," he said. "First female police detective and all. Decent record."

"Thank you," Emilia said, as if he'd actually complimented her.

The man's eyes finally travelled up to Emilia's face. "I understand you're on medical leave," he said coolly. "Should you be wearing that badge?"

"Call Lieutenant Silvio," Emilia said, matching his tone. She'd known him less than 30 seconds and was already second guessing the decision to call Hostage Negotiations.

They stood in the courtyard where two vans emitted a steady stream of plainclothes cops and boxes of equipment. The Suburban had been towed to the police chop shop. Emilia was driving Kurt's dark green SUV for the time being.

Plano introduced Hugo Chen Garcia, the Hostage

Negotiations unit's deputy and chief of operations. Emilia had met Chen during the murder investigation of Silvio's wife, but he apparently didn't remember and she didn't remind him.

Two men in overalls came out of the house, carrying Sophia's television. They put it in one of the vans.

"What's going on?" Emilia asked.

"Extraneous items will go into storage while the house is being used as our base of operations," Plano said. "For the duration."

Until that minute, it hadn't truly sunk in that Ernesto's kidnapping wasn't a relatively common express job. It would be a long nightmare before they got him back, with labyrinthine methods of communicating with the elusive kidnappers. Weeks and months of negotiations over the ransom amount. Threats sent by phone, email, and video. Body parts delivered by anonymous couriers.

For the duration.

"We have four days before we have to deliver the ransom," Emilia said.

"Correction," Plano said acidly. "Four days until your first demand for proof of life." He walked away from the circle of cops, orders to the movers coming out of his mouth at rapid-fire speed. It struck Emilia that he was fit, despite a thick waist and stocky legs. Plano was probably in his mid-40's, although there was gray in his hair. He wore jeans and a blue button down shirt.

"The team is already canvassing the neighborhood,"

Chen said. "Strangers acting suspiciously. Unusual curiosity about the victim. You know the drill."

"Ernesto," Emilia said, fuming at his high handed attitude.

"*Oye*?" Chen looked at her blankly.

"The victim," Emilia said. "His name is Ernesto Cruz."

"Sure."

Silvio's pal was a handsome mix of Chinese and Mexican genes but he was either too stupid to understand what she was saying or didn't care.

Plano came back.

"We'll be using the kitchen as the conference area," he said. "The living room is now the operations center. There will always be someone on shift in case the kidnappers call."

Inside, Emilia was amazed. The house now resembled something between a clubhouse and an electronics store. The living room furniture was gone, replaced by desks sprouting monitors and assorted gadgets. Cords snaked through a cut in the plywood covering the broken front window, ostensibly to feed energy to the octopus of equipment. A variety of duffle bags, baseball mitts and soccer balls suggested a team ready for both work and play.

In other words, the long haul.

The four settled at the kitchen table, but the room no longer belonged to Sophia. The counters were bare, the curtains gone, the homey scent of tea and vegetables replaced by a whiff of antiseptic.

Plano held out his hand. "Did you bring the phone?"

"Yes." Emilia reluctantly handed over Sophia's cell phone.

"Now," Plano said, his attention on Alvaro. "Let's walk through this to make sure we're all on the same page."

With little input from either Emilia or Alvaro, Plano succinctly summed up what they knew. Ernesto's previous life in Mexico City as a knife grinder married to Beatriz. Father to Ricardo and Rubén Cruz Parrales. The contract with El Cripo and Luca Diaz Alonso to guide the two boys to the border. Ernesto's arrival in Acapulco and subsequent life with Sophia. Yesterday's daring daylight snatch and the recorded ransom message from an unknown group calling themselves *Los Colectores*.

Plano summed up with a question. "Are we all agreed that Ernesto's kidnapping is connected to the *coyotes* who took Ricardo and Rubén Cruz to the border?"

"Yes," Alvaro said.

But Barrielos Luna . . .

"Yes," Emilia murmured.

"All right," Plano said, satisfied. "Now we can move on to how Hostage Negotiations works with the family in situations like this. If we follow the protocol, it's going to be much easier on everyone, including the victim."

"It's critical that we all stay on the same page," Chen added.

The situation was surreal. A war council going on in her mother's kitchen as the living room teemed with technical equipment and computer screens. Emilia missed Silvio. He was a *pendejo*, but she trusted him.

"First rule," Plano said, snapping his fingers for emphasis. "From this point forward, Hostage Negotiations is in charge. There's no family trying to circle around or negotiate independently. We can't risk confusing the hostage takers, which always hurts the victim."

"Understood," Alvaro said. After a moment, Emilia nodded in agreement.

A generator roared to life outside and she flinched at the unexpected noise.

"Second rule," Plano said. "The house will be the command center 24/7 until the hostage situation is resolved."

Resolved. A tidy way to say dead or free.

"Third. Before negotiations go forward, we need proof of life. A live video stream so we see the victim in real time. They directed the message to the victim's wife, Sophia—."

"My mother," Emilia cut in.

"So she'll have to be on the other end of the video connection," Plano ignored Emilia. "The kidnappers have to know that the victim's family knows the rules. It's the first step in establishing a basis for negotiations."

"Ahh." Alvaro glanced at Emilia. "Putting my aunt in front of a video camera could be a risk."

"I understand Sophia is taking the kidnapping hard," Plano said. "But if she wants him back, she's going to have to do her part."

"Could we ask for a photo of Ernesto with that day's newspaper instead?" Emilia asked.

The Hostage Negotiations chief frowned at Alvaro. "Pictures can be faked and it takes time to examine them. We never know how much time we have. Live video is always the first demand."

"The important thing is to see our man alive and talking," Chen added to Emilia. "They'll use an untraceable cell phone for live video. We see it all the time."

"And once we have proof of life?" Emilia asked.

"The proof of life is a signal to start negotiations." Plano again spoke to Alvaro. "We'll push to see Ernesto throughout what could be an extended period of negotiations. At the same time, we'll be investigating the hostage takers."

Emilia felt her blood pressure rise at Plano's refusal to acknowledge her in the conversation.

"If Los Colectores has kidnapped before, we'll find out," Chen said. "We're already in touch with Mexico City to validate the information from the ex-wife and see what we can turn up on the group."

Chen's confidence was reassuring, even if his boss was determined to be a *pendejo*. Given the murmur of voices coming from the living room and the thrum of the generator, Hostage Negotiations was throwing significant manpower at the problem. Short of hiring Pinkerton or another hugely expensive security company, there was no way Emilia could have brought this much effort to bear.

"I'm a detective," Emilia said to Chen. "I can help."

"There's the question of the ransom amount and how it

gets paid, of course," Plano said to Alvaro, ignoring Emilia's offer. "Hostage Negotiations cannot help raise funds or deal with banks. Our job is to keep the conversation open with the family as we negotiate with the kidnappers. The family's ability to pay has to be kept in mind when we close in on the final negotiated settlement."

Plano made it sound like they were buying a company, not stuffing cash in a bag to exchange for a man's life.

"Two million dollars is not a realistic amount," Plano declared. "Unless this whole thing turns out to be a case of mistaken identity, which the reference to his sons says it isn't, they know he doesn't have this much. Mark my word, this two million dollars is an opening bid. An attention-getter. They'll come down."

"It would be good to know more about Los Colectores," Emilia said. "Like how patient they are."

Plano snapped his fingers twice to signal a new turn in the conversation. "The last thing to clarify is family roles and responsibilities," he said. "Like I said, Hostage Negotiations takes point. We'll funnel status updates and requests through a family representative. A single point of contact. I'm assuming you, Sergeant Cruz, will assume that role."

Emilia held up a hand before Alvaro could respond. "I don't think that's been established," she said and turned to her cousin. "Shouldn't that be me?"

"You're on medical leave, *prima*."

"This is my mother's husband," Emilia argued. "My work status is irrelevant."

"We never do women," Plano cut in before Alvaro could reply. "No wives, sisters, or daughters. Women don't hold up when things get ugly. Girl tears and begging won't get your man back."

Emilia rocketed out of her chair. "Excuse me?" she exclaimed.

"No women," Plano said bluntly.

Emilia folded her arms as she stood by the table, feeling her pulse throb. "Lieutenant," she said, forcing herself to stay calm. "I'm a detective. I know Ernesto. His habits, his friends. This neighborhood. You need my expertise."

Plano stood up as well. "I've got enough expertise. My team runs like a well-oiled machine. I don't need some jumped-up patrol officer who got her job to meet a quota throwing her lipstick case into my gears. End of discussion."

"That's not an acceptable response," Emilia retorted.

"I don't care what is or isn't acceptable to you," Plano shot back. "I'm concerned with getting your mother's husband back to her alive. If we all stay in our lanes my experience tells me this might not turn into the tragedy you seem willing to risk."

It wasn't an outright accusation, but it felt like one: You think your career is more important than the victim's survival.

"*Prima*," Alvaro murmured. "We called Hostage Negotiations for a reason. Let *el teniente* do his job. Please. For Ernesto's sake."

Emilia forced her knees to bend enough to land her back

in the chair.

Plano sat, too. "Detective," he said. "I know how emotionally charged this can be for the family of a victim. It's one of the main reasons we all need to work within the framework I've laid out. Can we agree to play by these rules for now?"

The sun coming through the curtainless window fell across Plano's forehead. The silver hairs at his temples glinted in the light. The cool and brusque expression softened and there was a hint of sadness in the man's eyes.

Emilia wanted to take a deep breath but she couldn't. If the late Leonel Cardenas had lived another ten years, he would have looked exactly like Plano.

More mature, a little wiser, but still holding on to his leading man looks, brash confidence, and idiot views on professional women. She wondered if Plano was funny when he was off duty, if he liked to drink whiskey or sketch when he was bored.

"*Prima*?" Alvaro prodded.

"All right," Emilia said to Plano. "For now."

CHAPTER 7

Tía Lourdes gave a jerk of her chin toward the small apartment's living room, where Sophia was glued to the television. "You're at school and Ernesto is out, driving el señor to the office. She lost 30 years in a day."

As Lourdes rattled china and the coffee maker sputtered, Emilia watched Sophia through the open doorway. Her mother was entranced by a game show, silently mouthing answers to the host's jovial questions. Sophia's hair was plaited in a single braid that snaked down her back. She wore a favorite floral dress and the same flip flops as the day before.

"I brought the rest of her clothes," Emilia said, indicating the overstuffed pillowcase by the door. She began taking items out of the laundry basket used to hold the food from her mother's kitchen. "This is everything perishable I could find."

Lourdes opened the slim refrigerator to show Emilia how crammed it was. "The neighbors keep bringing food, as if Sophia eats like a horse."

Emilia mustered a smile. An express kidnapping would be over by now; a quick trip to the ATM machine, a cash drop, the victim released in a strange part of town. But an extended abduction would have ripple effects throughout the *barrio*. As negotiations over the ransom dragged on, neighbors who were initially shocked and supportive would distance themselves from the family. Fear of being asked for money would keep them away or they'd turn against the family in the mistaken belief that Ernesto had been left to die.

As a cop, Emilia knew that a family enduring an ongoing crime became isolated, turning into a little island of misery and false hope.

Lourdes swiftly put away the food and served them coffee. "Your mother's in her own world again, like before."

"It was bad when I was little, wasn't it?" Emilia ladled sugar into the steaming coffee.

"She's not hurting, at least." Lourdes hesitated. "But maybe a doctor should see her."

Emilia stirred the cup. "Tía, will you answer a question?"

"Of course." Lourdes smiled, clearly anticipating a request for a medical recommendation.

"Did Mama give away my brother before her mind broke, or after?"

"We don't talk about him in this house," Lourdes reproved her niece. "It's better that he never existed."

Emilia picked up her cup again. Lourdes did the same. Their uneasy silence was broken at intervals by the applause, rapid-fire dialogue, and a maddeningly repetitive musical jingle coming from the television in the other room.

As both women sipped their coffee, the specter of Rafa Gamboa hovered outside the kitchen like a dark shadow. The boy was a man now, but to Emilia's aunt and uncle, he was still a secret to be ignored, a family history to be rewritten.

"Do you want me to take Mama to the hotel?" Emilia asked at length. "She can stay with us."

"In your sin palace with a *gringo* and his fancy food?" Lourdes gave a snort. "What happens if Ernesto never comes back?"

Emilia shrugged. "We'll work out something."

"Sophia needs to stay here," Lourdes said. "It was her home once before. She's comfortable. Padre Ricardo is coming for dinner, too."

Emilia carried their empty cups to the sink, kissed her aunt, and went into the living room. "Hello, Mama. How are you?"

Sophia looked up and a vague smile spread across her face. "Emilia, what are you doing home from school so early?"

"It's a holiday," Emilia said. She'd used that answer for years.

Sophia's attention swung back to the television. "She won a washing machine."

Emilia leaned against Sophia's chair and watched the show with her mother. Contestants answered questions for the chance to slide into a ball pit. As the balls blew around, contestants were supposed catch one with a prize inside. The jingle played each time someone got a correct answer or found a prize. There was plenty of audience shouting and zooming camera stunts that elicited little gasps of excitement from Sophia.

"Mama, I brought your clothes," Emilia said. "You can't

go home for awhile. There are people using the house who are going to help us get Ernesto back."

"Should I tell them you're in Mexico City?" Sophia tore herself away from the game show to blink at her daughter.

"No, Mama," Emilia said. The game show jingle played relentlessly. "But you need to tell me if Ernesto made any friends lately. New friends."

Sophia tilted her head to see the television around Emilia.

"Was Ernesto going to Don Julio's?" Emilia pressed, naming a popular bar near the house. "After he finished working?"

"Why would he go there?" Sophia asked.

"I don't know, Mama," Emilia said helplessly. She'd promised Plano she'd stay in her lane. Yet here she was, asking questions of a woman who had no answers.

"Emilia, look," her mother said and clapped her hands in excitement. "That lady could win a vacuum cleaner."

The Sophia who'd admitted giving her son away was not at home today.

Surrounding the penthouse on two side, the balcony was as deep as the living room. From the bedroom, it overlooked the marina and the famous two-level Pasodoble Bar that formed the heart of the hotel.

Far below, a dozen ceramic lanterns, each as big as a barrel, created a flickering barrier between the water and the edge of the bar's lower terrace. Pinpoints of light bobbed in the inky sky beyond the shore, reflectors on the hotel's floating dock.

"From up here," Emilia said. "I can almost believe the last two days were a dream."

"I wish they were," Kurt replied, handing her a small glass of brandy. He wore a tee shirt, cotton boxers, and was barefoot. The bedtime attire did nothing to lessen the combination of natural confidence and personal power that he wore like a second skin.

Emilia took the glass, grateful beyond words at this resumption of the ritual she'd loved so much. A chat on the penthouse balcony before going to bed. A chance to unwind and share the day's highs and lows.

Kurt lounged next to her at the waist-high wall edging the balcony. "How is your mother holding up?"

The tile floor was cool under Emilia's bare feet as she told Kurt about the visit with Sophia and Lourdes, as well as the meeting with Hostage Negotiations.

"They're in charge of everything and they only want to deal with Alvaro," Emilia wrapped up. Her anger and frustration had bled off hours ago and she felt curiously numb. "Including waiting until the kidnappers contact us again. Or until Hostage Negotiations finds where they're holding him. But that would take a miracle."

"Your cousin's always come across as pretty sharp," Kurt said. "From what you told me, this Lieutenant Plano knows what he's doing, too."

"He implied I'm more interested in my career than in helping Ernesto," Emilia said.

"Did you punch him in the head?" Kurt gently nudged her with his shoulder.

"No," Emilia said. She bumped him back. "The stakes are too high."

The soft surge of the ocean, endlessly lapping at the shore, drifted up to the penthouse along with brief snatches of laughter and guitar music.

"You can punch him when Ernesto's back."

"I might," Emilia sighed. "Did I tell you—."

She broke off, distracted by movement below them. A figure halted on the path near the marina which was lit by fairy lights wrapped around the bordering palm trees in a continuation of the lobby's nighttime theme. Although she was too far away to see facial features, Emilia recognized the slender frame and dark suit, out of place so close to the water.

"Is that the Russian we met the other night with Sergei Porchenko?" she asked.

Kurt followed her pointing finger to the dark figure silhouetted against the glow of the fairy lights. "I think so."

As they watched, Andropov made a phone call, tucked the device into his jacket pocket, and disappeared into the hotel.

Kurt finished his brandy. "In a couple of minutes, he'll call Room Service and order tea and the dessert sampler."

"You can predict the future now?" Emilia raised her

eyebrows at him.

"Same order every night he's been here," Kurt replied. "In other news, I talked to my accountant in the United States today."

"Oh?" Emilia yawned.

"I think I can raise about 300,000 dollars for Ernesto's ransom."

Emilia gulped down the yawn, sure she'd misheard. "Three hundred thousand dollars? *Madre de Dios*, is that what you said?"

Kurt nodded. "I'm not sure how long it will take me to liquidate some holdings and get the money transferred to Mexico. I'll have to go to Las Vegas to sort out a few things but the money is coming."

"Liquidate holdings?" Emilia had no idea what sort of investments Kurt was talking about but she knew she couldn't ask him to do this. "No, no. They'll throw you in jail for trying to bring that much cash into Mexico."

"Good thing I know some cops."

Thanks to the drug cartels who always had plenty of dollars floating through their organizations, Mexico imposed draconian restrictions on international money transfers. To compound the problem, a freeze on withdrawing money to pay ransoms forced families to get more and more creative with how they obtained funds.

"Don't risk it," Emilia pleaded. "Ernesto isn't your responsibility."

"He's part of your family, Em," Kurt said. "That's reason

enough for me."

"It's too much, Kurt. To do this, when I can't even . . . I mean, I'm so sorry about the other night—."

"Don't go there, Em," Kurt interrupted. "This is us doing what's right for family, not some quid pro quo for sex."

Emilia put her empty glass on top of the wall and hugged Kurt fiercely, pressing her face into his chest. He wrapped his arms around her.

"There's no rush, Em." Kurt kissed the top of her head.

"You sure?" Emilia mumbled against the soft cotton of his shirt.

Kurt laughed. "Well, maybe. But when the time is right, we'll know."

Emilia was on the verge of falling asleep when her phone chimed from the bedside table with a reminder that she had a second appointment with the police psychiatrist tomorrow afternoon.

She turned on the light and opened the drawer. The gratitude journal she'd so unceremoniously dumped was still there, as was a pen. The psychiatrist expected to see three things tomorrow.

I am grateful for Kurt Rucker.
I am grateful for Kurt Rucker.
I am grateful for Kurt Rucker.

CHAPTER 8

Emilia opened her shoulder bag and took out the key with the paper tag that had been her talisman during the tribunal investigation. "There's something I wanted to talk to you besides Mama," she said.

"Of course," said Padre Ricardo Solis.

Emilia handed the key to the priest. "Does this mean anything to you?" she asked.

"Casa Odisea," Padre Ricardo read the little tag. "What's this?"

"It's an adoption agency," Emilia informed him, disappointed that he hadn't recognized the name. "Or maybe an adoption research service. Or both."

They were in the small sacristy behind the altar in the church of San Juan de los Pinos, sitting at the table that served as the priest's office. Emilia had been there a thousand times. First, as a fatherless young girl seeking counsel to deal with a mother perpetually caught in twilight, and later as a cop needing Padre Ricardo as a moral compass to help her cope with the crime and carnage on Acapulco's streets. It was natural to turn to the priest after the assault by Rafa Gamboa, too. When Emilia left Kurt, she stayed at the rectory for several weeks until the assignment to Mexico City.

"If you're adopted and want to find your birth parents," Emilia explained. "Supposedly Casa Odisea will help you.

But I haven't been able to find any contact information. No address, no phone or email."

"Ah." Padre Ricardo laid the key on the table. "This is something to do with Rafa Gamboa, isn't it?"

"An actress he dated in Mexico City told me he was trying to find his birth parents." Emilia stirred the mug of weak tea in front of her. She'd spent too much time lately drinking tea or coffee as a prelude to hard conversations. Of course, what was in the mug in front of her was neither.

Padre Ricardo reused tea bags until his recipe for a beverage was hot water and hope. Emilia had never seen him with a new bag. Or new clothes for that matter, only a succession of worn trousers and faded clerical collars.

"What about his foster mother?" the priest asked. "Karina Escobar de la Vega?"

Emilia smoothed the little cardboard label. "From what the old girlfriend said, Karina never knew Rafa Gamboa was trying to find his birth parents. I'm a little hesitant to tell her. She's been hurt enough by him."

Padre Ricardo sipped his tea. "Your mother and Karina probably never had any formal agreement over custody of the boy," he said. "He may have gone from being Ernesto Cruz Encinos to Rafael Gamboa Escobar without any legal action."

"So Casa Odisea wouldn't have been able to provide him with anything useful." Emilia sipped the liquid in her mug. It was completely tasteless.

"Probably not," Padre Ricardo said regretfully.

"I'd still like to speak with them," Emilia said. "Someone might have a way to contact him."

The door to the sacristy opened and a stocky woman lumbered in, dragging a suitcase with a box balanced precariously on top. "Padre, I got them things like you asked," she announced and let the box tumble to the floor.

"Hello, Berta," Emilia said. Despite being one of the neighborhood women who spent all their free time cleaning the small church and serving coffee after Mass, Berta Campos was a difficult woman who delighted in making others miserable. "How are you?"

"Fine without no help from you." Berta sniffed in Emilia's direction. "Lila never wrote me another letter."

"I'm sorry to hear that," Emilia said. A runaway, Berta's teenaged granddaughter Lila Jimenez Lata was last seen with El Acólito. "I'm still looking for the man I saw her with. If I hear anything, I'll tell you."

"No letters means she hasn't sent me any more money." Berta glared at Emilia. "You'd think she'd want to pay me back for keeping her long after her no-account mother ran away."

"Berta, thank you for getting Emilia's things out of the storage closet," Padre Ricardo said. "Will you join us for a cup of tea?"

"Huh." Berta pulled a handkerchief out of her sleeve and wiped her nose. "I'm taking the altar boy vestments home to fix. That Javier put his foot into the hem last Sunday and they all got candle wax on the sleeves."

"Thank you, Berta," Padre Ricardo said.

The older woman opened the armoire where the vestments were kept, extracted three small red polyester cassocks, and bustled out, slamming the door behind her.

"She doesn't show it," Padre Ricardo said sadly. "But Berta misses Lila terribly."

"I wish I had news for her." Emilia slumped in her chair. "If I find Rafa Gamboa, Lila might still be with him. But this key is my only clue."

"Casa Odisea." Padre Ricardo picked up the key again. "I've never heard of it myself, but any legal adoption service in Acapulco would have a relationship with the diocese."

"Is there someone I could talk to?" Emilia made a show of stirring the hot beverage in her mug. Next time, she'd bring her own tea bag.

Padre Ricardo got out of his chair and retrieved a box of papers on the windowsill that evidently served as his telephone directory. Emilia waited as he examined scraps of papers and the occasional well-worn business card.

"Here we go." The priest held up a creased card with satisfaction. He slid it across the table to Emilia. "Dora Machado Uribe. I met her a few years ago. She runs the family support office for the bishop."

Emilia picked up the card.

"Dora Machado Uribe," she read aloud. "*Asistente del Obispo*, Metropolitan Archdiocese of Acapulco, Family Support Services."

"Meet with her," Padre Ricardo urged. "If anyone knows

how to get in touch, I think she would."

"Anything I should know about her?"

Padre Ricardo sipped at his own mug, oblivious to the lack of flavor. "A caring woman, as I recall."

Once again, the session with the police psychiatrist left Emilia drained. She resuscitated herself with fish tacos at a stand she and Silvio used to frequent and made a quick visit to her aunt and uncle's apartment to check on Sophia. Her mother was the same as the day before.

Alvaro met her there. Standing on the sidewalk in front of her uncle's car repair garage, he gave her a disappointing update from Plano and Chen. Still no word from the kidnappers. Still no success getting information on El Cripo, Luca Diaz Alonso, or Los Colectores. Basically they were in a holding pattern.

Kurt was still in his office downstairs when she returned to the Palacio Réal. Emilia put away the items from the church and considered. If she stayed in the silent penthouse, thoughts of Ernesto and Rafa Gamboa and Barrielos Luna would sap whatever energy she had left. Emilia grabbed her phone and keycard and made a beeline for the Pasodoble Bar.

As she passed through the lobby, Emilia gave Christine, the head concierge, a frosty smile and got one in return. Christine Boudreau was from some European country where everyone was as skinny as a stick and had a personality to match. Luis Soto Rivera, who was much more personable, wouldn't rule over the concierge desk until the night shift. Steel drum music wafted through the vast space. The pianist came on later as well when the sky darkened and fairy lights turned the lobby into a romantic hideaway.

Emilia settled at a table at the far end of the Pasodoble, where she could watch who came in and out. From behind the long mahogany bar, the bartender recognized her and they exchanged smiles. Thirty seconds later, a perfect mojito arrived.

The cold blast of rum and mint was a godsend. Emilia tried not to guzzle as she looked around, taking in the famous blue mosaic, the gleaming expanse of bottles behind the bar, and the ocean lapping at the beach beyond the awning. The bar wasn't crowded. Her simple white tank and skinny black skirt didn't attract attention.

The sun hovered on the cusp of another beautiful sunset, as the sky prepared to trade cobalt blue for banners of pink and gold. At this time of the day, hotel guests were either napping in preparation for an evening out, playing tourist, or still on the beach. A few would be at one of the hotel's three pools.

A slender man walked into the bar from the lobby side. He wore a blue polo and white jeans. It took Emilia a second look before she realized it was Bogdan Andropov.

He accepted a frosty glass of beer from the bartender and looked for a place to sit. When he saw Emilia, he raised his drink in acknowledgment. Emilia returned the gesture and he approached her table.

"Señora Cruz?" Andropov smiled hesitantly. "Would you mind if I joined you?"

It took a moment for her brain to register that he was speaking English and what the words meant. "Please sit down," Emilia said in the same language. "But only if you call me Emilia."

"And I am Bogdan." He sat down and centered his glass on a coaster. "Are you waiting for someone? Mister Rucker perhaps?"

"Only the sunset. Kurt's still at work."

"Are you more comfortable in Spanish?" Andropov's seamless transition to her own language took Emilia by surprise, as did his accent. His Spanish was not from Mexico, but the language of Spain's Castile, the land of kings and conquistadors.

"Yes, I am." Emilia gave him a smile of relief. "I don't often speak English. But your Spanish is excellent."

"My mother was Spanish," Andropov said. "I grew up speaking Spanish with her and Russian with my father."

"Who taught you English?"

"School," Andropov said. "I took a course at Cambridge."

"Ah." Emilia assumed that was a school where they taught little Russians how to speak like a British television show.

"I took your advice," Andropov said. His face was slightly tanned and he looked heathier and more animated than over coffee with Porchenko. "I went to the dolphin show today at the CiCi water park."

"What did you think?"

"I know people complain about animal cruelty," he said. "But it was terrific. I really enjoyed it. Thank you for the suggestion."

"I'm glad you enjoyed it."

"If you don't mind, I could use a few more suggestions." Andropov took his cell phone out of a pocket and she was reminded again of his long, clever fingers. "What other places are popular?"

"Did you see the divers at La Quebrada?"

"Of course." Andropov tapped his phone screen and brought up a picture of a diver in mid-flight. He was a talented photographer.

"Divers and dolphins." Emilia grinned. "You're done."

"What about Acapulco's famous nightlife?" Andropov looked boyish and bashful as he drank his beer.

"Well," Emilia considered. "La Flor de Acapulco is the best club for a party vibe. There's salsa, rock music, lots of dancing. Oh, and you shouldn't miss Salon Acapulco. It's a floor show and a great bar all rolled into one. The cover charge is expensive, but everyone says it's worth it."

Andropov picked up his phone again. "I should make a note of this," he said, tapping the screen. "What about restaurants?"

"Acapulco has everything," Emilia said. "What are you looking for?"

"Something good but not too far."

"There are some nice places in Las Brisas," Emilia suggested. "It's not far. The concierge will call you a taxi if you don't have a car. Try Baikal or Casanova. Both are elegant and have excellent food."

"Are they tourist traps?"

The last sip of mojito was heady with mint. "More like where all the beautiful people go to see and be seen."

"What about the rest of us?" Andropov protested.

Emilia laughed. Without Porchenko in tow, Andropov was an amusing acquaintance and she was enjoying her new-found role as city tour guide. "This is the quiet side of La Costera," she informed him. "If you want popular beaches and hot clubs, you have to go west."

"All right." Andropov leaned back in his chair and grinned. "Where would I go on this side of the bay, if I lived here? Say, a little closer to the city."

"Real people go to the little *loncherías* and *taquerias* along the beach," Emilia said. She named several favorite spots.

Andropov used his phone's map application to find each suggestion and was satisfied with the locations. "What else is on this side of the bay? Where do people go when they aren't tourists?"

"The shops near the El Pueblito handicrafts market," Emilia proposed.

He made her find it on the map app. "Excellent," he said when the red marker appeared on the screen. "What else is in that area?"

Emilia jabbed her straw at the muddled mint in the bottom of the glass but there was nothing left. "You could watch jai alai."

"Jai alai?" Andropov put down his phone. "Is that like handball with baskets instead of rackets?"

"It's called a *cesta*." Emilia grinned at his description. "There's a jai alai *frontón* at the Emotion casino near the Hyatt hotel."

"Who goes there?"

Emilia shrugged. "Everyone."

"But it's a casino?" Andropov was clearly interested.

"You can bet on horses, play the slots, and watch some jai alai all in one place."

"How do they use those basket things?" Andropov pantomimed catching a ball with one hand and dropping it into a mitt held by the other. "Like that?"

"You only use the *cesta*. It's about this long and curved." Emilia spread her hands a meter apart. "The player uses it to hook the ball out of the air. It drops into a well in the *cesta* and they have to sort of sling it out. Some of the best players do this underhand rotation." She tried to duplicate the motion. "Well, anyway, the ball shoots out like a rocket. That's why jai alai is called the fastest sport in the world."

Andropov raised his eyebrows. "The fastest sport in the world? Now I absolutely have to go."

The waiter cleared the table and set down a fresh round of drinks.

"This is without a doubt the best hotel I've ever seen," Andropov said. He held up his beer. The foam was an inch deep and perfectly level with the rim of the glass. "No detail is overlooked."

"Will you mention the Palacio Réal in your article?" Emilia stirred her fresh mojito.

"Yes," Andropov said. "More than anything else, this hotel illustrates my theme."

"Which is?"

Andropov took a swallow of beer and savored it before speaking. "Despite the violence and the drugs, Acapulco is undefeated."

"Hear, hear." Emilia held up her glass in a salute of appreciation.

"This is not simply to justify my expense account," Andropov said, as if he needed to convince her. "The city has an enduring spirit and beauty that will not be destroyed."

Emilia liked him even more. "Thank you for not simply writing about crime."

"I'd like to come back in five years," Andropov said earnestly. "See how Acapulco is remaking itself."

Late that night, as Kurt pretended to sleep and Emilia stared at the ceiling wondering how Ernesto Cruz was faring in the hands of his kidnappers, she recalled the conversation in the Pasodoble. Sometimes it was good to talk to someone whose perspective was up in the clouds rather than below street level.

Acapulco is undefeated.

Emilia hoped those words applied to her, too.

CHAPTER 9

Kurt and Jacques raced each other to the swimming dock, leaving Emilia to stretch her muscles with a slow but steady stroke. It was so early that the sun had yet to warm the Pacific. The act of pushing herself through the chilly water cleared away the last vestiges of sleep.

Strong arms reached out as Emilia neared the platform anchored to the ocean floor. Kurt hoisted her clear out of the water and her legs bicycled the air.

Emilia landed on an upswell. Kurt grinned at her, sparking with energy, swim goggles around his neck, and tanned skin beaded with water.

If the Pacific came to life as a man, this is what he would look like.

Without thinking, Emilia went up on her toes and kissed him. The dock heaved and she clutched at Kurt for balance. The day felt like a new start. Ernesto's ransom was no longer an impossibility. She had a lead in the hunt for Rafa Gamboa.

"Children, children," Jacques reproved them as he shook water off his own goggles. "We have an audience."

Emilia looked over her shoulder at the hotel. On the edge of the beach half a mile away, a young man in the Palacio Réal uniform of blue floral shirt and khaki pants waved at them.

Kurt saluted the young man with his free hand.

The young man waved again, more energetically this time. He turned and ran toward the Pasodoble Bar.

"Okay, before the audience comes back, let the games begin." Kurt unstrapped his dive watch and gave it to Emilia. He stretched the rubber band of his swim goggles around his temples and adjusted the lenses protecting his eyes. "Jacques and I will race to the marina buoy and back. Em, you time us. First one that touches the—."

"Kurt, look," Emilia interrupted him.

Two hotel staffers pounded down the beach to the water's edge. They shouted, but the churn of the ocean swallowed their words. One waved, making sweeping *come here* motions. The other raised the seldom-seen red flag used to warn guests of danger.

"*Mon Dieu*," Jacques lapsed into French at the urgency radiating across the water. "Something is going on."

"We'd better go back," Kurt said.

Emilia felt a chill that had nothing to do with the temperature of the ocean. Had Alvaro called the hotel when she didn't answer her phone? Was Ernesto dead? Had something happened to Sophia? Was it something to do with Barrielos Luna?

The morning's euphoria vanished. The swimming dock felt miles from shore.

"Em?" Kurt's voice stopped the wheel spinning wildly in her mind.

"I can't breathe," Emilia whispered.

"Take my hand," Kurt said as Jacques looked at her with

concern. "I'll stay with you the whole way."

They plunged in. Kurt kept his promise but Emilia still sucked wind with every stroke. Her stomach was on the verge of cramping. When her feet finally touched, Kurt hustled her through the suck of the surf to the two young men waiting at the water's edge. She recognized them both as part of the morning set-up crew.

"Miguel, Jorge," Kurt acknowledged them as he yanked the swim goggles over his head. "What's going on?"

"*Jefe,* Christine sent us to find you," Miguel said excitedly as Jorge handed out towels. "We have an unresponsive guest. The doctor is attending to him now."

Emilia nearly laughed with relief. This wasn't about Ernesto's kidnapping. Barrielos Luna wasn't shooting up the hotel. The emergency didn't belong to her.

Or to Jacques. The chef quickly kissed Emilia, gave Kurt a sympathetic punch to the shoulder, and headed into the hotel.

"Doctor Palumbo said that you should come right away," Miguel urged. "What should I tell Christine?"

"All right," Kurt said. "Tell her I'm on my way. What's the room number?"

"Room 316," Miguel said.

Bogdan Andropov wasn't merely unresponsive. He was dead.

In hastily donned jeans and halter top, Emilia stayed by the open door. Memories of Leonel Cardenas dying on the metal floor of a shot-up van threatened to replace the elegant and airy hotel room with its Italian bed linens and expansive ocean view through French doors.

From the color and stiffness of the corpse she knew Andropov had been dead all night, sprawled facedown on the floor of his hotel room. He looked like a broken starfish abandoned by the waves and left to dry on the beach.

"Such a young man, but this appears to be a classic heart attack," Doctor Palumbo said sadly, kneeling by the body. A gurney waited nearby, boxes of unneeded lifesaving equipment strapped on top. "Probably felt the pain radiate down the left arm and folded it against himself as he fell. No one has moved him so you can see from his position exactly what happened."

Still in the blue polo and white jeans from their conversation in the Pasodoble, Andropov lay on the tile floor between the foot of the bed and the mahogany television cabinet. The left arm was tucked under his torso but the right was flung above his head. His feet were bare.

The doctor looked up. "I'd like to turn him over."

Emilia gave a start.

Kurt glanced her way. "Em?"

"Nothing."

She wasn't in the van with Cardenas, desperate to keep him alive as his blood drained away.

Wearing surgical gloves, the doctor and his nurse gently

rolled the body onto its back. Andropov's left arm flopped off his chest with a muffled thump.

Emilia took a step closer. Andropov's eyes were closed and his face was expressionless. There was no wound and no blood, but no life, either.

Without warning, she choked up. Yesterday afternoon he'd been drinking beer and planning the rest of his trip. Now, a nice man was dead. Did he have a family? Was someone in Russia waiting for him to come back? Emilia had an unreasonable urge to push the doctor out of the way, shake Andropov until he woke up, and take him to a jai alai tournament.

"I expect he had an undiagnosed heart defect." The doctor straightened up. "I'll be interested to hear what the autopsy says."

Emilia collected herself as the body was shifted onto the gurney. The carriage was raised and the sad burden wheeled out of the room to the service elevator. The hotel had its own clinic where the body could wait until the body wagon arrived from the morgue.

Kurt quietly conferred with Miguel. Emilia slipped into the bathroom and plucked a tissue from the holder, giving herself an excuse to look around, if for no other reason than to settle her mind.

Andropov's few toiletries were neatly laid out on the marble counter: razor, shaving cream, toothbrush, a white and blue tube of toothpaste with Russian lettering. A hotel bathrobe hung from a hook while a single hand towel was flung over the bar near the sink. All the other towels were folded and stacked on the shelf.

Emilia came back into the bedroom. The bed had not been slept in. The desk area was clean except for a pad of paper embossed with the hotel crest.

Using the tissue in lieu of gloves, she opened the closet door to see a suit and two shirts hanging above a soft sided suitcase, a pair of black dress shoes, and a pair of cross trainers. The dresser yielded underwear, socks, swim trunks, and two polo shirts. Andropov packed light.

A silver tea service was arranged for a late evening snack on a round table in front of the French doors leading to the balcony. Little silver tongs lay on the tray next to the sugar bowl and a small plate of lemon slices. A dessert sampler platter with a miniature chocolate mousse, slice of carrot cake and a fruit tart still looked fresh. A single cup and saucer waited for a pour of tea.

Emilia used the tissue to lift the lid on the teapot. She sniffed and was rewarded with the rich perfume of a tasty blend.

She looked up to see Kurt close the door behind Miguel.

"A dead guest isn't exactly the way I wanted to start my day," Kurt said. He spotted the tissue in her hand. "What are you doing?"

Emilia shrugged, feeling silly. "Old habits die hard."

The hotel staff handled the situation with consummate discretion. Emilia doubted that any guest even knew a man had died or that the police were there.

After Andropov's body was taken away, Emilia headed into Acapulco to see her mother. She returned late in the day, thinking longingly of a quiet swim, worn out by Sophia's obvious inability to accept what had happened to her husband.

The first person Emilia saw was Silvio, sitting by himself at one of the small tables along the perimeter of the lobby. Creased jeans, crisp white shirt, khaki bomber jacket, perpetual scowl.

"Hey, Cruz." Silvio raised a glass of cola to her in a dubious gesture of greeting.

"What are you doing here?" Emilia plopped into the plush chair across from him.

"Taking in the scenery," Silvio said. "Chen tells me that Plano handled you a little roughly the other day."

Emilia rolled her eyes. "Did you come to tell me that you and Plano are soulmates?"

"Nah, that's just the bonus." He turned serious. "I've got to talk to Ronaldo Olivas about Hollywood's dead Russian."

"I can show you where his office is," Emilia said.

As they walked, she gave Silvio a rundown on the hotel's chief of security. Olivas had been a detective in Monterrey and oversaw a large security team. Many of the floral-shirted staff roaming the hotel weren't waiters or beach crew but members of his team looking for trouble before any guest experienced it. Emilia often saw him in the hotel gym or walking the property. Approaching 60, with gray hair and a no-nonsense demeanor, Olivas was one of a handful of hotel employees who knew she was a cop.

Introductions made, Olivas got right to the point.

"Here is Señor Andropov's passport," he said, pushing a red booklet embossed with a gold eagle across his desk. "I can email you a file we've made with his check-in information, credit card used, and his habits while staying in the hotel."

Silvio rifled through the passport. "I'll take your professional opinion, too," he said. "Anything stand out about Andropov?"

"Only that we don't get many Russian guests."

"I've already spoken to the doctor who runs your clinic here," Silvio said. "Palumbo. He's sure it was a heart attack."

Olivas spread his hands. "Now you know as much as I do."

"We should have the toxicology results tomorrow," Silvio said. "The autopsy will be tomorrow, too." He tucked the passport into a pocket. "When we have the results, I'll notify the Russian Consulate that one of their nationals has died. Hopefully, they'll take possession of the body, but they're hard to deal with."

"We'd like to avoid an international incident," Olivas said.

"I'm sure the mayor would agree," Silvio replied.

They spoke for a few more minutes, Emilia in the

unfamiliar role of spectator while a death was being discussed. Finally, Silvio thanked Olivas for his assistance and said he had to get back to the station.

Emilia walked Silvio to the lobby. The vast space was bathed in early twilight. The fairy lights wrapped around the palm trees flicked on and Emilia changed her wishlist from a swim to a strong mojito.

Silvio slowed his steps. "About Andropov's autopsy tomorrow," he said. "Can you go? Get the initial results?"

"Me?" Emilia recoiled. "Why?"

"I figure Hollywood would like to know the results sooner rather than later," Silvio said. "Figure I'd do the man a favor and let you go."

"Let me go to an autopsy?" Emilia threw him her best *you're-so-full-of-shit* glare. "That's some favor, Franco."

Silvio scowled. "I've got no one else to send," he griped. "We're still babysitting that counterfeit seizure until the Secret Service comes to claim it, the situation at the airport is code red, and four people were murdered in the last two days. Some Russian heart attack doesn't make my squadroom's top ten."

"None of which is my problem," Emilia said loftily. "I'm on medical leave."

"Guess I could offload the Russians from the consulate here." Silvio gazed thoughtfully around the lobby. "Yeah, the Russians will want to spend some time here. Set up camp, eat free food, ask questions. Complain. Make statements. No doubt Enrique Santibañez from Carlota's office will rally around. Talk to the press about Russians in Acapulco. He strikes me as an attention hound. Not great for the hotel business, but that's life in the big city."

Emilia felt her jaw tighten. Silvio had no idea that his scenario could seriously hamper Kurt's ability to arrange Ernesto's ransom.

Silvio ran a hand through his bristly crew cut. "I might be able to spare Castro and Gomez in a couple of days," he said, pounding the last nail into the coffin. "To help the Russians. Here. At the hotel."

"Fine, fine," Emilia hissed. She hated both Castro and Gomez and Silvio knew it, the *pendejo*. "I'll go to the autopsy, you fucking blackmailer."

Silvio raised both hands in mock surrender. "As if you aren't curious about this Russian. I can read it all over your face."

"If I go," Emilia said, waggling a finger at him. "That means I'm working again. Done with doctors and medical leave. You have to give me back my gun."

Silvio snorted. "Nice try, Cruz."

He left her fuming in the middle of the lobby.

She'd be even angrier if she didn't feel she owed it to Kurt.

And Andropov.

CHAPTER 10

Emilia absolutely hated Acapulco's morgue. It was defeated but hadn't been allowed to surrender.

Gang fights in neighborhoods like El Roble and El Coloso meant that there was a never-ending stream of bodies waiting to be processed. Few got full autopsies, fewer still were ever identified.

As soon as Emilia pushed open the door and showed her badge, a mix of cloying sweetness and bleach assaulted her.

It was the smell of finality, Emilia thought as she followed one of the workers in frayed green scrubs. The hall was lined with body bags layered on tiered gurneys.

Obviously, the refrigerated drawers were full.

Emilia's eyes watered and she covered her mouth. Maybe it was the smell of despair.

"Doctor Prade said to show you in when you got here, Detective," the worker said. Emilia struggled to remember his name and failed. Before she could ask, he opened the door to an examination room where both Prade and an assistant hovered over a pale body on a tall examination table.

"Get a mask, Detective Cruz." Doctor Antonio Prade peered at her over tortoise shell reading glasses. A surgical mask covered his nose and chin. His lab coat was gray from too many washings.

Emilia had been there enough times to know where

everything was. She grabbed a surgical mask from a box on the long work counter where Prade kept supplies and paperwork as the door closed behind her. "I'm here for Bogdan Andropov," she said as she slipped the elastic around her ears and pulled the pleated fabric over her nose and mouth.

"The man who came in yesterday from the Palacio Réal hotel?"

"Yes."

"Your lucky day, Detective." Prade waved a scalpel over the torso. "Here he is. Third today and four more to go. I'm almost done."

Emilia edged closer to the table; glad she'd skipped breakfast. Andropov's body reminded her of a skinned rabbit, flayed open from throat to groin. Leg and arm muscles were relaxed and ropy. The long fingers curled around an invisible egg.

Prade and the assistant pulled a gooey mass out of the open cavity. Emilia's stomach lurched.

She backed up a safe distance and perched on a metal stool at the counter. "Did you determine the cause of death?"

"Heart attack," Prade said shortly.

"That's what the doctor at the hotel said, too." Emilia felt sad. Andropov had been her age. "He wasn't old. Did he have a pre-existing heart problem?"

"No," Prade said. He straightened and threw a humorless look over the top of his glasses. "He was pumped full of epinephrine."

"What?"

"I'll show you the toxicology report." Prade gave some instructions to his assistant, stripped off his mask and gloves, dropped them in a flip top trash can. "It's good to see you again," he said. "Welcome home."

"I'd say it's nice to be back but I'm not sure that would be a true statement today."

"It's where you can do the most good," Prade said. "You need to keep Lieutenant Silvio in line."

"Causing trouble, is he?"

"No more than usual, but I get the feeling he feels a bit constrained in his new role." Prade scanned the row of clipboards on the wall and unhooked one. "Bogdan Andropov," he read aloud. "Caucasian male, early thirties. Russian nationality. Approximate time of death between midnight and 2:00 am. Last meal some hours before, consisting—."

"I don't need to know everything," Emilia said hastily. "Just how he died."

Prade adjusted the reading glasses. "Cause of death. Massive cardiac arrest brought on by extreme levels of epinephrine in his bloodstream. And by that I mean enough to kill a race horse."

"Epinephrine?" Emilia searched her memory. Illicit drug? Heart medication? Primary chemical in oven cleaner?

"The hormone also known as adrenaline." The doctor put down the clipboard. "The medical community relies on it to treat severe allergic reactions. The correct dosage can save a life by stimulating the heart and lifting blood pressure that drops too fast."

"Was he having an allergic reaction?"

"There's no evidence to suggest he was."

"Do people use epinephrine injections the way a diabetic uses insulin?"

"No, it's only for allergic reactions."

"Do users abuse it?" Emilia knew that people stuffed all sorts of crazy things in their bodies to get high. Why not adrenaline?

"Even if he was an intravenous drug user, he could not have done this himself." Prade pulled on a fresh pair of latex gloves and returned to the exam table where his assistant stitched up Andropov's chest with thick, waxy black thread. "Come look at this."

Emilia reluctantly followed the coroner.

Prade lifted Andropov's right arm by the wrist. "There. See that? It's a curious place for an injection."

Emilia held her mask in place as Prade pointed to a needle-sized hole in the soft fold of the hairless armpit.

"An injection site," she verified. "Any other needle marks?"

"No, he's remarkably clean," Prade remarked. "No other needle marks, no tattoos, no scars, no sign he ever broke a bone, or had a medical procedure apart from dental work."

Emilia looked at the pinhole again. "Could he have done that himself?"

"No, not from this angle of insertion." Prade pointed

straight at the pinhole, then came at it from the side. "The needle went straight in. If he had reached around with his left hand, the angle of insertion would be different."

"He was right handed." Emilia recalled the way Andropov had stirred his coffee and worked his phone. "I'm sure of it."

"In which case, self injection is even less likely," Prade said. He gently laid Andropov's arm down by the man's side. "Was a hypodermic syringe found near the body?"

Emilia cast her mind back to the hotel room. Andropov on the floor, fully clothed. Left arm tucked underneath, right arm flung out. "No," she said. "Nothing."

"This was the most interesting autopsy in quite some time." Prade sounded bemused as he stripped off his second pair of gloves. "We get gunshot wounds, beating deaths, and meth overdoses. The occasional drowning. I've almost forgotten how else people can die. If we hadn't found the hole, a massive coronary would have been the logical conclusion."

"Let me get this straight," Emilia said slowly. "Someone came into his hotel room, made him raise his arm, and stuck a needle full of adrenaline into his armpit."

"There's a slight bruising on his right wrist," Prade pointed out. "His assailant probably held his arm up as he plunged in the needle."

"Any defensive bruising?"

"No."

That didn't make sense. "He was fit," Emilia protested.

"He would have fought back."

"With the dosage he received, his heart would have stopped almost immediately." Prade scribbled on the clipboard. "This was a cleverly planned death."

"A premeditated murder." Emilia pulled off her mask. First Ernesto is kidnapped, now this.

It was ludicrous to think that Barrielos Luna was behind the killing, but the drug cartel *jefe* had all the requisite ingredients: a never-ending income, a payroll full of killers, and a lust for attention. Who else would have gone to all this trouble—and risk—to murder a random travel writer?

"You should take his effects," Prade said. He handed her a plastic carrier bag.

Emilia peered inside at the wad of Andropov's clothing and underwear. "Everything's all together," she protested. "Nothing's in separate evidence bags."

"He wasn't a homicide when he came in."

The entire squadroom, including Silvio's office, was empty. Emilia dropped the autopsy and the toxicology reports on his desk. She was tempted to write *Now you have to give me back my gun* and stick it to his computer monitor, but the scent of lemon furniture polish lingered in the air. It reminded her that Silvio could still create a problem for Kurt with the Russian Consulate.

Emilia spent some time with her mother before returning

to the Palacio Réal. Kurt was in the penthouse, looking like he'd had a long day. Finding out that Andropov was murdered didn't help.

Room 316 was now a crime scene, but Emilia doubted that Silvio would bother to send the techs in to dust and photograph. The body was gone and half a dozen people had trampled through. The investigation would be hampered by the lack of forensic evidence as well as the tight staffing situation. Emilia knew Silvio would need help. Hopefully, she'd have her gun back by this time tomorrow.

Kurt opened the door to Andropov's room with his master keycard. Emilia walked around the room wearing a pair of gloves she'd stolen from Prade's supply at the morgue. Opened the closet and the dresser drawers. Andropov's things were still there.

The dresser top looked exactly as it had yesterday. The same pad of paper sat on the desk, alone and undisturbed.

"What are you looking for?" Kurt asked.

"I don't know." Emilia dragged out the suitcase, flipped it onto the bed and unzipped it.

Completely empty, except for several newspapers in English.

Kurt took them out and read the mastheads. "Wall Street Journal. Financial Times. The Enquirer."

Emilia let his voice flow over her as she searched the room again. This time she wasn't examining what was there, but searching for what wasn't.

"Eclectic reading taste," Kurt said.

The bedside table drawers were empty. Nothing on the floor behind the bed or hiding behind the draperies. She passed through the French doors to the balcony. Examined the potted plants and the teak loungers.

"What are you looking for?" Kurt appeared in the open doorway.

Emilia finally realized what was missing. "Where's Andropov's phone?"

As if to emphasize the question, her own cell phone rang from her back pocket.

It was Alvaro.

CHAPTER 11

In a floral dresses and flip flops, her hair trailing loosely down her back, Sophia looked out of place in her own house. Her youthful face puckered with worry.

Emilia had seen that expression before. It marked a problem beyond Sophia's ability to understand. In the past, it always kicked Emilia into action to find a solution before Sophia fell apart.

Today, however, Emilia was relegated to the sidelines. There was nothing she could do.

The living room was full of people. Technicians huddled over blinking equipment, wrestled with cables and tested audio levels. Little screens blinked icons and digital bar counters.

Alvaro gave Emilia a thin smile. "They're ready for anything," he said.

"Detective." Plano both acknowledged and dismissed Emilia with the single word before taking Sophia by the elbow and guiding her to a desk with a large monitor on it. "Señora, you'll sit here with me, in front of the computer. Whatever is displayed on your phone will also appear here on the big screen."

Sophia nodded.

"When the red light goes on it means they can see you." Plano rattled off the directions as if he'd said the same words 100 times. "You should talk to Ernesto like no one else is here. When the red light goes off, it's all done."

"Are you sure I'll see Ernesto?" Sophia asked plaintively.

"They promised you would."

Chen joined Emilia and Alvaro as they leaned against the wall where they could see over Sophia's shoulder. "We've got her phone juiced on a mirror app," he said. "Everything on the phone will be recorded. *El teniente* can type and the computer will appear to them as a text from her phone. They'll never know she's not alone."

"He just promised my mother she'd see her husband alive," Emilia said to Chen. "They promised a proof of life real-time video? You're sure? I don't want that light to go on and my mother to see something horrible."

"Show time," Plano announced loudly.

Chen flicked Emilia a thumbs up and took a seat at one of the workstations, leaving Emilia and Alvaro alone by the wall. Plano and his technicians went through an equipment check. It was a well-rehearsed exercise that cycled through various contingency steps. Hostage Negotiations knew what they were doing. Emilia clung desperately to the thought that these token displays of professionalism meant that Plano knew how to bring Ernesto home.

Last night, Alvaro had given her a wild flurry of hope and confusion. The kidnappers had texted Sophia's phone after only four days, not five, and it was hard to know if this was a good sign or not. Plano texted back the demand for proof of life. A short exchange took place, during which the kidnapper used an elaborate method of preventing a trace.

Each text to Sophia's phone came from a different number. Every attempt to trace a number came back empty, but they all knew it was a simple to remove the SIM card and battery from a phone. The kidnappers were also slow to respond, taking at least 20 minutes before replying to each text from Sophia's phone. Perhaps they were mobile, so their messages were routed through different cell towers.

Sophia gave a start as the computer in front of her emitted a ringing tone. Emilia wanted to rush over and substitute herself for her mother.

A message winked on the screen.

"All right, Sophia," Plano said softly and opened the connection. "Remember, we want to see Ernesto."

Emilia held her breath as a narrow, grainy image of a man in a black balaclava facemask opened in the center of the monitor. The kidnappers were using a cheap cell phone for the video feed. The connection would be untraceable, just as expected.

Sophia gave a squeak of distress.

"Ernesto Cruz is being held for the debt he owes," the balaclava intoned. "We will show him so you know we are honest people."

The balaclava moved away and was replaced by a rough sack. A blurry hand reached for a corner and pulled. Ernesto emerged, blinking and gasping.

"Ernesto!" Sophia screamed, half rising out of her chair. "Ernesto, can you see me?"

Alvaro grabbed Emilia's arm as she realized she'd taken

a step toward her mother.

"Sophia?" Ernesto had aged a decade. His eyes were bloodshot and unfocused, his mouth slack and rubbery. He was drugged.

"I'm here, Ernesto," Sophia gasped. "I want you to come home."

"Sophia, you should give them the money," Ernesto slurred.

Sophia gaped at her husband's image on the screen.

"The bank money." Ernesto had difficulty focusing. "Do you remember where we hid it?"

Alvaro threw Emilia a questioning look. She shook her head to indicate *I have no idea what he's talking about* even as Silvio's questions about Ernesto came rushing back. Did Silvio see something that Emilia didn't? Was Ernesto dealing drugs or acting as a lookout or courier for criminals? Maybe the reference to Ricardo and Rubén was only a smokescreen.

"I remember, Ernesto." Sophia had gone from screams to sobs.

Ernesto's drawn and bristly face filled the monitor screen. "Give it to them," he said. "If you don't they'll never let me come home."

"All of it?" Sophia asked.

"Yes." Ernesto looked as if he might cry. "All of it."

Ernesto disappeared and the screen went white. Off camera, he shouted Sophia's name. A heavy thump cut him off.

"What happened to Ernesto?" Sophia cried.

The balaclava reappeared. "Los Colectores gave the proof you asked for. Now it is your turn, Sophia Encinos. Two million dollars in cash. You have five more days. Pay the ransom or Ernesto will suffer for your greed."

The connection ended.

Emilia wanted to shout questions at her mother, even as Sophia wiped red-rimmed eyes. *Did Ernesto steal a fortune from Los Colectores in Mexico City? Where was the money?*

"Señora." Plano was obviously furious as he confronted Sophia, but his voice stayed calm. "Do you have the money your husband was referring to?"

"Yes," Sophia said, tears running down her face. "Ernesto has lots of money."

Emilia knelt by her mother's chair. "Mama," she said urgently. "What are you talking about?"

Sophia wiped her eyes with the back of her hand, like a child. "I told Ernesto about your hiding place."

"What hiding place?"

"What's going on, Detective Cruz?" Plano asked icily.

"Upstairs," Sophia said, as if it was obvious to all.

"Mama, you have to show me." Emilia grabbed Sophia by the hand and pulled her across the crowded living room and up the stairs, her mother's flip flops slapping the tiles as they went.

Sophia went into the bedroom that had been Emilia's before she moved away. Alvaro, Chen, and Plano crowded the stair landing.

"Ernesto put the money in your hiding place," Sophia said proudly. "He said nobody would find it."

"Mama, you have to show me." Emilia stared at Sophia, desperately trying to remember. They'd moved into the house after she got her first paycheck as a beat cop. Bought secondhand furniture. "I don't know what you're talking about."

"The broken floor tile." Sophia looked around as if she didn't recognize the room. "Isn't it still here?"

"*Madre de Dios*." Emilia shoved the bed away from the wall with a single adrenaline-fueled heave. One of the clay floor tiles was already broken when they moved in years ago and never replaced.

She fell to her knees and thumped the crack, dislodging a slice of tile. A depression in the crumbly concrete block subfloor held a fabric bag the size of a paperback book.

Sophia seized the bag. Coins rattled like castanets as she thrust it at Plano. "Give it all to the man in the mask," she said breathlessly.

"Where did the money come from, *tía*?" Alvaro caught Sophia by the arm as Emilia dusted off her jeans.

"Ernesto said it was our emergency money," Sophia said. "This is an emergency, isn't it?"

Plano hefted the bag. It was clear that it was heavy. "How much is in here?"

"I don't know."

Carrying the bag, Plano led the way to the kitchen.

He carefully loosened the drawstring and upended the bag on the kitchen table. Peso bills and a shower of coins poured out. A cloud of metal filings rose and swirled into greasy gray dust.

Plano grimaced as if he didn't like getting his hands dirty.

"I'll count it," Alvaro said.

"I'll help." Emilia already knew it was not enough. This wasn't some secret stash of millions that Ernesto had stolen and hidden. These grimy peso bills and smudged coins represented hours of pressing dull blades to a wheel that bit the skin off his fingers and filled his lungs with grit. Hours of walking around the neighborhood, calling out prices and hoping some housewife needed her knives sharpened.

Emilia and Alvaro worked carefully, checking each's other's math, their hands darkening as they made piles of bills and towers of coins.

"Three thousand seven hundred pesos," Alvaro said at length.

Less than 400 dollars.

"Can Ernesto come home now?" Sophia asked.

CHAPTER 12

"I blame you," Plano said, glaring at Emilia across the kitchen table. "You had one job. This is what happens when you give women responsibility."

"I had a job?" Emilia nearly came off her chair. "I distinctly recall asking you what my role was going to be. What exactly was your answer, again?"

"*Prima*," Alvaro murmured. Her cousin looked like he was going to be sick.

Plano jabbed a finger at Emilia. "You're her daughter!"

Everyone was gone, except for one of the techs in the living room, leaving Emilia, Alvaro, Plano and Chen around the kitchen table. The bag of emergency money was stashed in its hiding place again; the paltry amount was hardly worth considering in the face of a two million dollar ransom demand.

"You had four days," Emilia said in a voice like ice, eyes locked on Plano. "Four whole days to meet my mother and figure out her limitations. She deserved more than ten seconds worth of instructions before she had to face her husband's kidnappers."

"You should have prepped her," Plano shot back.

"You're the hostage negotiations expert!"

Chen raised his hands as if to break their eye contact. "I think we've learned some lessons here."

"The first lesson is that Sophia threw away a good start,"

Plano interrupted his deputy. "They contacted early. Agreed to a proof of life live video on the first try. That's two signals that the kidnappers aren't interested in dragging things out and are ready to negotiate the ransom demand. Well, that's all shot to hell."

"So we regroup," Alvaro said, obviously trying to be the peacemaker.

"The second lesson is that Sophia is out of the picture," Plano said, as if Alvaro hadn't spoken. "No talking to the kidnappers, no decisions, nothing. I don't want her around, making my team question her judgement and wondering if she's going to do something loopy. That's how people get killed."

Emilia nodded, it was the one thing she and Plano could agree upon.

Plano leaned back in his chair. "Nobody warned us she's soft in the head."

"She had a nervous breakdown several years ago," Alvaro apologized before Emilia could say anything. "We thought you knew that.'

"Any other family secrets?" Plano asked aggressively.

If you only knew. Emilia looked away.

"You said before you thought they were amateurs," Alvaro said. "Maybe that works in our favor."

Her cousin's deferential attitude toward Plano and Chen was starting to get on Emilia's nerves.

"This sort of hiccup makes amateurs nervous," Chen said grimly. "If they've got it in their heads that our victim is hiding a couple of million dollars, convincing them otherwise is going to be a problem.'

"Your problem." Plano jerked his chin at Emilia. "You've got five days to come up with an opening bid. And it better be good."

CHAPTER 13

The representative from the police benevolent society explained that they might be able to help if Ernesto was her husband or child. But he wasn't a blood relative. Such a shame.

The manager of the bank where Emilia had a savings account practically laughed her out of his office.

Which is why, the next morning, Emilia found herself in the white house in Las Brisas talking to the woman who raised Rafa Gamboa.

"Emilia, welcome back from Mexico City." Karina Escobar de la Vega was a trim woman with a sleekness Emilia associated with the spinning classes and spa treatments made possible by infinite wealth. Her shoulder-length auburn hair was pulled into a low ponytail that swished above a starched flaxen tunic, black pants, and jeweled flat sandals. A spectacular diamond ring flashed on her left hand, and a chunky sapphire decorated the right.

Her neck was about 50 years old, Emilia estimated, although her face was ten years younger.

They exchanged kisses in the perfunctory rite. Karina told the maid to bring *agua de jamica* into the *sala*. She led Emilia to the same room where the two women had first talked months ago. Pale aqua walls, white sofas, pastel occasional chairs, and gilt accents promised comfort and elegance.

The room was perfectly tailored to Karina, who invited Emilia to take one white sofa while she sank onto the one opposite. Not for the first time, it occurred to Emilia that her life would have been so different had she been the one to grow up in this house instead of Rafa Gamboa. If Karina had been her mother, Emilia would never have sold candy to cars at the Maxitunel toll booth. Never would have pounded a beat in a bulletproof vest. Never would have been pinned under Leonel Cardenas's body as bullets rained down.

"Is your assignment over or are you on a break?" Karina asked.

"The assignment is over." Emilia dug into her shoulder bag and pulled out two keys. "I wanted to return the key to Rafa's apartment. Thank you for lending it to me."

"How thoughtful of you," Karina said. She took a proffered key and placed it on the side table by her chair. "I'd all but forgotten you still had it."

Emilia held up the other key with its paper tag. "I found this in his apartment. I thought you might know something about it."

To her surprise, Karina reached across the coffee table and grabbed it. Her face flushed as she read the label. "Where did you say you got this?"

"It was stuck in the sofa cushion in Rafa's apartment," Emilia said.

"Casa Odisea." Karina's voice was strained. "Is this supposed to mean something to me?"

"You've never heard of it?"

"No, no never."

"I've done some research," Emilia said. "Casa Odisea is an adoption research service."

Karina wrapped her fist around the key. "Was Rafa adopting a child?"

Emilia gaped at the other woman. "That never occurred to me," she admitted.

"Well." Karina sat back and crossed her legs. "What else could it be?"

"I think he knew you weren't his natural mother," Emilia admitted.

The maid walked in with a tray. Karina put down the key to pour two glasses of *agua de jamaica* from the pitcher.

"What makes you say that?" Karina said and handed Emilia a glass.

"An old girlfriend." Emilia took a sip of the cold hibiscus tea; it was overly sweet and syrupy. "Rafa told her that he was adopted and he wanted Casa Odisea to find his birth family."

Karina's mouth tightened in distress. "Was he looking for Sophia?"

"I don't know," Emilia said honestly.

"Well, it really doesn't matter." Karina dismissed the issue. "If Rafa really has questions, he knows where to find me."

"Actually, that's something we need to discuss." Emilia took a deep breath. "You know that there's a warrant out for Rafa's arrest. Well, the *federales* aren't the only one looking for him. I have reason to believe that Diego Barrielos Luna is looking for him as well."

Karina looked genuinely horrified. "The man they call the Barrel Bomber? The one who escaped?"

"Yes." Emilia didn't know how else to warn Karina except by stating it plainly. "I'm worried that he'll seek you out. He may think you know where Rafa is."

"*Por Dios*," Karina gasped.

"It means that if Rafa tries to come home, he'll only put you and your husband in danger. You can't harbor him."

"I understand." Karina toyed with the key tag again.

"You've got tight security here. You'll be fine." Emilia waved a hand to indicate the high wall topped with razor wire that surrounded the house and its outbuildings, including the guardhouse which accommodated a fleet of private security guards. Senior bank officials like Karina's husband were under constant threat from kidnappers. No doubt their cars were all armored, too. "But if anything odd happens or you're approached by anyone asking about Rafa, I want you to call me as soon as you can. Better yet, call the police and ask for Lieutenant Franco Silvio."

"What did I do to deserve this?" Karina said quietly. She closed her eyes and her face tightened with the effort not to cry.

Emilia waited as Karina pressed a hand to her forehead, the key still clutched in the other.

"I gave him a home," Karina said at length, her voice choked with emotion. "Everything he ever asked for. As my reward I get to live in fear."

"We're all doing everything we can to find him," Emilia said. "It won't be long."

"And after?" Karina dropped her hand and stared at Emilia. "A trial? Prison? My family dragged through the mud? Our privacy and social standing gone?"

Emilia didn't reply.

Karina took a deep breath. "I'm sorry, Emilia. None of this is your fault."

"Karina, I have to ask a favor. It has nothing to do with Rafa, but it would mean the world if you could help us out.

"If I can."

"I told you before that my mother remarried," Emilia said. "Her husband's been kidnapped. We only have a few days to raise the ransom."

The temperature in the room plummeted to Arctic levels.

"You're asking me for money?" Karina asked in disbelief.

"A loan," Emilia said in a rush. "I'll find a way to pay you back."

"How much?"

"They're asking for two million dollars," Emilia said.

"Dollars?" Karina's hand flew to her throat.

"If you could help with half, I'll pay it back. We can draw up a contract and I'll pay you back a little bit every month."

"A million dollars," Karina said. "That's quite a lot, Emilia."

"It's a man's life," Emilia countered.

"You want a million dollars to pay a ransom for Sophia's husband." Karina dug her shoulders into the back of the sofa cushions as if to increase the distance between herself and Emilia. "What sort of man is this husband?"

"He's a decent man, a church-goer," Emilia said.

"Occupation?"

"A knife grinder."

"Not an educated man."

"I need your help, Karina," Emilia said, choking down a lump that tasted like pride. "He's a good man and he's good to my mother. Please help me save his life."

"Poor Sophia." Karina gave Emilia a brittle smile as she toyed with the Casa Odisea tag. "She always did have a taste for common men. First a chauffeur, now a fellow who sharpens knives. I'm sure Sophia can find another one if she has to."

It was such a callow remark that Emilia was sure she'd misheard. "What?"

Karina shook her head. "Emilia, you know there are strict banking rules against ransom payments. How would it look, my husband being the president of an investment bank, trying to break the rules for a knife grinder?"

"So if he was more important, say a rich businessman, the rules could be bent?" Emilia flushed with anger. She slammed her glass down on the tray and hibiscus tea swirled towards the rim. "But a knife grinder doesn't matter? He's expendable?"

"You're applying very convoluted logic to what I'm

saying, Emilia," Karina said, her voice staccato with annoyance. "I don't appreciate words being put in my mouth."

"I'll be going now." Emilia stood and held out her hand for the key. "Things to do, places to go. Got to catch Rafa. Save my mother's husband."

Karina gave a nervous sniff. "This key belongs to me," she said. "You found it in Rafa's apartment, which we still own. It's our property."

"It's evidence in an ongoing criminal investigation," Emilia replied.

"Surely not," Karina bristled. "It's just a key."

"You can have it when the investigation is over and Rafa is behind bars."

"It's hardly essential."

"That's not for you to decide."

"Given the police's poor track record, I think it is."

"Give me the key, Karina."

"I'd need a receipt."

Emilia grabbed Karina's wrist, found the pulse, and squeezed hard. The older woman squealed in fear and pain. Her grip loosened. Emilia snatched up the key.

"Get a piece of paper," Emilia said. She grabbed her shoulder bag. "Write it yourself."

"You and your brother are more alike than you think," Karina snarled.

Emilia whirled around.

"Don't ever come back here." Karina pressed herself into

the sofa, one hand massaging the other wrist.

"I'm sorry if I hurt you," Emilia said stiffly and beat the startled maid to the front door.

A few turns through the swanky Las Brisas neighborhood and Emilia was soon on the highway speeding toward central Acapulco, Kurt's SUV running like a stallion on steroids.

A thousand curses tumbled out of her mouth as Emilia drove. Karina was a *bruja* who believed she was entitled to judge who was worthy to live or die. Safe and selfish in her Las Brisas manor, far removed from the rest of the world, insulated by wealth and privilege.

When Emilia finally realized how fast she was going, she took her foot off the accelerator and let both the SUV and her thoughts slow. As she passed another closed PEMEX station emblazoned with signs reading *NO HAY GASOLINA*, she wondered why Karina wanted a key with a crummy paper tag as a souvenir of her son's past life.

After all, Karina still owned his apartment in Mexico City.

And everything in it.

CHAPTER 14

Ronaldo Olivas stopped Emilia as she came into the lobby of the Palacio Réal. "Detective, your vehicle was dropped off this afternoon," he said. "If you could step into my office, I can give you the keys."

"Someone left a car for me?" Emilia's spirit, bruised by the exchange with Karina, lifted at the thought of a new official vehicle.

"A white Suburban," Olivas affirmed.

"You're kidding." Even as the words came out of her mouth, Emilia knew Olivas wasn't playing a joke on her. The hotel's chief of security hardly knew her well enough to prank her. Moreover, he did not appear to have a sense of humor.

"Is now a bad time?" Olivas asked.

"No, no," Emilia hastened to say. She was going to pulverize Silvio if the Suburban was still an accordion.

They fell into step across the lobby, passing Christine at the concierge desk.

"I know you are dealing with a family situation right now," Olivas said. "But I would also appreciate a few minutes of your time in connection with Señor Andropov's untimely demise."

"I'm sure Kurt passed on the information about the manner of death. But I'm not assigned to the case. Yet."

"Still." Olivas gave her a tight smile. "I think this will be ten minutes well spent."

They went down the corridor which housed the hotel's administrative offices. Kurt's door was closed.

As soon as Emilia took a seat in one of the upholstered chairs by the desk, Olivas's secretary came in with a silver coffee service stamped with the hotel crest, like the tea set in Andropov's room.

"I'd like you to look at some videos of room service deliveries to Señor Andropov's room while he was a guest," Olivas began. "Each night he ordered the same thing."

"Kurt told me."

"The staffing complement is considerably smaller at night than during the day," Olivas said. He shook his head when Emilia offered to pour him a cup of coffee. "Pedro Lopez Ventura usually delivers room service orders on weeknights. He's been with us nearly two years. Young man, hard worker, comes on time, sailed through the training program with high marks."

"All right." Emilia felt a familiar prickle of excitement. The hunt was on. Olivas was a worthy partner.

"There's a security camera near the elevator on the third floor." Olivas tapped on his computer keyboard. "We have footage of Pedro wheeling the room service cart towards room 316 each night. That's what I'd like you to look at."

"I'd be happy to." Emilia set her coffee on the tray and nearly rubbed her hands together in anticipation.

A black and white video clip flickered into life on Olivas's screen, with the date and time in white letters on the bottom. The quality was a little better than Silvio's airport footage but not by much. A skirted cart rolled into the camera's view of a wide hallway. The wall was unadorned except for an ornate brass sconce shaped like a nautilus shell and mounted at eye level.

"This is the first night Señor Andropov ordered room service," Olivas said. "The sconce design is different on every floor, so we know this footage was taken on the third."

The entire cart passed across the screen, rolling from left to right. It was topped with a teapot swathed in a quilted cozy and a silver dome which Emilia presumed was the dessert sampler. The young man pushing the cart wore the hotel's signature uniform of floral shirt over khaki pants. He was clean shaven, his hair combed into a trendy pompadour, and he moved steadily but not swiftly. The young man's face was briefly illuminated as he passed in front of the sconce before passing into grainy shadow again.

Olivas clicked his mouse. "Now here he is leaving."

The video now showed the young man, minus the cart, moving past the sconce going in the opposite direction. The date and time stamp showed that two minutes had elapsed.

"He picked up the empty cart two hours later." Olivas clicked open a new video. The young man pushed the cart from right to left. Once again, his face was illuminated as he passed the sconce, as was the outline of his pompadour hairstyle. "Catering doesn't pick up until the guest calls to asks for the trolley to be removed. According to our call logs, Señor Andropov called about 5 minutes before the pickup."

Emilia nodded; the cart had been in Andropov's room for two hours.

"That's the first room service order." Olivas opened another video clip. "Here footage from the next evening."

The scenario was almost exactly the same except for the date-time stamp in the lower right hand corner. The cart rolled into view. The same young man pushed it across the screen from left to right. A few minutes later, he walked down the corridor in the opposite direction. Like the day before, about two hours later he returned to fetch the cart.

"Now that we have a baseline of Pedro's deliveries to room 316," Olivas said. "This is the last set of videos I'll ask you to sit through."

The third video began the same as the others. The date time stamp was of the night Andropov died.

The cart, once again laden with a tea service and a silver dome, travelled left to right across the screen. The man pushing it wore the hotel's signature floral shirt and khaki pants. As he passed the wall sconce he looked down, throwing his face into shadow. He passed out of sight and the footage ended. The next piece of footage showed him running in the opposite direction.

"He stayed longer," Emilia said immediately. "Pedro came back two minutes later at the most. This time it was five minutes."

"Correct."

"When they found Andropov's body, everything was still in the room."

"No one ever called to ask for the cart to be picked up."

"Play the previous day again," Emilia said.

Olivas complied.

When the young man walked past the sconce, Emilia asked Olivas to stop the video. They played with the timing until the young man was frozen on the screen a step before passing in front of the sconce. The swirl of the nautilus shell was even with the quiff of his styled hair. The floral shirt fit loosely. Olivas took a screen capture.

"Can you get the same shot for the night Andropov died?" Emilia asked.

It took a few minutes for Olivas to call up the other videos and find the best view of the man next to the sconce. In the end, the best he could do was a screen capture of the running man.

Emilia gazed at both printouts, her coffee forgotten. "It's not the same person," she said. Some image analyst could extrapolate height and weight from the image, but she could call on gut instinct and common sense. "The second man is at least ten kilos heavier. His shirt fits much tighter. He's also at least three inches taller. Different hair, too."

"Thank you for confirming my suspicions," Olivas said.

"Do you recognize him," Emilia asked. "Is this another member of the staff?"

"That was my first thought as well," Olivas said. "But every room service delivery from the catering staff is signed out. Pedro signed out Andropov's order, like every other time. The night catering manager saw him sign the book."

"So Pedro took the cart and you have the signature to prove it," Emilia verified. "But by the time the cart was on the third floor, someone else had possession. That person knew where the security camera was and made sure his face wasn't recorded."

"That would appear to be the case," Olivas said. "A serious breach of the hotel's security procedures."

"Have you talked to Pedro?" Emilia asked.

"Unfortunately, no." Olivas clicked through various tabs on his desktop. "He's on vacation and hasn't been in the hotel since the night Andropov died."

"I'll let Silvio know. He'll bring him in for questioning." Emilia took out her phone as she studied the screen capture of the running man. "This needs to go to Forensics. Maybe they can enhance it, get a cleaner view of his face. Maybe even do some facial recognition magic."

"If I may take the liberty, Detective," Olivas said. "It's good to have you back with us."

"That's very kind of you." Emilia was surprised; did the flinty Olivas have a softer side?

She left his office with the keys to the Suburban and the screen capture of the running man.

Thanks to the hotel security chief, she had a picture of Andropov's murderer.

CHAPTER 15

"You didn't have to come, Em," Kurt said. "But I think it's the right thing to do."

"Of course." Emilia buckled herself into the passenger seat of his SUV, hoping she didn't look as guilty as she felt.

In the middle of dinner, as they sat on the balcony, and ate swordfish from the restaurant, Kurt decided to go to the Pacific Lotus to tell Porchenko what happened to Andropov. Emilia nearly choked as the idea of blackmailing Porchenko for two million dollars popped into her head. By the time they finished the meal, she was feverishly weighing the risks.

Would Porchenko still be vulnerable once he knew Andropov was dead? Or was his liaison with the other Russian now imminently deniable to his wife, Magda?

What would Kurt do if he found out?

"Are you all right?" Kurt asked as he drove up the steep cobblestone road to the highway.

"Fine," Emilia answered. "I'm wondering how Porchenko will take the news."

At the top of the rise, Kurt turned left and they headed west toward the city.

The Pacific Lotus hotel had a prime spot along the rim of the bay. A rose-colored building, it stood out amid its white neighbors. Kurt navigated the churning downtown traffic with ease and pulled in under the hotel's pink and white striped awning. The scalloped edges flapped in the night breeze rippling off the water.

The doorman, wearing a white kimono-sleeved top and wide pleated black pants, sprang forward to open Emilia's door. As she climbed out of the car, he gave her short navy skirt and matching sleeveless top an admiring look. For a moment, the blackmail scheme was forgotten as Emilia took in the new experience of being ogled by a fake Japanese samurai.

Kurt handed the keys to the valet and took Emilia's hand as they walked into the hotel. "Let me break it to him, okay?"

"You're a good man, Señor Rucker," Emilia said.

"It was my hotel."

The lobby of the Pacific Lotus was decorated like the inside of a slightly manic geisha house. Every vertical surface was covered with rice paper panels depicting long-legged pink cranes, water lilies, or lotus flowers. All of the female staff wore pink kimonos; the waiters wore all black versions of the doorman's costume.

"Russia's version of Japan, executed by Mexico," Kurt muttered. "Remind me never to hire Magda's decorator."

The reception desk was straight ahead, cleaving the lobby in two. The left side was home to half a dozen groupings of plush pink chairs and marble-topped occasional tables. The right led to the bar. Although only part of the interior could be seen through an archway decorated with Japanese characters, Emilia could hear music and the clink of glasses. She wondered if they only served sake.

"We have an appointment with Señor Porchenko," Kurt said to the geisha girl behind the counter. He said their names and she nodded in recognition.

"Of course," she said. "Both el señor and la señora are waiting for you in his office."

She led them past the pink chairs to an office suite at the rear.

Porchenko looked the same as when he and Andropov had been in the Palacio Real's restaurant. Pasty, bloated, and falsely hearty. The bodyguards were noticeably absent; no doubt the Russian felt secure in his own hotel.

He extended his hand to Kurt. "Eh, Rucker, good of you to drop by. Show the girlfriend the gardens."

Porchenko had clearly forgotten Emilia's name, but Kurt smoothed the moment with casual introductions. Magda Porchenko, who had apparently forgiven the disastrous red wine incident, pulled Emilia into a traditional double cheek air kiss. The Russian woman was as wraith-thin as her husband was well-fed. Her blonde hair was scraped into a tight bun and she wore a purple caftan with absurdly tall wedge heels.

"Emilia and I wanted to speak to you in private, Sergei," Kurt said once the preliminaries were done.

"Of course, of course. Sit down." He ushered them to a round glass-topped table in the center of the office. Only once she was seated, did Emilia fully realize how magnificent the view was.

The entire rear wall of the office was floor-to-ceiling

glass, including massive iron-framed doors open to a lush garden. Slabs of slate formed a path edged with crushed coral that disappeared into a miniature forest of weeping cherry trees. Emilia saw pots of pink flowers and heard the sound of splashing water. Any garden with a waterfall had to be enormous.

Kurt stayed standing. "Magda, if you would excuse us," he said. "I'd like to speak to Sergei in private."

Porchenko sighed heavily. "You have bad news, no?"

"What have you done, Sergei?" Magda asked sharply, her claw-like hands clutching the back of a chair.

Porchenko shrugged without looking at his wife. "Magda stays," he said. "There is nothing she can't hear."

"It's about Bogdan Andropov," Kurt said.

"Who?" Magda shrilled.

Porchenko turned to his wife. "Sit, Magda."

Emilia's blackmail scheme died in a flash of Magda's purple caftan as the older woman flounced into a chair.

Kurt held out a chair for Emilia and sat next to her. "As I said, it's about Bogdan Andropov, the man you introduced to us a few days ago."

Magda's claw-like hands plucked at her husband. "What does this boy know about my Bogdan?"

"Magda, hush." Porchenko covered his wife's hand with his own as he glowered at Kurt. "What is going on?"

"Sergei," Kurt said. "I'm sorry to have to tell you, but Bogdan Andropov is dead."

"Dead?" Porchenko half rose from his chair. "No.

Impossible."

"He died as a result of a lethal injection of a chemical used for allergy sufferers." Kurt kept going but Emilia knew he was as nonplussed as she was. "It happened in his room at the Palacio Réal. I'm sorry."

"Bogdan? Dead?" Magda's voice came out as a screech.

Porchenko didn't react. It was as if he'd turned to stone.

Emilia reached for Kurt's hand and squeezed it under the table.

Magda turned to her husband. "What is he talking about? Why would he say such a thing about Bogdan?"

Porchenko licked his lips, starring at nothing, ignoring his wife's words. "He did not have allergies."

"An autopsy was done," Kurt ventured. "The police are investigating. I'm sorry to have to be the one to tell you."

Magda jumped to her feet and slapped her husband, the purple caftan billowing. The sound of her hand striking his flesh was as loud as the crack of a whip. "Tell me why he is saying that Bogdan is dead!" she shouted.

Porchenko slowly raised his eyes. "I thought he would be safe there. But they got to him."

"He was here? In Acapulco?" The color drained from Magda's face. "Tell me you didn't involve him."

"He knew what to do," Porchenko said simply, his face mottled with the imprint of Magda's spidery hand. "He wanted to help."

"You fool!" Silk swirled as Magda collapsed into her chair. Her shoulders shook with silent sobs.

Kurt squeezed Emilia's hand in a signal that they should leave. "Sergei," he said. "I think we'll leave you and Magda—."

Porchenko stood up. "Look at the gardens for a few minutes," he said, more as an order than a suggestion.

Kurt pulled out Emilia's chair. "I think it would be better if we left."

"Five minutes." Porchenko was either a good actor or he'd recovered quickly from the news of Andropov's death. He gestured at his wife as she slumped with her hands over her face, caftan puddled around her feet. "Magda will have questions."

Against her better judgement, Emilia felt sorry for them both. Bogdan Andropov had obviously been more than a traveler who needed his money changed at a better rate than the bank provided. Whoever he'd been to the two of them, the least she and Kurt could do was be kind for a few minutes.

Besides, Porchenko had information to share.

But they got to him.

Emilia and Kurt walked into the garden. Porchenko closed the iron-framed glass doors behind them, his bulky profile outlined against the glass as his wife remained at the table.

Something about the Russian woman's abject grief reminded Emilia of Sophia sobbing over Ernesto. "*Madre de Dios,*" she gasped. "Do you think Bogdan Andropov was their son?"

"Jesus, Em, I hope not," Kurt said. "Let's find the back door to this place."

"Are you kidding?" Emilia tugged at his hand. "Didn't you hear what Sergei said? He knows who killed Andropov. Think what Silvio will say if I gift him a closed case."

"You can come back tomorrow," Kurt said.

"Porchenko could be on his way to Moscow tomorrow."

"What? With Andropov's body?"

"He could claim it. No one else has."

The path widened and they crossed over a rounded footbridge lit with spotlights. Under the wooden planks, a waterfall cascaded into a burbling stream bordered by green bamboo, frothy pink azaleas, and waist-high flowering red ginger. A breeze rustled the cherry trees, their branches heavy with pink blossoms. Unseen bells chimed.

The air smelled like serenity.

The centerpiece of the garden was an enormous glass teahouse raised on iron legs and illuminated by soft uplights. The mirrored tile roof sloped into a pagoda shape and tiny bronze bells hung from the upturned corners. Through the clear walls, Emilia could see a Japanese tea service laid out on a low table like performance art. The stream ran under the unique structure, creating a moving tableau of delicate pottery and darting orange koi.

"They stage tea ceremonies on weekdays," Kurt said.

"There aren't any chairs," Emilia pointed out.

"You kneel for a Japanese tea ceremony," he replied.

"Like begging?" The teahouse could accommodate an

entire *fútbol* team, although Emilia couldn't imagine anything less appealing than kneeling on a glass floor to get a thimble of tea.

Kurt kissed the top of her head. "Never change, Em."

As they walked past, some trick of the dark night and glowing spotlights created a mirror effect and their reflection flickered on the teahouse walls. Kurt's white shirt looked luminous.

The stream widened into a circular pond, lit from the bottom like a shallow blue and white tiled bowl. Slabs of slate created a tall waterfall, more dramatic than the one under the footbridge, that filled the pond and provided a playground for more orange koi fish. A nearby ring of benches invited guests to sit and relax with a table-height zen garden complete with white sand and twiggy hand rakes.

Further on, a small building behind the benches was nearly hidden by a giant Buddha statue and a tall grove of bamboo. Emilia guessed that it was for the gardeners and maintenance workers. Anything this elaborate needed a dozen workers just to feed the fish and polish all the glass.

At the end of the garden, a discreet sign gave them a choice between exiting to the swimming pool or heading to the Lotus Bar.

They turned and strolled back to the teahouse, their reflections distorted and multiplied by the panels of mirrored glass. It was a carnival funhouse, but in semi-darkness and without a rowdy crowd of sticky-fingered children.

"Does Japan really look like this?" Emilia asked. Despite

the bad news they'd delivered, it was nice to be alone with Kurt in such a romantic spot, her arm linked with his. The garden was an oasis, light years away from Ernesto's kidnapping, Plano's cutting comments, and Bogdan Andropov dead in the morgue.

"I don't know," Kurt answered. "I've never been."

"Really? I thought you've been everywhere."

"Not yet."

They passed over the spotlighted footbridge, the waterfall splashing away the sound of their footsteps, and regained the slate path leading to Porchenko's brightly lit office.

An argument raged on the other side of the glass wall.

The stout Russian loomed over the column of purple silk that was his wife. Even from this distance, with branches of the cherry trees in the way, they saw Magda gesticulate angrily.

Kurt pulled Emilia to a stop. "We should give them—."

He broke off as both Porchenko and Magda spun around to face the other side of the office, backs to the glass. Porchenko shoved Magda away and she stumbled to the right.

Automatic gunfire ripped through the air, drowning out the gentle gurgle of the stream and whisper of the night breeze.

Porchenko's body juddered. Dark stains blossomed across the back of his shirt. Blood sprayed across the glass wall even as it disintegrated, one section at a time, until the entire thing collapsed with the deafening roar of an avalanche. Porchenko's body fell backwards as if punched by a mountain, crashing into the twisted remains of the iron door frame as glass showered down.

Magda's screams were obliterated by the continuing rip of gunfire. Her purple silk caftan swayed and then she was prone on the glittering mound like a body on an icy burial pyre.

The sudden quiet was broken by the crunch of footsteps.

Two men with long guns stepped over the carnage. Even from this distance, Emilia could tell they were *gringos*.

They crunched through the glass, heading purposefully toward the slate path and the cherry trees and Kurt's brilliant white shirt.

Kurt grabbed Emilia's hand. Together they dove under the footbridge and rolled into the bamboo bordering the stream. A burst of gunfire shook the wooden platform as the intruders fired into the footbridge, assuming their quarry was underneath.

Adrenaline sang through Emilia's body, sharpening her senses and pumping energy through her veins even as her ears rang. The heat of Kurt's body tight against hers, the two moving as one. The cherry blossoms smelled rich and heady. The stream was as cold as the ocean. High above the garden, the stars winked *good luck*.

It was crazy. It was exciting. It was a moment to remember forever.

If they survived.

Emilia and Kurt crept through the thick foliage in the

direction of the teahouse and koi pond, aiming for the exit to pool and bar. Halfway there, a scuffing step not 20 feet away caused them both to freeze. One of the gunman moved into the halo of light rising from the koi pond. He took his hand off the rifle slung across his chest and reached into a pocket.

A second later, Kurt slammed a rock into the back of his head.

The man crumpled. Emilia rushed forward to help catch him.

"Nice job," she breathed and they lowered the unconscious man to the ground. Crouched on her heels, Emilia unclipped the strap and pulled the long gun free. It was the same type of carbine she'd carried during the ambush.

A pinprick of light bounced off the glass teahouse. Emilia slowly rose to her feet, unsure of what she'd seen.

The tiny glow moved again.

Disappeared.

Reappeared. Became two.

Merged into one.

It was the tip of a burning cigarette, doubled and distorted by the reflective teahouse walls.

Emilia brought the carbine up to her shoulder, intent on the point of light, when a scrabbling flurry reverberated across the quiet garden. Kurt and the disarmed shooter were locked together, each struggling for leverage. Momentum carried them across the uplit koi pond with grunts and loud splashes.

From beyond the teahouse, gunfire tattooed the stones edging the pond. Water spewed into the air like thin streaks of rocket fuel.

Emilia fired back, aiming for the lit cigarette. The weapon in her hands bucked like a wild thing. The recoil slammed the stock against her shoulder hard enough to send sparklers across her vision. She staggered but kept firing, her teeth chattering and her shoulders vibrating with the force of the spitting lead.

Her rounds arced toward the spot where she'd seen the lit cigarette, chewing branches off the cherry trees and scything down ginger and bamboo.

The glass teahouse exploded into a plume of glitter, chased by the erupting stream. For a moment water and glass formed a geyser that hung in the night sky. Emilia had never seen anything so strange, yet so lovely.

Like a collapsing mushroom cloud, the geyser folded in upon itself. A roiling wave of glass and mirror cascaded over Emilia and the koi pond and the stone benches.

The rain of debris lasted forever, until it finally stopped with a last, sad rattle of broken glass against stone.

The silence was cool and ominous.

CHAPTER 16

"Magda, it's Emilia."

Emilia watched as Magda Porchenko's eyes fluttered open.

"Kurt's girl," the Russian woman croaked in English. "Emilia."

"Yes, that's right." Emilia gently squeezed Magda's bony fingers.

"Where is he?"

"Outside."

The hospital room was crowded with banks of equipment sprouting coils of wire and blinking screens. Magda looked completely different than she had four hours ago. Her blonde hair was plastered to her head and her face was as white as the cotton pillowcase beneath her. Clear tubes were everywhere—up Magda's nose, in the back of her hand, snaking from under the blanket covering her narrow frame.

The emergency room doctor said the victim had to be stabilized before they could attempt surgery to remove the bullet lodged in her chest. Given the circumstances, the police could question her for no more than five minutes. Emilia was the logical choice to question the critically wounded Russian woman.

"Sergei's dead, no?" Magda whispered.

Emilia winced. "He didn't suffer, Magda."

Sergei Porchenko was dead, nearly cut in half by the hail

of gunfire. The shooter Kurt struck with the rock was dead, too. Three rounds in the chest, courtesy of his friend.

Who had vanished, cigarette and all.

"It's finally over," Magda whispered. "We knew they'd come for him and they did."

"Who came, Magda?" Emilia leaned closer. The thousand tiny cuts on her legs protested and all she could do was ignore them.

Magda mumbled something in Russian.

"Magda, I don't understand."

"They said . . ." Magda closed her eyes and drifted away.

Emilia looked at the blinking equipment. The little green line continued to paint spikes and valleys.

"Magda," she said, a bit louder. "Stay with me. Help me find who did this."

Magda opened her eyes and looked around the room. Her gaze came back to Emilia.

"Magda," Emilia said urgently. "Sergei said he knew they'd come for Bogdan. Who did he mean?"

"Bogdan." Magda's eyes opened wide. "My nephew."

"Bogdan Andropov was your nephew?"

Magda's eyes filled with tears. "Sergei needed help," she croaked. "They said Sergei had betrayed them. But he wanted them to stop. Mexico is our home now . . . they'll ruin it."

"Who?" Emilia pressed. "Who did he want to stop? What are they doing?"

"Sergei never betrayed anyone. He wanted out." Tears

rolling down her cheeks, Magda grabbed Emilia's wrist with sudden strength. "Do you understand? No more. No more. That's why we came to Mexico. To escape."

Magda began to gasp, soft little puffs escaping her lips. Her hand relaxed. An alarm sounded from the assembled machinery. The room flooded with medical personnel and Emilia was unceremoniously shoved out of the room.

Seven minutes later, Magda Porchenko was dead.

It was nearly 2:00 am by the time a patrol car brought Emilia and Kurt back to the Palacio Réal. They stumbled into the penthouse, both nearly drunk with exhaustion.

"Are you hungry?" Kurt asked. He had a black eye and his shirt was ruined but he was alive and whole.

Emilia looked around the living room. She felt completely disoriented, as if she'd never seen this place before. Images of exploding glass and bloody bodies jerked through her head and collided with memories of Cardenas gasping his last breath as Barrielos Luna made his escape.

Her top and skirt were torn. Her sandals had disappeared in the garden and she wore paper slippers a nurse had given her.

"Em?"

"What?" Emilia asked blankly.

Kurt put his arm around her and guided her to the en suite bathroom attached to their bedroom. They stripped off their clothes and stepped into the enormous shower stall together. Emilia rested her cheek on Kurt's chest and let the hot water pound her. Kurt held her tight. She felt the pressure of his body and a raw, urgent need swept over her.

They made love on the wet tile, frantic for each other. The awkwardness of their first coupling was gone, burned away by the extreme experience and the knowledge that they had kept each other alive.

Emilia put pen to paper again that night.

I am grateful for Kurt Rucker.
I am grateful for Kurt Rucker.
I am grateful for Kurt Rucker.

CHAPTER 17

The shooting at the Pacific Lotus made all the headlines.

The *federales* descended on the Porchenko murders like locusts. It was the type of high profile case they liked and would fail to solve, with the usual perplexed excuses. Emilia had worked with a decent *federale* officer once, investigating a killing field. He was dead now.

As far as she was concerned, the rest were *pendejos*.

The Andropov murder investigation went along as an unfortunate footnote, related only because the three victims were Russian.

Emilia took the tranquilizer prescribed by the police psychiatrist. It knocked her out for two days and when she finally surfaced, Alvaro told her that Hostage Negotiations had a bead on Los Colectores, thanks to counterparts in Mexico City. The family should sit tight and wait to hear more. Perhaps something would break and a ransom payment would not be necessary.

With that positive news in hand, Emilia finally set up a meeting with Padre Ricardo's contact at the diocese's Family Services office.

Dora Machado Uribe was a big, brisk woman who settled Emilia into a chair by her desk, pushed a cup of coffee into her hands, and readied a pen. "Now, let's see. I think Padre Ricardo Solis told me you are looking for adoption records."

"Not exactly," Emilia said.

"You're single and want to adopt a child?"

"No, not that either." For a moment Emilia thought the woman was going to snatch away the cup of coffee. "Let me show you."

She took the key out of her shoulder bag and put it on Dora's desk. "I'm looking for Casa Odisea. I'm told it's an adoption search service."

"You want to give them back a key?" Dora asked.

"No, I'm trying to trace the owner of the key," Emilia explained. "This belonged to a fugitive criminal. I have reason to believe he was looking for his birth family and had engaged the services of Casa Odisea to find them. If they have a forwarding address or a phone number for him, I want it."

Dora touched the key gingerly, as if it was diseased. "When did you find this?"

"A few months ago."

She gave Emilia an assessing look. "Casa Odisea closed years ago."

It was the last thing Emilia expected to hear. The words hovered in front of her but she simply couldn't process them.

"Detective?" Dora's voice came from far away.

Emilia hauled in air. "When? When did it close?"

"I can check," Dora said. "How old is this criminal you're tracking?"

"Thirty-three."

"Well, it's possible they handled his adoption." Dora clicked a few keys on her computer keyboard and peered at the screen. She mumbled some numbers to herself, went over to a tall filing cabinet, yanked on a drawer and pulled out a thick file.

"He was trying to contact them relatively recently," Emilia said. "Less than five years ago at least."

"Let me see." Dora thumbed through the file, shaking her head slowly. "The original owner Doctoro Fernando Valdez passed away more than 20 years ago. His daughters took over Casa Odisea and remade the business into a research service. I anticipate they're both in their seventies now."

Emilia held out her hand. "Would you mind if I—."

Dora quickly closed the folder. "I'll look into it."

"I don't want to make work for you," Emilia said, wondering if she'd said something wrong. "All I need is contact information for either of them."

"It's no trouble at all," Dora assured her. "I'll do what I can to get that for you." She tucked the folder back in the filing cabinet and shut the drawer with more force than was necessary.

A caring woman, Padre Ricardo had called Dora.

As she left the office, Emilia wondered why.

Her cell phone rang with another call from Alvaro.

.

CHAPTER 18

"They sent two photos and a short line of text," Plano said. "From a new number. When we attempted to text back, the line didn't exist."

"Of course," Emilia said.

The war council was seated in Sophia's kitchen again. In the living room, the Hostage Negotiations' technical crew fussed over their computers and signal boxes.

Alvaro squeezed Emilia's knee under the table. She didn't know if it was a signal to shut up or a move to reassure her. She moved her leg.

Plano passed two printouts across the table. The first was a photo of Ernesto. He was hollow-cheeked and unshaven, squinting into the camera as if afraid of the light. A bold headline marched across the newspaper he held in front of his chest.

FUEL THIEVES CLOSE MORE STATIONS.

Kurt had read her the article that morning over breakfast on the balcony. Fuel thieves called *huachicoleros* were behind the rash of PEMEX station closings. So much gasoline was being siphoned out of illegal pipeline taps that PEMEX could not stock its stations. While *huachicoleros* were common throughout Mexico, the situation had now become acute due to PEMEX's declining capacity to refine crude oil.

Emilia picked up the other photo. "What's this?"

A long brown object filled the view. It was peppered with random holes.

"It's a coffin," Plano said. "They're apparently keeping him in a ventilated coffin."

Emilia's breakfast felt like lead.

"It's not uncommon in high stakes kidnapping to hold the victim in a confined space," Chen said. "Easily transported, too."

"They don't have to guard him," Emilia said. "He's locked in a fucking coffin."

"More evidence they're amateurs," Plano said. "They don't have a big enough team to babysit the victim."

"You said there was also a message?" Alvaro asked hopefully.

Plano swiveled his laptop to show the program which mirrored the texts on Sophia's phone.

He lives where he dies. 5 more days.

"A second proof of life," Plano said. "Before we asked. It's a good sign. But we haven't got anything definite yet from Mexico City. You're going to have to offer something in return."

"Sixty thousand dollars," Emilia said. It was the most Kurt could raise without going to *El Norte* to deal with his accountant.

"We can work with that," Plano said. "But it's a long way from two million."

Emilia looked at the photo of the coffin. "How long can someone stay sane living in a box?"

"That depends," Chen said. "Is Ernesto a resilient man?"

Emilia thought of the day she'd met Ernesto. Sophia brought him home like a stray dog and didn't even know how long he'd been in Acapulco.

"I have no idea," Emilia said.

Alvaro nodded to Emilia as the meeting broke up. They crossed the courtyard together but their steps slowed as they approached the Suburban. The vehicle wasn't the accordion it had been, but neither was it restored to assembly line condition. The police metal shop had fixed it with the automotive equivalent of chewing gum, aluminum foil, and a bad attitude. The paint on the repaired sections bubbled in the hot sun.

"The money," Alvaro said. "You're getting it from Rucker?"

"Yes." Emilia eyed her cousin. She'd known him all her life and knew his moods. "Is that a problem?"

"I've got a better idea," Alvaro said. He lowered his voice. "Franco Silvio stashed three million in counterfeit dollars in the evidence locker. Seized it a couple of weeks ago. We can take two for Ernesto's ransom."

Emilia gaped at him. "You want to pay the ransom with counterfeit dollars?"

"It's the perfect solution," Alvaro said seriously.

"What if the kidnappers find out it's bogus money and kill Ernesto?"

"Plano says they're amateurs," Alvaro argued. "They won't know the difference."

"Are you willing to bet Ernesto's life on that?" Emilia asked. "They're pretty savvy about using burner phones and different SIM cards."

"You can get all that from watching television," Alvaro said.

Emilia folded her arms. "Go back to the beginning of this conversation," she said. "Why does it bother you that Kurt's willing to help?"

"Look, *prima*," Alvaro said quietly. "You can't take his money."

"Why not?"

"If you do." Alvaro's voice lowered to nearly a whisper. "It's like you're a prostitute."

"What?"

"You sleep with him and you take money from him. What's that called?"

"A loan!" Emilia exclaimed.

Alvaro shook his head. "Are you really going to pay that off? It's bad enough that you live with him, but to take a pile of cash means something else."

Shock spiraled into fury. "I see you've been listening to your mother," Emilia said icily.

"Think about the counterfeit money, *prima*," Alvaro said. "Who knows when the Secret Service will show up to claim it."

"Sure, I'll think about it," Emilia said. "You think about what Silvio says when they come and want their fake money. All of it."

"This is Mexico." Alvaro shrugged. "The *norteamericanos* will assume it's just the *Mexicanos* fucking up again. Works every time."

CHAPTER 19

The rest of the day was soured by the exchange with Alvaro. Emilia went to her appointment with the police psychiatrist. When he pointed out that the entries in her gratitude journal were too few and all the same, she had no answer.

It was late by the time she got back to the penthouse. Luis was already behind the concierge desk and he gave her a wide smile as she went to the elevator. Emilia threw herself into the penthouse and dumped her shoulder bag onto the sofa. Kurt was not yet home.

She went into the kitchen, opened the refrigerator, and stared blankly at the well-stocked shelves. Fresh food magically appeared every few days. She never had to cook or go to the market. It was an unnatural way to live.

Emilia poured herself a glass of white wine and took it down the hall to the room Kurt used as a second office. She sat at the desk and turned on his computer. She searched for ransom negotiations. How much was demanded. How much was paid and how.

She was soon immersed in famous kidnapping cases. Few victims survived.

On a whim, Emilia typed "Bogdan Andropov" into the search bar and was amazed to get pages of links. Dozens of articles in English, Spanish, and Russian. She skimmed the Spanish language articles. Andropov wrote about tapas bars in Madrid. Magazine publishing in Colombia. Cuban slang in Miami.

Emilia finished her wine and thought about Magda Porchenko's last words. Bogdan had come to Acapulco to help Sergei.

He wanted out. No more. No more. That's why we came to Mexico. To escape.

Out of what? Escape from what?

How was a travel writer supposed to help?

She went to the hall closet, dug out the bag from the morgue containing Andropov's clothes, and dumped it on the floor.

White jeans with a waist narrower than Emilia's clothing. A polo shirt. A pair of men's white mesh bikini briefs.

She found a ticket stub for the CiCi water park in the pocket of the pants and paused to take a breath. At least he'd seen the dolphins.

The shirt had no pocket. Emilia checked the seams to satisfy herself that nothing was concealed in the fabric and set it aside.

"Bold choice," Emilia murmured as she picked up the briefs by the elastic waist. She gingerly ran the flimsy material between a thumb and forefinger. There was a distinct lump inside the waistband seam. Emilia tugged at the fabric and a tiny microSD card dropped into her hand.

Ten feet behind her, the front door opened. Emilia gave a scream before she realized it was Kurt.

"What's going on?" he asked. Kurt's black eye had faded

to a yellow half moon. "Are you cutting up my clothes?"

"These belonged to Bogdan Andropov." Emilia held up the tiny data storage card. "He had this hidden in his underwear."

Kurt squatted down next to her. "This is kinky, Em. Where did you get his stuff?"

"Prade gave them to me after the autopsy," she said.

Kurt held out his hand and she dropped the tiny chip into his palm. "I have a virus checker program loaded on my office computer," he said. "We can scan this and see if there's anything on it."

The lobby was lit up like fairy land again, making Emilia realize how long she'd spent upstairs glued to tales of kidnappings gone awry and Andropov's travel articles. Luis was behind the concierge desk and gave her a friendly wave as Emilia and Kurt passed by on the way to his office.

Emilia sat in one of the big swivel chairs around the conference table as Kurt tapped on his keyboard and eventually slipped the microSD card into a port.

"Three images," he announced. "That's all, just three images."

Emilia circled the desk to look over his shoulder. The screen showed a single folder containing three .jpg files. Each file name was a random string of numbers.

Kurt clicked on the first image. It was a snapshot of a page from an English-language magazine featuring a short article about a think tank called "Global Energy Study Group." A new branch office in Acapulco would join outposts in

Caracas, Rio de Janeiro, Panama, Moscow, London, and Riyadh. Kolya Bartok, an energy sector expert with over 20 years experience, would head up the new branch. An address in Acapulco was given.

"Ever heard of it?" Kurt asked. "Global Energy Design Group."

"No." The article hardly merited a hiding place in a man's underwear.

Kurt opened the next file. Lines of handwritten Cyrillic script filled the computer screen. The ink was smudged and creased.

"That's Russian, isn't it?" Emilia asked.

Kurt nodded. "The language of the moment."

"Look at the paper." Emilia was intrigued. "Looks like somebody wadded it up into a ball, smoothed it out and took a picture. I bet he found this in the trash."

"I think it's a code," Kurt said.

"For what?"

"No idea," Kurt confessed.

The third image was of a white business card decorated with a striking red and green logo, the same one plastered on every gas pump in the country.

Hector Calderon Rios
Director, GRUPO SUD ADMINISTRATIVO PEMEX

CHAPTER 20

"Did I call you?" Silvio asked.

"It was more like a subliminal cry for help." Emilia plunked her shoulder bag down on his desk, which was remarkably free of files.

"Yeah, sure." Silvio eyed her bag. "Any luck with the kidnappers?"

"They still want two million dollars and they're keeping Ernesto in a coffin," Emilia said.

"Shit." Silvio grimaced. "How about your mother?"

"Denial. Dreamland." Emilia regarded her former partner with suspicion. "Chen say anything to you lately?"

"Only that Plano is working his contacts hard. Thinks they could be holding Ernesto in Mexico City where the whole *coyote* contract deal began."

"So he said." Emilia opened her shoulder bag.

"If you brought me a fake letter from the police shrink, it goes in the shredder," Silvio warned.

Emilia sniffed the air, swiveling her head like a hunting dog picking up the scent of lemon furniture polish.

"How we've all missed your sense of humor, Cruz," Silvio said sourly.

"I know." Emilia showed him the microSD card. "At the autopsy, Prade gave me Bogdan Andropov's clothes. This was hidden in his underwear."

"That's a new one." Silvio's chair squealed as he sat bolt upright.

"It has three image files on it," Emilia said. "Nothing else."

She slapped down three printouts.

Silvio's expression went from puzzled to suspicious as he studied the pictures. When he finally looked up, Emilia knew he was in full investigation mode.

"Lemme see if I've got this straight," Silvio said. "Porchenko and Andropov do a money exchange in the Palacio Réal. Andropov's staying there, which is a good 30 minutes outside Acapulco and as expensive as shit for a travel writer."

Emilia perched on the edge of a chair fronting the desk. "Correct."

"The guy gets quietly murdered with a dose of adrenaline big enough to kill a horse." Silvio rocked back in his desk chair again. "Us clods here in Mexico are supposed to conclude a heart attack."

"Except we don't, thanks to the autopsy and hotel security cameras."

"What's more, we find out his aunt is married to Porchenko of the money exchange fame. Both of the Porchenkos get very publicly whacked by two *gringos* who don't bother to hide their faces. For the moment, let's assume they're Russian, too."

"Okay."

"All along, Andropov's got a chip in his panties with random shit on it, including the business card of the guy who controls all the oil and gas in this part of Mexico."

"One quiet murder," Emilia said. "Two public executions."

"You got that too?" Silvio rocked back in his chair again. "The Porchenko killing was a message."

"To?"

"Exactly."

Emilia propped her elbows on Silvio's desk. "At the hospital, Magda said Porchenko wanted out and that Andropov had come to help. So the big question is what did Porchenko want out of?"

"The Russian mob," Silvio said immediately.

"So killing the Porchenkos was a message to the rest of the mob? There's no out, *amigos*?"

"Unless Porchenko was being blackmailed?"

"By who?"

Emilia studied the printout of the business card. "Maybe Porchenko was the only person with a full tank of gas in Acapulco. Every other gas station is closed. Did you read the latest article on the fuel thieves?"

"Yeah, it was on the front page right above the news that the baggage handlers union is threatening a strike over the fucking privacy issue." Silvio rubbed his bristly crew cut. "Okay, say there's a connection between the Russian mob and PEMEX. What was some travel writer going to do about it?"

"I don't know," Emilia admitted. "Andropov was interested in ordinary things. What to do on the eastern side of the bay. Restaurants, clubs, that sort of thing. Nothing unusual."

"What if other Russians are involved?" Silvio scowled at the thought. "How many fucking Russians in Acapulco could turn up dead before we figure out what's going on?"

"Was that a rhetorical question?"

"Yeah. Shit."

"What happened to Andropov's things from the hotel?" Emilia asked. "There could be more stuff hidden in his clothes."

"We gave it all to the *federales*."

"*Perfecto*," Emilia said. "What part of this great big mess are the *federales* going to solve?"

Silvio snorted. "They're going to spend six months trying to ID the dead shooter from the Pacific Lotus."

Emilia slumped in her chair and pointed to the three images on Silvio's desk. "Are you going to give them this?"

"Is there any proof any of this is relevant to the hit on the Porchenkos?" Silvio obviously didn't expect an answer. "This is crap out of a guy's panties."

"*Federales* would laugh us out of our jobs if we gave it to them," Emilia ventured.

"I'll get this translated." Silvio studied the lines of Cyrillic print again. "Poke at it a bit. See if we can't get a better idea of what Porchenko was doing in Acapulco. That's still our prerogative."

His desk phone rang.

Emilia waited impatiently as Silvio grunted through a 10-second conversation. When he threw the receiver back into its cradle he stood up. "Your lucky day, Cruz," he said. "Macias and Sandor collared Hollywood's magically growing waiter, Pedro Lopez Ventura. Kid's been out of the country since Andropov was killed."

Most of the detectives preferred the privacy of the small cement-walled room where both suspects and witnesses could be intimidated the old-fashioned way but counterdrug funds from on-again-off-again partner *El Norte* came with a hefty price tag in terms of accountability.

So now they had a viewing corridor outside two new interrogation rooms, complete with one-way glass, audio controls, and a discreet signal system. Macias and Sandor waited in the viewing corridor.

The audio from the first interrogation room was on. Emilia heard the jerky, nervous breathing of the young man seated at the table. He was alone in the sterile space.

She recognized Pedro from the video in Ronaldo Olivas's office: trim build, square jaw, pompadour hair, alert and attentive. He looked like every other young staff member at the hotel, as if Kurt printed them in the basement.

"Got his phone?" Silvio asked.

"Yes," Sandor answered. "Ortiz is downloading everything now."

"All right," Silvio said. "See what story he tells us."

He parked himself in front of the big viewing window,

arms folded. Emilia leaned against the wall, ready to watch the show.

Macias and Sandor walked into the interrogation room. Sandor carried a slim laptop. Macias held a thick file folder, probably loaded with blank paper. Thin files never made an impression; thick files made suspects nervous.

The two detectives took it slowly, asking Pedro basic questions about his employment and family life. He wanted the night shift after his training class because it paid better than working days and he could hang around the catering kitchen. His goal was to go to culinary school and become a chef.

His father was a partner in a small fishing supply business. His mother was an aide in a school library. They knew he didn't want to work on the boats or sell bait but there was no money for culinary school. Pedro expected to parlay his job as a waiter into an internship with Jacques Anatole.

"What would you do if you lost your job?" Macias asked.

The young man's answer surprised Emilia.

"I'm not going to lose my job," he said. "I'm the best kitchen runner they have."

"Why isn't he nervous?" Emilia wondered aloud. Silvio shrugged.

No one in a Mexican police interrogation room was this composed unless they had a pile of money to buy them out. She wondered if Olivas had gotten it wrong. But no, she'd seen the videos and the log signed the night Andropov was killed.

"We've got six videos to show you," Sandor announced. He adjusted the laptop so Pedro could view the screen. "Please identify the person in each one."

"That's me," Pedro said, as his face passed the nautilus shell sconce in the first video.

"Okay, let's look at the next one." Sandor clicked to the video of Pedro walking across the frame without the cart.

"That's me again."

Sandor played another video of Pedro delivering a room service cart to the third floor.

"It's the same video as before," Pedro said.

"Similar but not the same." Sandor froze the screen and pointed to the time stamp. "It was taken the next day."

"Well, that's me again." Pedro looked from Sandor across the table to Macias lounging by the door with his arms crossed. "Is this some sort of sex approach? You're watching me because you're interested? That way, you know?"

"You fucking punk," Silvio roared at the glass, making Emilia jump.

"The kid's simply an asshole," she said dismissively.

Sandor ignored Pedro's remark. "Can you identify the person in this video?"

He played a video of Pedro walking toward the elevator alone, having left the cart in Andropov's room for a second night in a row.

Pedro lifted the corner of his mouth in a half smile. "It's me again."

"Thank you." Sandor tapped on the laptop keyboard.

"He's either a fantastic actor or has no idea what's coming," Emilia murmured to Silvio.

"Again, please identify the person you see," Sandor instructed the young waiter.

The next video came to life on the screen as the room service cart appeared. The figure pushing the cart approached the sconce. He looked down and to the left, hiding his face from the light at precisely the right moment.

"That's me, too," Pedro said in a bored voice.

"Are you sure?" Macias said from the doorway.

Pedro looked sideways at the detective. "Yes. You're interested in me that way, too, aren't you?"

Sandor tapped the laptop keys yet again. "Last video. Like the others, let us know who is in it."

The man ran across the screen.

"That was me, too." Pedro was matter-of-fact.

"For the record," Sandor intoned. "The witness claims to be the subject of all security camera videos." He gave the dates and times of each video before asking Pedro if that was a correct recap of their conversation.

"Yes, that's correct." Pedro smiled. "So?"

Macias came over to the table. "Between your deliveries on Wednesday and Thursday, you grew three inches. On your tall boy day, somebody murdered Bogdan Andropov, the Russian man in room 316 who liked tea and pastries."

"What?" Pedro sagged like he'd been hit by a bag of wet sand.

Silvio snorted.

"Gotcha," Emilia said.

Sandor replayed all six videos. The interrogation room was silent, except for the click of the laptop keys and Pedro's breath coming in scratchy gasps through the audio feed.

"Look at where your shoulder is in this video." Sandor spent a minute toggling between stills of the cart being pushed across the screen. "Twice it's below the level of the bottom of the sconce. In the last, your shoulder covers the bottom edge. A difference of at least three inches."

Pedro reached out to slam down the laptop lid. Macias caught Pedro's wrist and flexed it backwards until the younger man cried out.

"Who's in the video, Pedro?" Macias asked softly.

"Let go of me!" Pedro shouted.

"Just tell us who was in that video."

"Me, me." Pedro dangled from Macias's grasp, half in and half out of his seat. "I didn't grow. I . . . I was wearing different shoes."

"Different shoes?" Macias asked skeptically.

"Yes, please." The young man was panting in pain now. A tear slid down his face. "It was me, I swear."

Sandor gave his head a tiny shake.

Macias dumped the young man back into his chair. Pedro massaged his wrist with his other hand.

Emilia and Silvio exchanged a look.

"Let's talk about Señor Andropov," Sandor said mildly as if the painful altercation had never happened. "You delivered the same room service order to his room three nights in a row. Must have gotten friendly with him."

"No, he just signed the check."

"When?"

"Every night." Pedro edged his chair away from Macias. "He signed the check every night and I brought it to the kitchen like any other room service order."

"Why were you running Thursday night?" Macias loomed over the young man.

"There were more orders."

"We know how many orders the kitchen had in process," Sandor said. "None."

Pedro shrugged.

"Help me understand," Macias said nastily. "Thursday night. About midnight. You signed out the cart with Andropov's room service order. Brought it upstairs. He signed for it. You ran back to the kitchen because you were so fucking worried there were so many guests waiting for their room service orders."

"Yes."

"Did the exact same thing three nights in a row."

"Yes."

"But only in a hurry on Thursday."

"Yes."

"How many days of the week do you wear your tall boy shoes?"

Pedro opened his mouth to reply, reconsidered, and fell silent.

Sandor jumped up and went to the wall phone. Silvio grinned as the corridor phone rang. Emilia picked it up. "*Digame*," she said.

"Tell Silvio to send a car over to the Ventura Lopez residence," Sandor said, his eyes on Pedro. "Confiscate all the shoes. Bring the parents in for questioning."

Pedro began to cry.

Sandor hung up the phone and ambled back to the table. "We need a name, Pedro," he said. "We know the person in that video switched places with you. You signed out the order, gave him your uniform shirt, and let him deliver the order to Andropov's room."

"Please don't talk to my parents." Pedro hiccupped with the effort to stop sobbing.

"You must have been sweating blood because it took him so long." Sandor was relentless. "He knew he had to make it fast, didn't he? Ran like the wind down the hall to find you. Gave you the receipt to turn in. What's his name, Pedro?"

"No, that's not what happened."

"You gave him your shirt and the cart," Macias thundered.

"No." Pedro dashed the back of his hand against the tears running down both cheeks. "I took the cart upstairs and left it near the supply closet. That's all. I never saw anyone take it."

Macias slapped both hands on the table. "Who told you to leave the cart there?"

"Luis." Pedro teared up again. "Luis paid me to leave it.

He said if I didn't say anything, no one would get in trouble. We were doing Señor Andropov a favor."

On the other side of the viewing window, Emilia grabbed Silvio's arm.

"*Madre de Dios*," she said. "I know Luis."

By the time, Macias and Sandor dumped a sniffling Pedro into a holding cell, the squadroom was empty. Silvio made a beeline for the safe in his office.

Dying for some caffeine, Emilia made a pot of coffee and looked around while it brewed. The walls were segmented into depressingly similar crime scenes.

Bloody bodies crumpled on sidewalks or streets. Garbage cans and graffiti in the background. Most of the victims were male. Oddly enough, most wore rock band tee shirts.

Silvio came out of his office brandishing a folder as Macias and Sandor helped themselves to fresh coffee.

"I thought you gave everything on Andropov to the *federales*," Emilia said, surprised to see the file label.

"Not the actual case record," Silvio said, as if she was insane.

Sandor got to work pinning photos from the folder to a bare spot on the wall. Andropov's body. The room where he was found. The tiny hole in his armpit.

"Luis is a concierge at the Palacio Réal," Emilia said. "He and Pedro both work the night shift."

"Any Russian connections?" Silvio asked.

"No idea." Emilia thought back to the brief conversations she'd had with the personable night concierge. Weather, sunsets, special events in the hotel. Nothing significant jumped out.

"Here." Macias held out a printout stapled at the corner. "Here's the hotel's list of everybody who worked that night."

There were 124 names on it, organized by hotel department. Emilia had no idea so many people roamed the Palacio Réal while she slept. Luis Soto Rivera was listed as Assistant Concierge.

"Has he been working since the murder?" Silvio asked. "Or conveniently on vacation like the kid?"

"We can ask Olivas, but Luis has been around." Emilia was sure. "I saw him the other night. From what I can tell, he's good at his job. Everybody likes him."

"Good. He thinks he's in the clear so we've got time to dig around." Silvio pointed in the general direction of Macias and Sandor. "You two check him out. Background. Financials. Friends. Family. Links to the Russian community."

"Sure, *jefe*," Macias said.

Silvio inhaled some coffee. "Cruz, you follow up on that oil and gas outfit. What was it called?"

"Global Energy Design Group," Emilia provided. "But I'm on medical leave, remember? Dealing with a few family issues, too. Besides, no gun, no work."

Silvio grinned. "When you get a chance, call on Señor

Calderon Rios over at the PEMEX building, too. What's his connection to the late great Bogdan Andropov?"

It was infuriating how well Silvio knew her.

As Emilia drove back to the Palacio Réal, she passed another shuttered PEMEX station, a big banner stretched across the pumps. *NO HAY GASOLINA*!

If half the gas stations in Acapulco were closed, the clanky gas-guzzling Suburban was in trouble.

Perhaps she'd ask Señor Calderon Rios about those fuel thieves, too.

CHAPTER 21

Like so much of Acapulco hidden behind the white skyscrapers that ringed the bay, the El Coloso neighborhood bore testimony to the city's decay. As Emilia got out of the car, her glance picked out bullet holes in the walls safeguarding houses and shops. Rust from rooftop water tanks dripped down cracked and faded stucco. The razor wire topping every structure twinkled in the bright morning sun while vulgar graffiti spewed across broken sidewalks.

Dora Machado Uribe came around from the driver's side and joined Emilia in front of the pockmarked gray cement wall surrounding the home of the Valdez family.

"I haven't been here in years," Dora said. In contrast to Emilia's white blouse and skinny black pants, the head of Family Services wore a red polyester pantsuit. "This neighborhood used to be nicer."

"Lots of things in Acapulco used to be nicer," Emilia said.

Dora's call that morning trumped Emilia's plans to scout out the Global Energy Design Study Group offices or call Alvaro to ask for an update from Plano.

Today, finding Rafa Gamboa came first.

The key in Emilia's shoulder bag weighed it down as the two women walked to the rickety iron gate. White paint peeled off the posts and the hinges were coated with rust.

Emilia found a doorbell above a scratched metal speaker. When she jabbed her thumb on it, the button sizzled with an electric current. The shock tingled all the way to her elbow.

They waited. The street was deserted except for a few cars parked by the curb. No workmen, no shoppers heading to the market, no delivery trucks.

A tinny voice crackled through the tiny speaker set into the stucco. "*Bueno*?"

"We have an appointment with la señora." Dora yelled back.

"One moment." There was a loud buzz and the gate swung open in a shower of rust.

Dora passed through ahead of Emilia, her red suit jacket momentarily blocking the view. Emilia closed the gate behind them, moved aside, and swallowed a gust of involuntary laughter.

The two storey gray house was webbed with cracks and tilted like a cartoon. Buckled security grilles hung crookedly, partially obscuring the cracked windows behind them. Red clay tiles lay broken on the flagstone path, as if they'd raced each other off the roof like lemmings. The debris competed for attention with a healthy crop of weeds.

"*Madre de Dios*," Emilia said, surveying the wreckage of what had once been a nice piece of modern architecture. "The last earthquake to do this kind of damage in Acapulco was years ago. Why wasn't this place condemned?"

"Hopefully, Casa Odisea's records are still intact," Dora said.

A maid in a shapeless black dress waited at the door, seemingly as old and hunched as the house. She led them through what had once been a magnificent reception hall, her fabric slippers silent on the uneven marble floor tiles. Emilia picked her way carefully, as did Dora.

The ceiling sloped noticeably over a gold frieze that topped the walls like a bandage holding the house together. Long velvet curtains blocked the sunlight. A huge iron chandelier hung dangerously askew; the ceiling plaster bulged with the effort of holding onto it. Emilia edged toward a window to avoid walking under the dangling fixture and was rewarded with a lungful of mold from the draperies.

The maid deposited them in a flagstone courtyard ringed with flowering plants. Emilia gratefully inhaled a gulp of fresh air and noticed Dora do the same.

An elderly woman sat at a wrought iron table, wearing a black blouse and *rebozo* shawl across her shoulders despite the warmth of the day. As they approached, she eyed them with suspicion.

"Señora Valdez," Dora said warmly. "I'm Dora Machado Uribe and this is Emilia Cruz Encinos. I spoke to your attorney and he said you would be expecting us."

"He said something about it being of critical importance." The woman eyed her guests with dislike as the maid stood nearby, evidently waiting for instructions. "How exciting."

"Thank you for receiving us," Emilia said, extending her hand.

"I expect you want a seat and some hospitality." Señora Valdez gave Emilia's hand a withering glance and indicated the heavy iron chairs pulled up to the table. She told the maid to bring some water.

Emilia folded herself into one of the heavy chairs, wincing as bare arms touched sun-heated metal. Up close, Señora Valdez was only a few years older than Dora, yet she had the unkempt hair, protruding bones, and tatty clothes of an aged recluse who routinely forgot to eat and bathe. A pair of reading glasses perched on the end of her nose; one corner wrapped in a lump of white gauze tape. An old book with a leather cover lay on the table.

The maid brought three crystal wineglasses and a plastic liter of water and vanished back into the house. The rim of each glass was noticeably chipped.

"Now." Señora Valdez filled the stemware with water. "Exactly to what do I owe this visit?"

Dora nodded at Emilia.

"I'm looking for a man who contacted Casa Odisea some time ago," Emilia began. "His name is Rafael Gamboa Escobar and he was looking for his birth family. We hoped you still had his contact information, as well as a copy of whatever information Casa Odisea gave him."

"Impossible," Señora Valdez said. "For obvious reasons pertinent to our clients, Casa Odisea records are confidential."

"I completely understand," Emilia said. "I wouldn't ask if this wasn't such an exceptional circumstance."

"Everyone believes their situation is exceptional." Señora Valdez gave Emilia a brittle smile.

"Your attorney said you still have all of Casa Odisea's records," Dora interjected. "The diocese requires every adoption agency to keep records for 50 years."

"Yes, of course." Señora Valdez gave a twitch and her glance involuntarily slid to a door in the back wall of the courtyard before coming back to Dora. "They are only for the families involved. I can't help you."

As the other two women sparred over the confidentiality of Mexican adoption records, Emilia eyed the opposite side of the courtyard. A flat-roofed and windowless building backed to the wall surrounding the Valdez property. Parallel to the main house, it had a single door and straggly weeds grew against the stucco. Without windows, it couldn't be a residential apartment. It wasn't a garage, either.

Could that be Casa Odisea's office? As Emilia wondered if the key weighting her purse fit the lock, she realized that the conversation between Dora and Señora Valdez had become heated.

"My father created Casa Odisea out of nothing," Señora Valdez said, her voice shaking. "He sacrificed everything to help the less fortunate. Placing children into loving families. Helping people understand where they came from."

"Your father—," Dora's face tight with anger.

"That's exactly what Rafa Gamboa was looking for," Emilia jumped in before someone burst into flames. "Could you consult your records? We can wait. I'm sure whatever you provide will be helpful."

Señora Valdez squinted at Emilia, momentarily distracted. "What makes you so sure he came to us?"

"He told several people," Emilia lied.

Señora Valdez sniffed. "What's the name again?"

"Rafael Gamboa Escobar," Emilia provided. "When he came to you he was an actor using the stage name Rafa Gamboa."

"Gamboa." Señora Valdez adjusted her spectacles. "Was that his birth name or his adopted name?"

"The name of his adoptive father. His birth name was Ernesto Cruz Encinos."

"Cruz? Every third person in Mexico is called Cruz."

"I understand the difficulty." Emilia willed the woman to get up and go to the door in the windowless building. Rafa Gamboa's email address or cell number might be less than ten meters away. "Your help could truly be a life or death issue. He's a criminal fugitive."

Señora Valdez bristled. "Tell the police."

"I am the police," Emilia said. "A detective with the Acapulco municipal police."

Señora Valdez's eyes widened in sudden shock. She whipped off her glasses and stabbed them in the air at Dora. "Now I remember you," she shrilled. "Dora. *That* Dora. Of course."

Dora drew back. "This is a different day and time," she said. "We're here for Rafa Gamboa Escobar, that's all."

"No, you're not," Señora Valdez exclaimed. "After all

these years, you're still trying to strike at my family like a viper."

"Dora?" Emilia murmured. She had no idea what was happening.

Dora shook her head. "The past is what it is. We're not here to—."

"Get out, Dora," Señora Valdez shouted down the other woman. "Get out and take your little liar with you."

Emilia stiffened.

"I'm sorry you feel this way." Dora stood up. "We came seeking help."

"Go, go." Señora Valdez flushed with anger. "I never should have let you into my home."

Dora shoved her chair aside, iron grating against the flagstones. She stalked toward the house as Emilia stared at her retreating back in confusion.

"You." Señora Valdez hunched over her book like a vulture. "You go, too."

"I didn't come here to reopen some old feud," Emilia said, trying to project calm. "But to ask for help to find a fugitive criminal."

"You're here to do that woman's dirty work," Señora Valdez hissed.

"I don't know what transpired between you and Dora but it doesn't concern me." Emilia decided to throw out a last option. "I'm willing to pay for your time. Would 800 pesos be enough?"

Señora Valdez picked up Dora's untouched glass. Emilia

barely managed to turn her chin in time.

The cold water hit her cheek and ear. Emilia sprang to her feet with a yelp. The heavy chair fell backwards onto the flagstones with a bone-shaking clang.

"There." Señora Valdez's lips thinned into a taut smile of triumph as water dripped down Emilia's chin and soaked the front of her blouse. "Go away."

Emilia found Dora leaning against the hood of the car, a cigarette in hand. The older woman's jacket was off and the sleeves of her cotton blouse rolled to the elbow.

Dora waved a hand to dispel the smoke from her cigarette as she regarded Emilia's water-soaked blouse. "What happened?"

"First, you tell me why you're really here." Emilia jammed her shoulder bag on the hood of the car as anger sizzled through her veins.

"I expect I owe you an explanation."

"That's an understatement." Emilia yanked a tissue out of her bag and plied her face. "I don't like being played, Dora. I'm looking for a criminal and you fucked up my last chance to find him."

Dora took a last drag from her cigarette before flicking the butt into a clump of weeds trapped in a sidewalk crack. "She's still trying to preserve her father's legacy."

Emilia balled up the damp tissue. "And you're trying to

tear it down?"

"I'm trying to get at old truths."

"Old truths?"

Dora fiddled with a pack of cigarettes. "My first assignment as a junior administrator in the Family Services office was to investigate rumors about Casa Odisea."

"What sort of rumors?"

"Maybe rumors is the wrong word. Complaints, maybe. Families coming forward with complaints."

"This was back when Señora Valdez's father was still alive?"

"Yes, Casa Odisea was still an adoption service and Fernando Valdez was running it. On the surface, he was an angel and the diocese loved him. Nobody wanted to deal with the complaints but they couldn't ignore them, either. I was the expendable new *chica* sent to investigate."

"So?" Emilia still hummed with anger.

"Fernando wouldn't answer a single question. No access to Casa Odisea records. He denied all of the complaints. I talked to a dozen families but no one had any evidence to support their claims."

"Let me guess," Emilia said. "It was embarrassing to all concerned, so the diocese let it slide. Or Fernando paid people in the bishop's office to look the other way."

Dora nodded. "I always wondered. But it left a cloud over Fernando."

"So much so that when he died his daughters stopped facilitating adoptions and became a research service."

"Yes." Dora lit another cigarette and inhaled deeply.

"That's why you came today?" Emilia flicked the soggy ball of tissue into the street. "You didn't have to come and we both know it. You thought I could get you access to whatever evidence you were looking for years ago."

"Yes." Dora met Emilia's eyes. There was no shame in her face at all.

"You should have told me, Dora." Emilia heard the savagery in her voice but she couldn't help it. "You ruined my one shot to find out if Rafa Gamboa left a phone number or an address."

"Doctoro Fernando Valdez was buying and selling children, Emilia," Dora said quietly. She stared at her cigarette as if surprised to find she was smoking. "He'd scout out a poor village where there was nothing. No civil authority or telephones or decent schools. Find families with more children than they could afford to feed. He'd pay the family a few hundred pesos for a child."

"I'm a cop, Dora. This is hardly news." Emilia jerked open the car door and threw her shoulder bag onto the floor. As tragic as these stories always were, she'd heard them too many times to be shocked or even sad.

"Prospective parents gave him a list of what they wanted. Boy or girl, about how old." Dora paused.

"Let me guess." A light breeze played over Emilia's damp blouse and the resulting involuntary shiver didn't improve her mood. "Taking babies from *campesinos* and selling them to *criollos*. The children had to blend in with their new upper class families so he had to find children who looked right. Narrow features. Light skin. They had to pass."

"Bought a couple of kids each time he went to some dirt poor village. To those poor people, being a doctor was better than being a god." Dora gazed over the top of the wall at the second story of the house. "I think he brought the children here while the adoptions were arranged. I sat in that garden and could almost hear them. Confused. Crying. Little hostages."

Hostages.

Emilia thought of Ernesto and the care the kidnappers had taken to eliminate their footprint. If they were amateurs, they were savvy ones.

"What makes you think Señora Valdez still has the records?" she asked. "The family probably threw away anything incriminating years ago."

"She has them," Dora said. She opened the driver's door. "I think she's sat on them all these years, because in some twisted way she wants the records to clear her father's name."

"Why not let you look through them?"

"Because she knows they won't."

Emilia threw herself into the passenger's seat. "Bottom line," she said bitterly. "None of this has anything to do with me."

CHAPTER 22

"How did it go?" Kurt asked from the living room.

Emilia closed the front door to the penthouse behind her. "Don't ask."

She dumped her shoulder bag next to the door. Kurt sat on the sofa, glass in hand. Everything was off—lights, television, stereo. "What's going on?" she asked.

"Come watch the sunset with me, Em."

Emilia sank onto the sofa next to him. The white linen curtains were open and the floor to ceiling windows showed the full glory of yet another spectacular Acapulco sunset. Ribbons of gold and purple transformed the twilight sky into stained glass only to dissolve into the gently rippling ocean.

Kurt offered Emilia his glass. She took a sip of whiskey and coughed as it seared her throat.

"I have to go to London," Kurt said as he took back the glass. "Corporate isn't too pleased about a murder in their flagship hotel and me being involved in the Porchenko shooting."

A prickle of fear raced up Emilia's spine. "Are you getting fired?"

"This is business, Em," Kurt said. "They'd fire me over the phone, not pay for a first class ticket to London. No, this will be a face-to-face to talk about Andropov's murder and crime in Acapulco. What we're doing to shore up our security practices."

"When?"

"The day after tomorrow. I'll spend a couple of days there before heading to Las Vegas to meet with the accountant and get the papers signed. I know you need that money."

"Hostage Negotiations hasn't even pitched an opening offer, as Plano calls it."

Kurt finished the drink and put the empty glass on the coffee table. "They will."

"Thank you." Emilia pressed against him. "I don't know how you do it."

"Do what?"

"Run a luxury hotel in the middle of a combat zone and never lose your cool."

Kurt pulled her to her feet. "That sounds like a woman who needs a good meal."

"I'm starving," Emilia admitted.

She grabbed her shoulder bag, Kurt scooped up his phone, and they rode the elevator down to the lobby level. The doors opened with a whispered whoosh and they stepped out.

Into chaos.

Half a dozen uniformed police officers in full combat gear and long guns ran by, heavy boots pounding on the tile floor. Shouted commands and startled cries of guests and staff combined into a frightening cacophony.

"What's going on?" Kurt exclaimed in English. He shot across the lobby.

In the midst of the dark uniforms, Emilia saw Silvio. He was in jeans and a black blazer that covered his shoulder rig.

"Luis Soto Rivera?" Silvio thundered above the tumult as the phalanx of cops in SWAT gear surged toward the concierge desk.

Handsome face tight with shock, Luis spun around and sped through the doorway leading to the administrative offices. Two cops vaulted over the desk and pounded after him.

"Lock it down," Silvio barked into the radio clipped to his lapel. "We've got a runner."

Radios crackled. Multiple voices checked in. Silvio came with an army, Emilia realized, and had all the hotel exits covered.

Kurt broke through the circle of cops to confront Silvio. "What the hell is going on?"

Before Silvio could respond, there was a commotion in the hallway behind the concierge desk. Luis emerged, handcuffed, head bowed, and shoved forward none too gently by the cops who'd chased him down. Silvio flicked a finger toward the main entrance to the hotel and the grim parade made their way out of the lobby.

"My office," Kurt said to Silvio. "Now."

The two men locked eyes. For a horrible moment Emilia knew something very bad was going to happen.

Then Silvio shrugged. "Tell Olivas thanks," he said. "If he hadn't included the direct deposit information we wouldn't have found the 50,000 pesos deposited into Soto Rivera's bank account the day before Andropov was murdered."

"Fifty thousand?" Emilia marveled. That was probably more than Luis earned in six months.

"Jesus," Kurt said. "What's the charge? Taking a bribe?"

"Accessory to murder," Silvio said shortly. His eyes swung to Emilia. "Are you coming?"

Inside the interrogation room, Luis clasped his hands on the table.

"Okay," Silvio said. "You two see if you can get the story out of him."

Emilia flipped the audio switch as Macias and Sandor entered the interrogation room. They went through the preliminaries, introducing themselves and verifying Luis's name. He gave his name, address, and place of employment in a barely audible voice.

"This is going to be easy," Silvio said next to her, voice laden with satisfaction. He dumped his jacket on a chair.

Standing next to him, Emilia could almost imagine that they were partners again.

Macias and Sandor began to review the events of the night Andropov was killed. Luis congealed into a block of nervous ice. He stopped responding to the detectives' questions.

Silvio paced the viewing area, exhaling with impatience. Finally, he reached past Emilia and toggled the signal light. Macias and Sandor trotted into the corridor, leaving the frozen witness at the table.

"What the hell are you playing at?" Silvio demanded. "This is taking fucking forever."

"*Jefe*," Sandor protested. "It's been ten minutes. We barely got warmed up."

"*Rayos*," Silvio swore. "I'll give him ten fucking minutes."

He bulled past Sandor, rounded the corner, and a second later Emilia watched through the viewing window as Silvio charged into the interrogation room. He kicked the door closed and Luis cringed away from this new and volatile presence.

Emilia smiled. Everybody reacted to Silvio.

"Luis Soto Rivera." Silvio faced Luis across the table but did not sit down. He filled the confined space with menace. "Correct?"

"The other detectives introduced themselves," Luis said primly.

"Did they now?" Silvio said.

"*Madre de Dios*," Emilia murmured. Luis just bought himself 200 pounds of trouble.

"Well, let me introduce myself, too," Silvio continued in a dangerously reasonable tone. "I'm the fucking chief around here. I get to do what I fucking want."

Before Luis could react, Silvio reached across the table, hauled the young man out of his seat by his upper arms, and dragged him half across the table. Luis's eyes bulged in fear.

"You can tell me what I want to hear or I can butt fuck

you right on this table," Silvio roared. He shook Luis like a wet dog, the young concierge's arms pinned to his sides. "I'm going to have fucking fun with you until my cock is up your throat and you're broken in two. Whatever's left is going to tell me what I want to hear."

Luis's mouth worked like a fish out of water and then he spewed yellow vomit.

"Fucking shit!" Silvio yelled. He thrust Luis away and hopped backwards.

Emilia couldn't believe it. Macias and Sandor burst into laughter.

Luis threw up again.

Silvio barreled out of the interrogation room.

Hunched over the table, Luis retched over and over. He finally stumbled backwards and wiped his mouth with a shaky hand. Tears streamed down his face. A viscous yellow puddle spread across the table and dripped onto the floor

Silvio came into the viewing corridor. His white shirt was streaked with vomit. The stink was unmistakable.

"*Jesu Cristo, jefe.*" Sandor waved a hand in front of his face to freshen the air. "I guess you got everything out of him."

Macias cracked up at the double entendre.

"Need a clean shirt, Franco?" Emilia inquired sweetly.

She saw a muscle jump in Silvio's jaw as he regarded the three detectives hooting at his expense. "Make sure he doesn't go anywhere," Silvio growled and headed for the corridor door.

Macias snorted. Without turning around, Silvio made a rude gesture and disappeared down the hall.

Inside the interrogation room, Luis looked up, evidently assuming there were microphones in the ceiling. "Hello?" he called, tears still streaming down his face. "I need some help."

"Call the Russians," Macias joked.

"The room has gotten dirty," Luis explained to the ceiling. "Please send someone with a mop. Also, I need a glass of water."

Emilia trotted down the hall to the restroom reserved for detectives.

Silvio stood shirtless in front of a sink. The smell of vomit was strong and Emilia saw his dress shirt wadded up in the trash can on top of a pile of crumpled paper towels. A black tee shirt awaited, draped over one of the cubicle partitions.

He caught her reflection as Emilia came into the restroom. "*Rayos*, Cruz," Silvio swore. "I could have been taking a piss."

"Let me talk to Luis," Emilia said, ignoring his comment.

Silvio ran water over a length of paper towel. "Why?"

"Because he knows me from the hotel as Kurt's girlfriend," Emilia pointed out. "I'll be all sympathetic and he'll try to explain his way out."

Silvio snagged the black tee shirt. As he pulled it over his head, his abdominal muscles bunched and flexed. The man was a *pendejo*, but he'd obviously been spending hours in the gym.

"What if it doesn't work?" he asked, buckling his shoulder holster.

Emilia shrugged. "Give me an hour. After that, you can butt fuck him until he snaps in two."

"Butt fuck." Silvio's face creased in an evil grin. "Scared him pretty good, huh?"

"Sure." Emilia rolled her eyes. "Great strategy until he puked."

Silvio pushed past her out of the restroom. Emilia stayed on his heels back to the viewing corridor.

Luis was still alone in the interrogation room with his pool of vomit, talking to the ceiling as Macias and Sandor watched.

"I figure two hours in that stink will soften him up," Silvio said. He turned off the audio feed. "Long enough for a steak and a beer."

He ordered a uniformed cop to stand guard outside the door. No one in or out of the room until they got back.

Emilia took a last glance at Luis as they left. She wondered when it would dawn on him that no one was in a rush to clean up his mess.

It felt like old times to Emilia.

The four cops took over a table at an outdoor *parrilla* restaurant a few blocks from the police station, where the beer was cold and the catch of the day was grilled on an oil drum cut in half lengthwise. The cook whacked tentacles off an octopus with an enormous cleaver, dredged the meat in oil, and threw it onto the grill next to sizzling strips of beef. The smell of spices and hot charcoal made Emilia's mouth water.

"Video is the new DNA," Sandor declared as they dug into grilled octopus and *arrachera* steak. "If we can get enough cameras in shit places like El Roble, we can cut the crime rate in half."

"Sure," Silvio said sarcastically. He took a chunk of pickled carrot from the community bowl. "Because nobody's interested in privacy any more."

"Not every case is going to be like the airport fuckup," Macias pointed out. "Unless the gangs get a union."

"We had four cameras in the baggage handling areas," Sandor told Emilia. "Motion detection software. Remote control. We could sit in a parking lot a mile away with a screen and a joystick and zoom in when they went through the suitcases."

"Never had an easier stakeout," Macias added.

Sandor nodded. "Too bad it ended in a pissing contest between the unions."

Emilia cut off another bite of the succulent octopus. "Is it over? Who won?"

"Hard to tell," Silvio said. "When the baggage handler union threatened to strike, Chief Salazar ordered us to take the cameras out. We've still got the footage and the names."

They went back to the station to find a small knot of

uniforms clustered around the viewing window.

"What's going on?" Silvio demanded.

"If you had a plan, *jefe*," one of them said. "I think it worked."

The group dispersed amid chuckles and glances at the window.

Luis sat on the floor, his back pressed into a corner and his knees drawn up to his chin. His shirt was untucked and he covered his mouth and nose with the tail.

"Okay, here's what we're going to do," Silvio said. "Sandor, you get him cleaned up. Take him into one of the old interrogation rooms. Cruz will go in, make like Rucker from the hotel is worried about his boy. See what she can get out of him."

They decided that Macias would go with Emilia and play bad cop if her sympathetic approach didn't work. Ten minutes later, Sandor said he was ready.

Emilia put her badge in her shoulder bag. Macias kept his dangling from its lanyard. The two detectives went into the interrogation room.

"Luis, how are you?" Emilia tried to radiate concern.

"Señora Cruz?" Luis said. His face was washed, his hair slicked flat, and he wore a plain navy tee shirt. "What's going on?"

"Are you all right?" Emilia gushed. "No one at the hotel knew what was going on and of course the police won't say anything."

"I want to go home." Luis burst into tears.

"Luis, what happened?" Emilia sat across from him. Macias stayed by the door.

Luis drew a shuddery breath. "I'm sorry. I . . . I've never had anything to do with the police before and everybody knows what happens when you do. You disappear."

"You're not going to disappear, Luis," Emilia said. "There has to be a good reason why you're here."

Luis leaned toward Emilia. "They asked me questions about a hotel guest. Somebody I don't even remember. People come and go at the hotel so fast, you know. I want to go home. I don't know anything."

"Oh, Luis." Emilia managed a trill. "You're so good. You remember everyone. Who did they ask you about?"

Luis glanced at Macias again.

Emilia edged forward. "Luis?"

The young concierge's attention came back to Emilia. "Señor Andropov," he whispered. "The Russian who died."

"See, you do remember," Emilia said, as if impressed.

"I'm not supposed to be here," Luis said. "Do you think Señor Rucker can help me?"

"Maybe." Emilia smiled at his gift of a perfect opening. "If you tell me what the police are interested in, I could go back to the hotel and ask him."

"Look." Luis squirmed with embarrassment. "It was for a girl. That's all. A girl."

"For a girl? Your girlfriend?" If Luis had gotten Andropov killed to impress a girl, Emilia was going to strangle him.

"No, a girl for Señor Andropov."

Emilia hadn't expected Luis to say that. "He had a girlfriend?"

"Not, not exactly." Luis stammered. "Arnold promised to get Señor Andropov a Russian girl for his birthday. To visit him in the hotel."

"Arnold?" Emilia tried to keep the excitement out of her voice. "Arnold who?"

"Just Arnold." His natural confidence was coming back, as if the decision to cooperate put Luis in the driver's seat. "He's Señor Andropov's friend."

"And Arnold wanted to . . ." Emilia waited.

"Give his friend a girl," Luis finished the sentence. "A Russian girl. Arnold needed help to get a Russian girl up to the room without her being seen."

"Okay." Emilia glanced at Macias who raised his eyebrows.

Arnold had told a plausible story. Acapulco was full of hookers who specialized in visits to hotels. A Russian girl would be rare and in high demand.

"Was Arnold also Russian?" Emilia asked.

"I think so," Luis ventured. "He spoke Spanish but he had a funny accent."

"Did he come to the hotel?" Emilia asked. "Is that where you met him?"

"No, I was at the *taqueria*."

"Which *taqueria*?"

"A place on Prado Norte in my neighborhood that opens

early. I like to go there when I come off the night shift. Have breakfast outside. Read. Smoke.”

"So you were hanging out there after work," Emilia said.

"Can I have a cup of coffee?" Luis asked.

"In a minute," Emilia said. "Finish your story first."

"Arnold paid for my food," Luis said, now annoyed. "Said he'd been to the Palacio Réal for dinner and recognized me. He told me a friend was staying there and asked if I had any ideas how a Russian girl could visit him without it becoming a big deal. I guess everybody in Acapulco knows Señor Rucker doesn't like hookers."

Emilia gave him her best *damn-what-a-hardass* expression.

Luis nodded vigorously, agreeing with her theatrics. "I told Arnold if Andropov ordered the same thing again, she could pretend to be a waiter. He thought that was a great idea and we fixed it up."

"Fixed it up?" Emilia prodded.

"We met again the next day." Luis's face reddened. "He gave me an envelope full of cash and I gave him a master keycard and a shirt."

"Did you keep it?" Emilia interrupted. "The envelope, I mean."

"No, why should I?"

Fingerprints, you fool. Emilia bit back the words. "Never mind. Then what happened?"

Luis shrugged. "I asked Pedro if he wanted to earn a bit extra. We worked out a plan. Pedro took the room service cart upstairs and left it in the hallway. All he had to do was wait in the supply closet until the girl slipped the paper receipt under the door."

"How did you arrange the timing with the girl?" Emilia asked.

"Arnold gave me a number to text the next time Andropov ordered room service. He said it was the girl's number."

"You were supposed to text her? Was she waiting in the hotel?"

"I don't know." Luis had yet to realize that he was an accessory to murder. Despite everything, he still bought the story the Russian had paid him to believe.

"Okay," Emilia said. "Did everything go according to plan?"

"Yes." Luis straightened up, obviously proud of his organizational abilities. "The concierge desk has access to everything. When I saw the order from Señor Andropov, I called the kitchen and spoke to Pedro. Then I texted the girl."

"Did she text back?"

"She sent a heart emoji."

The irony wasn't lost on Emilia. "Did you see her?" she pressed. "Was she waiting in the lobby? Did you see her get in the elevator?"

"No."

The young concierge was staggeringly self absorbed. Emilia wanted to shake him until his brain rattled hard enough to start making connections. "You didn't wonder if she went up to Señor Andropov's room or not? Did you text her again or did she text you?"

"No. Pedro got the receipt and that was that." Luis pursed his lips in what Emilia had come to realize was a look of smug satisfaction. "It didn't matter, did it? Arnold had already paid me."

Emilia didn't know whether to laugh or cry. "What about Arnold? Did you hear from him again?"

"No."

"But the next morning Andropov was dead. What did you think?"

"I wasn't at work in the morning."

Emilia knew she was dangerously close to cuffing Luis on the side of his thick skull. "It never crossed your mind that the hooker and Andropov's death were related?"

Luis scratched his head. "Am I going to lose my job?"

CHAPTER 23

"We have a strict policy against prostitutes in this hotel," Kurt said for the tenth time that morning. "No exceptions. None. Never."

"Eat your food," Emilia said quietly.

Kurt pronged a forkful of the scrambled eggs he'd made and ignored as soon as they were on his plate. "Do you realize," he said across the kitchen table to Emilia. "What a fool I'm going to look like in London?"

"It's not your fault." Emilia poured them both another cup of coffee.

"I'm the manager, Em. Everything is my responsibility." Kurt put down his fork, the eggs still untasted. "First a guest is murdered, then stormtroopers invade my lobby, and next I find out two employees took bribes to sneak in a Russian hitman. Who was pretending to be a prostitute, no less."

Kurt's phone buzzed. He snatched it up. "Silvio's downstairs in Ronaldo Olivas's office," he said. "With Luis's phone records."

Fifty thousand pesos bought a lot of tone deafness when it came to the rules, Emilia reflected as they rode the elevator down to the lobby. The hooker story had been an easy one for the two Palacio Réal employees to swallow. Perhaps they hadn't been there long enough to realize that Kurt's rules were not to be taken lightly.

Silvio was in a chair next to Olivas's desk when they came in. He looked as if he had good news.

"We may have the killer, *jefe*," Olivas said to Kurt.

Kurt shook hands with Silvio before pulling out a chair for Emilia and settling into the one next to her.

"Luis's phone shows a text to an unknown number at the right time, if his story is to be believed," Silvio said. "We've already tried to trace the number."

"Out of service," Emilia guessed.

"No surprise," Silvio said.

"We've compared his cell phone activity with calls made to and from the concierge desk on the night of Andropov's death," Olivas said. A paper by his computer mouse was covered with numbers. "The room service order was placed at 11:20 pm. At 11:22 there was a call from the concierge desk to the kitchen. After that, Luis used his personal cell phone to send a text. He sent another immediately after Pedro signed out the order for Andropov's room."

His computer monitor filled with the interior of one of the hotel's elevators as Olivas clicked keys. "I've been looking through the footage from all of the hotel cameras for that time. We got lucky. This man got into Elevator 6 at the lobby level right after Luis's last text."

The camera mounted above the doors showed a three-sided box bisected by a waist-height brass rail. A man in a dark shirt and light pants walked into the empty elevator. With his back to the doors and thus to the camera, he slipped a keycard into the panel and punched a button. Then like any other passenger in an elevator, he turned to face the doors.

Olivas froze the video. The killer stood in the middle of the empty elevator, resulting in a near-perfect headshot. A *gringo* with light brown hair that fell straight across his brow. He had curiously light eyes framed by thin eyebrows and rimmed with dark shadows.

"We can get an expert to compare this to the videos from the third floor corridor," Olivas said. "But to my trained eye, this is the same man who pushed the room service cart to Andropov's room the night of his death."

"It's possible he's the second shooter from the Pacific Lotus," Kurt murmured to Emilia. "I never got a good look at him."

"There's a pack of cigarettes in his shirt pocket," Emilia pointed out.

A few hours later, Silvio called Emilia to say that Luis confirmed that the man in the elevator was Arnold, the Spanish-speaking foreigner who'd paid the night concierge 50,000 pesos to sneak a Russian hooker into Andropov's room.

"You and Hollywood think he's also the Pacific Lotus shooter?" Silvio asked. "The one who got away?"

"It has to be him," Emilia said. "I don't know how he survived, but he did."

"He's a *sicario*," Silvio replied. "Makes his kill and stays low until the next time. I sent the photo to the *federales* but they were less than impressed. Claimed the image isn't good enough for facial recognition comparisons with visa or passport photos."

"Did you tell them he's a chain smoker?" Emilia asked. "Needs it so bad he lights up in the middle of a murder."

CHAPTER 24

The building was a parfait of steel and glass east of the Diana monument. It glinted blue in the sunlight as Emilia parked in a space reserved for visitors. The sign in front was a huge sheet of curved steel, with the PEMEX eagle head and oil drop logo. Soaring letters spelled out GRUPO SUD ADMINISTRATIVO PEMEX.

Emilia stayed in the car for a few minutes, checking her makeup in the rearview mirror, smoothing the wrinkles out of her linen skirt and rifling through her notes for the meeting.

Now in charge of all PEMEX operations in southwest Mexico, Hector Calderon Rios was an engineer who previously held planning positions in other government departments before transferring to PEMEX 15 years ago. He rose quickly through the calcified PEMEX hierarchy in Mexico City and transferred to the important regional position in Acapulco two years ago.

Given his quick career gains, Emilia figured he was either an extremely good engineer or extremely slippery.

Or both.

According to an article she found online, he was the keynote speaker at the recent Congreso Mexicano del Petróleo annual conference. A captioned photo showed a short, middle-aged man on the stage at the big Forum de Mundo Imperial, a new hotel and conference center in the rapidly developing Playa Diamante area. The complex perched on a skinny sandbar with the Pacific on one side and the Laguna de Tres Palos on the other.

A guard in a bright green uniform came up to the driver's side of the Suburban. Emilia nodded at him through the window, stowed her notebook and popped the lock. The guard opened the car door and directed her to the entrance. Emilia was met inside by a young woman clutching a clipboard who announced herself as Betty, junior secretary to Señor Calderon.

"I'm in charge of *el patrón's* schedule," Betty said, exuding self-importance as Emilia was issued a visitor badge. She led Emilia to the executive elevator and pushed the only button on the display.

"A critical position," Emilia said.

"It is." Betty glanced lovingly at her clipboard.

When the elevator doors opened, the view nearly took Emilia's breath away. They were so high that the city lay below like a confection of white and blue gossamer. White skyscrapers gleamed against cobalt sky. White sails cut across crystal blue water. A gleaming white cruise ship berthed on the west side of the bay dwarfed the nearby Spanish fort of Fuerte San Diego. A line of beach umbrellas on Playa Hornitos were colorful candy dots sprinkled across the sand.

Emilia followed Betty past the guard, through inlaid rosewood double doors, and into a modern office suite where several women sat in front of computers, their desks separated by glass partitions. Betty's desk was closest to another set of double doors, one of which was ajar.

Betty knocked gently on the open door and was greeted by an affable male voice.

"Yes, Betty, come in."

Calderon's office offered magnificent view of skyscrapers, water, and sand. He rose from behind a vast rosewood desk and extended his hand. Emilia had an impression of quiet assurance and competence. He shook her hands as if greeting a fellow respected professional.

"This is Emilia Cruz," Betty said. "From the National Hydrocarbons Commission."

"Of course, of course," Calderon enthused before Emilia could correct the secretary.

As soon as he steered Emilia to a seat on a leather sofa, a steward wheeled in a breakfast trolley. Betty promised to escort Emilia back to the lobby.

"The Congreso this year was quite the success," Calderon said, as the steward handed Emilia a cup of coffee and a china plate of dainty pastries. "I'm so pleased we could follow up with this meeting."

"Actually, um." Emilia looked around for Betty but she was gone.

"Above all, I want to reassure you that PEMEX Sud will continue to regard the National Hydrocarbons Commission as a valued partner." Calderon accepted a cup of coffee and dunked a cookie into the brew. "The annual auctions for oil exploration and production partners will take place as planned, of course. The Commission will carry out the auctions and provide oversight. Your role is unchanged."

Your secretary made a mistake.

Emilia could say that. Or she could play along in hopes of finding out something useful.

She raised her eyebrows at Calderon, balanced the plate on her knee, and took a sip of coffee.

Calderon put his cup on the low table in front of the sofa. "As we both know," he said. "PEMEX will start importing around 100,000 barrels a day of light crude to supplement shortfalls in domestic Mexican oil production. While imports are unprecedented, this will help get our refining capacity back to the desired level of about 800,000 barrels a day."

"Ah," Emilia said knowingly.

"Well, it is below the desired national threshold but that's going to change," Calderon said. He opened a file on the table and handed Emilia a graph full of colored lines and numbers. "This gives you both national PEMEX levels and Grupo Sud's performance over the past five years."

The only reason Emilia knew she wasn't holding the chart upside down was the print at the bottom.

"Our refinery network should be able to accommodate nearly two million barrels per day, with a quarter of that coming out of the Costa Glorieta refinery after the upgrades." Calderon handed her a sheaf of charts and spreadsheets. Some were in red, others in blue, still others were in a bold font. All loaded with meaningless numbers and jargon.

Emilia blinked at Calderon's important papers and felt like an idiot. If only she'd been the one to grow up with Karina, if only she'd had the opportunity to go to college. Instead, she grew up with Sophia, who gave her nothing.

"Of course. The upgrades." Emilia had no idea what to say next. She gave up and laid everything on the table.

Calderon took a leisurely sip of coffee. Apparently, he'd been prepared for a more contentious meeting with the representative from the National Hydrocarbons Commission.

"Yes, I'll grant you that the upgrades are taking longer than expected," he said, as if Emilia deserved an explanation. "But Mexico's infrastructure market is still strong. Grupo Sud's negotiations to sell shares in the regional pipelines are still on track. Now, I know you want to discuss the *huachicoleros* situation. The global energy press likes to claim that oil and gas theft in Mexico is a billion dollar industry. That the robberies have crippled our refineries and closed our gas stations. Frankly, that's sheer media sensationalism to promote sales."

"Is it now?" Emilia murmured. He was finally talking about something she could understand. Everyone knew that *huachicoleros,* as oil and gas thieves were called, made a killing on the black market by undercutting PEMEX's state-controlled prices with stolen gas.

The profits were too good to pass up but energy theft was a high risk business. More than once, *huachicoleros* unintentionally set pipelines on fire or caused villages to be swamped with crude oil.

"Of course every oil producing country experiences energy thefts," Calderon went on. It occurred to Emilia that he was doing his best to downplay the issue. "Pipelines are an irresistible target. But we have doubled our on-site security presence. A new 24-hour drone program has tripled our real-time response rate."

"Good to hear." Emilia took a sip of coffee and wondered how to extricate herself from the conversation. "Perhaps some of the local PEMEX stations can reopen."

Calderon spread out more mind-numbing charts. "We'll be including some significant measures of success in our next status report to the Commission in about three weeks. The results of the production auctions will of course be tabulated, but we are most interested in showing a diagnosis of refining issues throughout the country, using industrial analysis tools applied against the entire value chain."

Emilia raised her cup in a tiny toast to analysis tools and value chains, whatever they were.

Calderon sat back, more relaxed now. "First Texas Reserve, one of the oldest private-equity firms focused on energy, has been selected as the principal underwriter for the proposed sale of shares in the pipeline in accordance with the new capital arrangement. Given that we are considering the first major midstream deal in which foreign capital—."

Between the charts and the business talk, Emilia eyes were glazing over. She couldn't put up with the charade any longer. "Señor Calderon, as interesting as this is, it isn't why I've come."

Calderon sat forward and put his cup on the coffee table. "Of course, of course, if you'd rather read the report—."

Emilia cut him off. "I'm here to ask if you were acquainted with a man named Bogdan Andropov."

Calderon paused, clearly nonplussed by the abrupt shift in the conversation. "Who? Andropov?"

"Yes," Emilia said. "Bogdan Andropov."

"I can't say that I recognize the name." Calderon raised his eyebrows. "Very unusual. Is he part of the *norteamericano* negotiation team from Texas?"

"No, a Russian journalist." Emilia dug out an enlarged copy of Andropov's passport photo and handed it to Calderon across the plate of pastries. "Did you meet with him? Fairly recently."

Calderon studied the picture for a moment, his face betraying nothing besides mild curiosity. "No, I don't think so."

"Are you sure?"

"Quite." Calderon handed back the picture, still relaxed and comfortable, the king in his statistics-filled castle of refineries and pipelines. "Why should I?"

"Señor Andropov had your business card," Emilia said bluntly. "When he was murdered here in Acapulco."

The PEMEX executive picked up his cup. "I'm sorry to hear that. Possibly someone in the industry passed it along."

Emilia showed him the picture of Arnold from the hotel

security camera. "What about this man? He may have called himself Arnold."

Calderon sipped coffee as he glanced at the picture. "No, I don't recognize him, either."

Emilia stowed both photos in her shoulder bag. "I won't take any more of your time. Thank you for the coffee and the most, err, enlightening conversation."

He led her toward the double doors. "As I said, the Commission will be getting our next report on current and future production as well as the proposed sale of pipeline shares in about three weeks."

"One last question." Emilia stopped. "Did you know Sergei Porchenko?"

"The man gunned down at the Pacific Lotus hotel?"

"Yes, Sergei Porchenko and his wife Magda were both killed."

"Why is this any business of the Commission?" Calderon asked, so abruptly it bordered on rudeness.

"I'm not from the Commission," Emilia said. "Your secretary made a mistake when she introduced us. I apologize for not correcting her."

"Who are you?"

"I'm a police detective."

"You're here for protection money?"

Emilia nearly laughed. "Let me assure you—."

"That's why you came here," Calderon accused her. "Pay the Acapulco police for the privilege of protecting my office or we all end up like Porchenko."

"No, not at all—."

"Don't bother to insult me with weak lies." Calderon's voice gathered strength. "Please tell your masters that PEMEX Grupo Sud is a state-owned corporation with sufficient security assets to protect itself. Betty will see you out."

The door closed behind Emilia with a forceful thump.

Betty's desk was littered with magazines and nail polish. She hastily swept them into a drawer. "I can take you back to the lobby now, if you're ready."

Emilia smiled uncertainly, her thoughts rushing like the ocean in a storm. Calderon's reaction was forced and she didn't know why.

"Are you all right, señora?"

Emilia eyed the double doors to Calderon's office. She didn't hear movement but the plush carpet would obscure his footsteps. "Betty, you said you kept Señor Calderon's calendar?" she asked, her voice low. "Is that right?"

"Of course," Betty purred.

"Can you tell me if Señor Calderon met with Señor Sergei Porchenko?" Emilia prayed the doors stayed closed and that her hunch was right. "I can spell the name for you."

"Porchenko? Such a funny name." Betty nodded vigorously, clicked her mouse a dozen times in rapid succession. "Of course, I know the day you mean."

A calendar application popped up on the secretary's computer monitor. Emilia held her breath as the curser selected a particular weekday.

Most of the time blocks were blank.

"*El patrón* deleted everything except the usual morning staff meeting." Betty played with the mouse, sending the curser zooming aimlessly around the page. "And lunch with his wife at Casa Cortez. That new place on Playa Hornitos."

Emilia's mouth was dry. "Were there other things on the calendar that he asked you to take off? A meeting with Señor Porchenko?"

"Señor Calderon took it off the calendar himself," Betty said as the cursor arrow drifted to the bottom of the screen. "That's why I remembered. He never does that. I always make the changes."

A light flashed on the console phone in sync with a grating buzz. Emilia jerked back but not before she'd seen the automatically generated notation at the bottom of Betty's screen.

"That's *el patrón's* office," Betty said. "He needs me." She clicked out of the calendar application.

"I can find my own way back to the lobby," Emilia said, offering a silent prayer of thanks to the Virgin for self-important secretaries.

Once in the elevator, she texted Silvio.

Calderon had erased his calendar the day after the Porchenkos were killed.

CHAPTER 25

"I'll be gone a week, Em," Kurt said. He took a suit out of the closet.

His suitcase was open on the bed, ready to be meticulously loaded with clothes Kurt rarely wore in Acapulco. Polished oxford shoes went into custom flannel bags embroidered with the word *Church*. Ties were folded in half and placed in a long canvas case to keep the silk from wrinkling. Shirts, starched and folded by the hotel's laundry to his specifications, went in a special section of the suitcase. A nylon frame folded out to accommodate suits, with clever inserts for jacket sleeves.

Emilia shucked her shoes, climbed onto the bed, and wedged herself between the headboard and the suitcase. "What time is your flight?"

"In about four hours," Kurt said. "Layover in Mexico City. I'll get into London about 10:00 am."

"Text me when you get there," Emilia said.

Kurt flipped the suit frame into place with more force than necessary. "I wouldn't go if I didn't have to. But at least I'll get that money for you."

"You're an amazing man, Kurt Rucker." Emilia hugged a pillow.

Just the sight of the suitcase made her queasy. When he was there, they lived together in this oasis in the sky. When he was gone, she was some *chica* freeloader.

"Anything you want me to bring back from London?"

"Just you." Emilia pressed her bare toes against the handle of the suitcase, wishing she could shove it off the bed. Tip it over the balcony wall and into the open maw of the ocean so that he couldn't leave. "So. A whole week of meetings with corporate types. Sounds grim."

Kurt took an armful of dark socks from the dresser. "I've proposed a new security program that could work for other hotels in the chain that operate in high threat areas."

"High threat areas," Emilia echoed. A rich person's way of saying that Acapulco was a combat zone.

"Apparently I've become our expert in high threat hospitality." Kurt arranged the socks in the suitcase.

Emilia nodded. Trust Kurt to turn crisis into gold. He dealt with bodies floating up on his beach, shootings on the road above the hotel, a stalker in the bar, and now a murder and the police in riot gear thundering through his lobby. Despite it all, the Palacio Réal ran like a precision instrument and was always booked to capacity.

It wasn't by chance. Kurt put in long hours, constantly anticipating and planning for the trouble that Acapulco dished out every day. His staff saw his example and followed it, and Kurt rewarded his employees well. With the exception of Luis and Pedro, the world-class hotel staff was remarkably loyal.

"You'll see some new faces in the offices downstairs." Kurt tucked in workout clothes and zippered the suitcase. "We've hired an outside security agency to take a second look at all the employees. They start tomorrow."

"Isn't that Ronaldo Olivas's job?"

"He's the one who recommended we do it," Kurt said. "The way Pedro and Luis were duped into the attack on Andropov showed our vulnerabilities. An outside consultant is part of the new security program."

His cell phone buzzed and Kurt checked it. "The car's waiting for me."

"Better go," Emilia said.

Kurt leaned over the bed and kissed her. "Will you be here when I get back?" he asked, his mouth still close to hers.

"Absolutely," Emilia murmured.

Kurt straightened up. "If anything worries you, for any reason, tell Ronaldo Olivas."

Emilia gave him a wry grin. "Kurt, I'm a cop. I don't need to bother Olivas."

Another kiss with meaning and Kurt was gone. Emilia changed into shorts and a tee shirt. The fridge was full of food. She poured a glass of wine, assembled a plate of cold lamb chops and bean salad, and plopped in front of the television in the living room.

In between bites, she clicked through channels, looking for something funny and mindless.

Alone in the penthouse, it was too easy to fall into dark places. Ernesto in his coffin, Andropov's hollow body in the morgue, Magda Porchenko uttering deathbed words, a killer coolly waiting for the elevator doors to close so he could pretend to be a busboy and murder a travel journalist.

Another click of the remote and Diego Barrielos Luna, the infamous Barrel Bomber himself, appeared on the screen.

Emilia gave a start that nearly dumped the plate off her lap.

She didn't even know which of the hotel's 150 channels she'd landed on, but the broadcast was a documentary on the cartel kingpin. His incredible wealth, his escapes from the law. Emilia dropped the remote as the show segued into an interview Barrielos Luna had given from the Multifoco prison a year ago.

Once again, he reminded her of a shark. Wavy black hair, a mouthful of white teeth, eyebrows like two dark slashes over drooping eyes, thick body constantly twitching with restless energy.

Dressed in a gray prison jumpsuit, Barrielos Luna opined that extradition was an excuse to destroy Mexico's sovereignty. He would never be turned over to Washington, because the people of Mexico would not accept it. A humble businessman who built schools and helped the poor. The charges against him were false.

Emilia stopped listening, mesmerized by the evil radiating off the man. The camera panned over Barrielos Luna's famous tattoo: a black Santa Muerte inked by a master. The skeleton saint held a scythe in one hand and a globe in the other. It was the exact same tattoo on Rafa Gamboa's chest. Barrielos Luna and Rafa Gamboa were two criminals with a devotion to Santa Muerte and a hunger for helpless women.

The documentary mentioned the reward for his capture. Twenty million pesos. At current exchange rates it was equivalent to the two million dollars that Los Colectores wanted for Ernesto's release.

Emilia stared at the television, food forgotten, hearing nothing but the frantic beat of her own heart. Like the unseen interviewer, she thought the Barrel Bomber would tell her something useful. In reality he was planning his escape and she played right into his hands.

When the show ended, she hit the remote, turned off the television, and took her wine out to the balcony. As the blood-red sun sank into the ocean, she knew Barrielos Luna was out there somewhere. He hadn't forgotten her or Rafa Gamboa but her hunt had come to a dead end.

I know where he is and I'll find him before you do. You'll trade for him.

Yes, mi corazón, you're going to be very useful to me . . . Whatever he is to you, you want him that much.

She felt helpless, like a sliver of driftwood at the mercy of the ocean until it ran aground on some gritty beach.

Lights flared and steadied along the beach as torches were lit outside the Pasodoble Bar. Steel drum music wafted up and Emilia was tempted by the thought of people and laughter.

But she knew if she went into the bar, she would sit alone, her senses on high alert. Everyone who approached her would be suspect. Ernesto's kidnappers, Andropov's killer,

Rafa Gamboa in disguise, an emissary from Barrielos Luna. Any one of them could be waiting for her.

Her thoughts were exhausting.

She climbed into bed, snuggled against Kurt's pillows, and opened the gratitude journal.

I am grateful for Kurt Rucker.
I am grateful for Kurt Rucker.
I am grateful for Kurt Rucker.

CHAPTER 26

A phone rang. And rang.

Emilia jerked awake and grabbed her cell phone off the bedside table. The screen told her it was 7:00 am but the instrument neither trilled nor vibrated.

The ring sounded again and she realized it was coming from the hotel house phone on Kurt's side of the bed. Emilia threw herself across the pillows and grabbed the receiver.

It was the receptionist in the lobby. A Lieutenant Silvio was there. Could they send him up?

Emilia rubbed her eyes. *Madre de Dios, why would Silvio have hauled all the way out to Puerto Marques first thing in the morning?*

"Yes, send him up," she croaked.

Five minutes later, when the doorbell rang, her face was washed and Emilia wore a tee shirt and jeans.

"What are you doing here?" she demanded in lieu of a greeting.

"You got coffee?" Silvio asked as he strolled in. His jeans were pressed, a white tee shirt strained over his pectoral muscles, and a black blazer hid the gun-shaped bulge under his left arm.

"Sure." Emilia blinked at him. "The rest of Acapulco run out?"

"I have to talk to Ronaldo Olivas."

"He comes in around 9:00 am," Emilia said. She realized Silvio was carrying a folder. "What's going on?"

"Where's the coffee?"

Emilia rubbed her eyes and led him into the kitchen.

Silvio left the folder on the table and took off his jacket. "Hollywood around?"

"No, he left for London last night." At the counter, Emilia filled the coffeemaker with filtered water and punched the button to start the brew cycle. "So what's so important you needed to drive all the way out here before work?"

"Andropov," Silvio said. He settled into a chair. "Looks like he wasn't a travel writer after all. Must have been a cover job."

"What are you talking about?" Emilia opened the dish cabinet.

Silvio shoved the folder toward her. "GRU. Russian military intelligence."

Mugs clattered together as Emilia nearly dropped them on the table. "You're kidding," she exclaimed.

"I put his name and picture into the pipeline, asking for any background information. Believe it or not, Mexico City took it to the *norteamericanos* and they came up with a pile of dirt on the guy. He got around. Spain, Venezuela, Panama."

"*Madre de Dios.*" Emilia opened the file to find a typed report, several photos of Andropov, both in military uniform and in civilian clothes, and facsimiles of five passports. The name in each was different, as was Andropov's appearance. Long hair, short hair, blonde hair, black hair, moustache, glasses. Two of the passports were Russian. The others were from Italy, Algeria, and Ecuador.

There was an identity card from Algeria as well. A stern-faced Andropov starred out from the bottom left corner. Green Arabic script marched across the top and down the right side, while several rows of black numbers occupied the middle.

"I don't like this," Emilia said. She sank into a chair.

Silvio went to the counter, grabbed the carafe and poured them each a mug of steaming coffee. "Hey, we should feel flattered. Used his real name here in Mexico."

Bogdan Mikhailovich Andropov, alias Egon Ivanovich Ivanov, alias Boris Andretti, alias Benyamin Haddad, alias Esteban Garza. Russian army colonel and GRU military intelligence operative. Age 37, unmarried, residence listed as Moscow. Swift rise through military hierarchy attributed to skill as well as family ties. Graduate of the prestigious General Staff Academy for top officers. Diplomatic postings to Venezuela, Panama, Morocco, and Norway. In each case, Andropov was carried on the diplomatic rolls as a low-ranking support officer in the office of the Russian defense attaché.

His father, the late Russian general Mikhail Andropov, served in Madrid, where he met and married Spanish socialite Celestina Porres. Bogdan was their only child. As a teen, Bogdan studied languages and military strategy at the

Moscow Suvorov Military School and graduated at the top of his class. English and Spanish language skills assessed as native-level.

Emilia studied the copy of Andropov's true name passport. "If Magda Porchenko was Bogdan's aunt," she said. "She must have been General Andropov's sister."

"Wonder if she knew he was a spy."

Emilia looked up to see Silvio staring into the open refrigerator. "What are you doing?" she demanded.

"You eat this *gringo* shit?" he asked.

From her seat at the table, Emilia stretched out a leg and kicked the door closed, forcing Silvio to hop back or get his head slammed. "You want breakfast," she said. "Go down to the restaurant."

"This hotel isn't going to make decent *chilaquiles*," Silvio said scornfully.

"You want *chilaquiles*?" Emilia huffed.

"Great, thanks." Silvio climbed back into his chair and guzzled more coffee.

If she wasn't starving, and curious to see what was in the rest of the folder, Emilia would have thrown him out. As it was, she slung oil into a frying pan, cut a pile of day-old corn tortillas into wedges, and heated up some *salsa verde*. Sophia had taught her to make the basics like *chilaquiles* years ago.

As she dropped the pieces of tortilla into the sizzling oil, Emilia had a flashback to the early years of her police career before Acapulco became Mexico's murder capital. Back when a shift meant easy things like sidewalk brawls, pickpockets, cheaters bailing on nightclub cover charges, and tourists who lost their passports or were too drunk to recall which hotel they were staying in. On her day off, Emilia and her mother would buy fresh, simple ingredients in the market, cook all afternoon, and fill the little kitchen with laughter.

"What about the PEMEX thing yesterday?" Silvio asked. "No tie to Andropov?"

"No." Emilia flipped the pieces of corn tortilla to crisp the other side. "Like I texted you, Calderon didn't react at all when I asked about Andropov and Arnold, but his fuse lit when I asked about Porchenko. They met a couple of months ago." She gave him a quick rundown on the calendar.

"So Porchenko, local Russian hotel owner, meets with Calderon, local PEMEX *jefe*." Silvio poured himself another cup of coffee. "You think they were talking about the price of gas?"

"That's probably the only thing Calderon thinks about." Emilia stirred the salsa verde. "He's a boring engineer. Obsessed with charts and graphs. No, not obsessed. In love with."

"So no connection?" Silvio asked. "Or blackmail?"

"I don't know." Emilia watched the skillet. The aroma of frying tortillas made her mouth water. "We need to know what they talked about. Why did Calderon erase the meeting?"

"He's the PEMEX regional *jefe*," Silvio growled. "I'm

not telling Chief Salazar we're digging into Calderon's particulars because you saw a blank calendar. While you were on leave."

Emilia gave the hot salsa another stir as she thought aloud. "Porchenko might have met with him to ask about . . . about . . . well, something unrelated. Calderon is so straitlaced he got the jitters when Porchenko was murdered. Remember, it was a broadcast killing."

"The message might have been for the rest of the Russian mob but it doesn't mean other people didn't hear it, too."

"What about informers inside the local Russian mob?"

"You bet," Silvio said sarcastically as he shoved the Andropov file aside. "We're up to our ears in Russians with a death wish who want to rat on their buddies."

Emilia stopped stirring. "Maybe that's what Porchenko was doing," she said. "Ratting out his buddies."

Silvio looked dubiously at the *salsa verde* in the saucepan. "You got any onions to go with that?"

"Are we dealing with a police investigation or your *maldita* stomach?" Nonetheless, Emilia stalked to the fridge, pulled out onions, eggs, and a round of soft *queso fresco* cheese.

She beat two eggs into the hot salsa. The mixture thickened into the perfect consistency. She added the tortilla pieces, gently coating them, before heaping two plates with the *chilaquiles* and topping the dishes with shredded cheese and chopped cilantro and onion.

The plates looked as good as her mother's.

Silvio grunted and shoveled in the food, which Emilia took as thanks.

"Maybe we're looking at this from the wrong angle," Silvio said when he came up for air.

"How's that?" Emilia took another bite.

"Venezuela."

"What about it?"

"Andropov spent time there." Silvio stopped chewing. "The think tank or whatever it is. Global Energy Design Group. They have offices in Venezuela and Russia."

He put down his fork, flipped through the loose papers from the folder, and pulled out a printout. "Speaking of Russians, I got the jumble from Andropov's chip translated."

The printout had twelve lines of text. Each line contained an indication of periodicity such as "three times" or "two times" or "six times." The rest was composed of digits punctuated with random periods and dashes.

"Cell phones," Emilia said immediately.

"Come on, Cruz," Silvio said. He forked up more *chilaquiles*. "You can do better than that."

Emilia saw her mistake. Although cell phone numbers in Mexico start with 55, there were too many digits in each row.

"Somebody wanted them to look like cell phone numbers," she said.

"That's what I figured." Silvio scraped up the last of the salsa on his plate with the edge of his fork. "Take out the first two numbers and what's left?"

"Bank account numbers," Emilia guessed. "A lock

combination." She mimed spinning a dial.

Silvio shrugged. "Russian shoe sizes."

"Wait a minute." Emilia retrieved her cell phone from the bedroom and opened a search application.

Silvio emptied the last of the coffee into his mug.

Emilia typed in the first string of numbers.

The search returned a jumble of nothing.

She tried again with the second and third strings. Both times the results were meaningless but brought to her attention how similar the strings were. Only one or two numbers were different in each one.

Silvio pulled out his phone and began searching against the last two strings.

Emilia typed in the first string of numbers again. This time she omitted the punctuation, leaving spaces instead.

Did you mean? popped up at the top of the results screen. The program had inserted single quotes in place of the spaces.

The first result was a map application.

"They're coordinates," Emilia crowed in triumph.

They plotted each string of digits and found themselves looking at a rough line some 60 miles southeast of Acapulco.

"You up for a road trip?" Silvio asked.

CHAPTER 27

Emilia tugged on the thick chain buried in the dust. It was half as thick as her wrist, yet the end was sliced through.

The opposite end was still attached to a metal stanchion leaning drunkenly by the side of the dirt road. Its twin was on the ground, obvious victim of a hit and run. Once upon a time, the chain had stretched between the two stanchions. Emilia raised the loose end of the chain to find a dirt-streaked metal sign still attached halfway along its length.

"Official Vehicles Only," she read aloud.

"Fucking helpful," Silvio observed.

Emilia left the chain and useless sign in a tangled heap at the base of the stanchion and jumped back in the car.

"You sure the GPS is right?" Silvio asked skeptically.

"No, but that's what it says." Emilia held out her phone so he could see the map application again. They were on an unmarked road, near a minor highway south of Acapulco.

Silvio shrugged and put the car into gear. They rattled past the stanchions and began a slow ascent. The dirt road was ridged with hard-packed earth and pitted with holes big enough to swallow an elephant.

"This is going to seriously fuck up my suspension," Silvio groused, swerving to avoid a crater. "Do you know how much paperwork is required to get an official vehicle repaired?"

"The same amount to slap paint over the dents in my Suburban?" Emilia inquired.

"More," Silvio said. "I'm a lieutenant."

Emilia grinned as she glanced again at the digital map on her phone. "Speaking of, *el teniente*, shouldn't you be in the office?"

"It'll be there tomorrow," he said.

Was he joking? Silvio had on dark aviator sunglasses and his expression was unreadable.

The car bounced through a shallow trench and was rewarded with a loud metallic crunch from the undercarriage. Emilia winced. Silvio swore. His vocabulary of crude curses was impressive.

For the next ten minutes they continued along a gradual uphill grade and eventually crested a rise. In the distance, a tangle of bright green and white slowly resolved itself into an intricate arrangement of pipes, some as thick as Silvio's chest. A small building anchored the scene and formed one side of a chain link perimeter.

Silvio stopped the car about a quarter of a mile away. The place looked deserted.

"It's a meter station for the Glorieta pipeline," he said.

Emilia dimly recalled the name from one of Calderon's charts. "How do you know?" she asked.

"Was in the news," Silvio said. "You were still in Mexico City. PEMEX doing something to bump up revenue. I don't remember what."

"They're selling shares in the pipeline," Emilia said. "Calderon talked about investors from Texas."

"Selling shares? Like it's a stock company?"

"I guess." Emilia leaned forward to get a better view of the strange landscape ahead of them. "This place looks deserted."

"Let's keep going," Silvio said.

The meter station appeared closed. The parking lot was empty and no one monitored the impressive array of pipes from the catwalk between them. The only evidence that it was in operation was a high-pitched electrical hum and the huge red PEMEX eagle and oil drop logo splashed across the building.

Less than a half a mile on, two yellow lines appeared on the horizon on their left. They sorted themselves into tall concrete signposts straddling a depression in the ground running parallel to the road.

Each post bore the strident warning NO EXCAVAR stenciled in vertical black letters on one side and NO CONSTRUIR on the other. Each post was topped with an elongated yellow metal pentagon. These spouted additional warnings into the hard blue sky.

DUCTOS, the pentagrams screamed in all capitals. *De alta presion bajo tierra. NO CAVAR.*

PIPELINES. High pressure underground. NO DIGGING.

Underscoring the words was the symbol of a skull superimposed on crossed pick and shovel.

"Nice of PEMEX to point out exactly where the pipeline

is," Silvio said.

"We're way out of our jurisdiction," Emilia said. The scrubby landscape was eerily empty in the afternoon sun. Little grew where the dirt was baked into a hard brown pancake by the relentless sun. A stunted tree thirsted for water. Cicadas put up a monotonous racket.

"No man's land," Silvio said.

They were less than a mile from the meter station when the GPS said they'd arrived at their destination. Emilia and Silvio tramped up and down the road but there was nothing but dirt and more dirt.

"You think Andropov was trying to fool somebody?" Silvio asked.

"Or somebody was fooling him?"

Silvio took off his sunglasses and squinted into the distance. "Only one way to tell."

They got back in the car and set off again, following the GPS to the next set of coordinates. This time the prize revealed itself before they arrived. Silvio brought the car to a jerking halt.

A mound of dirt announced a hole more than a meter deep. The claylike soil was heavy and brown. At the bottom, an industrial hose spigot, complete with a wheel for opening and closing the tap, sprouted from the smooth curve of the buried pipeline.

"*Huachicoleros*," Silvio said, jumping into the hole. "Not amateurs, either. This is a good quality tap."

Emilia slid down the bank of loose dirt. The tap was

bright metal, with the threads and clamping device that would attach to a fuel hose. Hot sunshine glinted off the handwheel. She listened for the gurgle of gas flowing through the buried pipeline, but there was nothing.

Silvio heaved himself out of the hole, stood on the edge, and looked around at the barren dirt track and distant hills. "You think all the coordinates are for taps?"

"Probably." Emilia flung herself over the lip of the hole, covering herself in grime. She dusted off her hands as best as she could, taking grim satisfaction that Silvio's white tee was now just as grubby.

They found the next coordinates near another set of yellow warning posts. More holes where *huachicoleros* had dug down to the pipeline, drilled through the layers of steel, and inserted a tap. Not far beyond the fifth set of coordinates, they came upon a cement shack adorned with the PEMEX logo. It was little more than a garage with a metal accordion door. Emilia rubbed dirt off the single window. The place was empty except for a trash barrel, a table and chairs, and a row of wrenches hanging above a cabinet.

"Maintenance shack," Silvio guessed after taking a look.

They walked around but there was nothing more to see. The rollup door was locked in place.

The next coordinate was like the others. A pile of dirt, a hole exposing a smooth section of pipeline, and a tap sunk into its steel skin. The air reeked of gasoline.

"*Rayos*," Silvio said from the bottom of the hole. "The fucker is leaking."

"*Madre de Dios*," Emilia exclaimed. "Get out of there before the fumes make you sick."

The rest of the coordinates contained taps as well, although the spigots in the last two were damaged and probably unusable.

Silvio swung the car around and they bounced along the pitted dirt road as the sun began to dip. "What I want to know is," he said. "How often do the *huachicoleros* come back to each tap?"

"Milking pipelines is usually night time work," Emilia pointed out. "They probably have some way of finding out when the gas is actually running."

"Why would a Russian military officer be so interested in Mexico's *huachicolero* problem?"

"He didn't even have a car." Emilia's attempt at dark humor fell flat. "Remember, he was here because of Porchenko. So Porchenko must have been involved."

They drew abreast of the maintenance shack. Silvio braked but kept the engine running. "What about that Global Energy Study Group?"

"I haven't gone yet."

"Go tomorrow. We don't know how it connects, so don't get too specific. Keep it light, get an impression of what's going on in that place."

"Okay," Emilia said. At this point, she was too curious to argue about medical leave.

Besides, Silvio was relying on her. Trusting her the same way as when they were partners.

It felt good.

"Those wireless cameras we took out of the airport can transmit their feed up to a mile," Silvio said thoughtfully. He tapped his hands against the steering wheel, a habit that Emilia knew meant an idea was percolating.

"So?" she asked.

"Macias and Sandor can plant them at a couple of the taps. Maybe on the warning posts." He lifted his chin at the lonely shack. "We can use this place for the stakeout. Couple of nights. Park inside, watch the camera feed, and wait to see what develops."

Emilia gave an incredulous laugh, sure he was joking. "And what? Apprehend a gang of fuel thieves in the dead of night and ask if they know any dead Russians? Us and what army?"

Silvio scowled at her. "That ambush with Barrielos Luna make you lose your nerve, Cruz?"

His words stung so hard it almost took her breath away. "More like all that paperwork made you lose your common sense," Emilia flung back.

"I was fucking wrong, excuse me," Silvio said in a voice laden with sarcasm. "You do have nerve. Just enough to walk into my office and ask for your gun back. But mention a stakeout and you're skipping for the hills."

"You are such a *pendejo*," Emilia said furiously. "You got no plan except anything that gets you out of the office and away from your responsibilities."

"Maybe it's time to think about a transfer to the Records

Department," Silvio retorted.

If Emilia wasn't wearing her seat belt she would have launched herself over the armrest at him. "You'd love that, wouldn't you?" she shouted. "Finally get a woman out of your squadroom. Well, too fucking bad. You want a stakeout, I'm in."

They drove back to Acapulco in silence.

CHAPTER 28

By the time Silvio pulled up to the main entrance of the Palacio Réal, Emilia was hot, dirty, and tired. She muttered something about texting him after she met with Kolya Bartok of the Energy Design Study Group. There was no need to wait for whatever *pendejo* crap Silvio might say in reply.

She slammed the car door, flounced into the hotel lobby, and saw Alan Denton, the Pinkerton agent.

"Detective Cruz?" he sputtered, stopping in his tracks.

Emilia recognized the sharp, dark features, nervous eyes, and execrable Spanish accent. "Alan Denton," she said. "It's been a long time."

"I hardly expected to run into you in a place like this," he said, recoiling at the sight of her dirt-streaked face and muddy clothes.

Time had not made the man less haughty or more pleasant. The Pinkerton Agency was the most well-regarded of all the private security firms making a fortune from the deteriorating security situation throughout Mexico and Denton wore his affiliation like a suit of armor. Emilia had run into him several times before. He always made it clear that he thought cops in Mexico were inherently dishonest and in thrall to the highest bidder.

"I could say the same," Emilia said, as he took in her. "I expect Kurt hired Pinkerton as part of the hotel's expanded security program."

"By Kurt, I assume you are talking about Kurt Rucker, the general manager here." Denton took a pair of sunglasses out of his suit jacket's breast pocket and put them on.

Emilia nearly laughed at this feeble effort at disguise. Denton was clearly uncomfortable speaking to a Mexican cop in plain sight. "He said the consultants would start today," she informed him. "But didn't mention Pinkerton."

"Nor did he tell us the police were involved," Denton said. He made a point of looking at her dirt-daubed jeans. "What's your role here? Undercover as the gardener's assistant?"

"I'm not working with the hotel." Emilia ignored the barb and threw him a shit-eating grin. "I live in the penthouse. With Kurt Rucker, the general manger here."

Denton adjusted his sunglasses to cover his surprise.

"What do you hear about the kidnapping business in Acapulco lately?" Emilia asked before Denton excused himself.

"Kidnapping?" Denton hesitated. "Nothing more than usual. Why?"

"My stepfather's been taken," Emilia said.

"Did the kidnappers make contact?"

"Yes." Emilia had his full attention now. "They've asked for two million. Dollars, not pesos."

"Denton took off the sunglasses. "That's high. Is he, ah, a

wealthy man?"

"He's a nobody," Emilia said softly. "An itinerant *macho* from Mexico City who sharpens knives and scissors for a living. They busted down the gates in broad daylight and put a bag over his head. I was there."

"Two million dollars is high. Could this be a case of mistaken identity?"

"No. The kidnappers claim he owes it on behalf of his sons. They've both been dead for more than two years."

Denton tapped the frame of the sunglasses against a trim thumbnail. "How did the kidnappers communicate the ransom demand?"

"Text messages to my mother's phone. They're keeping him in a coffin."

"Any idea who the kidnappers are?"

"They call themselves Los Colectores. Nobody here has ever heard of them."

"A few weeks isn't long when the ransom demand is that high," Denton observed. "Who is doing the negotiations?"

"Acapulco's Hostage Negotiations unit," Emilia said. "Lieutenant Javier Plano is the new *jefe*."

"We heard he's good," Denton surprised her by saying.

"What about Los Colectores?" Emilia prodded. Denton would have more to share from the deep well of Pinkerton's experience handling negotiations with kidnappers across Mexico. "Does Pinkerton have any experience with them?"

"Are you asking me for a favor, Detective?" Denton put his sunglasses back on.

Emilia swallowed hard. Denton never gave anything away, he only traded.

"What does Pinkerton know about Bogdan Andropov?" She tossed out the Russian's name to see if Denton was willing to play catch. "He's why you got this security contract, after all."

Denton pinched the bridge of his nose and surveilled the lobby. There were a few people lingering at this hour but most guests were either dining in the restaurant or having a pre-dinner drink in the Pasodoble.

"I'm listening," he said finally.

"Andropov was a Russian military intelligence officer," Emilia said, hoping it sounded juicy enough to matter to the Pinkerton Agency. "He had five passports. Five different countries, five different names."

Denton gave her an appraising look. "Those names might be useful."

"Los Colectores," Emilia countered.

"I'm sure we'll run into each other later in the week," Denton said.

He gave her a curt nod and strode out of the hotel.

CHAPTER 29

For the second time in two days, Emilia was woken by a ringing phone. This time it was her cousin Alvaro.

"*Prima*," he said as soon as she answered. "Plano is asking for a meeting at the house at 9:00 am today. Can you make it?"

Emilia scrambled to a sitting position against the bed pillows. "What's happened?"

"I don't know. Can you be there?"

"I'll make it."

Emilia threw on a blouse, jeans and sandals, getting to her mother's house a little before the appointed time. She found Alvaro in uniform, pacing the courtyard. Neither brought up their last discussion but her refusal to use counterfeit to pay the ransom was now a subtle wedge between the two cousins.

In the living room, two members of the Hostage Negotiations team drank coffee and tapped keyboards. The team's temporary desks and assemblage of computer equipment had an air of permanence. A large whiteboard propped on the chair cushions listed the dates and times of contact with the kidnappers. A picture of Ernesto taped to the top was a nice touch.

Emilia led the way into the kitchen where they found Plano and Chen at the kitchen table. Two laptops and three cell phones shared a power strip. One of the phones belonged to Sophia.

Sunshine slanted into the room through the window. The kitchen smelled like fresh coffee and happier days. Emilia half expected to blink and find that time had slid backwards. Sophia would be setting out mugs as Ernesto sharpened blades in the courtyard, the grinding wheel rasping noisily.

"Good morning." Plano abruptly cut short any wishful thinking. He gestured at the coffee maker. "Grab a cup. You'll need it."

Emilia braced herself. "Is Ernesto dead?"

"No."

"I'll get right to the point," Plano said. He swiveled the laptop around so Emilia and Alvaro could see the screen. "In response to our initial offer, the kidnappers texted this to Sophia's cell phone."

A vertical video display showed nothing more than a hazy shadow.

"Whenever you're ready," Plano said.

Emilia glanced at Alvaro before reaching across the table. He shrugged. She put the cursor on the icon and tapped the pad.

"Sophia." Ernesto's voice made Emilia give a start, although it was barely louder than a dying breath. "Sophia, they told me to tell you—."

Three sudden raps broke through, loud and sharp; triple the volume of Ernesto's muffled speech. The indistinct dark screen shuddered violently.

Emilia glanced at Plano. He stared back, his face

expressionless.

"Sophia," Ernesto said hoarsely, the screen still an amorphous brown shadow. "They're going to shoot me in a week if you don't pay the ransom. In the left leg. In another week, they'll shoot the other leg. Then my hands. I'll be a cripple."

Emilia began to sweat. Between the indistinct visual and Ernesto's disembodied pleas, she was watching a horror movie.

"Use the money, Sophia," Ernesto begged through weak sobs. "Please. Pay what they're asking. Please, Sophia, please. Don't let them do this to me."

The video blinked out. A second later it showed a coffin sitting on an unremarkable terra cotta tile floor. An unseen hand lifted the coffin lid to reveal an emaciated man dressed in a red tee shirt and boxer briefs.

His head was enveloped in a plastic bag taped snugly around the neck. The bag sucked in and out of his mouth as he breathed.

A gloved hand reached into the coffin and pried a cell phone out of the man's hand. A muffled protest was barely audible. The coffin lid slammed shut. The video abruptly ended, having revealed nothing about where Ernesto was being held.

"Was that . . ." Alvaro trailed off, hands clenched around his coffee mug.

"The first part was filmed inside the coffin," Plano said.

They played the video again.

"He doesn't understand how much ransom they're asking for," Emilia said bitterly after the second viewing. The film had been edited to reveal exactly nothing but what the kidnappers wanted to show.

"It's not uncommon for kidnappers to tell the victim one thing and the family another," Plano said. "It allows the kidnapper to pit one against the other in the ransom negotiations."

"Do you think that's what they're doing here?"

"Yes," Plano said. "This was their response to your initial offer of 60,000 dollars."

"This is a serious threat, isn't it?" Alvaro asked. "Do you think they'll really shoot him?"

Plano nodded. "Yes, I think they'll make good on their threat unless we can significantly up the offer. Once they make this kind of statement, they'll stick to it."

"This is crazy." Emilia slammed both hands on the table in utter frustration. "They have to know we don't have two million dollars. He sharpens knives. I pay their rent. There is no money."

"*Prima*," Alvaro said. He looked meaningfully at Emilia.

"I'll try to raise more," Emilia said, avoiding Alvaro's eye. "But I need time. Two weeks, maybe three. You have to stall them."

"It depends on our ability to stay in touch," Plano said. "Obviously, they are amateurs who don't have experience reaching a negotiated settlement. They rejected the first offer with a counter threat, not a counter offer. Our strategy may have to change to keep the lines of communication open."

What strategy? Emilia's head pounded with stress. "What are you doing to actually find Ernesto?"

Plano turned things over to Chen, who updated them on the latest developments in the search for the gang. The *coyote* called El Cripo, with whom Ernesto had contracted to lead his sons Ricardo and Rubén to *El Norte*, had died a year ago in a shootout in a Mexico City suburb.

Luca Diaz Alonso was likewise dead in a gang battle. The latter's ties to the Los Colectores gang, however, convinced Hostage Negotiations that Ernesto had been taken to Mexico City. More analysis was needed to find if Mexico City area cell towers had relayed the kidnappers' text transmissions.

Emilia listened but her thoughts were consumed by the image of Ernesto lying in the coffin, his head shrouded, desperately clinging to the cell phone. Hostage Negotiations might be doing all the right things and taking every opportunity to open a real dialogue with the kidnappers, but Emilia knew done of it was going to matter.

Los Colectores would shoot Ernesto and leave him to die in that coffin.

Sophia would remain a child for the rest of her life.

Plano closed the laptop. "I'm sorry the news wasn't better," he said. "These cases take time."

"I might have a lead on Los Colectores," Emilia offered, knowing that if Denton got burned, the Pinkerton agent would never speak to her again. "If it leads to anything useful, I'll let you know."

"An informant?" Plano asked dubiously.

"Something like that." She picked up her shoulder bag and angled herself out of the chair.

"This isn't the time to be keeping secrets, Detective," Plano said sharply.

CHAPTER 30

The frightening image of Ernesto in the coffin was still on Emilia's mind as she headed east on the airport highway. The Suburban groaned as she pushed the beast up to speed, but luckily she wasn't going far. The office of Energy Design Study Group was in the Puerto Marques neighborhood, north east of the Palacio Réal where she'd stopped to change. A think tank sounded as nice as the PEMEX headquarters so she'd thrown on a body-hugging blue knit dress and high heels.

More dubious sounds came from the Suburban's damaged front end as she passed the Instituto Leonardo Bravo. A low white wall surrounded the campus, emblazoned with LEONARDO BRAVO A.C. in huge maroon letters. A grove of royal palms all but hid the buildings and turned the hill behind the school into a protective canopy of leafy green. It was a private college, a place where she might have gone to study for a business career or taken a degree in information technology.

The *what if* game, the police psychiatrist called it. They'd have another conversation this afternoon about the dangers of *what if* and the importance of gratitude. As usual, Emilia wasn't looking forward to the session.

The road stretched on, past the Hotel Club Diamante, which was managed by a friend of Kurt's, until it became the Boulevard de las Naciones. A PEMEX station on the corner of Naciones and Paseo de los Manglares was open and a long line of cars snaked toward the pumps. She passed the Diamante *sitio* taxi stand and several of the outdoor restaurants she'd recommended to Andropov. The golf course stretched away to her right before her phone's GPS directed her into a U-turn and a quick right turn.

The Suburban protested the sequence of maneuvers. A curious rubbing sound began as Emilia navigated the loop of perpendicular street simply referred to as Interior.

The address was a modern six story building that overshadowed the trim white Hotel Olinalá Diamante next door, with its vaguely Spanish colonial architecture and sprinkling of palms and flowering trees across the lawn. It was a nice neighborhood, one that Acapulco's violence hadn't yet decimated, but off the beaten path.

Emilia parked on the street and showed her police badge to the guard at the building's gate. He was an ancient man in an oversized brown suit and looked surprised to see a visitor. The lobby proved to be an ample space with white stucco walls and a terrazzo floor. A green vinyl sofa stood guard next to a brass coffee table topped with a dusty vase of artificial flowers. There was a counter where presumably the concierge worked, but no one was there. Emilia punched the button for the elevator and was rewarded with a clank that sounded suspiciously like the Suburban's parking brake.

According to the press release, Energy Design Study Group occupied a suite on the third floor. Emilia stepped out of the elevator and into a wide hallway. The lobby décor had travelled upstairs, terrazzo floor, white walls, and a plain console table across from the elevator doors with another fake floral arrangement gray with dust. The place was silent.

The doors to the suites were carved and varnished wood, with brass suite numbers. She found Suite 301, her heels rapping on the terrazzo, and tried the door. It was locked.

Emilia knocked.

And waited.

She knocked again.

And waited.

Finally she took out her phone and dialed the number from the press release. A moment later, she heard a faint ring coming from inside the suite. After five rings the connection dropped.

The elevator gave a groan worthy of the Suburban. Emilia spun around. A man in a white linen guayabera shirt and dark pants charged out of the elevator with a wide, aggressive stride, a cell phone clutched in one hand. He stopped when he saw Emilia standing in front of the door to Suite 301.

"Who are you?" he asked in heavily accented Spanish.

"Detective Emilia Cruz from the Acapulco police," Emilia replied. "Are you Kolya Bartok?"

He looked her up and down, like a dog examining a bone. "What are you doing here, Detective Emilia Cruz from the Acapulco police?"

He enunciated each word, giving his question the cadence of mockery.

"I'm investigating a murder," Emilia said. Something

about the man set her alarm bells ringing and she decided that subtlety was not the way to go. "A Russian man named Bogdan Andropov was from Moscow and interested in the oil and gas industry. We thought you might be able to help us."

"I do not know of such a person."

Emilia guessed that the man was in his late 40's, with pale hair slicked straight back from his forehead and lacquered into place. A thick gold chain showed at the open throat of the short-sleeved shirt. His forearms were sinewy, like a blacksmith who twisted iron for a living. His pants puddled over shiny black loafers.

Bartok's eyes were dark blue and oddly expressionless. They were the only interesting feature in a face thickened by scar tissue, as if he'd been a boxer like Silvio but had never learned to block a right cross.

"Well." Emilia summoned up a rueful smile. "He knew about you. I understand you study oil and gas trends. Could you tell me about your organization?"

His flat stare was unnerving but Emilia was determined not to let it show. She gestured toward the locked office door. "Perhaps one of your clients might have known Señor Andropov. Could we discuss it?"

"We do nothing of interest to the Acapulco police," Bartok said. He launched himself at Emilia, forcing her to stumble backwards. Pinning her against the elevator door, he reached over her shoulder and hit the button. A heavy steel watch brushed against her neck. "You must go now."

The blue eyes were too close to her own. Bartok's breath smelled like fresh onions and stale cigarettes.

Just as she tensed her shoulders and readied to knee him in the groin, the elevator door opened. Emilia tripped backwards into the car. Bartok reached in and punched the button for the lobby level. "We are very busy," he said. "Do not come back."

As the elevator doors closed, Bartok stood like a sentry blocking the way.

Heart hammering, Emilia walked rapidly through the empty lobby to the Suburban. Gunned the engine out of the parking space and drove blindly around the Interior loop until she was back on Naciones heading east. *Madre de Dios*, she'd been a fool. Anything could have happened if Bartok had unlocked the door to Suite 301 and she tottered into the place in her *maldita* high heels like an overdressed lamb to the slaughter.

At the intersection with Calle Simon Bolívar, Emilia realized she was going in the wrong direction. Downtown Acapulco, where her next appointment with the police psychiatrist awaited, was due west.

Bartok had shaken her badly. She had not been prepared. What would she have done if Bartok had turned out to be Arnold the killer? She hadn't even considered that before prancing into an empty building.

Emilia got the car turned around and almost hit the curb when she realized why Andropov had asked her about places on the Puerta Marques side of Acapulco and been so interested in the type of people who went to see jai alai.

Where would I go on this side of the bay, if I lived here?

Andropov, the Russian military intelligence officer, had been stalking Bartok.

☼

"Where are you, Em?" Kurt asked.

"In the Pasodoble," Emilia replied. "I was too lonely upstairs without you."

The connection was so clear he could have been sitting next to her instead of in London.

"Did you get a mojito?"

"I had to," Emilia admitted. "It was sort of an awful day."

She was in a corner table, sandwiched between the wall and the end of the long bar with its elegant mosaic, providing her a direct line of sight to the ocean as well as everyone else in the bar. No one had approached her and no one was close enough to eavesdrop, so she told him about the video from the kidnappers and downplayed the run-in with Kolya Bartok from Global Energy Design Group.

"I'm sorry, Em." She heard the genuine feeling in Kurt's voice. "I wish I could hurry this week and get out to Las Vegas to talk to my accountant."

They talked for a few more minutes. Kurt made her laugh with funny stories about maintaining his training regimen for the Ixtapa Half Ironman, which meant running in places with funny names like Pall Mall and Kensington Gardens. When they hung up, she sat back in her chair, sipped her drink and felt the tight muscles across her shoulder begin to unkink. Talking to Kurt reminded her that living in the hotel was a gift. A respite from the cruelty on Acapulco's streets.

But if Kurt bankrupted himself for her family, would their relationship survive?

Her thoughts spiraled down again. Andropov's murder had happened here. Her oasis was violated.

Emilia dug through her shoulder bag resting on the next chair. Felt the outline of the key with the Casa Odisea tag before pulling out a pen and her well-worn police notebook. Flipping through her scribbles on Andropov's murder, she wrote out a timeline as if she was the lead investigator.

Energy Design Study Group, headed by Kolya Bartok, comes to Acapulco.

Porchenko meets with Calderon at PEMEX.

Andropov arrives in Acapulco, under cover as travel writer.

Porchenko meets with Andropov.

Arnold bribes Luis and Pedro.

Arnold kills Andropov, takes phone.

Arnold kills Porchenkos.

Calderon erases Porchenko meeting from his calendar.

Calderon denies ever meeting Porchenko.

Emilia put down her pen and looked at the chronology.

Everything happened after Bartok came to Acapulco.

CHAPTER 31

Two nights later, Emilia slumped behind the wheel of the parked Suburban looking at a laptop resting on the center console between the front seats. The screen was divided into quadrants, each showing a different green-tinged night vision view of a section of the Glorieta pipeline. The split screen display was courtesy of four hidden cameras which once graced the baggage handling zone in the airport.

In addition to being motion-activated, the cameras could be switched on and off remotely via the laptop. Macias and Sandor said the lithium ion batteries gave each camera 120 hours of service before needing to be recharged. Emilia hoped that didn't translate into weeks on stakeout with Silvio.

Unfortunately, Silvio was ready to go the distance. Repeating his refusal to tear up his official sedan's suspension any further, he'd loaded the Suburban with a cooler full of snack food, a case of bottled water, night vision binoculars, a digital camera with a long range lens, a couple of big flashlights, a rechargeable lantern, a bolt cutter for cracking the padlock on the maintenance shed, and extra handcuffs.

Emilia brought a bottle of iced coffee, a container of cut fruit from the penthouse refrigerator, a roll of toilet paper, and a blanket.

By 9:00 pm it was totally dark, with only a crescent moon

and a starry sky for light. They rearranged the detritus in the maintenance shack, backed in the car, and rolled down the garage door. The effect was immediate claustrophobia. Despite this, Silvio decided not to turn on the lantern, afraid the light could be seen from the window.

"Tell me again why we're here," Emilia said. "You know, waiting for somebody to start digging up the pipeline."

"Andropov knew something about these taps that got him killed," Silvio said. "When the *huachicoleros* come, we'll let them fill their tanks and follow to see where they go."

"You want to arrest somebody for stealing gas or for killing Andropov and the Porchenkos?"

"I want to see where this shitstorm is going."

Emilia threw up her hands. "What are the chances Andropov and Porchenko were a couple of *huachicoleros*?"

"*Rayos*, that would be excellent." Silvio gave a laugh. "Moscow's so cheap when it comes to paying their spies that Andropov comes to Mexico to help his aunt and uncle resell Mexican gas."

"Okay, okay," Emilia said. "It was just a random thought."

"That theory only makes sense if a Mexican killed him," Silvio said. "Say, somebody who owns the taps and whacked them to keep territory."

"I still can't believe we're doing this," Emilia said.

"Why?"

You're the lieutenant and I'm on medical leave. "Nothing."

Silvio reached into the open cooler and pulled out a bag of salted peanuts. He reclined his seat, made himself comfortable, and began to munch.

Emilia folded her arms and stared at the four static images on the laptop screen. It was going to be a long couple of hours until Macias and Sandor relieved them. The two teams would split the night watch; in this way, Silvio and the other two detectives could still grab enough sleep to work all day.

Silvio wadded up the peanut wrapper, lofted it into the backseat and made a call on his cell phone.

For the next two hours, Emilia stared at the unchanging laptop screen and listened to a dozen one-sided conversations while Silvio spoke to detectives about their cases. From what she heard, the squadroom had at least 70 open cases, mostly homicides of unidentified men. Without referring to notes, Silvio knew the details of every case, including what the forensic evidence had to say, and what the next steps should be.

Finally he pocketed his phone. "Tell me about Bartok," he said. "The oil and gas guy."

"The oil and gas thug," Emilia corrected him and flipped her notebook open. "He's at the top of the timeline. Everything happened after he arrived."

Silvio rubbed his chin. "Where did you say the office was?"

"In the Puerto Marques neighborhood."

"What's the address?"

Emilia read it off to him.

"New second theory," Silvio said, grabbing another package of peanuts. "Porchenko rents office space to Bartok."

"What?"

"Porchenko owned that building," Silvio said.

"You're kidding. A connection between Bartok and Porchenko." Emilia scribbled that interesting little fact in her notebook.

Silvio opened a bottle of water and drank half in one gulp. "We got a list of real estate he owned. Mostly commercial buildings, which fits the mob profile. Crime goes up, people move out. The Russians are buying up a ton of empty buildings in the city. Real estate is one of the easiest ways to launder money."

"I think Bartok is the only tenant, too," Emilia offered. "The building is a ghost town."

They talked in circles for the next hour, brainstorming the relationship between Porchenko, Andropov, and Bartok. There were any number of possibilities, each a different Russian puzzle. Yet when they threw in Calderon and the PEMEX angle, as well as the *huachicolero* taps, every theory became a wild card.

By midnight, they were out of ideas and energy. The laptop screen still showed four static images. Cameras 1 and 2 were hidden closer to the highway. Cameras 3 and 4 were on the far side, placing the maintenance shed between Cameras 2 and 3.

Emilia broke out her iced coffee and wondered if she

could make it last until Macias and Sandor relieved them.

Silvio opened her container of fruit.

"Any news about Ernesto?" he asked, fishing out a piece of mango.

"Plano isn't getting any traction," Emilia said unhappily as her snack disappeared down Silvio's gullet. "Los Colectores won't negotiate. They're holding out for two million dollars and we'll never raise it. They have to know that."

"What's the end game?"

Emilia felt sick again thinking of the last video. "Plano thinks they're amateurs who don't know how these things go. But I'm not so sure. They seem so . . . so." She trailed off, searching for the right word.

Silvio ate a handful of grapes.

"Prepared," Emilia said finally.

Right on time, Macias texted that he and Sandor were on the way. Thirty minutes later, the first camera flared into life and showed Sandor's SUV bouncing through potholes toward the maintenance shed.

"He'd better slow down," Silvio said. "Gonna flip his car if he hits a big hole in the dark."

The two other detectives arrived without incident and they made the switch quickly. Emilia was glad to be out of the claustrophobic shed as she carefully drove along the pipeline. The Suburban clanked and groaned but the night air was crisp and the sky glittered high above. They had the scrubby landscape to themselves.

"Want to get a beer?" Silvio asked as they hit the paved road and accelerated north towards Acapulco.

Emilia shot him a sideways glance. "We just spent seven hours in a car together."

"So?" Silvio grumbled. "You got something better to do?"

Emilia considered. He was really strong.

"Actually, I do," she said.

CHAPTER 32

At 3:00 am, the El Coloso neighborhood's decay was cloaked in darkness. Half of the streetlights were out, including the one closest to the Valdez residence. Bullet holes and graffiti were rendered invisible but the razor wire atop every wall swooped in deadly spirals against the milky night sky.

"You really think Rafa Gamboa stole a key to this adoption agency's warehouse?" Silvio asked skeptically.

"He's not exactly an honest man," Emilia pointed out. "Maybe he didn't like the information they gave him and planned to rob them in retaliation. Why else would he have it?"

"*Rayos*, Cruz," Silvio grumbled. "You should have told me."

"I'm telling you now," Emilia huffed. She slowed as they approached the gray wall surrounding the house. "Do you want to help or not?"

"What are we looking for again?"

"Rafa Gamboa's contact information," Emilia replied. "If he hired them to ask about his birth family, he must have given them contact information. A cell phone number, a forwarding address. The name of someone who could get in touch with him."

"This is a long shot, Cruz," Silvio warned but she knew he was hooked.

"The warehouse is on the other side," Emilia said as they slowly rolled past the rickety iron gate.

"Go around the block."

They were in luck. The Valdez property extended all the way to a narrow alley running parallel to the street. Emilia figured that the warehouse she saw during the testy meeting with Maria Teresa Valdez was on the other side of the perimeter wall.

As they drove past, Emilia could see that the wall was completely smooth. Silvio pulled out a pocket flashlight and aimed a narrow beam at the razor wire coiled along the top.

"We need a ladder," Emilia said, disappointed. Even if she stood on Silvio's shoulders, she wouldn't be tall enough to get past the wire without cutting herself to ribbons. If she could get over the wall, however, she'd probably find herself overlooking the roof of the warehouse. With any luck, she'd be able to jump down and unlock the door. Presuming the key fit, of course.

"Cut the lights and let me out," Silvio said. "Drive up on the sidewalk, as close as you can get to the wall."

The alley was narrow and the sidewalk was nothing more than a narrow strip sandwiched between the wall and the curb. Even with Silvio pantomiming directions, Emilia had to pull forwards and backwards several times, dinging the passenger side mirror in the process, before cutting the engine and killing the lights.

"Well, that was subtle," she said to herself.

In the darkness, the walls guarding houses on either side

and across the alley appeared to hunch forward, drawn by a common suspicion of a white Suburban intruding upon the quiet night.

The trunk of the car squealed as Silvio hauled out the bolt cutters. Emilia tucked her own penlight into a back pocket before climbing onto the roof of the Suburban. Silvio handed her the bolt cutters before vaulting up himself. The Suburban sagged under the big man's weight.

Dangerous loops of wire loomed overhead. Silvio made a basket of his fingers, bent down. Emilia put her right foot into his hands.

"Don't take my eye out with those," Silvio hissed as Emilia held the bolt cutters in one hand and braced the other against the wall. "Ready?"

"Ready," Emilia breathed.

He gave a heave. Emilia flew to the level of his shoulder and her nose almost touched dozens of tiny razor-like barbs knit into loops of razor wire on top of the wall. Moonlight twinkled on the slivers of steel; a ruse to make her believe they wouldn't slice her open.

Balanced on one foot in the cradle of his hands, Emilia shone the penlight over the wicked barbs. The coil of razor wire was affixed to rebar posts cemented into the top of the wall and spaced at one meter intervals. Trying not to tumble, she worked the jaws of the bolt cutters around the closest wire. Using the top of the wall as leverage, she sliced through the strand. Freed from the tension of the coil, the ends sprang apart, narrowly missing her cheek.

"Fuck." Adrenaline surged through Emilia's body as she jerked back and nearly dropped the bolt cutters.

"What are you doing?" Silvio hissed but kept her from falling.

Emilia got the tool into position again. This time she ducked before cutting. The wire skimmed over the back of her head but created a sizeable gap.

"I'm through," she whispered and got a grunt in response.

Emilia carefully dropped the bolt cutters and with a last heave from Silvio, got one leg over the top of the wall. A dark ledge appeared out of the gloom that had to be the flat roof of the warehouse. Beyond it, she saw the round iron table and chairs.

She squeezed between the broken loops of wire, turned so that she faced the inside of the wall, and lowered herself until she dangled over the roof at least two meters below her feet. The rough cement bit into her palms.

With a silent prayer, Emilia let go. She landed on something solid but unstable. Toppling to her knees, she faceplanted into a pile of shriveled stalks and broken terracotta; probably the ancient remains of a rooftop display of potted cactus. A chunk of pottery slid off the edge and smashed on the ground below.

Lights popped on in several windows. Emilia plastered herself flat against the roof and held her breath.

A bulb flared over the back door, which Emilia recalled opened into the kitchen. The light cast a large circle of light over the flagstone. Two female voices shrilled at each other.

Señora Valdez appeared in the kitchen window.

The back door opened. The ancient maid stepped out, clutching a threadbare coat around her shoulders.

Señora Valdez's querulous voice followed her. "Find out who's out there, girl. Chase them off."

The maid shuffled uncertainly towards the iron table and chairs, having obviously spotted the broken pottery at the warehouse end of the courtyard.

"Girl!" Señora Valdez screeched from the safety of the kitchen door. "What's out there? What are you doing?"

Still lying on the roof, Emilia meowed softly.

The maid stopped.

Emilia slung a bit of terracotta at the plants framing the courtyard and meowed again.

"*El gato*, señora," the maid mumbled over her shoulder. "Just a cat."

"Hit it, girl," Señora Valdez shouted back. "Scare it off. They're disgusting animals."

Emilia didn't move a muscle as the old servant half-heartedly flapped a dishtowel at the plants, then shuffled back to the kitchen. Eventually the lights went out. El Coloso was dark and quiet once more.

"Here, kitty, kitty," Silvio whispered from the top of the wall.

☼

The key with the Casa Odisea tag turned easily in the

lock.

They were in a narrow room. Emilia's penlight revealed more than a dozen metal filing cabinets lined along the long wall. A cheap card table and a couple of folding chairs occupied the middle of the space.

Emilia walked along the row of cabinets, shining the penlight at the fronts. The file drawers were labeled in alphabetical order.

The next room was more of an office than a storage facility, with irregular stacks of white file boxes here and there like broken teeth. A 10-year-old calendar curled away from the wall above a wooden desk. Cobwebs hung like a cordon of lace between the faded paper and the books and binders on the desk. The smell of mold thickened the air.

Half of the room was cordoned off by floor-to-ceiling chain link fencing secured by a rusty padlock.

"What's the deal here?" Silvio asked. "Looks like a holding zone for Customs."

Emilia aimed the beam of her light at the fenced area. The yellow circle revealed two iron bed frames with rotting mattresses, a crib, and a child-sized table.

I sat in that garden and could almost hear them. Confused. Crying. Little hostages.

"They, um . . ." Emilia wanted to sit down and bawl. Dora was right.

Señora Valdez's father, Doctoro Fernando Valdez, had kept children there until he sold them off to rich families.

"All right, let's find Casa Odisea's client file for El

Acólito." Silvio clicked on the battery-powered lantern from the stakeout. "We've got about 2 hours until dawn."

Emilia pulled herself together. "He wasn't El Acólito back then," she reminded Silvio. The echo of her voice made her shiver. "Just the actor Rafa Gamboa. They might have his file listed under Gamboa, or maybe Cruz, the name he was born with. Or even Escobar, his foster mother's family name."

"*Rayos*," Silvio swore. "Family name roulette. You take the file cabinets, I'll start here."

"Right." Emilia was glad to escape into the front room.

She launched her search with the first of several file drawers labelled "G." There were numerous folders bearing the name Garcia, but not one Gamboa. She moved ahead, looking for "C," and found more than ten drawers. Cruz was a common name and there were reams of folders. Emilia paged through half before she realized that the name on the label corresponded to the name of the family that adopted a child, not the child's original name.

"Come look at this," Silvio said from the doorway between the two rooms.

A number of the file boxes lay open. The lantern illuminated the contents.

Children's clothing. Tiny shoes and sandals. Ragged soft toys.

"What the hell was this place?" Silvio said. "A charity?"

"Take pictures," Emilia said around a lump in her throat. "I know someone who should see this."

She kept sifting through the Cruz files. Doctoro Valdez had been a methodical man. All the files were organized the same way. Each child's personal details were recorded in a precise copperplate hand and stapled to the left side of the folder. What village the child came from, names of the biological parents, any medical conditions that had to be treated before the child could be "processed."

The birth parents' compensation was also meticulously recorded. The amount was usually around 300 pesos. In a few cases they got a goat or a pig.

The right side of the folder contained details of the adoption, including how much was paid to Casa Odisea. It was about the cost of a new luxury car.

Emilia finished with the Cruz adoptions. If the file cabinets held only the old adoption records and the file boxes were full of children's clothes and toys, where were Casa Odisea's later adoption research service files? The only thing she could do was keep going, hoping they were mixed in, and quickly looked through the "D" and "E" drawers.

There was a single folder labelled Escobar. Emilia flipped it open and scanned the information stapled to the left side. It was the record of an adoption that took place long before Rafa Gamboa, or Emilia herself for that matter, was born. The pages were brittle with age. The ink had faded to brown but the precise handwriting was still easy to read.

Emilia was about to shove it back in the drawer when a notation at the bottom of the left side made her heart skip a beat. She dropped the folder on the card table and rummaged through the "E" drawer to find another folder, one she hadn't bothered to read.

The second file was equally as old, equally as disturbing. Equally as unbelievable.

The meticulously recorded notes flickered in front of her eyes. Emilia fought to take a breath.

Her lungs were stone. Her mouth was a parched canyon.

An hour later, they climbed back over the wall and reached the safety of the Suburban. Emilia wordlessly handed the car keys to Silvio. As he drove, she stuffed the two folders, edges crumbling with age, into her shoulder bag.

Neither cop spoke until they were well out of El Coloso and the rising run swathed the sky in a coppery veil.

"Well?" Silvio finally pressed.

"I don't think this was Rafa Gamboa's key after all," Emilia said quietly.

CHAPTER 33

The second night Emilia brought two containers of fruit.

As before, the laptop perched on the console between the front seats. The screen was again split into four quadrants, each showing a static green and black image from a hidden camera.

Silvio fielded calls as they watched the camera feed. He discussed a dozen cases before finally tossing his phone on the dashboard. "I hate this job," he said and rubbed his ear.

"You waited years to become lieutenant," Emilia exclaimed.

"Being a lieutenant is fine," Silvio snapped. "Being chief of detectives is different. It's a fucking nightmare."

"Looks pretty good from where I'm sitting," Emilia observed.

"Do you know how many fucking forms there are?" he griped. "I gotta fill out 20 just to take a piss on Tuesdays."

Emilia laughed.

"I'm serious as a heart attack," Silvio complained. "Meetings to discuss meetings so we can have a meeting with Carlota's new superman, Enrique Santibañez. And don't get me started on the unions."

"Poor you."

Silvio grabbed a package of peanuts and lapsed into glowering silence.

An hour of nothing went by but at least Silvio wasn't

asking her about the files she'd pulled out of the Casa Odisea warehouse. Emilia needed some time to digest her discovery before talking about it with anyone, even Kurt.

"Macias and Sandor want to get married," Silvio said out of the blue.

Emilia grinned. "They're both decent guys. Easy on the eye. They shouldn't have any trouble finding wives."

"To each other," Silvio said heavily.

"To each other." It took a moment before Emilia grasped what he meant. "Really? I never would have guessed. Can they do that?"

"I said I'd look into the regs." Silvio crumpled up the empty peanut wrapper. "Nobody else knows. Even if they can, doing it will kill their careers."

Emilia had nothing helpful to say in reply. Gay marriage wasn't popular in Mexico. It was legal in Mexico City but not really embraced elsewhere in the country. A ban on same-sex unions had been successfully challenged in the state of Guerrero, but the city of Acapulco did not issue marriage licenses for same-sex couples. If Macias and Sandor wanted to marry, they'd have to find one of the few municipalities in the state that would issue a license or try to arrange it in Mexico City. But the legal status of such a marriage would be dubious, given their residency in Acapulco, as would be their respective futures in a conservative police department already well known for favoritism.

Emilia and Silvio sat glumly, staring at the static

computer screen. Emilia finally uncapped her bottle of iced coffee and held it out to him. Silvio shook his head and opened a container of fruit.

"How's your mother holding up?" he asked at length.

"The same." Emilia sighed and reached for a slice of cantaloupe. "She's been in denial ever since they snatched Ernesto."

She told him about the coffin video and the threat to shoot Ernesto, limb by limb. "So far Los Colectores haven't negotiated at all. They still want two million dollars. They might as well ask for the moon."

"Yeah." Silvio found a wedge of pineapple. "Chen told me."

Emilia decided to launch a trial balloon.

"Alvaro wants to pay the ransom with some of the counterfeit money you seized a few weeks ago," she ventured. "Says the Secret Service hasn't picked it up yet and won't miss it when they do."

Silvio didn't immediately reply. He stared out the passenger window at the darkness beyond the car and licked pineapple juice off his thumb.

Emilia found a grape. "Well?"

"There's no counterfeit," Silvio said at length.

"The Secret Service already got it?"

Silvio finally looked at her. "There never was any counterfeit money. Or Secret Service."

"What do you mean?" Emilia was confused. "Even Obregon congratulated you on the seizure."

"It's a sting operation," Silvio confessed. "Internal Affairs set it up. Arrests, seizure. All faked. I'm a bit player."

"Why?" Emilia asked as her stomach turned into a knot of apprehension.

"Things keep disappearing out of the evidence locker," Silvio said evenly.

It was Emilia's turn to look away. Maybe Alvaro's unending well of mutual favors had run dry or Internal Affairs had a sudden attack of integrity. Either way, her cousin was in trouble. "Why'd you tell me?" she asked.

"So you wouldn't take it."

"Thanks," Emilia managed.

Madre de Dios. If she'd agreed to Alvaro's plan, they'd both be in jail and Ernesto would be doomed.

"Do I have to tell you not to talk about this with anybody?" Silvio broke into her thoughts. "Anybody at all."

"I know," Emilia shot back. "You don't have to say anything else."

Silvio munched his way through the rest of the fruit. Emilia imagined telling the police psychiatrist that she was grateful not to have stolen fake money out of the evidence locker and knew it was time for some overdue honesty.

"Do you know why I thought Barrielos Luna was behind Ernesto's kidnapping?" she asked.

"Because you're a cop and that means either paranoid or dead."

"That, too." Emilia braced herself for the plunge. "Barrielos Luna let me live after his *sicarios* shot up the convoy because he think he's got something to use against me."

"Rafa Gamboa."

"Yes. How did you know?"

Silvio shrugged. "Makes sense. Does Barrielos Luna know Gamboa is your brother?"

"Not as far as I know." Emilia's big secret shrank to manageable proportions in the face of Silvio's nonchalance. "He only knows I'm looking for Rafa Gamboa and thinks he'll catch him first and use him as fodder to get me to do whatever Barrielos Luna wants."

"Hollywood know?" Silvio asked.

"Yes."

"He did all right at the Pacific Lotus. Former military, didn't forget his training. I like that. He didn't panic." Silvio lobbed the empty fruit container into the backseat of the Suburban.

"I know," Emilia said. "I was there." A few more nights on stakeout and the car was going to look like a dumpster.

He unscrewed the cap on a bottle of water. "What about your friend Mercedes? She's a widow, right? Seeing anyone?"

"You're not seriously thinking of asking her out?" Emilia laughed.

Silvio shrugged, the heavy shoulders moving easily. "Why not?"

"Because you're a woman-hating *pendejo* and she's my best friend."

"Hey, I said something nice about Hollywood."

"Doesn't change anything."

"Seriously, is she seeing anybody?"

Emilia could not believe the turn in the conversation. Silvio was making her crazy way ahead of schedule. "Okay, say Mercedes doesn't think you're a caveman and actually goes out with you. She'll tell me everything. Absolutely every detail—."

The static image from Camera 4 burst into activity as a small truck bounced across the view.

Eight small pickup trucks passed Camera 4 before stopping in a line near the tap monitored by Camera 3. Two men bailed out of the cab of the first truck and went to the tailgate. Two big rectangular boxes filled the bed, each as big as a washing machine.

"They're using fertilizer tanks," Silvio said. He tapped the keyboard and the quarter showing Camera 3's feed filled the screen. "Probably holds 200 gallons."

The two men flipped down the tailgate and hoisted out the first tank. It was covered in the ropy netting used by fishermen, giving the *huachicoleros* something besides the smooth plastic to grip. They moved it easily. Emilia wondered how heavy the tank was when it was full of gas.

The tapping operation was swift and efficient. The men knew exactly where the tap was. They mated a hose to the tap and used a portable pump to fill the tank. The operation took about 10 minutes. When the tank was full, two more men stepped into the frame, presumably from the next truck in line. Using the rope netting, the four wrangled the full fertilizer tank back into the first truck and rigged the second tank into position. When that tank was full, it followed the other into the truck bed. Now fully laden with two full fertilizer tanks of gasoline, the truck drove off. A second took its place near the tap.

Two men with long guns wandered in and out of the camera view. They were the convoy's *halcones*, obviously on the lookout for law enforcement or a rival crew coming to seize the stolen gas.

Emilia kept waiting to hear the first truck drive past the maintenance shed, but there was only silence. "They're staying together," she said.

"This is a fucking professional operation," Silvio observed. "No wonder Andropov was whacked. Lots of money flowing into those tanks."

He was right. The men moved with military-like precision. As soon as one set of tanks was ready, the truck carrying them rolled off and was replaced by the next in line. The sentries were alert. Nobody wasted time. Every member of the *huachicolero* crew knew their job. Some of them even wore surgical masks to prevent becoming intoxicated by the gas fumes.

Emilia's jaw dropped when she saw the driver of the last truck get out.

He didn't bother with a mask.

"Is that the guy from the hotel?" Silvio asked. "Arnold?"

"*Madre de Dios*," Emilia gulped.

Even in the grainy green and black night vision image of the hidden camera, she could make out the man's high forehead, light eyes, and pale skin. Arnold was the only *gringo*. Unlike the other drivers, he did not approach the hole, work the hose, or bother to examine the tap. Instead, he lounged with his back against the driver's door and checked two different cell phones before taking out a cigarette and a big metal flip top lighter.

"He's smoking," Silvio exclaimed. "Next to an illegal pipeline tap."

One of the Mexican *huachicoleros* rushed toward Arnold. They had a brief conversation and Arnold stopped trying to light the cigarette.

"I told you, he's a chain smoker," Emilia said, unable to take her eyes off the screen. "The *cabrón* probably thinks he's invulnerable."

"He's insane," Silvio said. "He also speaks Spanish. Did you see that conversation? That *huachicolero* was comfortable. He was speaking his own language."

Emilia felt the impatience and excitement coming off Silvio in waves. He was ready for a fight; no, longing for a fight.

As the last tank was hoisted into the truck bed, Arnold made a call on one of his cell phones. Someone off camera must have scolded Arnold but he merely lifted a shoulder in response, climbed into the truck, and drove off. Camera 3's feed reverted to a static image of the hole.

Silvio tapped the laptop keyboard and the four quadrants reappeared. Emilia heard the hum of engines and a chill prickled the back of her neck. Silvio took out his handgun.

The ground shook as the heavily burdened trucks passed the maintenance shed. Fifteen minutes later, Camera 2 flared to life as all eight trucks trundled past the hidden lens, pitching and weaving through the deep potholes.

"They're moving slow," Silvio observed and holstered his gun.

The trucks were still in formation when they passed Camera 1, a full mile away along the dirt track.

"They'll be at the turnoff to the highway in about ten minutes," Silvio said. "We've got to let them turn before we get there or they'll know they were followed."

Her heart was in her throat when Emilia nudged the Suburban out of the shed. Silvio pulled down the garage door, replaced the padlock, and jumped into the passenger seat.

The night was completely black. The Suburban creaked along the track and the laptop showed them passing Cameras 1 and 2. Without the headlights, Emilia alternated between the windshield and the open side window to keep the Suburban from hitting the tall yellow pipeline markers or sliding into a bottomless pothole.

They could still hear the faint hum of engines as the Suburban bumped over the chain marking the turnoff to the paved road. Clutching the binoculars, Silvio leaped out and pounded to the edge of the highway. One swift look to the right and left and he was back in the car, ordering her to turn left and head south. Away from Acapulco.

They rattled onto the highway. With her foot on the accelerator, the red taillights of the *huachicolero* convoy were soon in sight. She stayed a mile behind the trucks.

They were at least two hours south of Acapulco, running parallel to the coast, when a glow in the distance lit the night sky.

"What's that?" Emilia asked.

"It's got to be the Costa Glorieta refinery," Silvio said.

The red pinpricks grew larger and Emilia realized the convoy was slowing down.

"Pull over," Silvio ordered.

Emilia coasted to the side of the road and they both jumped out of the Suburban. Resting her hip against the corrugated fender, she saw the line of *huachicolero* trucks approach the conglomeration of soaring pipe and bright lights.

One by one the trucks disappeared into the PEMEX-owned refinery complex.

"It doesn't make sense," Emilia exclaimed. "They stole gas that came from this refinery. Why bring it back?"

"Calderon." Silvio began to pace alongside the Suburban. "This is why Andropov had Calderon's card."

"Okay," Emilia said. A thousand erratic details swam through her confusion. "Arnold steals gas. Andropov finds out—."

"Porchenko finds out first," Silvio interrupted her. "I'll bet he found the coordinates for the taps and gave them to Andropov. Maybe he took them out of Bartok's trash. Would explain why the paper was so wrinkled."

Emilia threw both hands on the hood. "Right. Next Porchenko gets Andropov the spy to come and help deal with it."

"Porchenko wanted to shut it down," Silvio ventured. "Why?"

"Porchenko wanted out," Emilia reminded Silvio. "Maybe he thought it was a good idea at first, rented space to Bartok and later changed his mind because he wanted to get out of the crime business."

"Or maybe he wasn't getting a big enough cut." Silvio stopped pacing and stared at the refinery in the distance. "Is this a Russian mob operation? Real estate, hookers and money laundering aren't enough any more?"

"Stealing gas in a country that can't keep its gas stations open is a lucrative business."

"But they aren't selling the gas."

Emilia yanked her door. "I know. It's crazy. Why would the *huachicoleros* bring gas back to the refinery? That much gas is worth millions of pesos on the black market."

"Let's catch Arnold and ask him," Silvio said.

"Let's arrest him for three murders," Emilia exclaimed. "Andropov and both Porchenkos."

"That, too," Silvio said.

CHAPTER 34

The drive back to Acapulco wasn't pleasant. The middle of the night, on a dark and deserted road known to be frequented by armed bandits, was not a good place to be even if Silvio sat in the passenger seat with his handgun at the ready. Emilia fell into bed, glad for once that Kurt was still in London. She slept for a few hours, woke up thinking about the breakfast buffet in the Pasodoble Bar, threw on a sundress, and headed downstairs.

As Emilia stepped off the elevator, Alan Denton approached, briefcase in hand. "Detective Cruz."

For a moment, she couldn't recall why he would want to talk to her.

"I've got those names for you," Emilia said when the mist cleared.

"I have some information that I think you'll find enlightening as well," Denton said. "Perhaps we can find a cup of coffee."

They found a secluded table on the patio near the hotel marina and were immediately served coffee and breakfast rolls. The morning sun glinted on the line of powerboats rocking in their berths. It burned away the strange night chasing *huachicoleros* and trying to piece together a Russian enigma named Arnold.

"You first," Emilia said, tearing into a roll.

"It's not what I'd call good news," Denton said. He

extracted a slim folder from his briefcase.

Emilia grimaced. "It never is."

"Los Colectores is a parasite gang." Denton didn't open the file. "Operates out of Mexico City, but it has agents all the way to the border."

Emilia put down the roll. "A *coyote* gang, you mean."

"No." Denton hesitated. "A parasite gang lives off the *coyote's* leavings. Los Colectores buys *coyote* contracts, the same way that banks buy mortgages."

Emilia took a healthy slug of coffee and waited for more.

"In the United States, someone buys a house." Denton sounded like a teacher explaining the rules to a toddler. "They can't buy it outright, so the bank loans them money so they can pay over time."

"I know what a mortgage is," Emilia said, annoyed at his patronizing tone.

"Good. A mortgage is a financial instrument that can be bought and sold by banks." Denton paused. "Los Colectores buys *coyote* contracts the same way. They buy the contract, add interest, and put out a collection notice."

Emilia wasn't hungry any more. "But Ernesto's sons died. The contract is invalid."

"To Los Colectores, there's no such thing as an invalid contract, Detective." Denton drank some coffee. "Any *coyote* contract they buy is in force until it is repaid in full. Your stepfather made a contract. It wasn't paid. The debt was sold to Los Colectores like a bank sells a mortgage, whether or not the house is livable."

"But . . ." Emilia trailed off.

"Los Colectores buys contracts all the time," Denton said impatiently. "From hundreds of *coyotes*. You said they're asking two million for your mother's husband. The interest has been accumulating ever since the contract was first made. Who knows what interest rate they're using or maybe they make it up. But one thing is certain. They never take less than the full amount."

"That's why they haven't negotiated." Emilia pressed a hand to her forehead as her head began to throb.

"My assessment is that they know he can't pay up," Denton said. "They never expected him to."

"Why kidnap him in the first place?"

Denton selected a roll from the basket. "It's a matter of honor. Los Colectores owns a contract, ergo, they have to collect. Most likely, Los Colectores is holding someone who owes even bigger money and the family can afford what they're asking. They'll use your stepfather to show what happens if they don't."

"Another kidnapping?" Emilia sat bolt upright. "Here in Acapulco?"

"I'm not at liberty to say."

Emilia watched a pelican waddle along the marina. Something startled the big bird, which flapped its wings in agitation before resuming its promenade.

"Let me get this straight," she finally said. "You're saying Los Colectores will kill Ernesto as an example to others whose contracts are now owned by the gang."

"That's what my sources tell me." Denton was as relaxed as if they were choosing between dinner at Carlos 'n Charlie's or La Concha. "Payment in full or they kill the victim. They never negotiate. They only collect. Hence the name."

He was giving Ernesto a death sentence.

Emilia let her gaze wander from the pelican to the boats bobbing in the sunshine to the lobby. Guests strolled by on their way to the Pasodoble Bar while the staff in blue floral shirts made sure everything was absolutely perfect.

Another day in paradise.

Denton pulled out a slender gold pen. "I'd like those names now, Detective."

Emilia dug her notebook out of her shoulder bag. Without saying a word, she found the page where she'd copied down Andropov's aliases and showed it to Denton.

He copied the information and stood. "Good luck, Detective."

"Wait." Emilia took a deep breath, only now able to collect her thoughts and ask the important question. "Does Los Colectores release their victims?" she asked the Pinkerton agent. "If the ransom is paid?"

"I know of a few cases in which they did."

"And the other cases?"

"Time ran out," Denton said.

CHAPTER 35

"We received the same information, Detective," Plano said. "I wish you would have told me about your connection with Pinkerton. I could have saved you the trouble."

"What a coincidence," Emilia said. Had he been holding out?

The waitress set down two condensation-streaked glasses of pineapple juice and scurried off in her long black apron.

Plano inched his glass away from the cell phone on the table. It was Sophia's. Emilia was glad Plano was ready to connect with the kidnappers at any time, yet it felt strange to see a stranger handle something that belonged to her mother.

She'd called Plano directly, bypassing Alvaro, with a request to talk privately. Her cousin was turning into a liability, getting between Emilia and realistic solutions that didn't land somebody in jail. When this was over, they could reassess family relationships. Right now, however, she needed to go over his head.

Plano didn't mention Alvaro, either, but surprised her with the suggestion that they meet for a late breakfast at Los Metates, a 24-hour diner in the heart of Acapulco. It was a popular place with both tourists and locals. The food was basic but tasty. The décor was basic but comfortable.

The place was always crowded and today was no exception. Plano met her there, looking deceivingly friendly in a striped button-down and a pair of jeans, no gun in sight.

"Los Colectores is larger and better organized than we'd thought," he now admitted. "I wish I could say the information will help us, but unfortunately I don't think that's the case. If anything, it makes me less hopeful that there can be a successful ransom negotiation."

"When did you learn this?" Emilia pressed.

"Last night," Plano said, with a look that said he knew what she was thinking. "We finally got some solid intel from Mexico City. Nothing about the actual contract Ernesto agreed to, but details about the way Los Colectores operates."

Emilia drank some juice and the sweetness gouged a hole in her stomach. "My family still doesn't have two million dollars," she said. "I can raise less than a quarter and even that is going to take a few weeks."

"Are you sure you don't know anyone else who can help?" Plano asked.

Emilia shook her head.

"We haven't had time to get to know each other." Plano lounged back in his chair. "Tell me about yourself. What do you do when family members aren't kidnapped. And don't say work. We all have to have a real life."

"Easier said than done," Emilia quipped.

The waitress sashayed back, the black apron snapping around her legs, and slung down two breakfast platters. As Plano attacked his omelet, Emilia nibbled on a piece of bacon and wondered why he wanted to be her new chatty buddy.

In any other situation she would have been glad to be in the comfortably noisy restaurant, full of unvarnished wooden tables and chairs. The front was a series of arches open to the street, with pots of spiky plants forming a hedge between the restaurant and the sidewalk. Under the roof eaves, words in cursive yellow neon splashed against red lights, advertising *aguas frescas*, *tacos al pastor* and *pozole* to passersby. Lively mariachi music competed with the chatter of customers and the clink of flatware.

Plano wolfed down half his food in the time it took for Emilia to eat two bites. "Sorry," he said. "I'm a stress eater."

"Not a good thing for a cop." Emilia pushed a mushroom around her plate.

"If I didn't work out, I'd be the size of a refrigerator."

Emilia treated Plano to a frosty smile.

"We didn't get off to a good start, did we?" Plano actually sounded apologetic. "I didn't mean for that to happen. I hope you know that."

"Sure." Emilia didn't know if she believed him or not. Maybe he was embarrassed by how he'd treated her or maybe he was a lying sack of shit.

"Let's talk about what to do with this new information," Plano said, laying down his fork.

Emilia shrugged. "I don't have anything worth selling and no bank will give me a loan to pay a ransom. I told you how much I could raise. There's no more."

Plano was seized with a sudden coughing fit. As he reached for his glass, he dropped his napkin. Still hacking, he bent over to pick it up. A man at a nearby table was obviously annoyed that Plano's distress interrupted his texting. Emilia gave the man a frozen stare and he quickly went back to tapping the screen of his cell phone.

Emilia ate another bite of her omelet as Plano got himself together.

"Sorry," he said. "What were we talking about? What about the ex-wife in Mexico City?"

"She doesn't have that kind of money, either."

"What about your mother's family?" Plano gestured with his fork. "Her parents? Siblings? Perhaps—."

"There's no one else," Emilia pushed back. "Your job is to negotiate with the kidnappers, not play financial advisor."

"Right." Plano held up his hands in surrender. "I'm here to help, Detective. I'm not the enemy."

Sophia's cell phone vibrated against the wooden table. Plano snatched it up. One tap on the screen and his face tightened. "They sent another video."

"The kidnappers?" Unreasonable hope surged into Emilia's throat. There had been very few off-schedule messages.

Plano set the phone between their plates and opened the video frame. The screen was gray and fuzzy. A man cried out but the voice was weak and wheezing. "No, no."

The video blinked and the scene resolved into Ernesto lying in the coffin, naked except for a blindfold. His arms were stretched over his head and his wrists were duct-taped to the lip of the coffin.

"We are losing patience," a disembodied voice said.

"No," Emilia gasped. "They said five days. *Five days*."

A gloved hand holding a small pistol moved into the frame, hovered over Ernesto's thigh, and fired. The shot was loud. Ernesto screamed with the high pitched keen of a wounded animal. The hand with the gun retreated, revealing a neat black hole in Ernesto's leg.

Ernesto gagged and vomited. As his body convulsed, shoulders banging against the raised sides of the coffin, the voiceover resumed. "The ransom is two million dollars. If you do not pay soon, we will shoot him again."

The video abruptly ended.

"This is not a hopeful sign," Plano said heavily.

Emilia looked around the restaurant as she tried to slow her heart. Tourists chattered and the music was still lively. The man at the next table was gone.

"Ernesto won't survive if they shoot him again," she said, remembering Denton's grim pronouncement about victims who ran out of time.

"We'll keeping hammering at the negotiations," Plano said. "But if there's anyone you know, anyone at all who is in a financial position to help you, I strongly advise you to talk to them."

"Don't you think I would have done that already?" Emilia flung back. What was she going to tell her mother?

For the first time since the kidnapping, Emilia was genuinely angry at the way Sophia had blithely dropped Ernesto into their lives without knowing a thing about him.

Her mother was as naïve and trusting as a child. It always fell to Emilia to make things right. Well, this time, she couldn't unless she was prepared to go to jail for it.

"You have connections, Detective," Plano said. "There are people out there who could help you. Maybe you simply haven't considered every . . . angle."

He placed deliberate emphasis on the last word.

Emilia picked up her coffee cup with a shaking hand.

Was Plano telling her to take a bribe? Get a loan from a cartel moneylender?

Or was he in on the sting with Internal Affairs?

Maybe that's why they were sitting together at this cozy little table in Los Metates, pretending to be friends.

CHAPTER 36

Tonight, the plan was simple. If the *huachicoleros* came back, the detectives would follow them as before. This time, however, they'd wait for the empty trucks to come out of the refinery and tail Arnold. With any luck, they'd find out where he lived.

The interior of the maintenance shed was beginning to feel like Emilia's home away from home. The laptop was perched on the Suburban's console between the two front seats and Silvio's cooler was full of snacks. They finished the first container of fruit from the Palacio Réal as Emilia recounted the meal with Plano and the horrible video of Ernesto being shot.

"I can't tell my mother," Emilia said helplessly. "But if Los Colectores won't negotiate, Ernesto isn't ever—."

Silvio interrupted her. "They're back."

The convoy of trucks was loaded again with big fertilizer tanks. This time, they stopped in front of Camera 4.

"Come on, Arnold," Silvio muttered as they watched the *huachicoleros* start their well-coordinated theft operation.

Like before, the Russian drove the last truck and did not help the Mexican *huachicolero* crew. Arnold wandered in and out of the view, eschewing the surgical mask many others wore. Every time they saw him, he was either texting or clenching and unclenching his fists.'

"He needs a smoke," Emilia observed.

By the time all eight trucks filled their tanks and drove out of Camera 4's frame, Emilia was ready to scream from the tension. Silvio flipped the screen back to the four quadrants. They watched the convoy bump past Camera 3 along the rutted track and soon thereafter heard the hum of engines approach the maintenance shed.

Emilia fingers itched to start up the Suburban. She looked at Silvio. He was grinning from ear to ear, as ready for the hunt as she was.

Thirty seconds had barely elapsed after the last truck passed when a deafening *boom* shook the cement walls of the maintenance shack. The ground gave an enormous heave that made the Suburban rock like a child's toy. Camera 4's view filled with a giant fireball before the green and black night vision image dissolved into chattering snow.

"The pipeline blew," Silvio roared. He leaped out of the Suburban and raised the garage door.

When Silvio wasn't sucked into a wall of flames, Emilia scrambled out of the car, too.

Still a mile away, the fire blotted out the night with a two-story sheet of flame. The din was incredible, like a freight train bearing down on them, as fire sucked gas out of the pipeline and spewed destruction into the sky. Sparks carried on the night breeze showered down on Silvio's shoulders.

"We'd better get out of here," he said, as if they had all the time in the world.

Emilia practically levitated into the Suburban, gunned it out of the shed, and rattled onto the dirt track. Potholes forgotten, she pressed her foot down on the accelerator and they shot into the dark.

An alarm rang in the distance and a red strobe lit the sky.

"The meter station," Silvio said. He twisted to look back at the flames. "They must have sensors to detect fire."

Emilia glanced back, too, and never saw the vehicle lying on its side across the track until it was too late. The Suburban crashed into it with the force of a battering ram. Gas fumes enveloped her. Emilia barely had time to recognize the truck from the *huachicolero* convoy and its cargo of gasoline before her airbag deployed.

Mylar punched her in the face and pumped the breath out of her in a single blow. She heard the Suburban scream, or maybe it was her.

A second later, fire spewed out of the bed of the overturned truck with a *whoosh* of sucking oxygen. The Suburban shoved the *huachicolero* truck and its burning tail like a dead horse hooked to a burning wagon.

As Emilia's air bag deflated, one of the fertilizer tanks broke loose with the weight of a wrecking ball. Emilia threw her arms over her face as it careened toward the windshield. It thudded into the front grille of the Suburban and tipped to the ground in slow motion as flames licked toward it. As soon as the industrial plastic melted, it would become another fireball.

"Fuck," Silvio rasped. "We've got to see if anyone's still alive."

Emilia wrenched open her door and stumbled out, only to

be enveloped in gasoline vapor. Already dizzy from the collision, the stench turned her stomach inside out. She threw up an acidic mix of fruit and cold coffee, clinging to the open door for support.

By the time she stopped retching, Silvio was out of the Suburban and trying to open the door of the overturned *huachicolero* truck. Emilia caught the outline of a body lying in the road, a few yards away.

The dead Mexican *huachicolero* had obviously gone through the windshield. The man's neck was cocked at an impossible angle, the face pointed to the sky, limbs like broken puppet strings.

"He's still inside!" Silvio bellowed over the raging roar of the flames.

Emilia staggered through the heat to the wrecked *huachicolero* truck. The cab was crumpled like a cheap soda can. Jagged shards were all that was left of the windshield. The Russian lay crumpled against what used to be the passenger door.

The two detectives dragged him through the windshield opening, both of them burning their hands on hot metal. Retching again from the fumes and bludgeoned by the rising heat, Emilia and Silvio laid Arnold across the Suburban's back seat.

They both leaped into the front of the vehicle, seconds before the *huachicolero* truck exploded, along with the second fertilizer tank. Rockets of metal and gas rained onto the roof of the Suburban as Emilia threw it into reverse.

The Suburban slid backwards, sputtered, and died.

Emilia had visions of the vehicle melting around them and her skin scorching to a blackened crisp. The heat was unimaginable. She turned the key. Nothing happened.

"Get us the fuck out of here!" Silvio shouted.

"I'm trying," Emilia cried.

The vehicle was still in Drive. She shoved the gearshift into Park, mentally gabbled a prayer to the Virgin of Guadalupe, and tried again.

The engine caught. Emilia threw it into Drive and launched the Suburban toward the meter station. Potholes were forgotten as she drove like a Formula 1 maniac. The plume of smoke from the pipeline explosion followed them, expanding like a storm cloud.

Silvio catapulted into the back seat. "*Rayos*, Cruz," he said and whipped off his tee shirt to apply pressure to the Russian's neck. "There's blood everywhere."

The big vehicle careened through the craters, swaying like a ship in a hurricane. They passed the meter station, still emitting its piercing alarm and throwing a mayday call into the sky with the strobe. Otherwise, it appeared deserted.

The Suburban swept into a giant gouge in the track and came out the other side so fast that Emilia felt herself lifted into the air. She banged her head on the roof and came down hard.

Arnold screamed and flailed against the front seats. Silvio held him down.

Emilia glanced at the rearview mirror in time to see

Arnold, his face contorted in pain and desperation, latch onto Silvio's arm. "Juan, Juan," the Russian rasped. "Listen to me."

"Sure, sure," Silvio said to the Russian. "Here, press down here.'

In the rearview, Emilia saw Silvio guide Arnold's hand to the tee and make him hold it against his neck. "I'll head for Santa Lucia hospital," she said. "It's the closest."

"I need something for a tourniquet."

With one hand on the wheel, Emilia stripped off her tank top. She flung it over the seat and kept driving in her bra and jeans.

They were far enough away from the plume of smoke for the stars to be seen again. The vehicle crunched over the chain and Emilia swerved north onto the highway. She pressed the accelerator to the floor. The Suburban lumbered along the smooth surface like a wounded white elephant.

"Juan, take the gas to Costa Glorieta," Arnold groaned as Silvio tied a makeshift tourniquet around his thigh. "We have to be there tonight."

"Forget the gas," Silvio growled, trying to tighten the stretchy fabric.

Arnold mumbled something incomprehensible and his hand fell away from the blood-soaked cloth.

"Come on, *pendejo*," Silvio urged. "Stay with me so I can arrest your sorry ass for three murders."

Emilia took a quick look behind. Face tight with concentration, Silvio kept the pressure on the worst of

Arnold's wounds.

"Juan, Juan," Arnold moaned in confusion.

"Why did you kill Bogdan Andropov?" Silvio demanded.

"Andropov." The word came out as a bubbly rasp. "Juan . . . did you deliver the gas?"

"Yeah, it's me, Juan," Silvio lied. "We delivered the gas. Tell me why you killed Andropov."

Arnold made a gurgling sound. "He would tell . . . Moscow . . . Moscow . . . Kolya said . . ."

"Stay with me, you fucker," Silvio muttered. "What about Sergei Porchenko?"

"Porchenko." The name rolled off the Russian's tongue with agonizing slowness.

Emergency vehicles passed them, going in the opposite direction.

"Porchenko," Silvio repeated. "Why did you kill Porchenko, too?"

"Everybody saw . . . Kolya wanted everybody to see."

"Is Kolya in charge of the *huachicoleros*?"

"Hector . . . Hector and Kolya . . ." Arnold gave a gurgling cough. The sound trailed into eerie silence.

"Don't you die on me, *cabrón*!" Silvio roared.

"What's happening?" Emilia cried but her voice was lost as Silvio began chest compressions, shouting out the count.

The lights of Acapulco appeared on the horizon as a gentle glow against the night sky. Emilia heard Silvio blow rescue breaths into Arnold's mouth. The chest compressions began again. Silvio counted to thirty, his voice loud and strained. More rescue breaths. More chest compressions.

She saw illuminated billboards for the Liverpool department store and glass-bottom boat tours. The outskirts of Acapulco never looked so inviting.

Silvio stopped counting and blowing. He slumped onto the floor of the back seat.

"Shit," Emilia heard him mumble.

She let the Suburban slow to a reasonable speed and headed for the morgue.

CHAPTER 37

Arnold's fingerprints matched Secretaría de Gobernación immigration records. Arnold Ivanovich Sokolov arrived in Mexico on a Russian passport five months ago, according to his *Forma Migratoria Multiple* visitor's permit. Each permit was valid for six months. This was his second.

More importantly, Arnold's pockets yielded two phones.

The first phone's call log was full of short calls to and from unidentifiable numbers, which were probably those of Arnold's *huachicolero* crew. But Forensics quickly traced numbers corresponding to the Costa Glorieta refinery and the office of Hector Calderon Rios in the PEMEX building.

Arnold's text messages were even more revelatory. The exchange with Luis, the night concierge, was still there, including the heart emoji sent on behalf of the non-existent Russian hooker. But the preponderance of texts were in Russian with a number registered to Energy Design Study Group.

The second phone from Arnold's pocket belonged to Bogdan Andropov. The call log was intact, a record of calls to the Palacio Réal, Porchenko's office at the Pacific Lotus, Porchenko's personal cell phone, and Calderon's office.

"I remember you!" Betty exclaimed as Emilia and Silvio strode past the secretary's desk. "Wait! You can't go in there!"

Without breaking stride, Silvio smashed open the double

doors to the PEMEX executive suite. Betty squealed, Emilia grinned, and the doors crashed against the inside wall of the office. Momentum swung them back but Silvio had already passed through, leaving Emilia to clap them shut in Betty's face.

"Good morning, Señor Calderon," Silvio boomed. "Acapulco police. We need to speak to you."

Calderon was in the middle of a meeting, presiding over the head of his conference table, with five others ringed around it. Chairs were angled to watch a slide presentation.

A young man jumped up from his chair. Calderon rose more slowly and put out a restraining hand. "What is going on here?" he demanded.

With his enameled lieutenant's badge dangling from the lanyard around his neck, Silvio walked up to the executive. "Señor Calderon," Silvio said. "I'm Lieutenant Franco Silvio of the Acapulco police. We have an urgent matter to discuss. Adjourn your meeting."

"You." Calderon narrowed his eyes as Emilia stepped next to Silvio. "Your audacity in returning to my office is quite incomprehensible."

"I'll call security," said the man at Calderon's side.

"Go ahead, Ricardo," Calderon said. "These people are in gross violation of their duties as law enforcement officers. If that's indeed what they are."

"By all means," Silvio said, his eyes still on Calderon's face. "We can discuss Señor Calderon's involvement in a triple homicide and a Russian ring stealing gas from the

Glorieta pipeline."

Every face at the table went rigid with shock.

They were all *gringos*. One wore a bolo tie with a turquoise gem, two sported western cut jackets, and the last was bland and forgettable in an off-the-rack suit and tie.

The screen boasted a slide entitled *First Texas Reserve: Investing in Energy's Future*. Under the title, six graphs offered a complicated maze of black verticals and jagged red lines.

"Gentlemen," Calderon said stiffly. "There's been an evident misunderstanding. I'd appreciate a few minutes to sort it out." He turned to Ricardo. "Please take our guests to the visitor's dining room. Tell Betty to serve lunch. I'll join you momentarily."

The room emptied out, leaving Emilia and Silvio alone with Calderon. He scurried to his desk, making it a barrier between himself and the two cops. Anger revealed itself in the terse jerk of his chair before he sat, in the deliberate way he steepled his fingers and pressed them so hard together that the tips turned white.

"Now." The word was clipped. "I can give you exactly five minutes to explain your presence and ridiculous charge in front of my guests."

Instead of replying, Silvio ambled over to the conference table, selected the chair Calderon had used, and wheeled it over the carpet to the side of the desk. When the big detective lowered himself into the seat, Calderon leaned away.

Emilia decided she needed fortification before the

coming showdown. She went over to the table, where a tray laden with coffee and pastries beckoned, and poured herself a cup.

It was amazing that she didn't have an ulcer, given all the stress and caffeine she consumed.

"For several months a group of *huachicoleros* has been tapping the Glorieta pipeline." Silvio's tone was deceptively mild. "They always use the same taps and fill a convoy of trucks every two or three days."

"I'm glad to hear that our police are doing their job," Calderon said waspishly. "But I fail to see why you need to make such a production out of informing PEMEX."

Emilia angled a chair towards the show at the other end of the room. She sipped coffee, which was quite good, and watched Calderon. The steepled fingers gave way to playing with a slender gold pen, tapping it impatiently against the desk top.

"The thefts are organized by a Russian named Arnold Sokolov," Silvio said, still in that dangerously conversational tone Emilia knew so well. "What makes Arnold's *huachicolero* operation so unique is that instead of selling the gas on the black market, the trucks deliver it back to the Costa Glorieta refinery in the middle of the night."

"Return it to the refinery?" Calderon gave a nervous laugh. "You must be mistaken."

"You were warned about this by a Russian named Sergei Porchenko, during a meeting in your office."

Calderon's eyes flew to Emilia.

"You erased the meeting from your calendar," she said helpfully. "After he was murdered by Arnold Sokolov."

"You can't prove that," Calderon said. "I never met this Porchenko."

Emilia shrugged. "We can seize Betty's computer and do a forensic analysis."

Silvio kept going, obviously enjoying himself. "Porchenko asked his wife's nephew to come and investigate the gas thefts. A guy named Bogdan Andropov. Detective Cruz asked you about him."

"You labor under the impression that I have a remarkable number of Russian acquaintances," Calderon sniffed.

"Andropov was a Russian military intelligence officer." Calderon paled.

"Andropov was interested in three things," Silvio said. "The illegal taps of the Glorieta pipeline. Another Russian named Kolya Bartok who runs an outfit called Energy Design Study Group. And you."

"As I told her, this woman," Calderon floundered, obviously forgetting Emilia's name.

"Detective Cruz," Emilia supplied. The coffee was really quite good.

Silvio held up Andropov's cell phone. "This is Andropov's phone," he notified Calderon. "Recently confiscated from his murderer. The call log was extremely informative."

Calderon refused to look at the cell phone.

"Do yourself a favor, Señor Calderon," Emilia said

quietly. "Tell us about Kolya Bartok. What's his role in this scheme to steal gas and return it to the refinery?"

Calderon rose haughtily, clutching the gold pen as if hanging onto the tattered remains of his integrity. "I am the director of Grupo Sud and—."

"Three people have been murdered," Silvio thundered. "You're an accessory to murder."

He snatched the pen out of Calderon's hands and whipped it across the room. It smacked into the projector screen with the thump of a hollow drum.

Calderon slowly sat down again. "I . . . I recall Porchenko. We met at a Chamber of Commerce event last year. Played golf a few times. A crass Russian but an excellent handicap. I was surprised when he called to ask for a meeting here. Rolled up with bodyguards. All very awkward."

"What did you talk about?" Emilia prompted.

"He mentioned this Energy Design. Said the man heading it up was a bad sort, but influential."

"He called Bartok by name?" Silvio pressed.

"Yes, Bartok." Calderon nodded. "I could expect to run into him. Porchenko said PEMEX should keep him at arm's length."

"What happened next?"

"That's all."

Silvio put his boots on Calderon's desk and waited.

Emilia sipped more coffee.

"Bartok came to see me," Calderon blurted. "He had a young ruffian with him. An unsavory young man who wouldn't sit down and smelled like tobacco smoke."

"Arnold," Emilia supplied.

Calderon pursed his lips. "Yes, Arnold Sokolov. Bartok introduced him as Energy Design's operations manager. He said his group looked at the issue of pipeline vulnerability and solved it for Russia and Venezuela. He was sure he could apply the same techniques here in Mexico. If it worked for Grupo Sud, we could present the program to PEMEX at the national level."

"And you believed him?"

"Russians know the oil and gas business," Calderon said as if it was glaringly obvious. "The country is run by oligarchs. He knew we were contemplating the sale of shares in the Glorieta pipeline and that our funding partners were worried about the theft problem."

"His solution was to keep the *huachicoleros* occupied," Silvio said. "So you paid to keep them busy."

"We could stop the theft of premium gas from the Costa Glorieta refinery." Calderon looked triumphantly from Emilia to Silvio. "It was a genius short-term solution. There are only two refineries still open in Mexico that produce premium gasoline. Production is down 80 percent from five years ago. We have to preserve that capacity. We're an oil rich country with fuel shortages because we haven't recapped our facilities. Modernization starts with the pipeline share sale and there's no sale without the premium gas."

"You were paying thieves to steal PEMEX gas then

paying them to bring it back," Emilia exclaimed. "Why not pay to improve security?"

"We're already doing everything possible. Everyone knows that."

Silvio slammed his boots to the floor and stabbed a finger at Calderon. "Half the pumps in the country are closed because of the *huachicoleros*. We've been out there. PEMEX security is a joke. Was it really so much cheaper to pay Bartok than to buy real security?"

"Stop, stop!" Calderon slapped the desk for emphasis. "You don't understand. Bartok brought me an immediate solution validated by real numbers. The deal will go through. Modernization must happen."

The graphs projected on the screen above the conference table now made sense. "First Texas Equity," Emilia read aloud. "Bartok knew about the pipeline deal. He knew how vulnerable PEMEX is right now and made sure it would stay that way."

"The deal with First Texas Equity is critical," Calderon insisted. "The entire national modernization scheme depends on that funding."

"Does this Texas outfit know about the deal with Bartok?" Emilia asked. "How much did you pay him to steal the gas?"

"You don't understand." Calderon dismissed her.

"Bartok gave you a kickback, didn't he?" Emilia was relentless. "What about First Texas Equity? How much did the *gringos* promise to pass under the table for making sure the deal went through?"

Calderon's face reddened.

That was it. Everything—murders, thefts, the pipeline explosion—traced back to this deal and the money Calderon would pocket for making sure it happened.

"Did they promise you as much as three lives?" Emilia asked the PEMEX executive.

Silvio gave Calderon a withering glance. "Never mind this *cabrón*, Cruz. First Texas is across the hall, eating their nice lunch. Let's go ask them."

Calderon's face crumpled and he began to cry.

CHAPTER 38

Bartok was already in a holding cell when Emilia walked into the police station the next morning. He was dressed as before, in a guayabera shirt and baggy trousers. The blonde hair was slicked into a lacquered helmet.

He stood in front of the bars, not touching them, hands loose at his sides. The pulpy face was expressionless but the flat, cold eyes took in everything.

A corner of Bartok's mouth lifted in recognition as Emilia walked by. The expression was curious and lewd at the same time. She ignored him but couldn't suppress a shudder.

Silvio was in his office, tilted back in his desk chair. Macias and Sandor sprawled in the two visitor chairs. A bottle of tequila sat on the desk with a motley collection of china mugs.

"Hey, Cruz," Silvio said as Emilia poked her head in. "Come celebrate. Three murders off the books and the *federales* look like *estupidos*."

Emilia grinned. "Nice."

"Caught Bartok unlocking the door to his office about an hour ago." Silvio sloshed a generous amount of tequila into four mugs. "We took everything. Files, laptops, couple of cell phones."

He stood to hand around the mugs and propose a toast. The desk phone rang. Silvio scowled and picked it up.

He listened for a moment, grabbed a pen and scribbled

across a lined pad. *Santibañez.*

Emilia mouthed the name to Macias and Sandor and got two identical eye rolls in return.

"If what you claim is true, I'll need proof," Silvio said into the phone. "That's out of Acapulco's jurisdiction. He's under arrest for three counts of conspiracy to commit murder plus conspiracy to rob the Glorieta pipeline."

He held the phone away from his ear so that the others in the office could hear Santibañez's tinny voice going on and on.

"Well, if that's what you have to do, by all means do it," Silvio finally replied to the mayor's chief of staff. "But until such time, I'm not releasing the prisoner."

He slammed down the phone.

"What was that all about?" Emilia asked.

"Bartok has diplomatic immunity," Silvio said.

The police station quickly turned into a three ring circus. Enrique Santibañez from the mayor's office was the first to show up with two aides in tow. A team from the state government of Guerrero came next, followed closely by a disgruntled *federale* delegation. Emilia lost track as over the next few hours, as a parade of state and national officials came to complicate the situation.

Two unsmiling men from the Russian consulate in Acapulco showed up at noon, with documents in Russian that purported to verify Bartok's diplomatic status. During a heated argument one of the bulky Russians elbowed Santibañez and presto, Silvio had an unlikely ally. It was finally determined that nothing could happen until an official translation was obtained and provided to the proper authorities. The Secretaría de Relaciones Exteriores, or SRE, in Mexico City would make the final decision.

Alvaro called Emilia's cell phone as television vans and over-excited reporters formed a cordon around the police station. Plano had evidently told Alvaro about their conversation in Los Metates and her cousin didn't like being sidelined. Emilia told him to watch the news; she'd connect again later.

Sandor bought out the taco vender who usually parked his cart on the street in back of the station. A combination of goat tacos, tequila, and coffee kept the squadroom going.

Meanwhile, Bartok stayed in the holding cell.

In the middle of the commotion, the attorney general for the state of Guerrero sent an email to the effect that no charges were being brought against Hector Calderon Rios, who recently left Acapulco for an extended vacation.

Emilia thought Silvio was going to have a stroke.

Chief of Police Rodrigo Salazar and his usual phalanx of minions and bodyguards joined the melee as the sun set and the press people began rigging up spotlights. He escorted a three-person delegation from SRE which in turn escorted a Russian military officer. His green army uniform—complete with gold braid, red piping, and an enormous billed hat—

looked hot and uncomfortable.

SRE ruled that Bartok was indeed entitled to diplomatic immunity as a member of the Russian consulate staff. However, in light of the evidence against him, an agreement was reached between Mexico City and Moscow that Bartok would return to Moscow within 24 hours, escorted by Colonel Treblitvin from the Russian embassy.

Emilia smiled when she heard that Treblitvin was the defense attaché. He was probably a military intelligence officer, like Andropov. Perhaps they'd been colleagues, even friends.

She wondered what the penalty was in Russia for murdering a military officer, even if the killer was a minor diplomat.

Silvio wore an expression like granite as the holding cell sergeant unlocked the door to Bartok's cell. Emilia cut her eyes to the big detective as Bartok stepped out, but Silvio didn't move.

Bartok scanned the audience of Mexican and Russian officials. The head of the SRE delegation stammered on about friendship between the two countries being strengthened by the episode. Bartok's dead eyes met Silvio's stare.

"You sent your little girl to ask questions." Bartok spoke in English, directly to Silvio.

The SRE spokesman trailed off, annoyed and confused by the interruption.

Bartok's lumpy face shaped itself into a smile. "In Russia,

men are strong," he said. "But in Mexico they are babies, like you."

Emilia waited for Silvio to leap over the SRE delegation and strangle Bartok. But her former partner still didn't move. He stood with feet apart and arms crossed, massive forearms like a shield, eyes locked on Bartok.

Colonel Treblitvin said something in Russian. The delegation from the Russian consulate formed up on either side of Bartok and marched him out of the police station. A vehicle waited at the back of the building.

Chief Salazar and Santibañez accompanied the SRE delegation to a press conference in the mayor's office.

Emilia stumbled into the penthouse at the Palacio Réal a little after midnight. Kurt's suitcase was in the hall.

"Hey," he said groggily from the bed as she walked into the room. "What's going on?"

Emilia shucked off her clothes, left them on the floor, and climbed in next to him. "We won the battle but the Russians won the war," she yawned.

Kurt pulled her close. "What?"

But Emilia was already asleep.

CHAPTER 39

From the anonymity of his sedan, Emilia and Silvio watched Bartok and Colonel Treblitvin get out of a black SUV with diplomatic license plates. An Acapulco police cruiser idled in front of the SUV, lights flashing.

As other cars swooped in and out of the Departures lane in front of the airport terminal, the SUV driver opened the hatch. He lifted out a small duffel bag and a battered soft-sided suitcase.

He reached into the hatch again but Bartok shouldered him aside. One at a time, Bartok wrestled two big aluminum cases out of the vehicle.

Kurt had suitcases like that, each with four spinning wheels on the bottom. Emilia thought they came from Germany. The thick corrugated aluminum looked as if it could survive a nuclear explosion.

Treblitvin, still wearing his military uniform despite the heat, shook hands with the driver and picked up the small duffle, leaving Bartok to manage the other baggage.

Two uniforms got out of the back of the police cruiser and followed Treblitvin and Bartok into the terminal.

"Let's go," Silvio said to Emilia. "I want to make sure that *cabrón* gets on his fucking airplane." They left the sedan in the space reserved for official vehicles.

Three hours ago, Santibañez had called with Bartok's travel plans. Booked on the 5:00 pm flight to Mexico City.

From there they'd fly to Moscow, connecting in Amsterdam.

The uniformed cops who were supposed to make sure the two Russians boarded the aircraft waited while the men checked in at the ticket counter. Emilia and Silvio hung back near the security entrance, but still had a good view of the ticketing area.

Both detectives wore ball caps and sunglasses. Not really a disguise, but no sense in provoking a confrontation. All they wanted to do was make sure Bartok left Mexico.

The counter agent checked Bartok's passport. The aluminum suitcases tipped onto the scale. Bartok handed over a credit card.

"Over the weight limit," Emilia guessed.

"What do you think he's got in there?" Silvio said.

"Clothes, personal crap," Emilia said absently, her eyes on the little drama being played out at the ticket counter.

The suitcases were finally tagged and loaded onto the conveyor. Bartok and Treblitvin got their boarding passes.

With the two uniforms in tow, Bartok and Treblitvin headed for airport security control. Silvio raised a newspaper and Emilia turned sideways, hand to her sunglasses, as the men passed on the other side of the concourse.

Silvio dropped the newspaper on a bench. Emilia hitched up the strap of her shoulder bag and they strolled along, keeping the two cops in sight.

"Hey, honey," Emilia couldn't resist saying. "Are we having fun yet?"

"Big fun," Silvio growled.

The Russians presented their passports at the control desk and were waved to the front of the security line.

The two uniforms waited, as they'd been instructed to do, until Bartok passed through security and disappeared into the Departures terminal.

Silvio and Emilia stopped the two cops with a display of badges.

"The two Russians," Silvio said. "Did they check their baggage all the way through to Moscow?"

"Yes."

"You're sure?"

"The counter agent checked them through," the taller one said. "The tag on all their bags said SVO."

"That's the right airport code," Emilia said.

Silvio thanked the uniforms and sent them back to their normal duties.

"What do you think happened to all that PEMEX money?" Silvio asked.

"You don't think . . ." Emilia trailed off. She pulled off the stupid sunglasses and knew they were both thinking the same thing. "What do you want to do?"

"Come on." Silvio bulled his way through a posse of chattering travelers, scattering people to the left and right, and barreled his way up the first class line to the airline ticket counter where Bartok and Treblitvin checked in.

Emilia grinned in anticipation as Silvio held up his badge, informed the startled agent that they were on police business, and stepped over the luggage scale onto the agent side of the counter. Emilia clambered after him, her badge similarly on display, dangling from its lanyard around her neck.

They passed through the Employees Only door, down a short hallway, through another door marked with a caution sign and a warning to non-employees. Silvio set a swift pace, passing a line of doors before choosing one marked with a stairway sign.

"Are you sure you know where you're going?" Emilia panted as they clattered down a metal stairway

Silvio answered by shoving open the door at the base of the stairs. They emerged into a warehouse-like space with a vaulted ceiling latticed with steel beams. A complex arrangement of conveyor belts fed six metal boxes, each as big as a car and topped with colored lights. The floor vibrated with the thump and roll of machinery as luggage rode black conveyor belts through the boxes. Huge pinball flippers shot the emerging suitcases onto a steel-toothed conveyor rumbling toward the opposite end of the warehouse. Occasionally a light flashed atop one of the big metal screeners and a suitcase was hauled off the conveyor by hand.

It was a huge, mechanized ballet of suitcases and rolling cogs. Emilia wished she had hearing protection.

Silvio held up his badge as they jogged past a startled man in the uniform of an airport security officer, following the line of a conveyor laden with suitcases emerging from one of the behemoth screeners. Vibration from the machinery caused Emilia's teeth to chatter as she showed her badge as well. Thankfully, the sensation eased once they moved past the initial screening area.

The conveyor ended at the far end of the space, where suitcases were lined up in tidy rows. An enormous plastic curtain separated the end of the space from the outdoors but the smell of aviation fuel pervaded the air, a stomach-churning reminder of the night the Glorieta pipeline exploded. Half a dozen men in orange safety vests talked and joked, industrial headsets looped around their necks instead of protecting their ears, as they wrangled suitcases off the steel conveyor and onto baggage carts.

Emilia recognized the scene from the videos Silvio showed Obregon and Santibañez.

Silvio grabbed one man by the arm. "Javier Vargas, right?"

"*Oye*," Vargas exclaimed. He went to pull back and spotted the police badge. "You a cop?"

Emilia recognized the worker from the videos, too.

"That's right."

Two of the other workers dropped baggage and closed ranks with Vargas. They were all big men, hard muscled from hefting bags all day.

"I'm looking for two suitcases on their way to Moscow," Silvio said.

Vargas laughed. "Is this a joke?"

"Two aluminum suitcases tagged for Moscow," Silvio said. "Both over the weight limit."

"Those," Emilia said, pointing.

The two suitcases with white tags bearing the SVO trigraph lay on a baggage cart, ready to be hauled out to the waiting aircraft.

"Can you get them open?" Silvio asked Vargas.

Vargas folded his arms. "Is this a set up?"

"The cameras are gone," Silvio said.

"Those cases are going to the aircraft now," Vargas said. "Nobody touched them. Isn't that what you want?"

"I want you to open them," Silvio countered. "You're fast enough."

"You'll owe me a favor," Vargas said.

"Open it up and I'll lose the camera footage. What happens after that is up to you."

Three minutes later Vargas popped the first lock. The second lock took 30 seconds longer.

Silvio stopped Vargas from raising the lid. "Just the locks."

The baggage handlers retreated to the conveyor belt. Silvio and Emilia opened the cases to find books in Russian, a dozen new-in-box smartphones, three equally brand new laptops, and several plastic garbage bags stuffed with packets of dollar bills.

Silvio eyed Emilia. "How much money you got with you?" he asked. "Enough to buy a couple of bags to put this stuff in?"

"I doubt it."

Silvio took out his wallet and rifled through his cash. Emilia was giddy with the ridiculousness of hunching over sacks of dollars, counting up enough pesos to rob a Russian.

Clutching all of their combined cash, Emilia flew back up the stairs, and through the maze of doors. Knowing time wasn't on their side, she snaked past the startled counter agents, dodged suitcases on the conveyor, and popped out in the Departures concourse.

She bought two cheap duffle bags in a luggage shop and spotted a souvenir stand. Both of the suitcases had overweight tags on them. Without the money, they'd be suspiciously light en route to Moscow.

Emilia spent the rest of the cash on the heaviest souvenirs she could find, which translated into an armload of serape blankets, pottery plates painted with desert scenes, and a pile of tooled leather purses that proclaimed I ♥ MEXICO.

Back in the bowels of the airport, Emilia and Silvio substituted the souvenirs for the money, relocked the aluminum suitcases, and returned them to Vargas and his buddies. The last Emilia saw of Bartok's shiny cases, they were on a cart being towed out to the aircraft.

"Nice touch, Cruz," Silvio said as he hefted a lumpy duffle. "I especially liked the blankets."

"I hear it's cold in Moscow," Emilia said.

CHAPTER 40

"I have the ransom," Emilia announced.

Plano could not hide his astonishment. "You have two million dollars?"

"Yes." Actually, the money, which totaled over four million, was in Silvio's hands. Emilia and Silvio also had brand new laptops.

"Where did you get two million all of a sudden?"

"That's not important," Emilia said. She nudged her mother's cell phone lying next to Plano's laptop. "Let them know we're ready to pay. Now."

Hopefully, this was the last meeting of the war council in Sophia's kitchen. Emilia's thoughts couldn't help vaulting to tomorrow or the day after. Life would be ordinary again. Ernesto back at his grinding wheel, Sophia shopping at the mercado, Alvaro back to being a friend as well as a cousin.

Plano shook his head. "We've talked about this before, Detective. If you try to trick them with a bag of bricks, they will kill Ernesto."

"There's no trick." Emilia looked Plano square in the eye. "The full ransom in return for Ernesto. Today."

Plano texted the offer to Ernesto's cell phone and asked for delivery instructions.

Emilia looked at the time. It was early, only 9:00 am. She said she'd be outside and headed for the courtyard.

Last night, as she and Silvio counted Bartok's money,

they'd discussed the delicate matter of handing over the ransom. They both knew that kidnappers often seized the delivery person and held them hostage for a second payment. In worst case scenarios, an assembly line kidnapping scheme continued until every member of a family was ransomed or the kidnappers were convinced that the family fortune was completely depleted.

She needed someone who wouldn't disappear with the ransom or make separate deal with Los Colectores.

The fact that family members were cops complicated the situation even further. Every gang in Mexico that carried out kidnappings used informants. Plano might not have known about Los Colectores until recently, but that didn't mean the gang didn't have the skinny on every cop in Acapulco. A cop making a ransom drop had a guaranteed survival rate of zero.

By the time Emilia and Silvio repackaged the money, they'd narrowed the possibilities to three.

Tío Raul.

Padre Ricardo.

Kurt.

The sun was bright in the courtyard as Emilia slumped onto Ernesto's stool next to the silent grinding wheel and thought about the options. Silvio argued that Kurt was the only real choice. He wasn't a cop. Los Colectores wouldn't recognize him. He was cool under pressure.

The thought of Kurt walking into that situation made Emilia sick. Kurt was a wealthy *gringo*. It would be far too easy for Los Colectores to snatch him for an even bigger ransom.

Unbidden, Emilia's thoughts slid to Karina Escobar de la Vega. How would Rafa Gamboa's foster mother have held up if her husband was the victim of a kidnapping? Would she be stronger than Sophia or would her brittle façade crumble?

Alvaro approached. "*Prima*," he said. "Where did you get two million dollars?"

"It doesn't matter," Emilia said, squinting up at him. "I have it. That's all anybody needs to know."

"It matters to Lieutenant Plano." Alvaro squatted next to her.

"Get your head out of Plano's ass," Emilia said irritably. She resisted the impulse to shove her cousin onto the paving stones. "Don't be so worried about who can do you favors down the road."

"I'm thinking about Tía Sophia," Alvaro declared. "If Plano thinks you aren't being straight with him, he could pull the plug.'

Emilia narrowed her eyes at her cousin. "What makes you think he'd do that?"

"He doesn't believe you really have the money," Alvaro said. "I heard him telling Chen. We have to let him know where you got it."

"*Madre de Dios*." Emilia wiped sweaty hands on her thighs. She was dog tired from the craziness of the past few days and Alvaro's obsequiousness was getting on her last nerve. "Make up something. Anything. I don't care."

"Detective?" Plano shouted from the front door. "You need to see this."

Emilia sprang to her feet. "Did we get an answer?"

Los Colectores gave specific instructions. Sophia, wearing the pink apron Ernesto gave her for Christmas, was to bring the money to the Servicio Moderno car repair shop on Rio Colorado in the Hogar Moderno neighborhood at 1:00 am.

Emilia looked around the kitchen. Alvaro stared back, his face ashen.

Plano and Chen were expressionless.

"I can pass for my mother," Emilia heard herself say.

CHAPTER 41

It was a surreal experience. They were actually planning a ransom drop to kidnappers in the living room of the Palacio Réal penthouse. The setting sun threw glorious streaks of raspberry and tangerine across the sky as Maná's *Drama Y Luz* album played on the stereo.

Earlier, Plano and Chen briefed her on typical ransom delivery procedures, which boiled down to leave the money and get the hell out as quickly as possible. After a brief discussion Emilia ruled out a tracker in her pocket. If Los Colectores found it, the whole operation could go sideways. She would have Sophia's identity card and cell phone, which Hostage Negotiations would continue to monitor via their mirror app.

Plano's team would stay in the house in case Ernesto was released and found his way home or Los Colectores sent instructions where to find him. Alvaro would stay with Sophia and his parents in their apartment in case Ernesto appeared there. Emilia would be on her own.

Except what Plano didn't know wouldn't kill him.

Silvio brought the money to the hotel, one more person with a large rolling suitcase following the bellhop into the elevator. He also brought a tracker for the Suburban, chagrined that Plano didn't suggest it, and a burner phone so that Emilia had a second communications link. He would stay mobile, trailing Emilia throughout the night as she drove through the Hogar Moderno neighborhood.

Kurt would be on her tail as well, driving his personal SUV.

The color had drained from Kurt's face when Emilia told him that in a few hours she'd pretend to be her mother and deliver Ernesto's ransom. Now, as the three pored over a map of the city spread over the coffee table, Sophia's apron folded neatly on the sofa next to Emilia, he was uncharacteristically tense.

"Rucker." Silvio ran a hand through his crew cut. "You got a ball cap?"

Kurt raised his eyebrows. "Sure. You think Em needs a disguise?"

"You gotta hide the *gringo* hair."

Kurt left the room. Emilia heard the sliding door to the hall closet scrape along its track. She jumped up and ran after Kurt.

"I don't want you to do this," she said as he rifled through a box of sports equipment.

He turned, a navy blue ball cap in hand, some generic logo on the front. "I could say the same," he said. "But I won't. A man's life is at stake."

"Silvio shouldn't have asked you." Emilia clutched his arm. "If Los Colectores finds you, they'll hold you for ransom.

Kurt tipped up her chin. "When you went to change, I told Franco I was either coming with him or following on my own."

Emilia bit her lip, overwhelmed by his generosity and the fear that something would happen to him.

"You're not doing this without me, Em." Kurt pulled her close.

She rested her head against his chest, absorbing his strength until the shakiness passed. "I love you," Emilia said. "When this is over, I'll make it up to you."

Kurt kissed her. "You just did."

They left the hotel at 10:00 pm with the suitcase full of cash loaded into the backseat of the Suburban. Two million dollars weighed about 25 pounds. It would be easier and faster for her to pull it out rather than circle around and open the back hatch. Anything to keep her vulnerability to a minimum.

Emilia wore Sophia's smock-style pink floral apron over a long sleeved black tee, jeans, and cross trainers, making her feel like she ought to be hawking Chupa Pops from a cardboard tray at a downtown intersection. She filled her pockets with her mother's *cédula* identity card, the burner phone with earbuds for a hands-free connection, and a couple of pesos. Sophia's fully charged cell phone went into the console cup holder for communications from either Plano or Los Colectores.

They had three hours to get from Puerto Marques to Hogar Moderno, reconnoiter the neighborhood, and get into position for the 1:00 am ransom delivery.

Hogar Moderno was on the west side of the bay, well out of the tourist zone. The grid of one and two-story cement houses and low-slung commercial enterprises was boxed in by the wide Ruta 200 to the south and west, Avenida Constituyentes on the east, and Calle Ejido across the top. The streets were two ways, except for Rio Lerma which only flowed north. Unlike the El Coloso neighborhood, most of the streetlights still functioned.

All in all, Hogar Moderno was still a fairly decent neighborhood, although a car was torched there during a recent gang shootout. Emilia knew it well. She wouldn't get lost.

At 12:30, Emilia slowly drove up Rio Colorado and found Servicio Moderno. A block-long white building, the name was spelled out in huge red letters daubed onto the front wall, along with a menu of services: *Mecanica General. Hojalateria. Llantas*.

A torn striped awning fluttered from the second story balcony. No sidewalk separated the front of the building from the street, nor was there any gutter. The street almost certainly flooded during the rainy season.

Emilia veered to the left to go around the blackened hulk of a Volkswagen Beetle. The little vehicle's nose touched the tarmac; a cinder block substituted for the right front tire, giving the impression that the carcass was bowing to the nearby streetlight.

A blue metal garage door was rolled shut. Emilia caught

a few glimpses of Silvio's sedan and Kurt's green SUV as she drove through the quiet neighborhood a second time, arriving back at Servicio Moderno at 1:00 am.

The Beetle still genuflected its rusty subservience to the pavement but the big garage door was open.

"Going in," Emilia said into the microphone of the earbud that dangled from her left ear. Her hands were slick with sweat.

Silvio acknowledged.

Emilia nosed the Suburban into the garage and it rattled loudly in the confined space. Her headlights illuminated the bay, which reminded her of Tío Raul's shop. A workbench ran the length of the place on the right, rusted car parts were scattered along the left and stacks of tires rose to the ceiling in front of her. Her headlights revealed crumbling rubber; the tires weren't new merchandise, but old leftovers.

The place looked abandoned. No tools on the workbench. No cans of oil or brake fluid on the bare shelf above the work surface.

Silvio's voice rumbled through the single earbud. "What's going on, Cruz?"

"They're late," she murmured above the pounding of her heart. "There's no one here."

"Give it some time."

After ten minutes, she cut the engine. Silence settled on the Suburban like dust floating from the rafters.

Sophia's cell phone pinged.

Emilia plucked the phone out of the console cup holder.

A text message from an unknown number showed on the screen.

PEMEX 421 Ejido. 3 minutes.

She relayed the change to Silvio and Kurt, backed out of the empty garage, and headed north on Rio Colorado to the intersection with Ejido.

The PEMEX station was closed, but fluorescent strip lighting over the three rows of pumps allowed Emilia to easily read the big signs.

Cerrado por falta de gas.

Closed due to the gas shortage.

Madre de Dios. The irony of it all.

Emilia circled the pumps and coasted to a stop next to the station's storefront, praying to see Ernesto, but all she got was a sign on the glass door reading *Cerrado*. She kept the engine idling with the nose of the Suburban pointing at the street, ready for a swift getaway.

Traffic was light on Ejido, a four lane thoroughfare with businesses on both sides of the street. It was home to a colorful mix of flat-roofed blocky buildings. A few were offices for doctors and clinics and dentists, but most housed a mashup of *taquerias*, paper stores, used clothing shops, guest houses, and souvenir stalls for the tourists who wandered away from the beaches and downtown crowds.

She saw Kurt's green SUV come down Ejido, slow, and

turn right. Silvio was out there, too, keeping her safe. If Los Colectores wanted to play tag through the Hogar Moderno neighborhood, she knew both men would stay with her.

In fact, that had to be what Los Colectores planned. The PEMEX station was too brightly lit and too out in the open to be a drop zone.

Ten minutes later, Sophia's phone pinged. A new cell phone number showed up, with a much longer message.

Park at Rosa Linda Hotel on Velasquez de Léon. Walk through Palmas to Bar Tabasco corner Palmas and La Noria. Deposit package rear door brown van. 30 minutes.

Emilia's heart leaped into her mouth. Velasquez de Leon and La Noria were narrow one-way streets, both funneling traffic north away from the Playa Las Hamacas beaches. Palmas was little more than a pedestrian walkway between the other two, which ran into each other at a three-way intersection with Tadeo Arredondo Villanueva south of the major Avenida Cuauhtémoc. The triangle of skinny streets and heavy foot traffic would make it hard for Kurt and Silvio to keep her in sight.

That was going to be a problem because the three streets in the message were the epicenter of Acapulco's red light district. Every other structure was a hotel that rented rooms by the hour. *Machos* from all the rival gangs were faithful customers. Alcohol and sex fueled their fighting. Debauchery, drugs, and drunkenness ruled the night.

The morgue's body wagon made pickups in the morning when things calmed down.

The mayhem was tolerated because it was too dangerous to do anything about it. The city stopped policing Palmas years ago, although took care to warn tourists about going there. Nonetheless, more tourists hit the red light district than Acapulco's museums, inevitably encountering muggings, murder, and rape.

Emilia was heading into *La Zona de Tolerancia.*

The Zone of Tolerance.

A stringy man with a red rag waved her into a parking spot across from the Rosa Linda Hotel. It was a tall mashup of cinderblocks and flapping awnings. Music pulsed out of the ground floor. A sign advertised rooms for 70 pesos "for an hour of pleasure."

He rapped on the driver's window. Emilia rolled it down, the engine still idling.

"Sixty pesos," he rasped.

It was double what a street sweeper charged to safeguard a car anywhere else in the city. Emilia handed over the bills and he disappeared into a bar. She sat in the car, pretending to check her makeup, until she saw Silvio's sedan pull into a parking space. He'd follow her on foot, while Kurt stayed in his vehicle and cruised north on La Noria.

"Heading out," she murmured into the microphone.

When Silvio responded, Emilia stowed the earbuds and got out of the car, instantly feeling ridiculous in Sophia's pink apron. It was like wearing a beacon as she hauled the suitcase out of the back seat.

Trouble started as soon as Emilia headed up Palmas. The narrow street was lined with bars blasting music and electronic squawks of arcade machines. Tired looking girls lounged against doorways, all wearing the requisite Acapulco hooker uniform of spaghetti strap camisole, lycra mini skirt, high heels, and uncombed hair. They were neither clean nor pretty. The attraction was that they were cheap and plentiful.

A carnival atmosphere ruled as groups of young men roamed from bar to bar, occasionally congregating at a food vendor's wagon for tacos before the next round of girls and tequila. Apart from hookers, the few women on the street were sightseers, watching the show with arms wrapped around a boyfriend.

The suitcase full of cash weighed a ton as Emilia wheeled it down the crowded street, constantly maneuvering around meandering drunks and rowdy knots of *machos*.

"Hey, *mamacita*." A kid grabbed the hem of the apron, dragging Emilia to a halt. "Where you going so fast?"

She swatted his hand away and kept walking as fast as she could.

"My friend said he wants to know where you're going." A bigger kid danced in front of her, forcing Emilia to stop. "You running away from home?"

The words were dangerously slurred. Emilia prayed that Silvio was behind her.

Someone grabbed the suitcase handle. Emilia won a brief tug-of-war with a mighty jerk that caused her to stumble into the kid in front of her. He got a fistful of apron and pulled her close. "You're the prettiest girl on the street." He brought his face next to hers. "I gotta get me some of your ass right here, right now."

His friends whooped. Emilia drove an elbow into his neck but almost lost control of the suitcase. It tipped over, slamming the weight of two million dollars into the circle of drunken *machos*. Somebody tripped and sprawled with a roar onto the sidewalk. Another snagged Emilia around the waist and she kicked like a mule, desperately clinging to the suitcase.

Silvio joined the party. As he waded in, Emilia tore down the sidewalk toward the intersection with La Noria, the suitcase banging behind her until she managed to flip it back onto its wheels.

She saw Bar Tabasco from the street corner. La Noria wasn't quite as congested as Palmas, but the same tired girls waited for the next customer in front of the same cheap hotels and noisy bars. Music and lights pulsed down the street, except for Bar Tabasco.

There, the windows were dark behind iron security grilles and a row of empty cement planters blocked the entrance. The shabby low building wasn't bunched with the rest of the hotspots but separated by a dirt lot on one side and a narrow alley on the other.

Emilia followed a faded sign that pointed to a parking lot.

The suitcase was hard to pull over the uneven gravel surface. A van was parked in the darkness behind the bar. The sliding door was open. The interior was dark and empty.

This was it. With a silent prayer to the Virgin that the next text would be instructions for picking up Ernesto, Emilia collapsed the telescoping handle of the suitcase and heaved two million dollars of stolen Russian money onto the floor of the van.

She heard footsteps on the gravel. Before Emilia could turn around she was lifted bodily into the van. The door slammed shut, the engine roared, and the van sped out of the alley.

CHAPTER 42

Two men in balaclava masks swiftly enveloped Emilia's head in a plastic bag and secured it in place with a wad of duct tape. Her hands were cuffed behind her back and her ankles taped together, leaving her face down on the floor of the moving vehicle.

A scream rose in the back of her throat as they groped through the front and back pockets of her jeans, removing Sophia's cell phone and identity card. The hands didn't touch her again but a heavy foot kept her jammed into the carpeted floor.

No one spoke as the van rumbled along. Emilia fought panic as the plastic bag pressed against her face with every breath. She mentally chanted to stay calm.

Two breaths in. Two breaths out.

As the vehicle turned, Emilia flopped like a dolphin caught in a fishing net. The duct tape collar rubbed against her neck. Maybe it wasn't tight enough to suffocate her.

Two breaths in. Two breaths out.

The car picked up speed and Emilia realized they must be on a main artery. She tried to fix the map of the western side of the city in her mind

The van had headed north out of the Bar Tabasco parking lot at the end of the alley. The choices off the upper end of La Noria were either a right turn south toward the beach and Avenida Costera Miguel Alemán or a left to connect with

Avenida Cuauhtémoc. Both choices were main roads. They ran roughly parallel as they flowed over the middle of the bay but Cuauhtémoc eventually turned north while Miguel Alemán hugged the curve of the bay all the way to Punta Diamante on the southeast tip.

From the faintest tang of salt, Emilia guessed they were on Miguel Alemán. She tried to gauge the speed and visualize where they were. When the car swayed to the right, she imagined it was because they were coming around the Diana monument, passing the Pizza Hut and the shuttered hulk of what used to be the iconic restaurant, Señor Frog's. The van picked up speed and it seemed incredible to Emilia that she was being carried along like this, next to a suitcase full of dollars, not knowing if she was helping to release a kidnapping victim or becoming one herself.

About 15 minutes later, the van slowed and made a hard left turn. Emilia heard the suitcase slide along the floor. The man holding her down grunted as she rolled, too. They were going up a steep hill. They made a series of turns; right, left, right, right; all while climbing higher and higher.

The salt tang faded and the air smelled like pine. They slowed and turned right again. The engine strained in low gear. Emilia realized they were driving up the mountain that brooded over Acapulco like a vanguard between the Pacific and the rest of Mexico.

The van finally stopped.

The sliding door opened and Emilia was dragged out feet first like a stevedore handling a bag of onions. She was hoisted onto a shoulder. The air rushed out of her lungs and the plastic bag wrinkled against her mouth. Her head bobbed against the man's back and blood thumped in her ears. Emilia tasted acid in the back of her throat and knew if she threw up in the bag she would choke to death.

There were few clues to tell her where they were bringing her. The slap of rubber soled shoes against a hard surface. Tile or terrazzo. The suitcase wheels squeaked. The man carrying her began to breathe heavily. The sound of the suitcase faded.

She heard the release of a lock. The pop and clang of a metal fire door. The man stopped to adjust her on his shoulder and mounted stairs, Emilia's head snapping with every jolt. Whatever stairway they were climbing turned twice.

Another door groaned open, but the sound was softer than the others. Emilia felt herself swinging off the man's shoulder only to be dumped onto a clammy tile floor. Her left shoulder hit first, sending a searing bolt across her chest. Her cheekbone slammed into the floor. A bone cracked, the sound magnified in her ears by the plastic shroud. She gasped in pain and the bag ballooned into her mouth.

A door closed, making the air shudder.

The plastic bag rippled in the draft. Emilia lay without moving and let the pain swallow her whole.

CHAPTER 43

She came awake slowly, choking on the taste of blood. She opened her eyes and saw nothing.

Blinking made it worse. Her eyelashes dragged against something pressing against her face. She gasped and shook her head, trying to rid herself of the suffocating sensation.

Instead of freeing herself, her breath drew it in and her mouth filled with a rubbery film that tasted like blood. Emilia gagged. A forest fire of panic swept through her before she remembered what happened.

The situation was blindingly obvious. She was the kidnappers' next victim, the same as happened to so many other families.

She managed to spit out the slack in the plastic bag enveloping her head. Shallow breaths calmed her enough to take stock. She was lying like a fish on a slab, tipped on her side. Still handcuffed behind her back, ankles still taped together.

The silence around her was complete. No voices or footsteps or even the sound of breathing beyond her own.

No cars. No wind. No rustling of trees or rush of the ocean.

It took every ounce of concentration to ignore the choking panic and work herself into a sitting position with her bound ankles in front of her. The bag sucked in and out as Emilia breathed, but she didn't pass out again and that in itself was a small, bitter victory.

The handcuffs left her fingers relatively free. She could feel that she was sitting on a tile floor. Emilia slowly scooted backwards, arms extended as far as her burning shoulder would allow, straining to reach something, anything that would give her a clue as to where she was.

Her fingers touched something rough and vertical. Stucco.

She rested against the wall, out of breath, the plastic bag rattling against her face. By now she knew that her nose and possibly a cheekbone were broken. Her entire face hurt and her eyes watered from the pain, but the next time she inhaled and the bag pressed into her mouth, Emilia bit into it, worrying the plastic between her teeth. The slippery material puffed away when she exhaled, but she managed to catch it again on the next intake of air.

She drew her knees up and rested her unhurt cheek on them. The bag slid around less. Six bites later, she made a ragged little hole in the bag. She kept at it until she could stick her tongue through the hole.

Emilia greedily hauled in a deep breath. The bag pressed against her lips but didn't plaster itself against her skin. The air smelled like sewage but the extra oxygen steadied her.

With renewed energy, Emilia resumed her groping tour of the black hole she was in, blindly scooting herself along on her butt and her heels, hands straining to encounter a recognizable shape. It occurred to her that she might be in the same place as Ernesto's coffin.

"Ernesto? Ernesto?" Her voice sounded like an echo from far away.

Her circuit of the wall stopped abruptly as her fingers encountered first a smooth ridge and then open space. A doorway. The tile floor changed from big squares to tiny coins. Her fingertips traced grout lines.

She was in a bathroom.

Emilia kept going, trying to identify what she was encountering. She felt the sharp edge of a wooden cabinet and a protruding handle jabbed her in the arm. She slowly hitched around until she was facing the cabinet. Sliding to the floor on her stomach, Emilia pushed her head against the handle in a blind attempt to snag the bag.

Her muscles screamed and she nearly knocked herself out as her head rapped against the cabinet. Emilia kept at it, tears in her eyes, until she hooked the hole in the bag around one end of the handle. She slowly forced her chin down. The plastic stretched upwards . . . and slipped off the end of the handle.

The third time she tried, the bag ripped.

Emilia sat up, breathing heavily from the tension in her body and the sustained effort of pulling her head down. She put her head against her knees and rubbed hard to push the split bag away from her face. The plastic settled around the back of her neck like a hood, held in place by the duct tape collar.

She could see. Moonlight shining through a small window revealed that she was in a modest bathroom, with a toilet, tub, and the vanity cabinet which so thoughtfully provided a handle. The plumbing fixtures were gone, leaving only exposed pipes. The tile surround was slick with mold and the walls were riven with cracks.

The toilet was intact, although the seat was gone and the bowl glazed with brown slime. Emilia slid backwards along the floor and jammed her feet against the foul smelling ceramic. The sharp-edged threads of a thick screw protruded from the base of the toilet.

Emilia breathed in the same two-in, two-out cadence as she scraped her taped ankles against the screw. Her leg muscles shook with the repetitive motion and sweat soaked her tee. The pain forced her to stop twice before the tape gave way and she could pry her ankles apart and clamber awkwardly to her feet without the use of her hands.

The first room was little more than a white box. Lines of pale moonlight sliced across the emptiness, thanks to old plastic vertical blinds. The door was smooth, with a plastic picture on it.

Emilia pushed down on the door handle with an elbow. It was locked. She pressed her ear to the door. No voices, no footsteps.

The picture on the door was a complicated triangular diagram. She stared at the faded ink until her brain processed what her eyes were seeing.

It was a floor plan of a wedge-shaped hotel, directing guests where to go in case of fire. The masthead revealed that she was in the Hotel Monte Vista, enjoying the comforts of "Acapulco's Deluxe Mountain Hideaway!" The copyright at the bottom was from 1965.

The Monte Vista had been abandoned for years, victim of the cartel violence that shrank the tourist zone to the rim of the bay. But tucked halfway up the mountain on the eastern side of the bay, miles from the beaches, the Monte Vista had been doomed the day it was built. It was on the end of a hilly street called Villa Vista, looking down on the sports clubs and condo complexes on Lomas de Mar.

It was the perfect location, Emilia thought grimly. Remote and abandoned.

Los Colectores could see who was coming up the narrow Villa Vista, but why would anyone? The old hotel was so decayed that even Acapulco's squatters stayed away.

A lizard darted up the wall and Emilia flinched at the unexpected movement. But it shook her out of her reverie in front of the floor plan.

The window was covered with tattered vertical blinds that Emilia pushed aside with an elbow. No one shouted or otherwise indicated that her movement was seen from the outside. Emilia realized that she wasn't looking out of a grimy window, but out of a grimy sliding glass door.

Thrilled at this piece of good luck, she turned her back and managed to find the latch with her fingertips. With a little encouragement from her knee, the door slid along a rusty metal track.

Emilia stepped onto a narrow balcony. The view confirmed her test of Acapulco's geography. The entrance to the hotel was fronted by a circular drive. It created a dead end for a steep and narrow street that could only be Villa Vista.

It gave Emilia a measure of control to know where she was. In the distance, city lights created a welcoming glow. At sunrise the view would be breathtaking.

Acapulco was always breathtaking from a distance.

The balcony was surrounded by a filigreed iron railing. Identical balconies marched across the building to her right and left, as far away as China.

Palm trees rustled in the night breeze. They framed an enormous swimming pool yawning below, surrounded by a dark stone patio. An overgrown hedge had probably once been an attractive bit of landscaping.

The fear of staying was greater than the fear of smashing into the pool. Clinging awkwardly to the iron railing with her cuffed hands, Emilia got her legs over one at a time, until she was balanced on the slim ledge.

She let go and kicked out at the same time.

The shrubbery rushed up. Emilia tumbled into a mess of twiggy plants and dry palm fronds, scattering them in all directions. She ended up on the rim of the pool, gasping in pain.

Emilia rolled to her knees and got to her feet by bracing herself against the wall of the hotel. Pain ripped up her right leg when she put her weight on that foot. Her ankle was either twisted or broken.

It didn't matter. She had to get away from the Monte

Vista before Los Colectores put her in a coffin and sent Kurt the video. Time wasn't on her side, either. Eventually someone would come to check on her. Emilia hobbled forward, staying close to the side of the building. Fire lanced up her leg every time she put any weight on her right foot. She didn't know how she was going to get down Villa Vista. The street was pitched like a rollercoaster, without sidewalk or railing.

Maybe she could roll like a sausage or inch down on her ass.

As Emilia crept her way towards the circular drive and the street beyond, her uneven shuffles broadcast through the quiet night. Small stones skittered away and dry fronds crackled, as slippery underfoot as ice.

The corner of the abandoned hotel was her last refuge. Emilia took a deep breath and hobbled out in the open. Her nose wasn't working at all. The night air was heavy and humid in her mouth.

The streetlights blazed like Christmas. It was ironic that the lights worked here, an abandoned and overgrown no-man's land at the base of the mountain, but nothing worked in populated areas like El Coloso. If only she wasn't wearing Sophia's *maldita* apron. The pink smock was easy to spot in the dark but with hands cuffed behind her back, even a contortionist couldn't take it off.

Emilia was nearly in tears from the pain but she managed to hobble down the driveway. The hotel was eerily silent. No one shouted or ran after her. She looked back once, but none of the windows showed a light. The kidnapers' van was the only evidence that someone was inside.

Her right ankle swelled to twice its normal size, straining against the hem of her jeans. Emilia expected to fall headlong on the steep street at any moment. Picking her way along Villa Vista was going to take forever.

Without warning, a car sped toward her at racetrack speed. Headlights bathed her in white light. The car screeched to a stop as Emilia desperately tried to run but her ankle collapsed and she fell to her knees.

A moment later, someone grabbed her upper arm. Emilia twisted but couldn't get away.

It was Plano and he was livid. "You fucking *puta*," he snarled.

"What are you doing here?" Emilia gasped. "How did you find me?"

He yanked Emilia to her feet and marched her back the way she'd come, cursing into his cell phone all the way. Again, Emilia's ankle gave out. Plano dragged her the last few feet before dumping her near the hotel's front entrance. A man with a flashlight ran out of the dark doorway.

"I found her on the road, Chavo," Plano raged. He grabbed the duct tape still wound around Emilia's throat. "Another five minutes and she'd be gone. What the fuck were you doing?"

"What the fuck are you doing here?" the man called Chavo shouted angrily.

"She turned over fake money," Plano said furiously. He

wrenched Emilia's head back and shoved his handgun in her face. "You stole counterfeit out of the police evidence locker and tried to pass it off as ransom money. "

"It's not fake, you liar," Emilia choked.

"Your idiot cousin told me," Plano insisted.

"Alvaro made that up." Of course, Plano wasn't there to rescue her. He'd teamed up with the kidnappers, like every other *cabrón* in charge of Hostage Negotiations. "You're a kidnapper, too."

"Shut up, *puta*," Plano snarled.

"It's all there," Chavo said. "Two million. If it's fake, it's real good fake."

"We'll test the cash," Plano replied.

"Test your share when Luca gives it to you."

"We test it all," Plano said angrily. "I'm not going to walk away with a worthless share."

Chavo shrugged. "Go tell Luca. What about her?"

"I'll get rid of her." Plano yanked up on the duct tape, forcing Emilia to stand swaying on her left foot. He grinned at her. "I can leave your body on the mountain and in three days the vultures will pick it clean. Not even your idiot mother will recognize you."

"Were you in on it from the start?" Emilia croaked.

Plano slapped Emilia with the barrel of his gun. The broken bones in her face ground together, blotting out coherent thought. She fell backwards, landing on the handcuffs. He hauled her to her knees, again using the duct tape collar like a handle.

"Hey. Hey. Dudes." A figure trotted up the drive, caught in the glare of Plano's headlights.

Emilia barely recognized Kurt, shirtless in a pair of board shorts and sneakers, a bottle of tequila in his left hand and a tee shirt in his right.

"Dudes. You all hablo English, *amigos*?" Speaking English with an exaggerated accent, Kurt shook the bottle as if to share. He reeked of cheap tequila and his blonde hair was mussed as he grinned like a confused drunk. "Hey, a dude down at the fort told me this was the best place to get blow. Yeah, right?"

"Get lost," Plano exclaimed in English.

"Get rid of them both," Chavo said tersely and disappeared into the hotel.

"Hey." Kurt swayed. "Hey, he only know Spanish?"

"Get lost," Plano repeated in English. "Tell your buddy he made a mistake."

Kurt came closer, the epitome of the sozzled surfer. He wiped his nose on the back of the hand holding the bottle. Tequila sloshed out, the smell pungent in the warm night.

"Just here for the blow, man," he said earnestly, ignoring Emilia kneeling next to Plano. "A little blow for me and my buddies. I got dollars, too. Waddaya say?"

"Go back the way you came," Plano said evenly. "There's nothing for you here."

"Fucking negotiator, I can respect that." Kurt nodded sagely and swayed closer. "Hey, you two having a private moment? How about—."

Plano extended his arm with the gun and pointed it directly at Kurt. "Get out or I'll kill you."

Kurt dropped the bottle of tequila. Liquor and glass sprayed across the drive. "Dude! Look what you made me do!"

Emilia saw the muscles in Plano's forearm tense as his finger curled around the trigger. She launched herself against his shins as he fired, knocking him off balance.

Kurt rolled across the driveway. Hidden under the boozy tee shirt, a handgun barked three times.

Plano staggered; his face painted with surprise. He dropped his gun and slumped against the car.

Emilia watched as Plano slid down the fender and toppled sideways onto the ground. His mouth was open as he stared sightlessly at the abandoned hotel.

CHAPTER 44

"Em, are you all right?" Kurt asked urgently, pulling Emilia into the shadows by the side of the crumbling hotel. "How do I get these things off you?"

Shock hit her all at once. Emilia's teeth chattered as she spoke. "We need a key. Check Plano's pockets."

"Who?" Kurt propped her into a sitting position against the wall.

"You shot Lieutenant Plano. The head of Hostage Negotiations."

Kurt came back with a handcuff key, a pocketknife, and Plano's gun. A minute later, Emilia's hands were free, she was armed, and Silvio was on the way.

That's how Emilia and Kurt ended up in ringside seats for what happened next.

Silvio drove up Villa Vista like a madman in time to intercept the kidnappers' van heading out with the two million dollar ransom. He spun his car into Plano's vehicle, forming a barrier that blocked the kidnappers. A short and deadly gun battle ensued.

When it was all over, the two kidnappers were dead. Silvio retrieved the ransom. After a breathless reunion with Emilia and Kurt, he explained how they found her.

Chen called Silvio when Plano got a call on his personal cell phone and rushed out without an explanation. Silvio, in turn, alerted Kurt. In separate vehicles, both men followed

Plano into the abandoned neighborhood as far as they could. Thinking fast, they cooked up the drunken surfer act and Kurt ran up the steep street the way only a world-class athlete could, looking for Plano's vehicle.

Silence settled over the ruined hotel as if three dead men weren't sprawled on the driveway and gunfire had never torn the air. The survivors were alone at the end of the winding street. If anyone still lived in the ruins along Villa Vista, they'd learned long ago how to be invisible.

"What about Ernesto?" Emilia asked. "Did Chen say they found him?"

Still breathing hard, Silvio shook his head. "You think he's inside the hotel?"

"Yes."

Silvio tipped his head back to contemplate the Monte Vista. "You said he was being held in a coffin. This place won't have a working elevator. They wouldn't have hauled a coffin up too many flights of stairs."

Emilia hobbled as fast as she could as they entered the hotel. The Monte Vista was nothing more than a carcass. Anything of value in the lobby had been torn out and carted away, creating an echoing chamber of ruin. As Kurt played the beam of a flashlight from Plano's car around the space, they saw big holes in the walls along with rivers of cracks and gouts of rust.

Scavengers had picked the first floor clean. The reception desk was gone and the tile floor demolished. Even the sinks and toilets in the restrooms were gone, as were the interior doors, although carved wooden frames remained, homage to an unknown craftsman.

The focal point was a curving stairway that vanished into darkness. Emilia could imagine a filigree banister to match the exterior ironwork but it was long gone.

"Ernesto Cruz," Silvio shouted.

The only response was an echo.

Emilia leaned on Kurt, too jazzed to feel pain, and hopped up the stairs. The smell got worse the higher they climbed, as did the heat.

"*Rayos*," Silvio swore as they got to the top of the stairs and found themselves on an open ledge overlooking the lobby. The floor tile was rubble and the mezzanine rail was gone. The floor sloped toward the edge. One misstep meant a tumble into the pitch black lobby far below.

"Over here," Kurt said.

A typical hotel hallway led off the mezzanine, but in this case most of the room doors were gone. The few doors stood out, even more because they were fitted with shiny new deadbolts.

Silvio threw back the bolt on the first door and kicked it open. Kurt's flashlight picked out the silvery remnants of duct tape and a balcony on the other side of the open sliding glass door.

"I was here," Emilia said, hardly recognizing her own voice.

The next room was unlocked. Plastic shrink-wrapped cases of bottled water were stacked against a wall. A piece of furniture that might have once been a dresser lay on its side, flanked by two cheap white plastic chairs and topped with a propane lantern and a couple of rolls of duct tape. Old newspapers littered the floor next to a plastic grocery bag full of empty beer bottles. The stink of urine made Emilia's eyes water.

"Fuck," Silvio said. "Amazing they didn't burn the place down."

Two rooms away, another deadbolt caught the gleam of Silvio's flashlight. A coffin rested on the floor near a wad of clothing and a bucket that stank of feces. It was latched, preventing anyone inside from being able to raise the lid.

"Ernesto!" Emilia screamed.

Kurt and Silvio jimmied the latch and opened the coffin.

A naked man lay inside, his face covered by a plastic bag secured at the neck with duct tape. The bag sucked in and out as he breathed. Kurt ripped the plastic away.

In the light of Silvio's flashlight, they could see that it wasn't Ernesto.

The man blinked but his eyes didn't focus, nor did he speak.

Silvio took out his phone. "I'll stay with him."

Kurt and Emilia kept going down the hall. They found a second coffin.

It was empty but redolent of urine and abject terror.

Emilia slipped out of Kurt's arm and sat on the floor, unable to stop a flood of tears.

"What's that?" Kurt said.

"Patrol car." A faint siren was getting closer. "Ambulance."

"No, a knocking."

"What?"

"Em, listen."

She heard it. A faint tap. Hope surged into her bones. The throbbing in her leg was forgotten.

The very last door along the hallway was locked.

Kurt turned the deadbolt and shoved the door open, revealing a third coffin. They unlatched it and pried up the lid. Another naked man lay inside, his head covered with a plastic bag and secured with duct tape. One leg was bandaged.

Kurt tore the bag.

A slow smile spread over the man's face as Emilia hovered over the open coffin.

"Can I go home now?" Ernesto asked.

CHAPTER 45

Hostage Negotiations cleared out, leaving behind the stink of cigarettes and stale coffee, as well as an automatic opener that controlled the gates from inside the house. At least Plano got one thing right.

Ernesto was released from the hospital a week later. Sophia fussed over her husband, making all his favorite foods and reading magazines to him.

An X-ray revealed that Emilia's nose was broken and her cheekbone suffered a hairline fracture. Two black eyes and a purple stain across her cheek made her look like a masked bandit. Fortunately, her ankle was twisted, not broken.

Kurt brought her home to the Palacio Réal where she spent three days in bed with ice packs. When Silvio extended her medical leave by another six weeks, she didn't argue. Talking about the ransom delivery with the police psychiatrist brought relief. Kurt came with her twice and she knew the sessions were cathartic for him, too.

Alan Denton called to thank her. He wouldn't tell her the name of the second man held hostage at the Monte Vista, but that the family wished to express their gratitude with a monetary amount. According to Denton's sources, moreover, Los Colectores never took a hit like what happened at the Monte Vista. The gang was in disarray.

Emilia knew another parasite gang would take its place, but for now, the police could declare victory.

As the bruises faded, and her ankle healed, Emilia lounged around the penthouse, ate delicacies that Jacques sent up, played with her new laptop, read the ancient files from the Casa Odisea warehouse, and thought about her family. The rift with Alvaro needed to be mended. But if he fell for the Internal Affairs sting and took the planted counterfeit money out of the evidence locker, she wasn't going down with him.

That relationship could wait while other issues were sorted out.

When the worst of the discoloration across her face was gone and she was ready to drive again, Emilia brought Ernesto some videos. He was still recovering and napped for most of the day. After they talked for a few minutes, Emilia went into the kitchen and helped Sophia make *frijoles de la olla*. Ernesto liked the tasty bean recipe ladled over rice.

Wearing a new floral apron, Sophia chopped cilantro at the counter for the *pico de gallo* relish. Emilia gave the beans, onions, garlic, and diced jalapeños a final stir and closed the lid. The mixture needed to simmer for at least an hour but already the delicious fragrance reminded her of happier days cooking with her mother.

"Mama," Emilia said as she washed her hands. "I need to ask you something."

Sophia paused, knife held over leafy green stalks. "Ernesto's going to be all right, isn't he?"

"Yes, he'll be fine." More nervous than she anticipated, Emilia wiped her hands on a dishtowel, glad that it gave her something to hold. "I wanted to ask about when you were a little girl."

"When I was little?" Sophia smiled, relief lingering at the corners of her mouth. "Why are you interested in that?"

"Do you remember a man called Doctoro Valdez?" Emilia asked.

Sophia frowned. "Is that the name of the doctor who talked to Ernesto at the hospital?"

"No, Mama." Emilia twisted the dishtowel into a damp wad. "When you were a little girl, he took you and your big sister away from your village. A place miles away from Acapulco."

Sophia's smile faded.

"You were called Maria Josefina." Emilia wondered how much her mother remembered. "Your sister was Consuela. She was three years older than you."

Her mother carefully put down the knife, collected all the minced bits of cilantro off the cutting board and dropped them into the *pico de gallo* bowl on top of a mound of chopped white onion.

"He brought you both to Acapulco." Emilia watched Sophia closely. "Arranged for both of you to be adopted. You went to the Encinos family. They weren't rich but they wanted a child very badly. Your name became Sophia and you never saw your real parents again."

Sophia blinked at Emilia.

"Your sister was adopted by a different family. Their name was Escobar." Emilia paused but Sophia still didn't react. "Mama, Karina Escobar de la Vega is your sister. Your older sister, Consuela."

To Emilia's surprise, Sophia went to the stove, lifted the lid and stirred the beans.

"Mama?"

"Why are you telling me this now?" Sophia asked as the scent of beans and garlic wafted through the kitchen. "Did you think I didn't know?"

Emilia gaped at her mother. "*Oye,* Mama. I never—."

"Consuela made up a silly game because I was sad," Sophia interrupted. She smiled at her daughter as if sharing an old secret. "We were in a cage because we were parrots. We flapped our wings. Walked like birds. Pretended to peck at seeds."

I sat in that garden and could almost hear them. Confused. Crying. Little hostages.

The lump in Emilia's throat was so big, it was hard to breathe. "But if you knew," she floundered. "If you knew Karina was your sister . . . All these years. She was my aunt. She raised your son. My brother. But we never knew them. Why?"

When her mother began mixing *masa* to make fresh tortillas, Emilia knew she would have to find the answers somewhere else.

CHAPTER 46

Kurt offered, but Emilia decided to go alone.

The white house in Las Brisas looked the same. The maid showed Emilia to the big *sala* at the back of the house with the grand piano and the white sofas and the expensive knickknacks.

Beyond the French doors, the pool twinkled in the midday sun. The perfectly pruned border blazed with color. The pink pillows on the white chaise lounges matched stacks of pink and white striped towels. Emilia wondered if anyone actually used the pool.

Wearing white pants and a black silk turtleneck, Karina stalked into the room, her stiletto heels ringing on the tiles. She stopped by the piano and folded her arms.

"I assume you're here to apologize." Karina said.

For the first time, Emilia saw the family resemblance. The same cheekbones, the same thick-lashed eyes. But there was a kindness in Sophia's face that Karina's lacked.

"I'm returning your key." Without waiting to be invited, Emilia sat and opened her shoulder bag. She found the key with the cardboard tag and set it on the coffee table between the two sofas. A copy of the key was already with Dora Machado Uribe at the diocese's Family Services office, along with a letter of explanation and Silvio's photos. "It's yours, I'm guessing. Not Rafa's."

Karina lifted her chin. "You could have sent it by

messenger."

Emilia couldn't help but smile at this oblique dismissal of the key's ownership. "I thought you should know," she said. "Rafa never talked to anyone at Casa Odisea. Whatever he remembered about his own birth family had nothing to do with the key."

"Thank you for returning our property." Karina indicated the doorway. "The maid will see you out."

Emilia didn't move. "I think Rafa took the key to hurt you," she said. "He knew it had some special meaning for you."

"Shall I ask the chauffeur to see you out instead?" Karina's voice shook slightly.

"I think you should sit down, Karina, and listen to me." It took all Emilia's self-control to stay calm instead of hurling questions at the other woman. "According to Casa Odisea's records, you were born Consuela Ramos Duarte. Your little sister was Maria Josefina."

Karina sucked in her breath.

"Your family lived in a village called Santo Domingo," Emilia revealed. "When you were six years old, Doctoro Fernando Valdez from Casa Odisea paid your father a goat in return for you and Maria Josefina. Valdez took you both to Acapulco where he put you in a cage in back of his house. You pretended to be parrots to keep your sister from crying."

Emilia had to stop for a moment to force down the lump in her throat.

"Valdez was an animal," Karina said.

Tears threatened. Emilia blinked them back.

"One day we were playing in the dirt. The next day we took a marvelous ride. It was the first time I'd ever been in a car." Karina hugged herself. "Two days later, Valdez raped us both."

Expectation didn't make those words any easier to hear.

"I was six!" Karina shouted, startling Emilia.

The elegant woman scooped up the key and hurled it across the room. It smacked it into a vase on an antique gilt table and plinked onto the tile floor. The arrangement of tulips shivered but didn't tip.

"You must have been terrified," Emilia said.

Karina sank into a damask armchair and pressed a hand to her face. The diamonds on her fingers flashed in the light. "He gave us candy laced with drugs and he raped us," she murmured.

"Did you ever tell anyone?" Emilia asked. "Later, after you were adopted?"

"No, never." Karina gave a shake as if a sudden draft swept the room. "After awhile I convinced myself that it was a bad dream. I had everything. Parents who adored me. Parties. A pony. I was the golden child."

"What about Maria Josefina?" Emilia wondered. "Growing up, did you see her?"

Karina closed her eyes as if the memories hurt. "When I got married, I told my husband about her. He hired a private detective. That's who gave me the key to that horrible place. As if I'd ever go back there."

"Your husband's private detective found Maria Josefina? I mean, Sophia. You must have been thrilled."

Karina reverted to the here and now, with a glare meant to put Emilia in her place. "He found her in a hovel. Eighteen years old with two babies on her hip and not a peso in her pocket. Thought the sun and the moon revolved around her smart-mouthed mechanic of a husband. We saved her. Cleaned him up. Gave him a job."

"That's how my father became your chauffeur?" Emilia had no memories of her father. Tío Raul occasionally mentioned his dead brother, but never in front of Sophia.

"You think he could have gotten a job like that on his own?" Karina dug her manicured nails into the chair's upholstery. "Self-taught, my husband used to say, may his soul rest in peace. A big talker, I said."

"But you and Sophia—."

"It was hard for me to see what had happened to her," Karina told Emilia. "When we brought them to the chauffeur's house, she carried on like it was a palace. She simply didn't know any better. The Encinos family gave my sister nothing."

"But was she happy with Ernesto?" Emilia leaned forward, curious about the father she didn't remember.

"Sophia married Ernesto because he was handsome," Karina declared. "Too handsome for his own good. Full of self-confidence and swagger. He didn't know his place."

Emilia sat back, disappointed at Karina's answer. "Did people know that Sophia was your sister?"

"Of course not." Karina drew back, clearly surprised. "She was the chauffeur's wife. I was the daughter of a prominent politician. My husband was a well-known doctor."

"But when my father died," Emilia argued. "Why didn't you help her? Take her in?"

"I told you," Karina said impatiently. "She was the chauffeur's wife."

"But she was your sister!"

"I helped out the best way possible by taking Rafa and moving to this house where he could have a better life." Karina sniffed. "Sophia had two children and I didn't have any. It was an equitable arrangement."

Emilia slid to the edge of the sofa. "Tell me the truth, Karina. Did Mama really ask you to take one of us?"

Karina propelled herself out of the armchair and went to the French doors, her back to Emilia. "I'm sure you understand what painful memories these are for me. I'd like to be alone now."

"I think you lied to me," Emilia said slowly. "Made me think my mother didn't want her children."

"Her children." Anger crept into Karina's voice as she faced the swimming pool and row of lounge chairs. "Sophia talked of nothing else but her children unless it was her husband. How clever you were, how pretty. How Little Ernesto had his father's smile and charming ways."

A shiver ran up Emilia's spine at the way Karina mocked Sophia. "Were you jealous?"

"Of course not." The answer came a little too quickly.

"So why didn't you ever let my mother see her son again?"

"It was Rafa's fault," Karina said as if she'd rehearsed the answer for 30 years. "He was a difficult child. It would have confused him."

Emilia had been in far too many interrogations not to recognize a lie. "I don't believe you."

Karina spun around, eyes blazing. "I had to protect him," she insisted. "He was high-strung. Exactly like your father. Headstrong. Difficult."

"Why do you keep mentioning my father?" Emilia asked.

Karina's face flushed. "No one's talking about him. He's in the past."

"You were in love with my father, weren't you?" Sadness closed in as Emilia realized the sordid truth buried under years of lies.

"I would never soil myself with a chauffeur," Karina said indignantly.

"When he died, there was no choosing between me and my brother, was there?" Emilia flung the charge out as a fact, not a guess. "*Madre de Dios,* you stole your sister's son. He must have reminded you so much of my father that you just had to have him."

Karina pointed a shaking finger at the doorway. "Get out."

"You were so rich you built a wall around Rafa and there was nothing my mother could do except lose her mind."

Rage built inside Emilia like steam in a boiling kettle. The beautiful house probably hid as many terrible secrets as the Casa Odisea warehouse. "What did you do to Rafa inside that wall? Did you touch him? Pretend that he was his father?"

"Get out," Karina shouted. In that instant she was the mirror image of Señora Valdez in the lopsided mess in El Coloso. "Get out of my house!"

"Doctoro Valdez hurt you." Emilia snatched up her shoulder bag as she heard voices in the hall and the stamp of running feet. "But that doesn't excuse what you did. You ruined my mother's life. You turned Rafa into a monster! His childhood must have been a nightmare. You're a horrible, damaged woman."

Emilia shoved past a uniformed security guard and fled before she was infected by all the lies.

CHAPTER 47

On Saturday, Mercedes came with Emilia to watch the Ixtapa Half Marathon. Kurt made the top 20 and came first in his age group. Jacques finished 11 minutes behind Kurt. Emilia tried not to laugh when Mercedes rebuffed Jacques's obvious flirting before the race. The French chef was attractive enough, but Mercedes found the cultural gap too wide. Most of the time, she confided to Emilia over iced coffees as the runners flashed by, she had no idea what he was saying or why he was making all those silly, dramatic gestures.

It was late now and Kurt was sound asleep. Hoarse from cheering the race, Emilia sat on the balcony with the gratitude journal open on her lap and a pen in her hand. Yesterday's entry was the same as the day before and the day before that and the day before that.

I am grateful for Kurt Rucker.
I am grateful for Kurt Rucker.
I am grateful for Kurt Rucker.

She was alive because of Kurt. His military training. His cool head when things looked rough. His fearlessness at the Pacific Lotus. The risk he took running up the hill to the Monte Vista in the middle of the night, with a bottle of tequila in one hand and Silvio's gun in the other.

Without Kurt's courage, Plano would certainly have killed her and Ernesto would have died, too.

As the night breeze fluffed her hair and strains of music floated up from the Pasodoble Bar, Emilia was sure she'd never met another man like Kurt.

He adapted to the language and culture of another country, while skillfully integrating the best practices of his own.

He accepted all the crazy baggage that came with being a cop in Acapulco. He understood her faults and fears and let her have them. He was strong enough to confront her past and refuse to let it destroy either of them.

When Emilia told him about the scene in Las Brisas with Karina, he cut right to the heart of the issue.

"That bitch betrayed your mother," Kurt said. "Stole half of the only thing she had left after your father died. I'm thankful Karina didn't steal you."

"Me, too," Emilia said. She wasn't going to waste any more time playing the *what if* game while envy gnawed on her like a dog with a bone.

She'd spent hours wondering what if she had been the one to grow up in Las Brisas with Karina. What if she always had money for fancy clothes and parties? What if her stepfather ran an investment bank? What if she went to college instead of a police academy?

She wanted all the advantages that Rafa Gamboa threw away.

But Karina's version of events was a carefully forged lie.

Sophia had never offered up either of her children.

If she'd grown up with Karina, Emilia would have turned out like Rafa Gamboa. Warped. Angry. Manipulated and abused by a sick woman.

Karina would have taught her to be cruel. Selfish. Ruthless.

Emilia's childhood was one of poverty, but she'd never once doubted that she was loved. Unlike Rafa, she grew up surrounded by supportive, caring people like Tía Lourdes, Tío Raul, and Padre Ricardo. Her cousins defended her on the playground and paved the road into the police department for her.

But it was Sophia who made sure that love was abundant, even if money never was. There was pride and excitement at Emilia's accomplishments, no matter how trivial. Compliments and hugs, ribbons for her hair, a hand to hold onto, cooking lessons full of laughter, prayers at night.

By example, Sophia taught her daughter how to love. And without that lesson, as poorly as she applied it, Emilia knew she'd never have Kurt.

Her pen scratched against the paper.

I am grateful for Kurt Rucker.
I am grateful for Kurt Rucker.

I am grateful for my mother.

CHAPTER 48

The next day, Emilia took a big hamper of goodies from Jacques and a basket of herb seedlings to Sophia. Mother and daughter puttered around the patio, planting the herbs and sweeping the cement. The Hostage Negotiations team had used the outdoor space as a smoking zone. It took an hour to pick all the cigarette butts out of the plants.

They lunched on cold shrimp ceviche, mushroom tarts, and roasted potatoes with capers and olives, all washed down with bottles of French lemonade. Ernesto ate well, but the highlight of the meal for him was the triple layer chocolate cake for dessert. He was healing well and gained back some of the weight he'd lost, but would only talk about his ordeal with Padre Ricardo.

After they finished the meal, Emilia kissed her mother and pressed the button to automatically open the gates. No more manual opening and closing, which was nice for Ernesto.

The afternoon was glorious, warm and bright. Perfect for a swim when she got back to the Palacio Réal.

Emilia climbed into the Suburban, checked her rearview, and saw that the rear window was half obscured. A large manila envelope was trapped beneath the windshield wiper. Addressed to her, it contained a single sheet of paper with a short, typed message.

Her blood pressure rose so fast that Emilia's vision

darkened at the edges.

No one had been through the gates that day except for her, yet obviously someone else had access. Emilia made sure her mother and Ernesto locked all the doors and promised to stay inside. Fifteen minutes later, she slapped the paper onto Silvio's desk.

"Read it," Emilia said, trying to suck enough air into her lungs to keep from passing out. "I was right. I was right all along."

Silvio gave her a dirty look but snatched up the paper and read it. "Where'd you get this?"

"Someone left it on my car at my mother's house," Emilia said. "Inside the courtyard with the gates closed. Plain envelope. My name on it. I kept it but I already know there won't be any prints."

"*Rayos*, Cruz," Silvio swore. "This is bad."

"I told you it was him." Emilia began to pace, fighting to stay calm. "*Madre de Dios*, it was him all along. He tried to use Ernesto to get to me." She stopped and pressed both hands to her head. "He set up Los Colectores with Ernesto's *coyote* contract so I'd come running to him for two million dollars. Plano was his man and he played me like a song."

"Plano was working the ransom with the kidnappers for himself, too," Silvio pointed out. "That man got what he deserved."

"Franco, are you listening to me?" Emilia demanded. "He manipulated us all like pawns on a chessboard and he'll do it again."

Silvio went to the two-drawer safe on the other side of the office, worked the combination, took out a handgun in a shoulder holster, and thrust it at Emilia.

"What about my medical leave and all the paperwork?" she asked, shrugging into the rig.

"I'll make it look like a database malfunction." Silvio took his jacket from the hook on the back of his office door. "Good thing I happen to have a couple million dollars because we need to get your mother out of that house now. We'll buy something but keep your name off the bill of sale."

Emilia paused as she adjusted the leather strap. The gun was a comforting weight on her left side. "You still have Bartok's money? You didn't turn it in?"

Silvio snorted. "With what explanation?"

"But—."

"Life's full of emergencies that require cash, Cruz. Like today."

Emilia was astounded. Once they had Ernesto safe and sound, she didn't give the money a second thought. "When were you going to tell me? Or share?"

"You want to talk?" Silvio glowered. "Or go find your mother a house?"

Emilia took a step towards the door before swinging back to him. "I want a new car," she announced.

"Yeah, maybe." Silvio rubbed his chin as he regarded her thoughtfully. "What's your friend Mercedes's phone number?"

Emilia weighed a new car against a phone call. Silvio was

the complete opposite of Jacques. Plus, Mercedes was pretty tough. If Silvio acted like a *pendejo*, the dancer would let him know.

"I want an SUV like Kurt's." She grabbed a sticky note and scribbled a string of numbers. "A dark color, too. Not white. Nothing that stands out."

Silvio took the note. "You're not the only one who needs a car, Cruz. My official ride got totaled, remember? I'm driving some wreck from the impound yard. I'm thinking a little Korean smartie car will do you just fine."

"One of the numbers on that sticky note is wrong," Emilia informed him. She opened the office door. "When I have the keys to a nice new SUV in my hand, you'll find out which one."

"It's like you don't trust me," Silvio rumbled.

He shut the door behind them, leaving the paper on his desk.

You are very clever, Detective Emilia Cruz. How did you pay such a high ransom without my help? Javier Plano underestimated you, but I won't. I am glad to have such a clever friend. Until next time, DBL.

DBL.
Diego Barrielos Luna.

El Fin

You're invited

You're invited to stay up to date with Emilia and the team in the Mystery Ahead newsletter. Get behind-the-scenes details and must-read recommendations every other Sunday.

Subscribe and receive the Detective Emilia Cruz Starter Library with 2 novellas and the Who's Who guide to the series.

Go to carmenamato.net/starter-library.

There are extra goodies ahead, too.
- ✓ A favorite recipe from a meal featured in the book,
- ✓ Glossary of Spanish words, and
- ✓ An excerpt from the next Detective Emilia Cruz novel.

Frijoles de la Olla

(Beans with Pico de Gallo)

Adapted from Saveur Magazine

Ingredients for beans
2 cups dried pinto beans
1 tablespoon chopped garlic
¼ cup chopped canned jalapeños
½ cup minced yellow onion
4 cups water
4 cups chicken stock
Salt and black pepper to taste

Ingredients for pico de gallo relish
1 tomato, finely chopped, no seeds
1 tablespoon chopped canned jalapeños
¼ cup chopped fresh cilantro
½ cup minced white onion
Juice from 1 fresh lime
Crumbled cotija cheese (optional)

Instructions

Bring all the bean ingredients to a boil in a big pot. Lower
heat and simmer 2-3 hours until you can easily mash a bean

with a spoon. You can also use a crockpot. Stir occasionally. Add water to keep the beans from getting dry. They should be somewhat soupy, like chili con carne.

Mix all the relish ingredients except the cheese. Serve over the hot beans. Top with cheese, if desired.

I like to serve this over rice as a side dish.

Glossary of Spanish Terms

Words and phrases commonly used in the Detective Emilia Cruz mystery series

Abarrotes: snacks

Agua de jamaica: cold tea made with dried hibiscus

Alcaldia: town hall and/or mayor's offices

Amigo: friend, buddy

Barrio: neighborhood

Cabrón: slang meaning dumbass

Campesino: subsistence farmers, country dwellers

Casita: little house

Cédula: identity card

Chica: girl

Comida: the main meal of the day, usually eaten in early afternoon

Conchas: sweet rolls topped with sugar and shaped like a conch shell

Dios mio: my god, an exclamation

El Norte: the United States

Federales: slang for the Policía Federal Preventiva, federal law enforcement agency

Guayabera: men's button-down shirt with a straight hem and multiple pockets

Halcone: word meaning falcon, used to mean a person acting as a lookout

Hombres: men

Jefe: chief, person in charge

Jitomate: tomato

Libraría: bookstore

Libro: book

Loco: crazy

Lotéria: lottery

Madre de Dios: Mother of God, used as exclamation

Maldita: damn, damned

Mercado: market

Mujeres: women

Muertos: papier maché skeleton figures used to decorate Day of the Dead altars

Narcomanta: banner bearing a message from a gang or cartel

Norteamericano: North American

Ofrenda: altar

Palapa: traditional Mexican shelter roofed with palm leaves or branches

Papel picado: streamers of tissue paper cut into silhouette designs

Parrilla: grill for food, usually assumed to be for meat

Pastelería: pastry shop

Pendejo: asshole, jerk

Permiso: excuse me

Placas: license plates

Prima: female cousin

Privada: enclosed subdivision and/or the gate to the property

Prohibido el paso: "Keep out" warning
Queso fresco: soft cheese common in Mexican recipes
Rayos: exclamation, similar to "oh hell"
Reina: queen
Salsa verde: tart green salsa usually made with tomatillos
Sicario: cartel henchman or assassin
Talavera: hand painted pottery from Puebla
Taqueria: taco restaurant
Telenovela: television soap opera
Tiendita: little store
Tío/Tía: uncle/aunt
Zocalo: town square

An excerpt from NARCO NOIR, the next Detective Emilia Cruz mystery

Emilia Cruz Encinos had never met Lieutenant Bolivar Campos before. Neither had any of the other detectives gathered around the squadroom's conference table. Campos was the head of Acapulco's small Financial Crimes unit, established a year ago by Chief of Police Rodrigo Salazar. As far as Emilia knew, Financial Crimes had yet to make an arrest.

Campos was a small bespectacled man in a suit and tie with a terse expression as if he resented the need to be slumming with cops in tees and torn jeans. He tapped on a laptop as everybody waited, connecting it to the television mounted on the wall.

Across the table from Emilia, Lieutenant Franco Silvio silently fumed at the waste of time. *El teniente* was a formidable presence in his everyday uniform of jeans, white shirt, shoulder holster, and bad mood. Two teams of detectives, Macias and Sandor, and Castro and Gomez, slurped coffee, cracked jokes, and waited for the show to begin. Three suits who came with Campos sat behind him, their chairs against the wall.

Fresh from an extended medical leave, Emilia was still getting used to the new dynamic in the squadroom. Previously her partner, Silvio was now her boss. The last few days were a non-stop argument over the cases she would handle, the delay in getting her a new partner, and if she'd be allowed to assist the *federales* hunt for escaped cartel druglord Diego Barrielos Luna, known as the Barrel Bomber.

Emilia and Silvio went at it again that morning, wrangling over a report that another fugitive, the murderer and human trafficker El Acólito, had been spotted in Veracruz. Like a *pendejo*, Silvio refused to let her go, saying they didn't have funding to chase rumors halfway across Mexico. Emilia retorted that El Acólito was her brother and she had the right to find him before Barrielos Luna did.

Then Campos arrived and the discussion went into limbo.

"Sorry for the delay," Campos announced. "We're ready now."

Silvio glared down the length of the table and the detectives settled down.

Campos tapped the laptop keyboard and a video player opened on the television screen. "This is from a Bancomer Bank ATM machine's security camera," he said. "As luck would have it, the camera was installed incorrectly and captured the street in front of the machine instead of the touchpad."

The silent black and white video showed a *sitio* taxi stand. Waiting nose-to-tail for customers, the line of parked cars represented a quintessential part of urban Acapulco life. *Sitio* stands were usually near large intersections. A ride in a licensed *sitio* was always safer than taking a chance on the unlicensed taxis roaming the streets looking for fares.

The passenger side of each car was to the camera, showing off the *sitio* stand's stenciled logo. The curb was shaded by soaring palm trees that broke up the expanse of sidewalk.

The intersection with the cross street was partially in the frame. Traffic flowed in both directions. Pedestrians strolled by while others crossed the street in front of the first taxi in line. It was a typical downtown Acapulco scene.

"The *sitio* drivers are getting extortion threats from Los Mozos," Campos said and froze the video. "The gang is loosely affiliated with the Knights Templar cartel. We opened an official Financial Crimes file on Los Mozos about six months ago."

"Got some names we can cross reference?" Silvio asked. "Knights Templar is a big problem for us here in the homicide business."

Campos looked pained. "We're still in the evidence-gathering phase."

"But now Los Mozos has upped the ante." Silvio looked questioningly over the rim of his mug as he took a swig of coffee.

"Well, yes," Campos said. "I guess you could put it that way. The day before we got this video from Bancomer, Los Mozos left a *narcomanta* message on the wall by the *sitio* manager's station, which is out of the picture. They threatened to kill drivers unless they pay protection money."

Campos clicked and the video played again. Judging from

the angle, Emilia guessed that the camera was mounted some 12 or 15 feet above the level of the sidewalk.

Two men, in the white short-sleeved shirts and narrow black ties that identified them as *sitio* drivers, leaned on the third taxi in line. As they talked, one smoked and the other held a cell phone. Their faces were striped by the shadows of palm fronds stretching into the sky above them. More pedestrians walked by. No one appeared to be in a hurry.

"Here we go," Campos murmured.

A dark shape popped into view at the top of the video frame. As it crossed the street and headed for the line of taxis, the figure resolved into a slender man in a hooded sweatshirt that obscured his face.

At the same time, a woman carrying a plump shopping bag approached the *sitio* stand. One of the drivers noticed and appeared to call out to her. The woman spoke to him, then got into the back seat of the first taxi. The driver flicked away his cigarette, trotted over, and slid behind the wheel.

Before the taxi could drive off, the hooded man opened the door behind the driver. His face was lost from view as he leaned inside, but a second later, the woman scrambled out of the taxi from the opposite side, in full view of the camera. Still clutching her heavy tote, she ran down the sidewalk and disappeared.

The man in the hood straightened, took a handgun out of the kangaroo pocket of his sweatshirt and shot the driver at point blank range. From the recoil, Emilia knew he fired three times. He pocketed the gun, tossed something into the car, and loped off.

From the rustling around her, Emilia knew she wasn't the only police detective in the cramped office who noticed the speed and efficiency of the kill. The assassin had been on camera less than five seconds.

Intermittent traffic flowed past the *sitio* stand. No one went to look at the dead driver for another 30 seconds, although a commotion must have ensued that the camera couldn't see. Eventually, a *sitio* driver in white shirt and narrow tie opened the passenger side door and looked inside. He backed away, abruptly sat down on the sidewalk and put his head in his hands. Two female pedestrians opened their mouths in soundless screams. More *sitio* drivers came to gape at their dead colleague.

Campos stopped the video.

"What did he throw into the car after he shot the driver?" Emilia asked.

"A note wrapped around a rock," Campos said. He tapped the laptop and the video player was replaced by a message clumsily block-printed on white cloth.

You men of the taxi syndicate must pay your dues to LOS MOZOS! We know what you do.

Protect your women and children and bring safety to Acapulco's streets. This is a warning.

"Okay, so Los Mozos made good on their threat," Silvio recapped for everyone at the table. "It's officially a homicide and they'll probably strike again unless the drivers pay. I told Chief Salazar we'd help and we will. Send over whatever you've got on Los Mozos and we'll take it from here."

Campos frowned. "Chief Salazar said that you would lend assistance."

"We will," Silvio agreed. "We'll open a homicide investigation."

"The drivers haven't changed their minds," Campos said. "They won't pay, which means this crime is still our jurisdiction."

"Financial's got no jurisdiction over a homicide investigation," Silvio pointed out.

"Chief Salazar ordered me to fold the driver's murder into the Financial Crimes investigation into Los Mozos," Campos said.

Emilia gave a start, as did everybody else around the table. Financial Crimes was three accountants and a calculator. They didn't have the resources for a homicide investigation. Gomez and Castro actually laughed, but shut up after getting the eye from Silvio.

"Exactly how would Financial Crimes plan to catch the killer?" Silvio asked, his voice larded with skepticism. "Hypothetically. Also, keep in mind you'll need to protect the drivers at the same time."

The television screen blinked as Campos threw up another still photo, an enlargement of the woman who exited the taxi moments before the drivers was killed. As she emerged from the vehicle, her expression was composed, although Emilia recalled her moving swiftly.

"Based on this image," Campos said. "We don't believe the killer threatened or frightened her. That matches up with the sympathy in the message toward women and children."

"So you think the killer is a skinny guy who likes women?" Gomez asked and was rewarded with a cackle of laughter from his partner.

"We don't think Los Mozos will shoot a woman," Campos said. "Our plan is for a female taxi driver to join the *sitio* stand."

"You're talking about an undercover operation," Silvio said with a scowl.

"Well, yes."

"Is Financial Crimes equipped to do that?"

"Actually," Campos said. "We'd like to borrow Detective Cruz."

Find NARCO NOIR on Amazon or at your favorite bookstore.

ABOUT THE AUTHOR

Carmen Amato turns lessons from a 30-year career with the Central Intelligence Agency into crime fiction loaded with danger and deception.

Starting with *Cliff Diver*, her award-winning Detective Emilia Cruz mystery series pits the first female police detective in Acapulco against Mexico's drug cartels, government corruption, and social inequality.

The series was awarded the Poison Cup for Outstanding Series from CrimeMasters of America in both 2019 and 2020 and has been optioned for television.

Her Galliano Club historical thriller series was inspired by her grandfather who was a deputy sheriff during Prohibition.

Originally from upstate New York, Carmen was educated there as well as in Virginia and Paris, France, while experiences in Mexico and Central America ignited her writing career.

Subscribe at carmenamato.net.